BETTER
BETTER

THAN
THAN

HEISENBERG
HEISENBERG

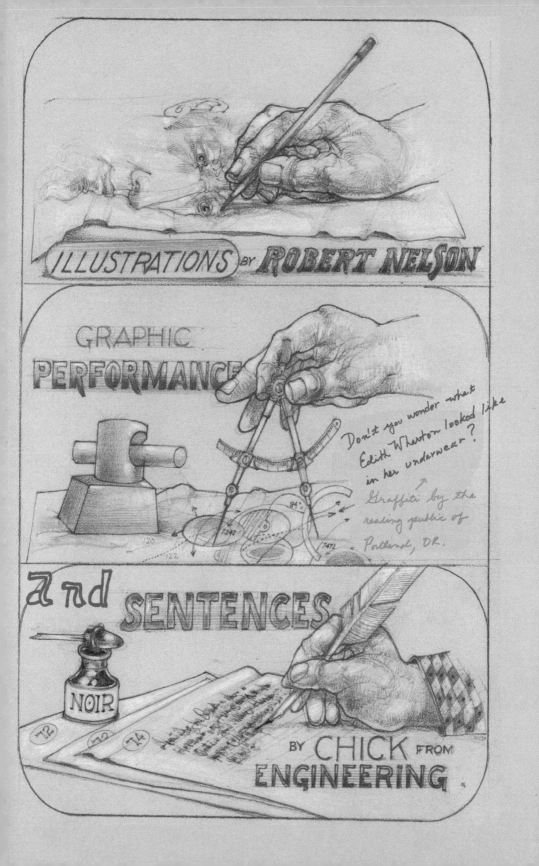

Portrait of the Author as A Young Man

"Entering a gambling town is a lot like going down The Labyrinth looking for the Minotaur. Let's take a tour around Jake, Nevada. I'll be your Theseus, laying down colored elastic from a big ball to save our way out of the cowboy Minos. We'll slice some chips off the big red bull and get the hell out with some new money and a huge erection." *Chick from Engineering*

"I've known Chick longer than anyone because he knows his casino stuff. He's not faking it like these newspaper jerk-offs." *Jack Bullock*

"Who among the gamblers, hookers, and bomb physicists is the Minotaur? The brilliant ball of elastic is reversing into Theseus's hand while shedding pretty little rubber shards like early ejecta from a nuclear event. You've read yourself into a tunnel where the escape twine is raveling up an implosion which will confiscate the past." *Phil Grethlien*

"From a ΣN graduate of Faber College we get a sinkfull of rage in a style which burns away any academic hair which might clog the drain to reader understanding." *a waitress at the Sahara*

"Here in the art of writing is confused with the science of physics, and the thrill of shooting craps is bundled into the adventurism of inventing the Hydrogen Bomb."
Emil Lillo-Furon

"In my home town the best people wind their plans onto a shrinking pirn that becomes so small there is soon nothing left to knit with." *Erving Lehman*

"Don't trust any of this gamblespeak. The more you and Chick try to slash the beast with that big ego you think is a sword, the more you will resemble the Minotaur, not Theseus."
Pollyte Allen

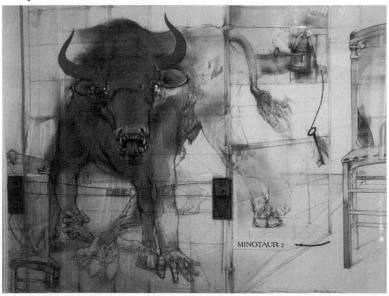

MINOTAUR-2

Jake, Nevada
1950–1968

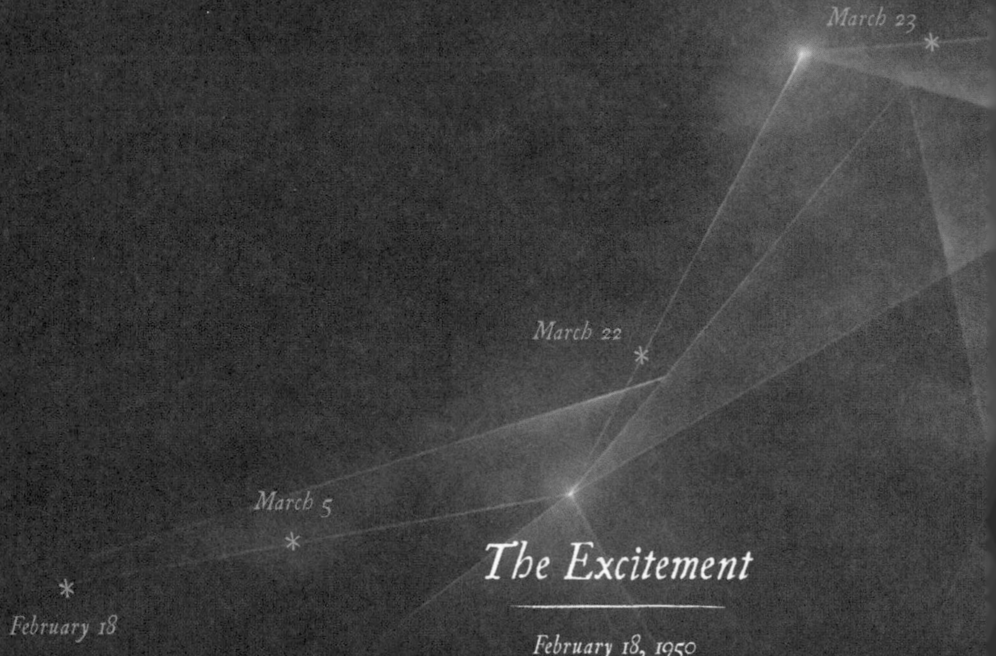

March 23 ✳

March 22
✳

March 5
✳

February 18
✳

The Excitement

February 18, 1950

N

The Loss
___
March 25, 1950

* *April 12*

April 14 *

* *June 14*

September 1 *

November 2
*

The Repair
___
November 1, 1950

August 19,
1961
*

August 26,
1961
*

October 19,
1968
*

August 25,
1961
*

February 27,
1967
*

THE SCENE

JAKE

A gambling town on

Trembling Peak

in southern Nevada,

THE CHARACTERS

Phil is so mysteriously intelligent, thoughts of surpassing value fly out of his head, amazing himself and those around him, who can't help falling in love with his gentle brilliance

Lehman, the owner of the grand hotel Ziraleet, introduces crooked dice which favor the tourists

Spike, a young golfer, already a has-been, wanders into Jake and mines a rich vein of experience

Erving is Lehman's teenage son, who leaves town in a red Cadillac wearing a brilliant Rolex

Viner's brain is as busy as Phil's, but the number of jakes who credit the damaged shit it issues is tiny and does not include himself

Lineheardt, a new physicist from Columbia University, has a remarkable academic record and a beautiful mouth

Starzinchger: The great physicist's agile mind feeds with a vast appetite of scholarly greed

For eons Trembling Peak sweat rich deltas of silver down its huge stone forehead. In 1850 the 1st jake scooped up this freckled ooze with wondrous ease. He believed 4 ancient moons had sent this filthy silver down to Nevada in cold maculate light to chill the peak's volcano.

The mining enterprise became grand. Deep twisting tunnels were opened down into the mountain. Jake's 1st luxury hotel, the Ladies' Heel, opened in 1914. More followed. It was widely believed that everyone in Jake was devoted to easy money. But a lesson was coming.

In 1940 the men who owned the mining companies pointed down to the tailings of their work, now too widely scattered across the flats to collect for profit, and said it was over. That wasn't the lesson.

The lesson was that half the whores, miners, and gamblers, who'd thought they would evacuate Jake as if cholera had broken out the moment they detected the end of easy money, found Trembling Peak too beautiful to abandon. They floated the town along on its usual cloud of mania and euphoria as if nothing had changed.

1 jake said that if they all hadn't been adept at dreaming up euphoria out of nothing, they never would have become whores, miners, and gamblers in the 1st place.

In the middle forties a new troupe of prospectors, the nuclear physicists, arrived in Nevada. They set up their business down in the flats and came up the mountain to live in Jake. It was a lot like Los Alamos, herds of buildings and homes clashing with each other as if construction had run around the mountain in a stampede while the town planning official cowered behind sage. The human climate was also familiar what with most every jake believing his personal candle of genius burned much brighter than physicists whose only trick was the taming of stars.

1950

March 5

Through the winter of 1949, 43 feet of snow fell on 4th Street. The hotels, the gas stations, the houses, and everything else in Jake were lumpy mounds of white. It was so hard to keep ahead of the constantly falling snow not much could be kept clean of it. Neon had a significant enough priority to be kept clean. Parking lots were thought important enough, too, at the beginning.

But by February the fight for the parking lots was abandoned and the Jake which Phil Grethlien saw from his upstairs bedroom was nothing but snow, ice, and huge pulsating mists of nearly edible color.

March was hot so an early run-off tumbled down the rough gravel of the mountain's wide stream beds. Spring rains

11

mixed in with the gushing runs of melting snow. Rivers as potent as the Colorado formed in hours.

They rushed down the mountain for several hundred turbulent yards only to fall through the bottom of their own beds. Phil knew the mountain's mining fissures opened adits down into caverns large enough to store Lake Mead vertically, so what brought him out of his house in the morning was not curiosity about the swift disappearance of so much water.

He came out to gape at the argentite the water had found in the bottom of the mountain. Everyone else had come out to look, too.

It was exciting and distressing to see a fortune in precious metal the hundred years of mining had missed come sluicing out across the alkali plain to form a beautiful radioactively contaminated lake of wet mountain silver shit.

Late that morning, after the flood had already disappeared into the alkali sink, Phil walked cautiously toward the herd of sheds which made up the labs and offices of 52. He didn't want to go in. He stretched up on his toes to see how far north the sparkling argentite reached up 52's grey sands.

His view of the new silver was blocked by Starzinchger's latest cyclotron housing. Phil laughed at him. Starzinchger's title for his bomb vibrated Phil's funny bone.

Starzinchger called it "The Super." He had been building bigger and bigger cyclotrons to provide more and more tritium which in turn required larger and larger cryogenic housings because liquid tritium boiled away at 20 degrees above absolute 0, and all of this was supposed to be a bomb. Bombs were supposed to fit into the bellies of airplanes. "The Super" was a mountain range of industrial plants.

Phil turned back towards the doorway to 52 with effort. He had difficulty making his eyes focus on the door. He had to make himself walk. He didn't want to go in. Holy shit, he felt like Freud terrified at the entrance to his father's graveyard.

Well, he made himself better than Freud. He went in.

Renza was waiting. He had called Phil earlier to warn him that Starzinchger was racing up from L.A. to see if the flood had damaged the new cyclotron.

"Where is he?" asked Phil.

"He's touring with Huke," said Renza.

Lineheardt came rushing in. She'd been working for Phil only 2 weeks before he'd begun hiding out at home. She said Huke was planning to usher Starzinchger into Phil's empty office in order to justify firing Phil.

Renza's face crinkled with warning. Starzinchger and Huke were outside the door. Lineheardt stopped in mid-sentence, but they went into the lab across the hall. Lineheardt paced with excitement. Phil wanted to explain to Renza why he'd disappeared. He wanted to talk about how bent off he had become.

It had started with his being ordered off the rail cannon to work on the hydrogen bomb. At 1st, it had been no problem. He had decided his contribution to fusion research would be to prove the H-bomb impossible.

His enthusiasm for this strategy had been great. Holy shit, he'd told himself, he would make the 1st negative discovery great enough to attain the popularity history books noticed. It could be so damn popular it was the stuff whole new eras were made of. The hell with finding fabulous new possibilities for natural law. If he could prove fusion impossible, for the next hundred years physicists would glory in dead ends. The Grethlien Feature, it would be called.

13

Oh, yes! For the next 1,000 years, whenever nature hit the wall, someone would feel compelled to tell a story about when Phil Grethlien proved there was such a thing as the impossible when he'd demonstrated there would be no Hell-bomb no matter how much money Starzinchger squeezed out of Truman.

He hit his fist into his palm. Lineheardt flinched. Why hadn't he followed through?

Right after starting on the proof, he'd found himself hiding out in different nooks of 52 or sneaking up to 4th Street to hang out at hotel bars and chat with girls.

{You people are crazy. You are treating world depopulating weapons like they are entertainment. Do you know what you are risking?"

"I sure do," responded the bar girl at the Ondine. She looked half-good in her red satin swimsuit, which all the girls in the Ondine lounge wore 1 size too small. "We aren't risking anything. People here don't really have that much to care about. This big super balloon bomb thing is fun. Plus we are making money off of it. That's what jakes do. They make money off of fun."

"It can blow up in your face and leave you without a nose," said Phil.

"I see. Ok." laughed the girl. "I'm supposed to be afraid of taking chances."

"Yeah, I know." Phil gave up on reasoning with her and watched her breasts bobble. "Me, neither."

"You look really tense," the whore changed the subject, noticing the change of direction in his eyes. "Wouldn't you like to release some tension?"

"No thanks," said Phil. "I'm not really interested in sex with a whore."

"I'm not really a whore," said the whore. "I just think you are really tense."}

14

We're Back!

AND THRILLED TO BE
"HOME AGAIN"

C'MON OVER AND SAY HOWDY!

COOPER SISTERS
(AUDREY AND BLANCHE)

After numerous similar interviews, Phil had figured out that talking to whores in hotel bars wasn't going to produce any deep understanding of Jake and jakes. He probably needed to actually live Jake out for real.

He watched television a lot. It became the most interesting thing in his life. He could watch anything tv showed him.

Then the reading started to go. Nobody believed him

15

about that. People aren't supposed to forget how to read. But that's what happened. He could see the letters, but he couldn't get them parsed into meaningful bunches. He would look at the spaces between the words and get stuck there, and soon all he saw when he tried to read were the spaces.

The next stage was picking up blank pieces of paper and staring at them for as long as an hour at a time, as if they were profoundly interesting. As bad off as he was then, he knew he was staring at the white sheet of no meaning only for the exquisite relief it provided.

The snow was falling then as if it were being sprayed down on Jake from a huge sten gun on top of the peak. He stopped coming into work. He didn't call. It was like having the flu.

Except instead of invading his sinuses, this virus localized in his mind. He spent all of January and February at home with this long white cold in his mind. Before the phone had rung this morning, his head had been so cold and so white it was as if that snow sten gun had been put at his ear and all the winter's heavy snows had been shot inside.

Renza's frantic appeal to his pathological fear of getting fired was the only thing in the world that could have persuaded him to come out and down the mountain. Now that he'd come, and proved himself better than Freud, he wished he hadn't. What was so bad about getting fired?

"Phil!" Frederic Starzinchger strode in and grabbed his hand. Lineheardt studied the great physicist respectfully.

Huke, disappointed Phil was present, asked curtly if Phil had any work to interest Starzinchger.

"You have no work to talk about?" he said to Phil's silence.

"None," said Phil. "Other than the obvious perception."

"Which is?" asked Starzinchger.

Velson, Robt. A. 2013

"There has to be a more direct route to a flyable bomb than building mountain ranges of cyclotrons and cryogenics," said Phil.

"Of course the cryogenics are large now; that is irrelevant. I will miniaturize the refrigeration," decreed Starzinchger, as if he were god and Phil as gullible as the President of the United States.

"Suppose 1 produced tritium inside the gadget itself with lithium compounds," said Phil. "There, Fred, bang! Let's junk your stupendous refrigeration for a simple chemical reaction. The lithium****"

Starzinchger was enraged and moved towards Phil like a boxer. He hated what Phil was saying, and suddenly he hated Phil himself even more than this blinding idea.

Phil saw and heard himself from a distance. The way people experience themselves when they are dying. Lineheardt was staring at him with awe. He felt a beautiful insect beating purple gauze wings inside of him, getting ready for a desperate rush out.

Starzinchger pushed him over the chair Lineheardt usually sat in. He fell backwards and hit the floor without interrupting the pestilent physics gushing from his mouth. The insect was out and darting around on its terrible wings. Still crazy with jealously, Starzinchger picked up the second chair and flung it across the room as if he could see the bug and was trying to hit it in flight. This beautiful thing whose birth was giving Phil and Lineheardt so much pleasure was Phil's invention of the H-bomb.

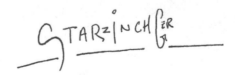

The pleasure of Lehman's customers filled him with an intense thrill. Before that teenager had pointed a huge shotgun at him, only 2 weeks ago, his eyes would reach out to his men like the tongue of a snake, touching and feeling everywhere for the texture of something sharp. His mind had been enveloped by cheaters.

All his adult life he had seen only dealers and bosses, gambling paraphernalia and agents inside a casino, and all he thought about was how to catch them at the instant of their criminality. He had been only dimly aware there was such a thing as tourists, and he'd had no idea they could sing such arias.

He recalled with pleasure how, once he had begun to hear his customers' song, he'd soon gotten the idea to fuel it with crooked dice. 1 morning he'd gone into the vault and replaced all the dice with new 1s which had been edged to favor the customers.

Though no1 knew for sure, it was now widely believed in Jake that Ziraleet was on a losing streak. Many many players were walking out winners. But astute Lehman watchers sniggered at such a rumor. Lehman could be seen walking his joint night after night, beaming with satisfaction.

The night the shaved dice went into play, Lehman fell in

love with his new kind of reverse gambling. He hadn't realized it was going to happen. It was his policy to never be around when something illegal started so he went over to the Chute to play craps while his bosses turned his new dice loose. When he came back and heard the songs his funny idea was creating, the pale thrill of his own gambling against his competitors made him laugh. In no way did it compare to letting money go out through his own tables. In no way did it match the thrill of reversing a process as old as civilization.

And in no way did his own most intense shout of crap shooting pleasure measure up to listening to the ziraleets of his customers. Not that he was going to give up striding into joints on 4th street to scare the piss out of his competitors, but the kid with the gun had opened a window to things he never would have seen if he hadn't come so close to the mouth of death and almost fallen in.

"Paging Bill Kearns," the public address system called. Bill Kearns was Lehman's paging name. "Bill Kearns, telephone please." They never paged him by his real name because people would line up near the house phones waiting to pepper him with requests. "Bill Kearns."

Alexander Viner came to Jake with some men 5 years ago and stayed. It wasn't a plan he had made. It was an accident. Like an auto accident. He had been run over and then rolled up in pretty oozing light like a mummy. He was as dead as a mummy. He didn't feel anything about anything. Except that this morning before his show he had felt points of shame spreading across his skin like ants biting.

He loathed himself. Actually, what he loathed was the sexuality which had exploded a purple wart onto the end of his dick in his 1st hours among Jake whores. His stupid affection for trotting out his pork chop in the company of sexual business women, 2 and 3 at a time, had stained him.

He knew during his 1st afternoon in Jake he wasn't going back to Blunt to drive a tractor in a straight line for 3 miles at a time. It had taken him until 4 days after the other men had returned to South Dakota to call his wife.

His sex bingeing had impaired his person so badly he couldn't take himself home to his young daughters. No matter how far he hid its images in the back of his head, he couldn't give it a ride home. He had explained it to his wife poorly.

{ **S**ex drunk? she asked. Was she supposed to come to Jake?

He got a job selling hardware. He convinced the owner to sell televisions. And then he got a job at the tv station. So well did he understand the marriage of television and journalism, he was awarded his own show for which he wore exotic costumes to mesmerize 9 year old boys.}

Was she supposed to come to Jake? He heard her last question from years ago. Why did this question keep coming back to him like a ghost? Linda come to Jake alone? Not, don't, not, no. He had said good bye without getting anything explained at all, severing his wife and girls to become something he could really hate. And sex had given him this gift of self loathing. Thank you sex for taking my daughters away from me. He had used his new hatred of himself to swear off whores. But Linda's question still kept coming back to him 3 times a day.

{"Do you want me to come out there without the girls and stay with you for awhile?"}

Maybe he should have let her. Probably he should have told her to bring the girls. To Jake?

This morning he had found himself making frequent references to God on the air. And now he was sloshing colored bourbon across his cheeks in the bar at Greek Hell, hoping Lineheardt would come in.

Lineheardt wouldn't notice he was a braying jackass. He would though. He could tell when it was happening. Right in the middle of a beautiful sentence, it would suddenly dawn on him that he was barking shit.

But Lineheardt didn't care when he barked his shit. She liked it.

The red Cadillac pulled up under the glowing green overhang. Erving tingled with delight. The pleasure of returning home from military school was always greatest when he 1st entered Ziraleet to find his father. He climbed out of the car and admired the new sign. However it was done, the arc of silver dollars was noisy. It was driven by a loud engine deep below the ground. Erving speculated it was quite new because the random silver dollars thrown onto the grass were being picked up by surprised passersby. The slot bums had not heard about it yet.

"How did he build this?" Erving asked his mother, unable to keep a note of tourist admiration out of his voice. How much had he paid how many physicists from 52 for this?

"Oh, I don't know," Sonia dismissed it, bored.

His mother's indifference irritated him. He loved his father for things like this and all the other things Ziraleet was. The other hotels were all feeble jokes compared to Ziraleet. This was what all the other morons were reaching for.

Pat O'Brien, Ronnie and Nancy Reagan

He rushed ahead of his mother into the lobby. At the casino entrance a waiter was handing out silver chalices of champagne. Erving recognized them from the trophy room where Lehman kept his silver collection. A stupid tourist took 1, turned around, and ran right into Erving in his hurry to get away with his fabulous souvenir.

Lehman raised his hand to the glasses on the tip of his nose. He seldom lifted them up to his eyes because he didn't like the way they magnified his brilliant blue cataract. (His eye looked like a cloud of sparkling blue gas behind the heavy prescription of the lens.) But he only hesitated for an instant before moving his glasses up to see if it really was his son approaching him.

"Hi-ya, Pop," said his son with a big grin, delighted to see his father.

"Plant 1," Lehman indicated his cheek. Erving kissed the cheek. It was rough with stalky whiskers which meant he had been up all the previous night gambling and still hadn't gone to bed.

"Z!" a voice shouted out to Lehman across Craps #2. "Can't I get in to see Reagan tonight?"

Erving looked at the tourist with a glare which would have made a PFC run the length of the Army dorm and hide in the showers. Lehman only nodded in the direction of the sound.

"Who is Reagan?" Erving asked.

"Movie star," reported Lehman, "Ronnie Reagan."

"How is his show?" asked Erving planning for a great first night home.

"He started with the monkeys from his movie on the stage, but they went out into the audience and people gave them their drinks. The monkey's got looped and we had to fight them back into their cages."

Erving laughed, thinking about monkeys jumping from table to table around the Ghaz. "I guess you got rid of the monkeys?"

"He wanted to bring them out again and control them with promises," smiled Lehman. "Hollywood. They're all drunk monkeys themselves."

"So what does he do without the monkeys."

"He talks a lot and sings a little."

Erving decided he wouldn't be going to the show. He would have Maryland fried chicken in the coffee shop. 3

make it a movie!

legs, 3 wings. Or 3 legs, 5 wings.

"Pop, do you think I need a paging name this vacation?" Erving had been thinking about the status of his own paging name all winter.

"What for?" asked Lehman, which meant no.

"How about Chick Evans?" asked Erving, hoping the name of a cool golfer might change Lehman's mind. He hated being summoned with 'Master Erving Lehman.' "Can I tell Margaret to page me as Chick Evans?"

"Nah," Lehman said, studying Erving's military appearance. "Nobody is going to bother you now. Just listen to them. They don't give a damn about you."

"Oh," said Erving. Three months of trying to figure the right name wasted. He probably should have tried Charles Stuart, the gambling king of England.

Lehman liked that Erving had returned home wearing his school uniform. The uniform was dark woolen blue, decorated with officer epaulets, a fruit salad of conduct metals, and a Sam Browne belt looping over his right shoulder. There were many Jews who dressed their sons up in bright suits like their own. These Jews had even taught their mafia friends to wear them. The Italians were all wearing these bright suits because they thought it gave them class. They often demonstrated their class by getting drunk and drooling wine all over their bright fabrics. 1 such bastard had sent a young gunman to kill Lehman. This killer youth had looked puzzled, as if he didn't understand what he was trying to do.

"The jerk, he had a gun that looked as big as the pipe underneath your sink," Lehman had told Ariel Stern. "He put it right up to my mouth."

Lehman, going back to his fighting days as a bootlegger, had stepped on his assassin's instep, broken his foot, and taken the shotgun away.

"For 70 years old you must have fantastic reflexes," congratulated Stern.

"I feel great!" laughed Lehman, feeling another spurt of invulnerability and well being. Such flashes had started the instant he'd taken the gun away from the kid, and they kept coming back.

After probing all the important men in his industry, Lehman still didn't know who was mad at him. But if he hadn't discovered the identity of his enemy, he had discovered something in his search. All of his business colleagues, besides being sensitive, quick to rage, and childishly paranoid, believed that none of those adjectives applied to them. They talked about the criminal element in Jake as if it were someone else.

S pike saw Trembling Peak off to the Northwest. A brilliant sun had pierced the grey roiling clouds blowing up over the mountain. The sun was low in the sky, but it wasn't pink, or even the 1st rich yellow of a beginning sunset. Balancing just above the peak, it was beaming out a penetrating silver. It made the mountain look like a giant volcanic chimney spewing swift grey clouds across the sky like ash. He realized the sun looked so low only because Trembling Peak was so tall.

Billboards for casinos and hotels began to block his view. The big rectangular signs had sexy Western girls endorsing hotels for their opportunities in skiing, competing in a canasta tournament, watching A-bombs, and even playing golf.

"He can really hit it, folks," he said to himself.

Just as he reached its turn off, Spike decided he'd see Jake. He turned and the billboards disappeared. The desert highway became a black aisle between sandy basins dotted with purple blooms. It was spring in Nevada. He passed through a forest of Yucca trees, the tips of their prickly Y's and W's all capped with pineapple-like flowers. He felt like Jason heading uphill through a foreign land towards the Golden Fleece.

27

"He can hit it."

He drove on up through piñon pines into a line of cheap motels where the ponderosas began. Past the motels many tents had been staked against the ponderosa trunks, a neighborhood known to jakes as yurtville. The sagebrush grew scarce as he drove higher. The taller and taller ponderosas looked like giant spinal columns with furry transverse processes. He came up over a ridge into a large mountain meadow thick with clusters of trembling aspens. Houses were tucked in between the groves of aspens wherever there was room. The air was cool and fresh.

He stopped to get out and look back down the mountain. Far below, Testrange 52 was surrounded by the Mojave's cactus and creosote. The specks of green and yellow went right down to a sea of grey dust and stopped. The monochromatic dust looked like the outreaching of an immense lunar ocean hidden up north beyond the mountains and buttes. It reached southward in a deep killing fjord to flood the Mojave and suffocate all its prickly life with grey dust. He stared at the dormant spiral whorls left by underground explosions with revulsion. No wonder the Army fired bombs into it.

He turned around and looked up through stands of some new pine with long graceful arms he'd never seen before. This new 1 was quite different from the thick and bushy spruce. Its limbs were spare and slender but still drooped from the weight of their fine needles. It was the most beautiful maudlin conifer he'd ever seen. He felt as if there were 2 expanding balloons in his lungs.

"He can hit it," he told himself. Usually when Spike heard himself singing his own praises, he got angry and frustrated, but not this time.

"He can really waffle it," he whispered, suddenly reversing his private disaffection with his golf game. Maybe he could

VERSION Nº III   NELSON. ROBT. A.

"STEALING THE GOLDEN FLEECE - SUMMER - LAKESIDE - OREGON - 2006

hustle up a golf game, win enough to parlay into a run of 21 which could feed him for a couple of years. His 1 iron would be his sword. Jason and the golden payoff. He could feel it in his lungs.

"Can he nail it!"

He got back in the car to resume the climb. Big drop-offs began to appear off the side of the road. The trees were getting shorter. He was coming to a turn-around in the highway. The mountain had been too sheer to bed the road about, so cars had to stop 1 at a time to turn around and continue. He watched the forest trying to scale the mountain alongside him. In pain from the effort, the trees bent over and shrank down to gnarled shrubs. He stared at the dwarfed spruce and pines with pity. 1 of his new favorites with the sad drooping arms was only half a tree. Its 1 arm flailed up and down spasmodically in the wind. Beyond it was a slope of sterile white gravel. He had reached the timberline. It took the last of his breath away. He could see up the white gravel to the mountain's towering stone face. At its base was a mining tunnel with a tilted mirror in its entrance. All the white gravel was coming out the mine shaft and down to the timberline as if the mountain were drooling stones out of a small shiny mouth.

Finally it was his chance to turn. He drove back down a long slope to a boulevard of weird hotels. They were bizarre buildings with odd motifs. They, too, seemed to reach toward some agonizing forbidding climate, some architectural timberline where the high winds of damaged imagination blew buildings into preposterous twisted shapes. Only 1 hotel, called Ziraleet, was as beautiful as it was strange.

He inched down the boulevard behind the heavy Friday traffic. Ziraleet was a face of glass worked into the mountain like the polished facet of a jewel, the jeweler's 1st careful effort on a bulky raw stone. Ziraleet's sign was an arc of gleaming silver dollars blowing a hundred feet up across its facade. There was no container or tube for the twirling silver. He couldn't imagine how it was done. The high arc of twirling coins was 6 feet in diameter.

The boulevard was jammed with cars, trucks and buses waiting to get into hotels. He couldn't wait out the traffic to get to Ziraleet. He turned into the 1st hotel. It was a tall pyramid with **"ANNUIT COEPTIS"** spelled out in lights over pink eye-like circles. The circles were a glowing soft neon tubing, as flexible as garden hose. He stared at the pink neon eye as the doorman yanked his suitcase from his trunk. The neon began to look less and less like an eye, and more like something familiar.

Inside he found a howling casino. Beyond it, up a few carpeted steps, was a bar lined with women. The tourists had parked their wives at the bar while they howled in the casino. The hotel was hosting a convention because the wives were all wearing the same high necked dress. The dress had a black stripe all the way down the front so that the pink satin looked like wet butterfly wings.

He walked around the side of the casino to the front desk. The desk clerk had a dollar bill folded up in his collar as a paper bow-tie. The doorman had been wearing 1. The bell boys had them. All the hotel employees had them. He fished a dollar bill out of his pocket. The hotel was the same as the pyramid on the bill, with the motto Annuit Coeptis over the eye. On the way up to his room, he asked the bell boy why the eye out front was on the bottom of the pyramid instead of the top like on the dollar bill.

"I'm tired of that question," he sighed.

Spike waited for the answer to the tiring question, but it never came.

The room had a double bed with a bedspread that looked

like somebody's old bathrobe. He undressed, took a shower, and sat down to read the hotel's guide to Jake. There were whores in Jake. Fornication was an approved industry here. He dressed and went downstairs to see.

He walked around through the casino looking up at the conventioneer's wives along the bar. Maybe there was no convention today. He stepped up from the casino floor and sat down at an empty section of the bar. The smell of crushed oranges rode the casino smoke. Fluorescent bulbs were shining up from the depths of the bar making a long well of white light. The bartenders were glowing from beneath their eyebrows. He looked down the line of pink satin women. The 1 on the 1st stool was looking at him very little like a conventioneer's wife. There definitely was no convention here today. The dresses were the whores' uniforms.

She hopped off her stool and walked towards him. She had a round soft face that looked like pudding. The satin dress had buttons halfway down the black stripe. She kicked her leg gracefully up over the stool next to him and the satin split from the buttons down. She wasn't wearing any underwear.

Her name was Patsy. She wasn't tired looking like the whores in Camden or Atlantic City. Probably because fornication was an approved legal industry here. But she wasn't pretty either. None of the other whores at the bar were pretty. He wondered if there was such a thing as a pretty whore. He wondered if there was such a thing as an attractive whore.

"So!" she said.

"So what?" he asked. Wasn't she going to sell him on it like a used car salesman? He was horny but he would need some sales work to screw this 1. Suddenly he wanted to go back down into the casino and play 21. He tried to apologize gracefully for not wanting to do business. Patsy

jumped off the stool and left with a look of sorrowful hostility.

He went down into the casino and sat down at a 21 table next to a blonde.

"He's a student," the pit boss was telling the blonde. The boss indicated a player at the next table. The blonde laughed a single clean note.

"A student?" asked Spike.

"They case the deck," said the pit boss.

"A student thinks he can beat the game by remembering the cards," said the blonde, as if she were describing someone who had begun to consider himself Napoleon.

Spike wondered why it was crazy to think you could beat 21. The blonde was probably over 30. He studied where the edges of her purple silk dress mixed in with the shadows along her deep neckline. Her skin was fair. She had light blonde hair. He wondered if her nipples were pale.

He tried to get a look when the loose purple silk wafted forward, but he saw only the rounded grey-white and shadows in between. He told her his father was a veterinarian.

"A veterinarian?" she asked, faking polite interest.

"Yes."

"I'll bet you know a lot of interesting things about animals," she said.

She was bored shitless with the possibility that he might know something interesting about animals.

"I do."

"What's the most interesting thing you know about animals?" she challenged him.

"The most interesting thing I know about animals is about pigs," he said.

"No fooling," she said. "Pigs."

"Pigs have grooves on the end of their dicks that fit into a sow's cervix like dowels," he said, "When they shoot, none of their sperm leaks out."

"What?"

"It's all stoppered up inside the womb, every drop of it, and it's not just a couple of teaspoons like a man either," he added. "A pig comes a pint of semen in an incredibly long orgasm."

"A pint?" her shoulders jogged up and down as she tried to not to laugh.

"My father is a veterinarian."

She laughed her clear laugh. The pit boss gave Spike a look of envy and left. She began asking him genuine questions about himself. He explained he'd left New Jersey on a whim 3 days ago. She told him she knew how it worked in gambling towns.

"Everyone is brimming with urgency and familiarity," she said. "When you meet people, it's like a weird combination of talking to someone you feel like you've known for years, and having to make a good 1st impression right away."

He liked her. She was smart.

"Everyone is walking around with their secrets hanging out so you feel like you have to unzip, too," she said, "but you don't, you know."

"What are you doing in Jake?" he asked her.

"I live here," she said. "I'm a dental hygienist."

He laughed.

"What's funny?"

"You're not kidding?" he asked.

"There are professionals in Jake besides those in the casino-related industries," she said in a withering monotone.

"I know," he apologized. "I meant****"

"Sometimes people who live here actually come out at night," she interrupted. "Like bats."

He'd touched something sensitive.

"I like to gamble at the Dog," she added.

"The Dog?" he asked. "Where's the Dog?"

"Here," she said. "This is the Dog."

"I thought it was called," he looked at 1 of his dollar bills, "Annuit Coeptis."

"Your father is a veterinarian?" she asked.

"I love dogs," he said. "I'm in the Dog?"

"The gut of it," she said. "Are you dumb?"

"No," he shook his head.

She waved at the pit boss and asked him to watch their chips while they went outside.

"Come on," she said. "Let's see if you're dumb or not."

He followed her through the casino towards the hotel entrance.

"This won't be a math question, will it?" he called after her. It was unlikely he would be able to prove himself smart with a math question.

She just kept walking. Her cocktail gown was tight around her ass. She had a perfect globular fanny and long legs. The purple silk around her neat ass made her look like a walking Darwin tulip. She took him across the street and turned him around.

The sky was starting to dim. Somewhere behind lower mountains many miles to the west of Trembling Peak, the sun was finally setting. The clean backless sky was a huge silver grey.

36

"They can call it 'Annuit Coeptis' all they want," she said.

He looked down from the sky to the grandiose triangle of cement and its meaty red neon eye.

"It's called the Dog because it looks like the back end of a beagle with its tail up," he said.

"So you aren't dumb," she laughed.

He laughed along with her, grateful to have dodged a math question. He watched the Dog spin its pink mist out into the huge silver sky like woolly atomized cotton candy. He turned and gaped down the street at all the other joints pulsing out their equally weird auras in neon mists. It was all so thick he felt like he was trying to breathe in a cloud of colored talcum. There was Ziraleet, still the most amazing, sunk into the mountain in burnished glass, and now behind the arc of silver dollars, 1,000 emerald "z"s were tumbling down the facade like teddy bears rolling down stairs. He was breathing in short gasps. He wasn't coughing but very little was going down his air hole. He felt like he was going to suffocate.

"What's your name?" he gasped at her.

"Noreen."

"I'm Spike."

He put his hands on her silk tulip hips. It was wonderful to feel their sharp outward slope. Her scentless breath tickled his face, and suddenly he began to breathe again. He kissed her. Her mouth was clean. He kissed down her long neck. She'd gotten hot inside the casino and the cool outside air had brought on a flush of perspiration across her neck. It was spreading along her bare shoulders in lucent bubbles. He nuzzled in close to her skin, breathing in her light perfume as if it were the purest oxygen for his shortness of breath.

"Holy work, you smell good," he said.

37

She looped her arm around his head and kissed him back. His lips felt like they were being pressed against warm glass. He pushed her away and held her by her bare damp shoulders.

"Do you like sex?" he gasped.

"Yes, I like sex," she laughed.

They went right up to his room. She got out of her dress while he was still unbuttoning his shirt. She jumped up and down on the bed like it was a trampoline.

"You're athletic," said Spike.

"What?"

I want athletic socks for Fucking.

"Will this be athletic fucking?" he asked.

She jumped off the bed and remounted it as if she were a gymnast. She flipped onto her back and over onto her stomach and onto her back again. She kept it up, twisting like a high diver and giggling wildly in the middle of all the turns.

"What the hell are you doing?" he shouted to get her attention.

"It's been a good day for me all day," she breathed, stopping to sit up and tie her long pretty legs together like a yogi. "Now I find someone like you who just happens to want athletic fucking."

She let loose her pretty laugh. Something about her good day was even funnier than the story about the student who memorized cards.

She untied her legs and flopped back on the bed. The nipples he'd been so anxious to see in the casino were spongy pink buttons. She had a fine light brush. From the waist down she still looked like a tulip, a naked snow peak with fine light stamens. Maybe the fleece God had sent him up the mountain to find wasn't gold. Maybe it was this silver silk surrounding a fabulous pussy.

He sat down on the bed to kiss her. When they parted, she wiggled her tapered legs proudly. Close up, he noticed she didn't use any eye make up. The eyes were her pride. That was her scheme. They soaked in the middle of all her faded colors like big drops of shiny blue ink on light paper.

"I like your eyes," he said. "Let's get married."

"Okay."

"I'm not being funny," he insisted.

"Okay."

"Come on," he said. "Let's get married."

"Now?"

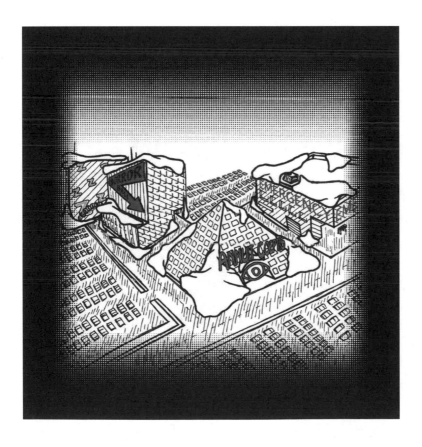

The Dog restaurant offered 6 different kinds of curry. Noreen explained that curry was sweeping the restaurants of Jake because everyone was imitating the Indian motifs of Ziraleet. She boasted that last week she had dined at Ziraleet with Lehman himself. Lehman was the owner of Ziraleet.

{She told Lehman how all the other hotels were serving curry to steal some of Ziraleet's magic. Lehman smiled and said there was no curry in any Ziraleet restaurants.

He'd raided the Indian culture for decorating concepts because every word that meant wealth or

Howard Kheel

happiness and started with a 'Z' belonged to India. The Indians might have colonized the rear of the dictionary, but that didn't mean he had to love their sandy food.

She laughed and told him that 1 of his competing hotels, Leo Gilberg's Hospital, was serving a curry that came out in yellow-green with black flecks floating on top. It looked like peppered snot.

Lehman's bad eye lit up in electric blue as he whispered to her that Gilberg liked the many fluids of disease because he found their colors charming.}

After dinner Spike waited at the bar while Noreen went to retrieve their chips from the pit boss and cash them in. He noticed the whore Patsy looking at him. He went over to share the good news with her. He wanted to cheer her up and lessen the insult of refusing her earlier. She said she didn't like good news. Now her face looked like curdled pudding. Noreen came back with the money.

"Patsy, meet Noreen Krieder," Spike introduced her. "I was telling Patsy that you and I are going to find a chapel and get married, and maybe she'll come with us, and we'll make it a party."

Noreen looked at him as if he were nuts.

"I'm working," Patsy refused.

"I'll pay," said Spike, lifting the $300 in winnings Noreen had just fetched for him.

"No thanks," said Patsy, looking at Noreen with hatred.

"Do you 2 know each other?" asked Spike, suspicious.

Patsy snickered.

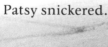

"We've never met," said Noreen distantly, like a banker cooling a bond salesman.

"We all know the Noreens of Jake," Patsy burst out jealously.

Spike frowned at Noreen. Another trick was being played on him. This 1 wasn't as funny as the cotton candy coming out the Dog's neon asshole. Maybe there was such a thing as a pretty whore. Maybe there was such a thing as a supernaturally beautiful whore and maybe he had just asked her to marry him. This wasn't funny at all. He was gasping again. He felt dizzy.

"Is she saying you're a whore, too?" he asked.

"I'm a whore?" demanded Noreen, her eyes jumping up her brow.

Patsy grinned at that. Spike wished this had come up earlier when they had been alone in his room. He could adjust to it, but he wished it had come up earlier in private. Noreen's blue irises were vibrating. Tears bubbled up out of them like carbonated water.

"Is that what you want, Spike?" Noreen didn't want him to want it.

He didn't say anything. Was that supposed to be an answer to the question? She turned and hurried away through the lobby.

"She's a whore, isn't she?" he asked Patsy.

"A whore?" scoffed Patsy, his stupidity turning her grin into laughter. "There is nothing pro about her. What does she know about being a good boff? They can look into her eyes and come. I'll bet she lays there like a dead moth."

"Not really," said Spike. "It's more like screwing a bucking horse. And when I came, she made her cunt squeeze my dick like it had fingers."

Chick

"She can do that?" Patsy was astonished.

"She can do that," affirmed Spike.

"No kidding," breathed Patsy, her hostility suddenly dissipated by admiration. "If I were beautiful like that Noreen****" She stretched her hands up over her head as if she wanted to take a nap. "Hey, Spike," she put her hands on her hips, struck with a wonderful idea. "Let's get married, you and me."

"What?" Where the hell was this coming from, he wondered. He heard his own spirited proposal to Noreen in the back of his head. Was there something in Jake which made everybody propose to everybody? That's why there were wedding chapels everywhere.

"You could have girl friends," she offered.

Patsy saw Spike looking at her with confusion and new interest. She could see it was possible. But maybe Spike hadn't been in Jake long enough to understand she was serious.

"Go out at night and come home drunk. Just be nice to me and a good step dad to my daughter."

Sometimes they came to town in a hurry to get married, as if their bachelorhood were a glowing nugget they had to extinguish before it burned a hole in their scrotum, Patsy calculated. They'd marry anyone who seemed faintly attractive.

"I won't sit there and stare at you with blue eyes while you do all the work," she embellished her offer. "I used to be a bank teller. I'll get a job in a bank. Are you an actor?"

"An actor?" Spike liked this wondrous strange civilization he had found by accident. Marriage here was a different. Even for a novice like him.

"You're good looking," she said. "Lots of actors come here. What do you do?"

"Not much."

"You can fuck anybody you want," she guaranteed.

"You're serious?"

"Dead."

He looked way across the casino to the lobby where Noreen was walking out into the cotton candy night.

"You bastard," Patsy sighed, giving up on him as he hurried away after Noreen.

"He can hit it," said Spike with the crackling sarcasm he reserved for mocking himself,

"He can really waffle it."

Perhaps it could be pancaked???

yum!
make them
for Breakfast
please!

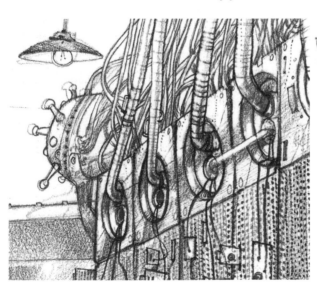

45

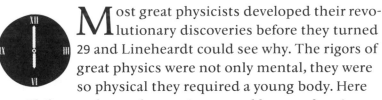 **M**ost great physicists developed their revolutionary discoveries before they turned 29 and Lineheardt could see why. The rigors of great physics were not only mental, they were so physical they required a young body. Here was Phil, 31 and past the magic age; and he was showing the strain.

Working the way only physicists could work, 20 hours a day for weeks, their minds staying focused and sharp on the exhilaration of progress, they had worked the critical mass for a fission burst down from the 19 kilotons of Trinity to 5 kilotons. They were ready to fit the whole new gadget inside the plastic cube Phil had designed for the new rail cannon.

Phil still didn't know where his radiant idea had come from, but the moment it had started coming out, he had known his 2 white months at home had been a fight to keep it in.

All his life Phil had believed that if offered the choice between the distinctly right and the distinctly wrong, he would have no trouble rejecting the wrong. But it hadn't worked out that way. A hydrogen bomb was wrong. That gram of reality was easy enough to weigh. But the choice had contained some-

46

thing more pressing than the business of right and wrong.

The choice had been between madness and ambition, and now that it had been made, right and wrong would never be invited to snow their cold weight inside his head again. Even as he had showered Starzinchger with a sparkling meteor storm of perceptions, Phil had realized that his long white cold of the mind with its daily episodes of shrieking wildly about the kitchen while May and his sons looked on in terror was worse, far worse than being the man who brought the H-bomb into the world.

Perhaps because Phil had shot the ideas through Starzinchger like poison darts and because Starzinchger had his years and billions invested in gigantism, he had been unable to see into Phil's small idea. He had entertained it with scorn. (After picking up the busted chairs and apologizing for beating Phil up.) But Phil didn't mind now. Whatever Starzinchger's reaction had been, the idea had taken Huke, and Huke could do whatever he wanted to with 52's money while Starzinchger screwed pricey women down in LA.

"I've got to get a memo off to Starzinchger before I do my taxes," said Phil. "I'm going to tell him that the 1st H-bomb will have cryogenics on a scale he's familiar with. The scale of the ice-box in his kitchen."

Lineheardt laughed. She watched Phil sit down on her stool and twirl around. His arms swung like the iron struts on an amusement park ride when it's just beginning to spin. She could see the strength in them.

Some experimental physicists were physically strong because they were always lifting and bending things, but Phil was exceptional. When a screw had to be bent only a tiny bit by hand, while it was still screwed into something delicate, there was never any discussion about whom to send for. It was always Phil, even if he were 2 miles of corridor away.

The interesting thing about his strength was how skinny he was. He was over 6 feet tall but weighed less than 130. His bone structure was fine and wrapped with films of muscle so thin Brady would have trouble measuring them, and yet so tensile people had to be warned about shaking hands with him.

She stopped looking at him and picked up the newspaper Phil had put down on the counter. He got off the stool and began to fool with 1 of her oscilloscopes.

"It says here in the Mercury," she called to him. "Recent underground tests might have punched the start of a hole in the earth's crust."

Phil laughed.

"You don't believe it?"

"Did you flunk geology?" mocked Phil. He was fond of making fun of her perfect scholastic record.

"Damn it, Phil."

His teasing about her scholastic excellence made her feel strange. She'd caught him with her employee file mooning over her grades once. Hers, he had said, were the kind of grades Kepler or Newton would have gotten if they'd been admitted to a great American university.

Renza came in, and because she was annoyed with Phil, she went off with him to the party in the mess hall.

Everybody was jolly as hell at the party. She didn't stay long. She felt a punishing sense of helplessness, as if suddenly things had arranged themselves so that there was nothing she could do to make her work or her life turn out right.

She found Phil back in his own office reading a memo. Her

bad feeling became sharp. He was rubbing his forehead with 3 fingers. He had short fine fingers. The pink half moons beneath his small nails turned smoky orange as he

A pilot from Nellis contracts with Ziraleet to parachute into the hotel pool

pressed them across the paler skin of his large brow.

She stared at him, adding up his neat hair, the 3 small fingers pressed along his brow, his smile bowed out from the corners of his great mouth up to his eyes, and she got angrier and angrier.

Men were no different than women. Whenever Phil looked in the mirror, he combed up the things he loved in himself. In this way he must have developed his style of moving his hand up and down the corner of his big brow. He'd painted himself up for the world to see with years and years of work no artist could match; and he'd turned out something wonderful because such work, like his physics,

49

came directly from his secret thoughts. It all added up to his sensitivity and his originality which were exactly what she loved in men, and it pierced her like a bullet that what made her angry was that she loved it because she couldn't have it for herself.

That originality. She would always be quick. She could learn like Lillo or Starzinchger. But where was the thing that sparked up in Phil, who couldn't even do The Calculus, that thing which gave off ideas such as firing projectiles with forces related to the velocity of light rather than expanding gas, and more, a hundred ideas a week, all coming out of Phil's peculiar way of understanding things, and each, at its very least, challenging and new?

She would never have it. She couldn't remember ever producing anything anyone wanted to call beautiful. She didn't even get the symptoms, which she guessed were tingling spears of awareness winging their way about the body at speeds far beyond the slow circulating thrills of solving problems. Phil didn't solve problems. He wasn't even a visionary because he had no visions.

"It's physical," he had explained. "I'm tense, like I'm vibrating almost, and it can go on for awhile, and then there it is. It's wonderful and it's strange, and I have no idea where it came from. It's not a vision. I've never had a vision. I see it finished. There's nothing nebulous about it and no part of it is in the future. It's all coming out right in front of me, Whoosh!"

He had made it sound like something was making love to him without his knowledge or consent, and then suddenly he'd have his rush of pleasure.

As he finished Huke's memo, Phil became aware of Lineheardt's stare.

"You know what the worst thing about fusion is?" he asked her, holding up the memo.

"No."

"The shortfall of genius in the idea itself," he said. "The

potential consequences are so big, the idea should be as demanding and inaccessible as Relativity. But it isn't inaccessible at all. Even Huke can understand it."

52 Security

She wasn't listening. Phil had noticed that she had begun to pay him back for his constant study of her mouth. She often looked at him as if she were taking notes on his mannerisms. She had breezed through most of his physics as if it were high school algebra, and now she was moving on to other things.

"If I had started in physics before Bohr, or maybe even before Newton, no, Kepler, way way back before all the laws were wrinnen, it would have all come out different," he said.

Lineheardt laughed.

"You know what I'd like to do, now?" he asked her. "I'd like to prove that our current physics is an artificial map we've made up to explain terrain we don't really understand at all. And never will. It's all self-contained, self-fulfilling Gödel flavored bullshit."

She frowned. Phil thought back to how he'd pronounced 'written'. He had his worst problems with the double t. He couldn't hear the difference between some ts and ds. Maybe she was beginning to listen for his speech problems instead of his meaning.

"Is that what you were doing at home all winter?" she asked. "Invalidating physics?"

He laughed. "Not exactly."

"What were you doing?" she asked. "I come to work for

you, and a week later, you disappear for months."

Phil was amazed. "You took that personally?"

"I schemed for a year to get a job with you," she said.

"What do you do when you go mad, and you know you're mad, but you're not so sick that you can let yourself be dragged away to a nut house?" he asked her.

"Are you talking about you?"

"You can't go there and let them treat you like you're crazy," he said. "What do you do?"

"You mean you went crazy?" she said.

"You go home," he said. "You stay inside like you have a cold, a long bad cold in your mind. You hang on until it passes."

She seemed dumbfounded.

"My lord," she whispered.

"It had nothing to do with you," he said. "Working with you is great. Don't think it had anything to do with you."

"But how did you know it would go away?"

"I didn'd know."

"Why are you laughing?" she asked. He was laughing the nearly hysterical laugh he always let loose when someone was praising him. He found praise very very humorous.

"It's funny," he said.

His laughter died down. The creases of his big smile circled up from his spread mouth all the way to the corners of his eyes. 2 very big very infectious furrows.

"I wonder how you made it."

He looked at her as if he didn't understand.

"I mean I want to know what you said to yourself," she said, "when you woke up every morning and knew you were still mad."

"What?"

"What did you say to yourself to make yourself keep going?"

"I dinnid say anything to myself," he said, shaking his head as if she should know better. "I've had the discipline of physics. I've seen problems before which require indeterminate expenditures of energy and patience."

When she went back into the party, the long grey mess hall was still buzzing with happy physicists. Alfred Jenks, the X-ray specialist, came up and demanded an explanation of Phil's rail cannon.

"The history of ballistics has been gunpowder," he said, interrupting her explanation before she could get started. "The ignition of gunpowder releases expanding gas which pushes the projectile down the your barrel. Now here comes Phil, and he implodes 2 copper rails together to compress an electromagnetic field down to something so dense and energetic it flees along the closing rails pushing its plastic cube out its mouth in the same way gunpowder creates gas to move bullets."

Jenks puffed on his pipe, looking at her for approval.

"Yes," she agreed.

"In the instance of gunpowder, the velocity of expanding gas is related to the speed of sound," Jenks continued. He held onto his pipe bowl with his fingertips as he lectured. He was pleased with himself. "The movement of electromagnetism, however, is governed by laws pertaining to the speed of light."

"Which is why a rail gun can fire projectiles at speeds 150 times faster than gunpowder," put in Lineheardt like a good little listener.

"Why didn't anyone think of this before Phil?" asked Jenks.

"Implosion," said Lineheardt.

"Yes," agreed Jenks, nodding with respect.

Implosion belonged to Phil. The laws of electromagnetism had been around since Faraday's beautiful experiments, but nobody had ever thought of using them to fire shells and bullets because nobody but Phil spent morning, noon, and night thinking about all the things that could be done with implosion. Of all the Byzantine plots physicists had dreamed up to manipulate physical phenomena, there was none more elegant than the addition of implosion to electromagnetism.

"When you implode 2 copper rails together," said Jenks, "you not only create an incredible force field, you give it direction at the same time. I imagine a rail cannon could fire a gadget from Kansas to Korea."

"We're not ready for that," Lineheardt said quickly.

"No?" asked Jenks, disappointed. "But you shot 1 at the moon."

"The size a gadget requires would create friction problems in the atmosphere," said Lineheardt. "The 1st cube presented only a small surface area to the atmosphere."

"And there is the problem of aiming a square projectile accurately," she added.

Phil's plan to startle the world by hitting the moon and sending up a 1,000-mile plume of dust had failed because the plastic cube had wobbled through a few

*unexpected vectors before escap-
ing the earth's atmosphere. After
missing the moon it pierced Orion
through the gut and was current-
ly speeding towards the Sombre-
ro galaxy where it would arrive
about the time men eliminated
war from politics.*

Jenks rumbled on about the potential for the rail principle
as if he were introducing her to ideas she'd never heard
before. He sounded like Huke reciting Phil's dreams. There
was however a small snag Jenks had missed in his readings of AWB memos. At the moment there was no way to
prevent any construction of a rail gun from blowing itself
into a million metal groats at the same instant its projectile
exited its mouth.

"What are you looking at me like that for?" asked Jenks.
"You're awfully short tonight."

Renza came over to tell her the same secret Huke had told
her earlier. She had a martini. It made her feel better. Even
good.

She watched Renza sharing his excitement with Jenks. She
had a 2nd martini. She felt hot and sweaty and angry again.
The gin was turning on her.

She asked herself what she had to feel so good about. The
party buzzed around her. She was suffocating. She wondered if Phil were attractive looking in the nude. She imagined him with his back to her. She gave him a cute ass. She

felt stupid and angrier still. She wanted to see him from the front too. Did he have a long dick, tensile and strong like his handsome forearms?

She arched her neck like a bird swallowing water, trying to get rid of the tension across her shoulders. She wanted to weep a hot stream of disgusting boozy tears.

This line is fantastic

It pained Phil that he hadn't been invited to the party. Why would they exclude him from parties? He went out into the main passageway. The noise of the party, wherever it was, couldn't find its way through the corrugated hallways of 52 to him.

He walked down to Lineheardt's lab. He went in and tread slowly past the row of her homemade CRT's. She made her own oscilloscopes out of tv tubes because tv's had very fine powers of resolution. She was frugal. She used old tv's she got from a former tv salesman she liked to tour Jake bars with.

He looked out 1 of her cow-eyed windows. The desert seemed calm. He opened the window wondering if he could detect the location of the party from noise coming out an open window.

The party's windows would be open because Huke loved to open windows. But the desert was quiet. Whatever meaningful noise there was in the world seemed to pass over the Mojave in swift high clouds while 52 thumped sullenly about its secret work. Only Jake was watching, and they had started to lose interest. Especially since the Helldorado had just started and they were all having Western fun pretending to be cowboys in fancy tack.

He went over to the other side of the lab to look up at Jake. A jet from Nellis was flying across the top blue stripe of the sunset. The jet slowed sharply as it passed over Trembling Peak. Something came rocketing up out of it.

The pilot had ejected. There was a problem with the plane. It was going to crash. A huge lavender parachute opened up out of the tumbling metal pilot's seat.

The jet zipped around and climbed like a silver humming-bird. Nope, it was only a stunt. Some guy had been shot up out of the 2nd seat to parachute down into Ziraleet's

2nd Lieutenant Erving Lehman, just under the neck of Buck's Nugget, back from ENMS for Helldorado

swimming pool for Helldorado. The cone of lavender slid down the sunset's layers of blue and fiery pink towards the brilliant beads of 4th Street's neon jewel work.

Jake, the only town in America where both whoring and gambling were legal, had been prospering making a show of 52's gadgets. The mountain's beauty had never been powerful enough to attract the throngs required to make a thriving resort until atomic testing began, and all the noceurs could look down on the purple roiling dust of fission and be amazed.

At 1st they hadn't even understood that they were looking at A-Bombs. The bursts were originally described to tourists by Jake's native experts as magical seismic events whose startling visual effects were natural mysteries.

Stories of the unusual earthquakes brought many visitors

into Jake looking for something novel to see on the sleepy Western weekend. The mystery lost cogency, however, as the bursts became ordinary and atomic secrecy cheapened.

It became known among the residents that their whoring and gambling were thriving on reproductions of the A-Bombs which had destroyed the Japanese. Lately, even the tourists had begun to get bored with 52 because all the new testing was underground. An underground was only a loud whump, followed by sand falling into a spiral maw.

The lack of interest up on the mountain dismayed the physicists. Having Jake up there full of jaded whores and cynical dealers staring down on them with intense absorption had made them feel like they were doing something very exciting. They had arranged flashier shows for Phil's last tests, putting the small gadgets closer to the surface. But as far as Jake was concerned, a geyser of dirt was better than a dull whump in much the same way that cholera improved constipation. Perhaps Jake was never going to care about them again, no matter how big a blam they sent up when fusion was ready.

Phil heard shoes rustling across the floor behind him. Lineheardt had returned from the party. She was drunk now. He smiled at seeing her tipsy.

"I've been celebrating," she said. "We've all been over celebrating. Exactly what we've been celebrating I'm not supposed to say. It's an officious secret."

"Official," said Phil.

"No," Lineheardt corrected him back. "Officious. Right from the Huke itself."

He looked up from her sharp lip to mischievous eyes. Now that they were boozy and intense, they were even more interesting than the neat line of her lip.

"The Huke invited Renza and me to something secret on

59

Sunday morning," she said. "Do you think he wants to make me 1 of his WACs. Maybe I'll be allowed to wear a lab duster instead of 1 of those astonishing uniforms."

"You wouldn't work for him," said Phil nervously. "Doing what? Sums to back up BOIR8Min?"

"Oh, no!" she agreed loudly, shocked at Phil's nervous response. "I want to work for you. I'm in love with working for you."

Phil laughed happily.

"Huke hates Lillo, you know," said Phil.

"He hates Lillo," repeated Lineheardt.

"What is there to hate in Lillo?" begged Phil. "Lillo wants only to be loved for his work. He doesn't care by whom, whether it is Truman, Huke or the janitor. He wants it from everybody. But Huke hates him and loves Starzinchger."

"But how can Huke hate Lillo?" asked Lineheardt drunkenly.

"Because Huke's hero is Starzinchger," said Phil.

"His hero is Starzinchger" said Lineheardt, trying to get it.

"Take Huke's attitude towards our current work," said Phil. "He tells himself that since the cyclotron was patched into existence almost by accident, why then fusion can be the same kind of experiment. If it goes partly wrong, what the hell, we fix something and try again until it comes out right. It worked for Starzinchger, dinnid it?"

"Starzinchger did invent the cyclotron," argued Lineheardt. "Starzinchger is a worthy hero. We must allow Huke his worthy hero."

"Starzinchger didn't invent the cyclotron," said Phil, surprised at her ignorance of the well known gossip.

"What?" asked Lineheardt, alarmed.

"He stole it," said Phil. "Jim Hetzel got it working in 1 single inspired night while Starzinchger was at home asleep. He was Starzinchger's assistant at UCLA then. It was only the 2 of them."

“I’ve never heard of Jim Hetzel,” said Lineheardt.

“As soon as he saw it in the morning, Starzinchger began to talk as if the crucial conception was his,” said Phil. “Hetzel spent the day in torment. What should he say? In the afternoon, the University Regents came around to be amazed by the revolutionary instrument. Hetzel called Starzinchger a liar right in front of them. He was expelled from the university. Starzinchger won the Nobel Prize.”

“No,” said Lineheardt, dumbfounded.

“No?”

“He couldn’t get control of modern physics because he stole an idea from somebody I’ve never heard of,” she said.

“I guess not,” laughed Phil.

“He stole it,” she said. “Amazing.”

“It’s part of why Starzinchger can make no progress developing fusion,” said Phil. “He’s still working through the cyclotron because it’s the only idea he can call his own. It’s all he has.”

“And he stole it,” she echoed.

She felt feverish. She paced up and down her lab ticking off points to herself as if she were examining stages in a new formula. The cyclotron was the only way to produce tritium for liquefaction. Liquid tritium was necessary for fusion in the orthodox view. But the orthodox view was orthodox only because it was Starzinchger’s view.

“And the cyclotron gets bigger and bigger,” she said. “That’s the attraction of fusion for Starzinchger, part of why he’s always been so eager to produce the Super. It’s a way to keep on building new cyclotrons, but he doesn’t really know their future because they aren’t his. He believes in magic!”

“Yes!” agreed Phil vindictively. “He doesn’t know what he’s doing. He’s only tossing stuff out and hoping for the best.”

Lineheardt touched the wet roots of her hair. Huke's hero was a plagiarist and a thief.

"I'm not supposed to tell you," she said. "Renza isn't going to tell you, so don't tell him I told you or he'll tell Huke that you know and he didn't tell you and that only leaves Inez and Huke won't think I'm attractive after all. He leered at me, Phil. Can you imagine what color his complexion turns when he's leering?"

Phil was looking out the open window. The air coming in was cool on his cheeks. The desert air always cooled quickly after the sun went down. It was late twilight now. The sky was purple. So was Jake. The dark purple twilight looked like a mist just thick enough to condense on Jake like dew. He quivered nervously when he realized what she was telling him. Her reason for returning from the party wasn't loyalty. It was guilt.

"Where is the party?" he asked after Lineheardt finished explaining. The burst had been scheduled for Sunday morning, and no 1 was to tell Phil. "I have to talk to Huke."

"Oh, he's not coming back to the party," she said. "He went back to his office. He had 30 or 50 phone calls to make."

Phil hurried through the crinkled metal corridors towards Huke's office. He took numerous wrong turns on a route he knew by rote. Why were they firing it without him? The significance of their keeping it from him was terrifying. Holy shit, had he pulled this awful thing so far only to be excluded from watching?

After Phil had begun to read again, it was never the same as it had been before everything had gone white. Sometimes he'd be reading along and he'd get stuck on a word like **TUBALLOY.** For several moments it would bounce around inside his head like a photon inside a reflecting cube. Even after finishing what he was reading, the word would tic away in the back of his head. Then at night it would zing through his sleep, leaving tracks across his dreams like white mesons in a cloud chamber.

TUBALLOY had been uranium's secret name during the war. It was the code word designed to prevent stray Germans from overhearing any loose conversation among scientists and making a connection between uranium and the best of America's physicists. Of course, if any such connection had been made, word would have reached Hitler inside of an hour and he would have ordered Heisenberg to have an A-Bomb ready by the end of the week.

After the war America's best physicists never got out of the habit of calling uranium **TUBALLOY**. Now everyone at 52 called uranium **TUBALLOY**, even though the A-Bomb was nobody's secret and few of them had been in Chicago. They all invoked **TUBALLOY** like 14 year old boys saying that a girl's private areas smelled like fish, as if citing the mystery of the odor proved they'd been there with their noses.

This morning Huke had made Phil go over everything with him again. Now that the experiment itself was close, Huke seemed to want to actually understand it.

To Phil's amazement Huke had understood it. Fueled by affection for Huke's detailed interest in the work, Phil had found himself telling him how wonderful Lineheardt was. He had told Huke she had the stuff to become the next genius in physics.

"No, sir," Huke had said painfully, as if Phil were rubbing a sensitive wart. "There's no such thing as genius or intuition."

Phil had laughed.

"Nobody is a genius," Huke had said. "Starzinchger and Lillo have superior mental mechanics. Nothing more."

Huke had then gone out to look at the rail cannon, which seemed to interest him more than the gadget itself. Phil had sighed and let him go.

Now in full panic from Lincheardt's drunken confession that Huke was going to show the H-bomb on Sunday morning, Phil hurried down the long aisle of files towards Huke at his desk.

Phil wondered if he should go to Washington to raise the alarm on Huke. There was no point in going back to the White House though. Nothing could be done with the righteous Truman. Phil would have to explain to the entire Senate, 1 senator at a time, exactly why the Lillos of science had abandoned the AWB and only the Starzinchgers and their Hukes remained.

He would tell them that Starzinchger was in this only to take his intellectual pleasures with the Huke's of physics, to take it like sex since Huke was a poser whose mind had the same utility as the core asset Starzinchger often rented from sexual business women in Jake.

In his thoughts Phil was eloquent, but every senator was sitting behind a desk covered with the same grey desert dust as Huke's, and all across their blotters dead flies were lying with their legs up.

The cow-eyed windows in Huke's office were open. The office felt even hotter than usual. The windows were always opened as soon as the sun went down. According to Huke the nighttime air cooled BOIR8Min. But the huge office was always very hot.

Behind Huke were the 200 arithmetic teachers turned WAC. They were working 4 to a desk in the astonishing uniforms Huke had manipulated the Army into making them wear. They were supposed to help them stay cool. They were nothing more than khaki colored negligees. It was obvious Huke was interested in their bosoms.

Like Phil, they had not been invited to the party. They had too much to do. They were working frantically to catch up with the hulking BOIR8Min on the other side of Huke's office.

BOIR8Min's large modules lined the walls in 20 huge telephone-like switchboards. The switchboards were fed by large cables which hectored noisy electricity into them at gargantuan rates. From the WACs' point of view, the most salient quality of BOIR8Min was the way it gorged on electricity.

The WACs were too hot to see that the computer was a miracle. To them it was a fatuous 8 year old, which, because it

was too young to be trusted, forced them to work around the clock in Army underwear to check work it had finished 2 weeks ago.

They had to re-calculate everything because few scientists were willing to take this miracle's word for anything. Only Phil, out of his deep hatred for mathematics, and Lineheardt, out of her great admiration for BOIR8Min, accepted computer data without reservation.

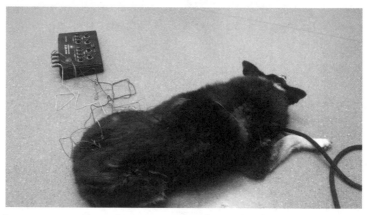

Huke was wearing a baggy suit and a cream colored bow tie with plum polka dots. Though he was sweating, his hands were venous and would be cool to the touch. Phil hated shaking hands with him.

Huke liked to shake hands hello, shake hands good-bye, and sometimes in the middle of a meeting he'd shake hands for a false parting and then take special pleasure in the final handshaking as if it were an encore.

Phil watched Huke talking on the phone. Suddenly he felt a stupid fondness replace his hostility for him.

"*Phil!*" Huke exclaimed when he hung up the phone.

Phil clasped the blue lattice work of the hand. The pulsing veins felt like cold worms.

Huke rambled for 20 minutes. He complained of anxiety about the scheduled test. He said that Phil was the only 1 at 52 capable of relieving his anxiety. Nobody at the party had understood. Not even Phil's pretty assistant.

"Phil, I'm tired of years of safety experiments and undergrounds," he said. "Where's the glory in spreading plutonium across the flats like salt? We have the right to do something meaningful before Truman forces Starzinchger to come up here full time and make everyone miserable. We're the 1s who've been sweating over nuclear weapons technology for 5 years out here in the desert. Why don't you stop contesting everything with me, and let's take our glory together."

He held out the cool venous hand again. Phil felt his thoughts wander into a black pool of sadness. He wanted to take Huke's hand. He hated him, yes, but he wanted very much to take his hand and end ten years of animosity. Holy shit, what a wonderful feeling it was to have it offered up by Huke himself on a plate of genuine affection.

"We'll go out to the bunker together Sunday morning," said Huke happily, as if Phil had taken the hand already and agreed.

"How far up range will you put the rail cannon?" asked Phil, his hand trembling at his side.

"We'll fire the cannon within sight of the bunker," said Huke. "We'll make up for the moon shot by letting everyone see the rail cannon fire the 1st H-gadget."

"You shouldn't fire it that close," Phil said. "I think you have the gadget's radius of destruction wrong."

"No! No!" Huke was offended by Phil's objection.

"If you're going to have the rail cannon that close, you should fire the shell much farther up range; and there may be problems with that****"

"Don't be silly," differed Huke energetically. He was bright with confidence. "That's not a problem."

69

Huke had no doubt that the radius of the gadget's destruction would be less than 5 miles. He had fed some formulas through the 200 WACs several times, and the WACs had awarded a 5 mile radius the status of reality.

Phil imagined himself going to the party to argue such figures with his colleagues. Upon hearing that Phil wanted to argue mathematics, they would line up in a gauntlet to entertain his opinions. He would debate his way down a corridor of 50 physicists, all batting away at him, each with his own personal club leaving its own little stamp of numerical reality on Phil's head. Who was right would not be the issue. No. Not at all. The issue would be the fact that these Indians would bounce enough wood off his skull to make him forget how reality actually was put together.

"You don't have to add anything together, Steve," said Phil, his hatred of their math suddenly venting itself. "You don't even have to think. Just let the sight of fission and fusion exploding together play up on that feeble screen of pictures you call your imagination, and you'll get a powerful conviction it has to be at least ten or 15 miles. Before you even write down any numbers, you have to feel 10, 15 miles."

"I don't believe in intuitive calculating, Phil."

"He doesn't believe in intuitive calculating," Phil called to the WACs. 1 of them looked up from her work. Phil turned back to Huke. "Do you know how powerful fusion might be?"

"Of course I do," said Huke, his voice colored with exhilaration. "The potential for this weapon is unlimited. We'll add whatever power to the burst we want. We can have 50, 100, 200 megaton bursts. Megatons, Phil. Theoretically, it is even conceivable that we might possess the power to turn the Earth into a star."

Phil stared at Huke in horror. This filthy piece of pride

Elise is the keep knees of it

had been his 1st a decade earlier. Hearing it from Huke
dislodged the memory. He could see himself making this
same speech about turning Earth into a star, with this
same exhilarated enthusiasm, to Lillo when he had been a
young graduate student. Lillo, he now remembered vividly, had looked at him with despair. It was a look which
said something useless and heinous had just flown out of
Pandora's box. The instant he understood Lillo's revulsion,
the idea for a lithium fueled fusion fell down inside himself to wrap itself in silk.

It had hibernated down there for years. It had taken a
white winter in his bedroom and a confrontation with
Starzinchger for it to molt and fly. And now it was buzzing all over the place. It had grown a bomb in his rail
gun. It had thrown Lineheardt into a frightening spin
that reminded him way too much of his dead best friend
Barbanel, and here it was, now, the most disgusting thing
he had ever said in his life, winging back to him as proud
original Huke wisdom.

"No, I don't think you will be there, Phil," said Huke,
coming to a decision. "I'm withdrawing my invitation. I'm
sorry I have to be the 1 to tell you this, especially since our
association goes back to Chicago, but everyone agrees that
your presence at this facility has become counter productive."

"Counter productive!" shouted Phil. Several WACs looked
up this time.

"Your association with the AWB is terminated, Phil," said
Huke.

Phil felt a terrifying loss of orientation. How could the
computer be so wrong? It hadn't even gotten close. Huke
was still talking, telling him more about being fired.

"Since this is a top secret urgent priority government and
military installation," Huke was saying, "I'll have to ask you

to take whatever in these facilities which you value personally to the director of security to be inspected before 9 o'clock, and that you absent yourself from the facility at 9."

Phil saw himself rifling his drawers for something of value, searching wildly to find something, anything of personal value. Before 9.

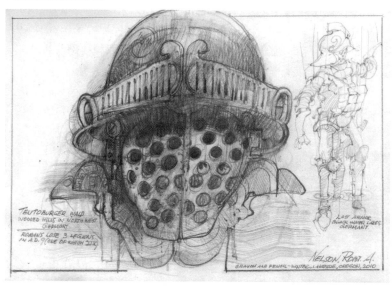

"And I must warn you never to communicate again with anyone who works at this installation," continued Huke in his Wednesday morning meeting tone.

Phil wondered if this termination of his association with the AWB hadn't been the inevitable destination of this interview. It was coming out of Huke so exactly, in such a bored official tone, it was obvious it had been worked over in his mind for several days. Terror dropped out of the bottom of the black pool in his head and flooded his body. In an instant the flow of it spilled into his right forearm triggering a painful cramp which turned his right hand into a claw.

"Prior to 9 o'clock I further enjoin you to limit communications with anyone at this installation to transmitting farewells of the permanent and unbridgeable nature required by atomic secrecy."

Huke came around his desk and held out his hand. He was offering up the real-parting handshake. His pallid cheeks were flooded with happiness. At last he was getting rid of Phil. He was his own experimental physicist now. He wanted to be congratulated, never mind that he was asking it of the injured party. Phil, now that the last membrane between his hatred and Huke had been torn, took the cool hand as if it were metal in need of re-alignment and crushed it.

What test? Starzinchger had asked himself when Sensenig had called after lunch.

"Huke told me you were eager for this," Sensenig had said, smelling something in Starzinchger's confusion.

Starzinchger had hung up amazed. Huke was trying to finesse him. Huke. On the drive up, Starzinchger speculated Huke was trying a small lab exercise intended to seduce

Sensenig away from refrigeration.

"Don't be ridiculous," Starzinchger sighed with exasperation when Huke told him they were trying the entire fission-fusion reaction plus the idiotic rail cannon. "Now I have to tell Sensenig I'm going to stop the test."

"You may stop this experiment," granted Huke. "If you have no fear of discussing your absence, your neglect, and your jealousy."

"My jealousy?"

"You heard the solution to fusion from Phil and you rejected it," Huke was pointing at him with his left hand. When Starzinchger had arrived, Huke had given Starzinchger an annoying left-handed handshake, as if Huke were Bing Crosby and Starzinchger a fan. "There isn't a physicist in 52 who wouldn't see your attempts to stop this experiment as arrogant disrespect for scientific truth."

Starzinchger wiped his lips and looked at Huke like a doctor. Good job. Huke had this all planned down to exactly what he was going to say to everyone.

He tried to show Huke why it wouldn't work. Huke's certain failure dissolved any anger the feeble vindictiveness might have stimulated. They went over the material, point by point, and the hopelessness of it should have become obvious, but Huke defended himself with Grethlienese, an impenetrable and bogus school of thought if ever there were 1. It was hot in the office. Starzinchger decided to take a walk in the cool night. He passed the physicist with a pretty mouth on the way out.

He hoped to see some of the last rich purple of sunset. When he'd 1st arrived, the clouds along the mountains had been blue-grey and the sky had turned lavender above them. It had annoyed him to have to hurry inside to confront Huke. Now back outside, there wasn't a hint of purple left.

He walked around the outside paths of 52. He saw yellow light billowing out of a long row of open windows. He walked up to look in. He found himself nearly on top of a desk full of Huke's arithmetic women. He studied the closest 1. The yellow light made her large bra visible beneath her fantastic evening uniform.

He walked out into the night. It was only a few hundred yards to the edge of the alkali sea. There were several stars beaming down between the seams of the swift clouds. The stars provided enough light to see the outlines of the massive towers on the flats. They looked like black tongues. He felt a flutter of alarm. Something was changing. His sense of being right was leaving. He was wrong.

It frightened him that it could change without his consent. He didn't believe in the cyclotron anymore. He had been wrong. Suddenly he felt exhilarated. He was letting it go now. He'd had decades of fame and work invested in the cyclotron, but he was letting it go. He'd been wrong. He trotted out across the black alkali dust towards the buildings. He wanted to touch them. He'd been wrong. He wanted to feel the cool flanks of his monumental error.

The cinder blocks were pimpled with rough peaks. He drew his palm excitedly across the toothy surface. He'd been wrong. He wished it were in man to recognize when he was wrong without putting up huge buildings filled with machinery worth billions of dollars to prove it to himself.

"But it's not possible," he said to himself. *"What*

makes man great is his ability to make huge wrong investments and then walk away from them as if they aren't there."

He started back for his car. He'd have to lie to Sensenig again. Sensenig didn't know Starzinchger hadn't been back to 52 since his argument with Grethlien. Looking back on it, Starzinchger realized that his argument with Phil had been the 1st step towards realizing he'd been wrong. Resisting Grethlien's ridicule, he had been dreaming of

General Sensenig decorating his driver in a private ceremony

an atom collapsing inwards and sucking the heat out of everything around it with ferocious energy. The image had repeated itself in other forms. He had seen the state of Nevada chilled to decimal points above absolute 0 by a lump of collapsing beryllium the size of a lima bean. But it was only the image of a solution. There was nothing in physics which would allow such a thing. He'd spent a lot of time and energy trying to find a link between this handsome fantasy and the laws of physics, but there was none. He'd been wrong.

He got into his car still nursing his feeling of exhilaration. He drove up the mountain towards Jake. A jack rabbit, jumped by his headlights,

FEELINGS

raced up the slope ahead of him. He accelerated, trying to catch it, but the rabbit laid its long ears down flat and squirted out of sight. He sighed with admiration for such speed, and his mind turned back to how to present this situation to Sensenig.

"Huke thinks he's going to outshine Lillo now," Phil told Lineheardt, back in his office.

"Lillo!" she cried. "He can't believe that."

Phil looked at his desk, wondering if he should really search it for something valuable.

"He's had lessons to the contrary," he said. "But they didn't take."

"What do you mean?" she asked.

"Lillo loved to talk theory with everyone," said Phil. "He used to instruct Huke at lunch back in Chicago. Day after day Lillo would patiently lay out the frontiers of physics and Huke would struggle to get it. It was a function of Lillo to give fresher perspectives to himself simply by talking. Huke would come back and parrot what Lillo had said the day before, only to hear Lillo reply 'Yes, but,' and reel off a host of new contradictory perceptions, and there was Huke**** confused."

Lineheardt let out a crisp laugh. Now she found denigrating stories about Huke more enjoyable than ever.

"In fairness to Steve though," added Phil, staring away and pressing 3 fingers to his brow.

"What?"

"Sometimes Lillo's truth was so inaccessible, it was like**** I don't know****"

"Like what?"

"Physics is like a rabbit hunt," said Phil. The 3 fingers left

Abbe Lane

his forehead as if he'd touched something hot. "It's like a rabbit hunt on my uncle's farm; and, when we were all standing out on the cold edge of the woods, we'd hear Lillo shoot, and we could see the rabbit lying dead in the woods, and we could see Lillo leaning over his kill, his hand feeling around inside its entrails; but we were always so far away, way back out on the edge of the woods waiting, we could see the steam coming out from the truth inside, but we had to take his word for what it was he felt in there."

Phil avoided telling May he'd been fired. He found himself rambling on about Barbanel to her. Barbanel had introduced him to her when she was a graduate psychology student. It was at a cocktail party for Johnny Von Neumann.

Von Neumann had a crowd around him, mostly graduate students, and 1 of them, some Brad or other, was asking him a long question about reducing social hand signals to binary code.

Von Neumann's answer was succinct and inaccessible. It was normal for the graduate student to be faced with dense sentences from someone like Von Neumann. It could take 3 weeks of head scratching to understand them.

But this time, May, the psych student, cleared it all up for the group in 2 minutes, with Von Neumann nodding his approval of her every utterance. From that moment Barbanel and Phil had biffed each other about for weeks in pursuit of her hand.

Now as he paced around talking about Barbanel to May, Phil waved the round plastic scale Barbanel had created to measure the range of destruction for fission bombs. Barbanel had made his little plastic wheel 5 years ago. While everyone at Los Alamos had been preoccupied with making the gadget work, Barbanel had dreamed about what it would do when it did.

So strong was Barbanel's curiosity, he wanted to go along in the airplane on the bombing run itself, but Lillo wouldn't ask Sensenig's permission for him. The instant they knew the burst had been successful, Barbanel badgered Lillo mercilessly to let him go inspect the victims and crushed buildings of Hiroshima. He was furious when Lillo refused.

When the doctor's reports and pictures came back from Japan, Barbanel was the 1st to borrow them from the statisticians. For weeks he alternated between brooding motionlessly over the reports and taking notes so intense the lead of his pencil cracked. Out of all this came the plastic wheel he gave to Phil near the end of the week he spent dying.

Barbanel had sort of accidentally-on-purpose killed himself with a tiny neutron bomb. Barbanel's job on the Hill was to project the critical mass of the different batches of bomb metal. To get his projections he pushed 2 little samples of fissile uranium towards each other with screwdrivers.

The closer the lumps got to each other the more excited they became. The idea was to push them closer and closer until he could extrapolate a rate of accelerating activity and thereby predict critical mass. But he had to quickly separate them before the little chain reaction got out of hand. When the chain reaction went too far, a lethal geyser of neutrons resulted.

Phil had seen it happen in another lab with much smaller

lumps of U235 than Barbanel used. There was a small puff of brilliant purple ionization. Everyone felt a weird mixture of euphoria and dread. The disorienting mood, they all agreed afterwards, had no origin in their thoughts or feelings prior to the accident. It had been shot into them by the neutrons.

Barbanel's accident came after Hiroshima. He teased too huge lumps of bomb metal too close. They hissed like punk and washed the lab with a brilliant ionization cloud. The room was crowded when it happened. Barbanel always had a large following for his work. His fellow physicists were fascinated by his bravery and wanted to share in it. Several of them were looking right over his shoulder when the lab lit up in brilliant purple.

They all scrambled from the lab in terror. Barbanel threw his body across the radiating material and groped it about beneath his stomach, struggling to tear the reacting lumps apart. Billions of neutrons pierced his guts like darts.

This morning when Phil had taken Lineheardt to see some of the Hiroshima pictures in 52's files, they had stumbled across some medical pictures of Barbanel. The ring finger on Barbanel's right hand was the most swollen. His middle finger was blown up around the center knuckle only, looking like an anomalous balloon taking its shape at its middle instead of the far end. His pinky was swollen on top where he usually wore his silver ring. He had a crown of puffy flesh instead of the ring. The pictures were taken in black and white with a brilliant flash so it was difficult to see how his skin had turned ugly purple. The pictures showed only the bulbous gross swelling which suggested he had cradled the fissioning material in his 3rd finger, and the reaction had bloated all the flesh around it like a flame carbonizing sugar.

His calm expression in the picture reminded Phil how eager Barbanel was to pose, delighted to contribute to the

elepHAnt MAn (handwritten)

medical literature on nuclear weapons. He was even more
delighted that everyone came by to visit him in the hospital.

It was a duty they hated but none dared shirk. ~~One~~ *old fashioned* after another, Barbanel's fellow physicists came into his room to
find him euphoric.

Phil offered to bet anyone 3 to a million that Barbanel had
teased the lumps too close sort of accidentally-on-purpose.
There were no takers. It was becoming obvious that the Hiroshima Complex could be fatal. Physicists began to leave
the Hill for universities.

He told May he had to go out for a walk. He took Barbanel's
wheel with him.

Although Lineheardt was drunk, she wasn't finished
drinking. She met her friend Viner at Greek Hell. Viner was
her best pal outside 52.

Lineheardt loved the damaged compass of Viner's peculiar
intellect. He was the signal jake.

His mind was a blackened negative of Phil's, mesmerizing
but stupid. He was a geyser of confusing images and wild
claims. No matter how dopey his ideas proved, he always
raised his newest inverted notion with loving hope.

Viner was talking about God tonight. She learned that
Viner didn't actually love God. He didn't even like Him.
God's need for Viner to foul himself in Jake proved that
God was something of a sadist. But Viner had to show Him
respect because he wanted badly to help people with their
lives, and that was how you helped other people, by using

God kindly.

Lineheardt took in this numb-tongued nonsense as a doctor would listen to a favorite patient about ghostly pains, but she wondered how he could help others when he was so busy with the boiling reformulations of his personal legend.

It was a legend she refused to damage with rebuttal. That would be like throwing rocks at the gold tinted Apollyon over Greek Hell's bar, her favorite indoor buzzing of Jake's mystifying neon noise.

  Spike couldn't sleep. He had the half daydreams that come just before dropping down into deep sleep. But every time he got to the edge of deep sleep, he didn't fall over. What grit Noreen had. She had saved up enough money from household expenses to secretly pay her way through dental-tech school.

85

Spike got up out of the big bed. He padded through her rented house looking for signs of her past. He went into the guest room.

There were 30 small boxes on the bed, each had a number written on adhesive tape. There were more larger boxes stacked up in the closet. He opened 1. He found a hat with fruit and bananas tacked all over the brim. The next 1 had an Australian cowboy's hat with a beautiful violet scarf tied around it.

How long would you have to save from household expenses to secretly pay your way through dental-tech school?

Each of the boxes on the bed had a pair of shoes inside. He went back into the bedroom and quietly opened her closet door. There were as many dresses inside as there were shoes and hats in the guest room. The hangers all had numbers on them too. Each number was an outfit. Dress, shoes and hat.

Maybe it wouldn't take all that long to pay for dental tech school if your household expenses were huge.

"What are you doing?" she asked behind him.

She was sitting up in her lilac nightgown. She stretched her sleepy arms up and her wonderful breasts pressed up against the slick fabric.

"You're rich," he said.

"Rich?"

"You've got a dress, a pair of shoes, and a dumb hat for every day of the month," he said.

"I am not rich," she yawned. "I like clothes."

"You said you went to Shipley," he was annoyed she was denying it. "I know Shipley is a Philadelphia prep school."

She looked at him with cool blue eyes. She could see where he was going. She didn't like it.

"You said you play golf, too," he said.

"What does golf have to do with anything?" She flared.

She feared him now that he was getting close to the weird mud puddle of her self-esteem.

"You don't play golf because you love it," he said. "You play it because you're rich and everybody at prep school played it."

She scrambled across the bed and ran at him like a billy goat. He was too shocked to defend himself. It fooled him that someone who owned 30 pairs of expensive shoes could ram her head into his stomach like a goat.

His breath went out of him in a whoosh as she slammed him up against the wall. She pulled away and rammed him again. He grabbed at her to throw her back, but she was too slippery. She wriggled around inside his arms and keep slamming at him. Finally he stopped trying and let her slam away.

"Don't you ever say that to me again!" she shouted, giving up on the slamming because he wasn't fighting back. Her pale face was so purple with emotion her head looked like an over-animated shouting eggplant.

"Say which?" he asked quietly.

"That I'm rich!" she screamed. "That I play golf and went to Shipley because I'm rich. I told you about Shipley because men think preppies are horny. That's why I told you that."

"Men think what?"

"And don't you ever throw anything up to me because I'm smartly dressed," she added. "You wanted to marry me because I was smartly dressed."

They made love a 3rd time, but he still couldn't get to sleep. She said newcomers to Jake often have difficulty sleeping.

They went out for a night walk. He was interested in the mountain and asked her about it.

"It's 3 climates," she told him. "The Yucca and creosote you saw 1st was Sonoran Desert. The Mojave is an example of Sonoran desert. Then the sagebrush, grease-wood and winterfat was the cooler Great Basin of northern Nevada, did you feel the temperature change? The 3rd 1 is the Coniferous Forest, which occurs around here only on Trembling Peak because it's the only mountain high enough to make the clouds rain on it regularly."

"What about the grey dust at the bottom?" he asked.

Jimmy and Tommy Dorsey

"That isn't a climate," she answered. "That's a dead sink."

Her body was humming. He had launched her several times now, all as if he loved her. He was making something pleasurable twirl up and down her abdomen like a yo-yo. The last time he had screwed like an ape. He was all over her, twisting in and out of her limbs and when he came, his eyes went up into the back of his head and saliva bubbled out the corner of his mouth to drip on her chest bone. She had run her thumbs up the ridges of his spine and strained up to kiss his wet drooling mouth.

"What's this 1?" he asked.

"A Utah Juniper."

"You know all of them, don't you?" he asked, reaching around her hips to hug her to him. "What do you like about me?"

"I like the way you screw," she said.

His hands went down the small of her back to crumple her levis against her ass.

"I think you like my ass."

"I love your ass," he said, swearing on it.

"I'm 35."

"You told me that already," he said.

"I might be in love with you because you're 9 years younger than I am and good looking."

"I'm in love with you because I don't give a shit why I'm in love with you," he said.

"Didn't we come out to look at trees?"

"We did," he agreed happily.

He let her ass go and took her hand. They walked around the night-time streets. He looked at her with intense curiosity, lighting up with every new shrub and tree she named. He was especially excited about the sad limber pines. He said they were holding up religious arms to god. He very much enjoyed her knowing things. Not once did he look away from her when she was talking.

She snuck looks at his hands. She'd thought them shocking when she'd 1st seen them at the Dog, but they were attractive now. She wanted to take his hand and hold it, gently, like a manicurist, and press carefully about the lumps. There would be something precise and loving in sending gentle spurs of pain up his fingers.

[handwritten: How do you know me so well?]

"I'm sorry I said that stuff before about golf and your being rich," he said.

"I hate that," she said with venom. "I have a job that pays well. Maybe I spend my salary on clothes. And I hate the way golf is encrusted with etiquette. The manners you have to learn before you can play are staggering. Then there are all the spasms of social prestige which run through all the members as soon as they pull into the club parking lot. What does that have to do with long walks on pretty turf?"

[handwritten: he shouldn't be talking with pessimistic snakes — slim so hateful.]

"This is it! We've got to get married!" Spike exploded. "Sacred work, this is it!" He jumped up and down pulling her arm. "Sacred chuck work! This is it!"

After walking 4th Street for hours, Phil gave up on instructing the tourists and decided to convince jakes further down the mountain. After a lonely half-hour he found himself approaching a handsome couple.

The man was tall and athletic looking, and his girl friend was a beauty with striking hips. They were having an animated conversation and didn't notice him approaching. He stopped and listened.

"Sacred work, this is it!" the athlete was shouting. He went on but Phil couldn't make it out. Phil walked slowly towards them to get close enough to hear more.

"None of the chapels are open now," the beauty was laughing, letting herself be pulled along. "It's 4 o'clock in the morning now."

The athlete stopped pulling. He let go of her arm. He stared at her with ferocious emotion. Phil could tell she loved the way he looked at her. It was plain the guy saw something inside her he liked. Something he liked a lot because it seemed as if his thrilling stare was burning in through her eyes, going straight through her skull and was about to make exit wounds the size of silver dollars out the back of her head.

"What's wrong?" he howled. "Why don't you want to get married?"

Phil had gotten too close. The beauty had noticed him.

"You're not saying anything!" the athlete demanded as Phil passed.

Phil quickened his pace, turned the corner, and hid behind a limber pine.

"You're only pretending when you say you hate money and social prestige," he said bitterly. "You're rich. I'm middle class."

She looked at him as if she were discovering a new creature. "What's this 'middle class' deal?"

"You wouldn't marry anything less than a Philadelphia lawyer," he said. "Member of the Union League, and so. Right?"

She let out a laugh. "So that's why you keep talking about how rich I am."

"Yeah," he said. "And that's why whenever I say let's get married, you say okay, and then make up something you have to do right away instead, or lie. There must be ten wedding chapels open 24 hours a day up there."

He pointed up where Jake was burning with colored light.

"I'm out here on a divorce."

"You're married?" The color drained from his face.

"My family won't have anything to do with me because I'm out here on a divorce," she said. "Dad frowns on divorce."

"It never occurred to me that you were married."

He looked sick.

"Oh, no!" she shouted angrily. "You're not supposed to get

a divorce!"

"Sacred chuck."

He was looking at her with his hot admiring glance again.

"I guess you're not really interested in getting married again, then," he said glumly.

"Why not?" she argued. "The divorce is final on Monday, and we can go from the lawyer's office to a wedding chapel."

He took her shoulders to kiss her. She turned a happy face up to him and blew her wonderful clean breath right up his nose.

Watching the athlete kiss her, Phil felt wonderful. As if he were the 1 who had just become engaged.

"You shouldn't really stay here until Monday," he announced, approaching them again.

They jumped with fright.

"What?" said the athlete. "You scared the living chuck out of us."

"Do you 2 look like you're in love?" Phil asked, nodding his head yes. "I couldn't help noticing when I walked by. You're both glowing."

There was an awkward silence.

"Oh," said Phil, holding out his hand. "Phil Grethlien."

The athlete's name was Spike, his fiancée was Noreen.

She stared at Phil's hand when he offered it to her.

"What are you spying on us for?" asked Spike.

"I'm not crazy," said Phil.

The girl laughed, won over by his smile. Or maybe his small hand, which she kept looking at with interest.

"I apologize for interrupting something so private," Phil

said, "but the AWB is setting off a fusion burst after dawn Sunday morning. I think it might knock over every wooden, brick and block structure in town. Maybe only part of the Dog, which is constructed with reinforced concrete, will remain standing. What the blast wave blows over won't matter much anyway. The thermal radiation will come through 1st and incinerate everything alive in Jake and melt everything that isn't. I think."

"What are you talking about?" asked Spike. "You might as well be gargling as talking. Do you live here in Jake?"

"He's a physicist," said Noreen. "I'd recognize 1 anywhere. You're from the AWB, aren't you?"

"That's right," said Phil, pleased she could tell. "Now you 2 look at this. I estimate the yield will be something near ten megatons. Look for yourselves."

He held out Barbanel's disc to Spike. It was a measuring scale with several overlaid transparent wheels. There was red and blue lettering and figures all over it. It looked like a pocket roulette game.

"What is thermal radiation?" asked Spike, noticing several spirals for measuring it.

"Radiant heat and flames," said Phil rotating the wheels for Spike. "See? Ten megatons is off Barbanel's scale."

"What does this thing measure?" asked Spike. "What is it?"

"It's Barbanel's wheel," said Phil. "It measures only fission bursts. What you're going to have on Sunday is a fission-fusion burst. It will be 1,000 times more powerful than the burst over Hiroshima if I'm right."

"Sacred work," said Spike.

"Spike, do you know how dumb you sound when you use expletives like 'sacred work' and 'holy chuck'?" demanded Noreen. "Do you really believe in god? I can't believe you believe in god."

Barbanel's Wheel

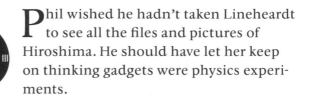

Phil wished he hadn't taken Lineheardt to see all the files and pictures of Hiroshima. He should have let her keep on thinking gadgets were physics experiments.

He looked down the mountain past the glowing windows of Jake homes, to the cheap motels below them. *Maybe it was silly to try to save Jake. But it would be nice to save something,* like some pair that had a nice reason for living, such as the sexy Noreen and Spike waiting till Monday for her divorce. But they had gotten into an argument about religion and walked away. He felt acutely lonely.

Phil stopped in front of a familiar house. Maybe he should ring the bell and talk to them. Maybe with someone he knew he could be more convincing.

"Phil!" a familiar voice called behind him from down the street.

"Inez?" he turned quickly around. "I called you at your apartment, but you weren't there."

"I was out bar hopping," she said, smiling with radiant happiness at finding him. She had been looking for him up among the hotels on 4th Street for an hour.

"I'm working on jakes now instead of the tourists," he explained.

"Are you doing any better?"

"No."

"I think you can get on tv," she said. "Remember my drink-

96

ing pal who sold us CRT's."

"The television salesman."

"He doesn't do that any more," said Lineheardt, "He has his own television show at 7 o'clock every Saturday morning."

"Really?" Phil looked at his watch. It was 6 o'clock. "7am Saturday. That would be Mr. Festival, the children's show."

"How do you know that?" Lineheardt was dumbfounded.

"I watch a lot of television," said Phil, feeling stupid because he knew too much abut tv.

"He wants to meet with you at the station right now."

KJK was behind Horror Hall. Ariel Stern, who owned the hotel, also owned KJK. Lineheardt took Phil into a small room with a soda machine and a coffee maker on a small patio table. The only furniture in the room was 3 lawn chairs. A tv fastened to the ceiling was blank. The show Lineheardt hoped to get him on was the 1st of the programming day. Phil paced nervously about the bare canteen.

"What's Mr. Festival's real name?"

"Alex Viner," answered Lineheardt. "You'll like him. He's a very sweet man."

"Where is he?"

"He told me to wait for him here," she said.

"What happens if I can't get through to him?"

"Phil, you sound terrified," she said nervously.

"I am terrified." He stopped pacing abruptly and looked at her. "I'm sorry I took you to the files and shoved all those pictures at you. I'm sorry, Inez."

She got up and took his arm. She looked desolate, as if she could see his Hiroshima Complex was going to kill him.

"I should have quit them," he said. "How could I keep on going until an asshole like Huke fires me. This is awful! He's planning to stand up after the burst and say, 'Look at me, I'm your next Lillo.'"

"Nobody will let him do that," her head shook like a paint mixing machine.

"Who can stop him?"

She looked at him, thinking about it for a long time. "No 1."

"Exactly."

She let go of his arm. He began walking about the small canteen again. He longed to call Lillo.

"I've figured out there is an evolutionary process at work," he said. "That's why everyone I respected was driven out of the AWB."

"What do you mean?" she asked.

"Everyone that can make sense is gone," he instructed her. "It's the end result of an evolutionary process. They've been chosen out to kill themselves because they're dumb dinosaurs, and I'm 1 too."

"You're not like them," she argued.

"The Army, from the start confounded and alarmed by the ungovernable luminaries of physics and their unintelligible work," he said, as if making a speech, "was delighted to see the Lillos flee to universities, sucking their brilliant assistants along behind them like comets following suns. What a wonderful solution to the heinous Hiroshima Complex. The bastards left and the delightful weapon remained behind in the hands of 2nd rate obedient clucks."

"Are you going to say that on tv?" she asked.

"Why not?" he said. "I wanted to leave, but no college offered me a chair. After all I can't even do The Calculus.

But I should have tried the old boy network anyway. I could have got a job with Hetzel at Colorado maybe. But the Army has a way of finding out about such inquiries, don't they? Their intelligence officers are good at that. Stopping Commies from getting the specs for Fat Boy? No can do. But they love to smoke out the sufferers of the loathsome Hiroshima Complex and send them on their way, job waiting or not."

"You're so nasty to yourself," said Lineheardt.

"I should have taken the chance," he said. "All the other did. The 1st string. They took the chance and made out right."

Lineheardt looked at him quietly. The clean line of her upper lip was trembling. "You can go to Columbia and get funding for the rail gun," she said, naming her school eagerly. "They'd be delighted to have you. I know they would."

"It used to be I worried about if I was going to get a Hiroshima Complex," he said, "because if I had 1, I didn't know what it would do to me since I knew I'd be afraid to leave, which is the standard cure. Then I knew I had 1, knew I'd had it from the beginning, holy shit, I was Barbanel's best friend, and the worry became whether the Army would figure it out. And when they did, would they deal me the same savage blow they gave to Lillo. Inez, where am I going now? What am I doing? They're going to humiliate me like they did Lillo, and I can't take it the way he does. I'll shatter. I'll just crack and shatter."

"Do you want to leave?" she asked with her pretty trembling mouth. "We can walk out. You don't have to go on tv."

"Oh, no, let everyone in Jake be incinerated by my gadget because I'm afraid of the Army?" he asked.

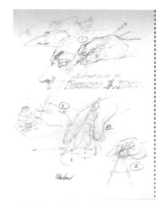

Alex Viner was broad shouldered and muscular, but a little short. He said his show was a magazine type near-news show, not knowing Phil had already watched him many times and knew he was using a children's show to explore the nerterology of medicine men. *One morning Viner had done a series of weird bends which helped supine Apache warriors hop the twig into the long home of the grave.*

Viner had shown an engaging generosity in his tv manner, and Phil liked Viner's off camera persona, too. He was like an adulatory younger brother pretending to be a ring master. He was naive about science, but he interrogated Phil with a pleasing intensity. Phil began to feel better. He would go on tv, which he had wanted to do for a long time. He would convince Jake to evacuate. *The 2nd-rate physicists would destroy only themselves and there would be some profit to the world in that.*

They went into a vast empty room. A dozen 9 year old jakes were sitting on a bare mock grandstand. 2 tall stools were set out in front of it.

The cords feeding the cameras their power were huge. Here was a technology as hungry for current as physics. But where was everyone?

Instead of a crowd of scientists and their proteges, this lab had only 2 technicians. 1 moved the camera, and the other bundled its huge train of cables behind it. The clean studio looked like 1 of Starzinchger's cold rooms. The floor was all dull linoleum and the walls were a sick grey. He, Viner, and the kids were a very small ensemble in this vast grey solitude.

He'd loved watching television at home. It was the only thing in his life outside his work that excited him. He felt wounded by its impoverished secret interior. What an ugly contrast to the exciting population and busy appliances of his own work. He'd been swindled here.

He answered Viner's questions like a robot. He felt a spark of shame. He'd loved and believed in this bullshit television. He began to burn with embarrassment and anger.

Viner's excitement soon smothered the worshipful half of himself with the manic ringmaster personality. Phil felt like a bug wobbling drunkenly across the hot glass of a Jake searchlight, its wings vaporizing in the white heat.

It was well past dawn when Starzinchger ran out of money. He had been playing panguingue all night. He had been in ten different hotels. He went to the desk of the 1 he was at and asked for a suite.

He dismissed the bellboy with a wave. He had no luggage and nothing to tip him with anyway. He found the suite himself. It was decorated with French chairs and a long curving sofa of yellow satin. He walked across the deep pile of the cream rug and absentmindedly turned on the television.

He sat down on the sofa by the phone. He picked it up and asked the operator for the Vogue House apartments. The Army kept an apartment there for VIP's and congressmen. Sensenig always stayed there.

All night Starzinchger had been telling himself he'd wait until Sensenig got up in the morning to call. The phone at the other end of the line began to ring. Starzinchger hung up before anyone could answer. He'd get some sleep 1st.

He stared at the test pattern on the tv. Suddenly it was

replaced by brassy music introducing a morning magazine program. Film clips showed a Mr. Festival posturing
in different festive costumes while kids in a bare peanut
gallery behind him watched like students. Starzinchger
told himself to turn it off and get some sleep, but he was
too weary to move.

How dumb could he get? he asked himself. He was going
to sit and watch a kiddie program on Saturday morning
because he was too tired to move.

The live program began with a view of Mr. Festival and
some kids behind him eating watermelon. Mr. Festival
wasn't wearing a costume yet. Maybe it was part of the
show to watch him put it on. Someone familiar was sitting
next to him, somebody Starzinchger knew he should recognize.

But he was too tired to rifle through his huge mental card
file of identities. He watched in a daze of post gambling
shock, not comprehending what they were saying. It took
him several minutes to realize their topic was fusion.

He laughed at himself for not recognizing Phil Grethlien.
He was so out of context on a kid show, talking destruction perimeters of H-bombs with this idiotic Mr. Festival
imbongi.

"The whole town of Jake will be reduced to 0 when they
test this H-bomb," said the imbongi. "What does H stand
for?"

"Hydrogen," said Grethlien. He looked very different on tv.

"Isn't hydrogen the male component of water?" asked the
imbongi solicitously.

"Yes, hydrogen is part of water," granted Grethlien.

"What's the other part?" asked the imbongi.

"Oxygen," responded Grethlien.

"So what we're going to have is a giant hydrogen explosion up there in the sky where there is a lot of oxygen, the female component of water, and you say that your innovention is going to result in a curtain of flame," said the imbongi. "I don't think that's what's going to happen at all, Phil."

"What do you think is going to happen?" asked Grethlien, interested in his male female imagery.

"I believe you about how powerful it is," said the imbongi seductively. "But I think it's obvious that what will happen to all this hydrogen when it explodes will be for it to transmate into all the oxygen up in the air and make water."

"What?" asked Grethlien.

"Isn't it obvious that what we have to fear is a tidal wave of rain coming directly out of the sky and crushing Jake under 40,000 feet of water?" asked the imbongi gently.

"How???" Phil's voice trailed off in confusion

"We had our warning from God in March," said the imbongi, turning to the camera. Starzinchger liked the beautiful kindness in his manner, even if he was making no sense. "From time to time the new silver glitters on the alkali plain to remind us the bigger flood is coming."

"You know, Lex," said Phil, in pain from seeing someone suffering from a familiar disorder, "You have now crossed over into idiosyncratic delusion."

Viner burned with shame as he listened inside his head to a replay of what he had just said. Where did this junk come from, these pretty thoughts he believed so truly when they were running up his throat, but sounded as smart as the feeding squils of a porcupine the instant they were out?

 It was a struggle for Lillo to come to the phone. His wife watched him anxiously. Suddenly he began to feel better. Phil was terribly upset, but Lillo was too busy thinking to share Phil's distress.

There was something different about this confession. They had started the instant after the 1st burst when Klewitt came to him with hysterical babyish tears about all the innocent Japs who were going to be torched. After Klewitt physicists came to him in rapid succession, some somber, some ironic, all getting a needle into him to feed him long agonizing packs of intravenous guilt.

They were standing in line to get to him those 1st few hours. Then there was some rest, and he could measure their aggressive litanies by days, and finally months. Sooner or later nearly every physicist from the Hill had asked Lillo to excuse him from the guilt.

Now Lillo's wonderful mind, which had been counting all along, without his even knowing it was counting, was notifying him it was over. Phil was the last 1. He would never have to suffer this again. Phil, whose guilt and pain had

Jimmy Durante

been so visible from the start, had held out the longest and was last

"Huke fired me," said Phil. "I think he wants to steal it."

"Starzinchger will steal it 1st," Lillo reassured him, and they laughe
together.

"Why did you hate Victor Barbanel?" Phil asked.

"Because he liked to get so close to death, Phil," said Lillo, gently, but unable to keep the tide of euphoria out of his voice. The last.

"You know what was the beautiful thing about our 1st gadget?" asked Phil.

"Yes," said Lillo. This was his 849th time through this dialogue. He knew what was the most beautiful thing about the 1st gadget.

"What was it?" tested Phil. It was his 1st time through. He had no idea there had been 848 before him.

"The clarity," said Lillo.

"Yes!" said Phil, delighted Lillo understood so exactly. "That light, what an amazing light. I was looking at your face and it was lit up so bright I could see your whiskers."

Lillo laughed. His face was smooth and his whiskers white. Most people thought he didn't have to shave.

"I saw a hundred grey-white whiskers on your cheeks," Phil said. "There were lines coming out the corners of your eyes, like tiny strings of washed sand on the flats. I could see your age. I saw everything in your face in that instant. Everything."

"I know."

"Will you come up here?" asked Phil.

"I guess so, Phil," responded Lillo. "But it doesn't matter what you or I say or do about these things. Weaponry has its own **animus** and it's too powerful to be controlled by men."

"**Animus**," said Phil, struck with wonderment. **TUBALLOY** fell to the bottom of his thoughts like an exhausted star. God damn it. **Animus**.

Phil considered the **animus** of the Dog, where he had taken a room after the disastrous tv appearance in order to make this call to Lillo. He hadn't gone home because he still couldn't bear to tell May he'd been fired. Lillo said good bye. Phil stared at the phone. Where had Lillo found that word? What was the **animus** of people who found the Dog amusing? Of the people who'd built it? These people hadn't understood a word he'd said last night. Just like Viner. They all seemed to speak the same English as Phil, but the **animus** of it was different. Phil smiled at himself. He had to study and comprehend the underlying **animus** of Jake to save it.

But what if he became like them, became 1 of them, what would that mean? He would give up his gentleness to other people for a grasping rude rush at pleasure without interruption? That would be giving up himself.

Since it was for them, this risk of himself was good, he argued with himself. In 2 ways. To save them and to erase the pain of his achievement.

He would do it. He would visit criminality if he had to, and he would ask for the bill. He would prove he had meant nothing cruel by his ambition to create weapons. He would swallow their **animus** though it was a sea urchin with nasty spines protecting its soft inner core. He didn't care how much it hurt, he would chew it all to get to their soft yielding core. Jesus, where was he going? He was on a bus with no brakes.

He could do it. He was trembling with pleasure. For the 1st time in months he'd found a thought which was generating physical pleasure. Here was a demanding project worth giving his inexhaustible scientific energy to. The result of this research would be unequivocally virtuous.

He heard a key in the door. At 1st he thought it was the

Don't fuck with Hoppy

maid, but it was Lineheardt. She'd gone home to shower and change while he called Lillo. He was ignited by his desire to research the **animus** of Jake. The 1st step would be to go the bank and get out all his savings so that he could gamble like a sailor.

Lineheardt had put on a pink blouse with an open slit down her bony solar plexus. He realized how genuinely sexy she was in her lab duster. He looked away from her as she talked. He didn't want to see her this way. He tried to see her in her lab coat in his imagination, beaming at him with admiration and praising the rail gun.

The other part of Jake's **animus** besides gambling was to try to fuck everything that had a warm hole between its legs.

Lineheardt, while inquiring eagerly with the fine lines of her pretty mouth if Lillo was coming to Jake, was asking for something else with her bony solar plexus; and Phil's marriage spilled out across that bony solar plexus and fried like an egg busted onto a hot skillet.

 "There comes a moment in life when you realize that what you do is up to you," Phil blurted out as he jumped up out of the bed, their fucking over. "You realize that other people care about themselves in such an utterly selfish way, they're never going to care about you."

Phil was different nude than Lineheardt had imagined him. He had tufts of hair on different parts of his body which stuck out like pine needles. Under his arms, on the ridge of his long thigh, lining the sides of his calves, across the top edge of his shoulders, and in the middle of his chest were the same stiff black hairs. The rest of him was pink and white. He came back and sat down on the bed next to her. He touched her upper lip. He was fascinated with her lip. He gave her a long soft kiss.

"Did you ever stop to wonder why people hate their shit?" he asked.

She giggled like a teenager.

"That's what I like about Freud," said Phil. "He writes honestly about shit. What's so funny? Why is shit funny?"

They both laughed. It was a relief to laugh after their intense fuck.

She got out of bed and started getting dressed. He began putting his clothes on too. Hers were piled up on the chair. He watched as she pulled her girdle up over her panties. It had amazed him when he'd seen that girdle. What did she need a girdle for? She was so slender.

"You know what Starzinchger and I have in common?" he asked her.

"What?"

"Poverty," he said, stepping into a sock. "Physics is a rich man's sport. On the Hill so many of them had money, you wouldn't believe it. A lot of them, when we were in Chicago, came to work every day in chauffeured limousines. They worked hard, we all loved the work; but they never had to make it pay. When they got bored or got into a fight with somebody they didn't like, they just left. Now these same sons of bitches criticize Starzinchger because he's always drumming up gigantic money for his projects, and its always part of his projects that he gets free rent and big feeds. The bastards!"

Lineheardt, who came from a modestly wealthy family, blushed with embarrassment and quickly buttoned the slit of her pink blouse.

"They look down on him because he takes cash from physics buffs." Phil's anger changed to sadness. "People give him money, you know. Rich people who admire scientists the way restaurant owners love baseball players, they come right up to him and press money on him. I've had dreams about people doing it to me. I wouldn't refuse it either. What for? So I can pretend I'm as honorable and above board as all the bastards who come to work in limousines?"

There was a polite tapping at the door.

"If that's the maid," said Phil, buttoning his shirt. "Tell her we'll be gone in a couple of minutes."

Lineheardt opened the door to Phil's wife, May. She was wearing costume pearls over a cheap white lace blouse. She didn't know how to use make up very well.

"I have a telegram for Phil," she said, looking right at him past Lineheardt. "It might be important. It's from the AWB."

"*The AWB!*" Phil shouted. He ran across the room to snatch the yellow envelope. He didn't open it. He held it out in front of him as if it were a delicious dessert he couldn't bear to begin.

"Is it important?" asked May. Her lipstick color, a weird orange, clashed with her purple sweater.

"They have to have me back."

"What do you mean?" asked Lineheardt. She felt a chill in the pit of her womb. She had a good idea what the telegram was.

"They can't make it work without me," Phil said.

"But you said you wanted to save Jake," Lineheardt said. "That you were****"

"Isn't this the best way to save Jake?" demanded Phil. "Now I can make them move it up range."

"And if you can't?"

"Can't what?" asked Phil impatiently.

"If you can't make them move it up range," she said. "Will you still help them set it off?"

"What kind of question is that?" he asked, wounded.

"It's only the 24 hour telegram, anyway," she said.

It was routine AWB procedure to send a telegram to all its scientists, engineers and employees 24 hours before a burst.

"Oh, yeah," said Phil. "The 24 hour."

Lineheardt noticed that May was staring at her. She and Phil were dressed now but the mussed bed was in plain view. May had obviously dressed to please Phil. It was clear this was a new tack for her, as she looked as if she had been dressed from the closets of 3 different people who had never met each other.

"What's happening, Phil," asked May, her voice high. "Why didn't you come home last night?"

"I've been fired."

"Oh, dear," she said.

Phil opened the telegram.

"You're right," he said to Lineheardt. "It's just another burst telegram. They forgot to take me off the list."

He slumped down in the easy chair, the wrong news making him drowsy.

"Phil, I'd like you to come home to breakfast now," said May.

Phil noticed how short his wife was. She had pale mottled cheeks. He wanted to embrace her and make her feel bet-

113

ter. But she hated hugs. She always murmured no when he went to put his arms around her.

"No," he said. "I'm not going to come home now."

"What are you going to do?"

"I'm going to become an architect," he said.

"Please, Phil," she said.

"All right, I'm not going to be an architect. There's no money in that either, is there?"

May looked at Lineheardt awkwardly. She was hoping for some sympathy, but was confused to find Lineheardt studying her shoes with a creased brow.

"I know what I'll do," said Phil. "I'll invent a Reality machine."

"Will this be like your poop machine?" May asked angrily.

"You remember Korman from Berkeley, May?" asked Phil,.

"Yes, I remember him," said May.

"Korman used to come down to 52 to look at Starzinchger's gigantic machinery and make wisecracks," Phil said to Lineheardt. "The 9th cyclotron was such a prodigious machine, Korman loved to taunt Starzinchger. 'Why bombard the tiny atom he'd ask. 'Such a simple task for such gigantic paraphernalia. Why don't you make it into a time machine?'"

Phil laughed a geyser of hysteria to himself.

"Phil," said May, looking not at him but to Lineheardt. She wanted a partner with an interest in getting Phil to make sense.

"Obviously a time machine is out of reach," said Phil, feeling professorially serious. "What I must invent is a Reality machine. Something that will accelerate the flux of fantasy in faster and faster circles until its electron cloud of decoration is spun away and the only thing that remains is a core of Reality at the center."

"Phil, you're not making any sense," said May, almost begging.

"Not to you now," said Phil. "But once I build it and put Huke in for a little ride, and we see the real Steve Huke, instead of the fantastic weavings between his ego and the military's need for weapons, you'll see how valuable such a machine could be. Of course we won't get rich on this peculiar tilt-a-whirl. Reality isn't a profit making commodity. But we'd get into the history books. Right after Lillo. There I'd be. The man who peeled the assholes away from Reality so we could see it."

May turned pale with apprehension. It made the lines of color on her face darker.

"You agree it hasn't been isolated yet?" he asked her, ignoring her acute discomfort. "Reality?"

"You sound mad."

"I do," he agreed, "but I can't come back home and sweat it out there again."

"Why not?" she was hurt. "Have I been so bad for you?"

"Yes," he nodded. "I think."

"I'm sorry about wanting more money," she said. "I grew up wanting it, believing I'd have it. I'm sorry. I can't change that."

"Why did you marry me then?" he asked. "I never talked about getting rich when we were falling in love."

"I know," she said. "I don't know why I married you. I don't know why."

"Yes," he said.

"But I am a good wife to you," she said. "I've been a wonderful wife."

"I knew you'd say that," he said angrily.

"Say what?" she asked. "What did I say?"

"Forget it," he said.

"What did I say to make you so angry?" she asked, getting angry again herself. "I want to know what I said."

"You were supposed to do something that was part of saying 'Yes, I love you, we'll get married.'"

"What didn't I do?"

"I have no sense that anyone has ever had a deep feeling of caring for me," said Phil. He turned away from her and looked at the window. "No 1. I guess people like me, but nobody has this thing like they care deep down inside themselves somewhere that makes it hurt when I hurt. You, you feel affection for me sometimes. When you're happy. And sometimes when I'm happy because you like my mood. But it's not deep. It's always as if there's manipulating and figuring going on in the back of your mind when you're affectionate with me, like you've got 1 eye open when we're kissing, trying to figure out some way to make a profit for yourself off the affection."

"That isn't me, Phil."

"You know what hurts the most?" Phil asked.

"No, Phil," she said sarcastically. "What hurts the most."

"You don't like my work," he said.

"That's not true!" she protested, stung.

"You think it's the biggest bunch of bullshit in the world."

"No, I don't," she complained. "What's the matter, don't I praise you enough? Is that it? When you come home with your trophies, don't I polish them all through dinner with you."

"That's not it," Phil shook his head. "You're full of praise

116

when I come home with enthusiasm for something. You think it's your duty to be enthusiastic too. But what about when I feel like shit? When you feel like shit, I try to pick you up. I tell you you're a wonderful mother, that we have a good family, you're doing a good job and you're really good at it."

"I know there is a class of sinners that love things that can't love them back," said May. "Gamblers. They're trying to make love to their crap game but it just takes a nasty piece of them almost every time they go to it. That's you and your physics. You're in that set too."

"Yes, that's it now," he said. "You think physics is a bunch of bullshit. It's for the idle rich, and I have no business in it. You hate it, and you'd like to see me crushed by it because you want me to quit."

"You mean there is something that'll make you quit?" she challenged him. "What would that be?"

"You know what it's like living with you?" he asked.

"That would be when Lillo-Furon calls you on the phone," she declared. "And tells you how much smarter you are than he is. That's when you quit."

"It's like living near the parkway," he said over her answer. "They live in those houses right next to the parkway in Brooklyn, and all that traffic goes whizzing by all the time and it sounds like an ocean of cars and trucks because the noise of it never stops. They get used to it. After awhile they don't hear it. But then they go somewhere in the country and they can hear birds calling and squirrels running across leaves and they realize it's not the car noise that hurts, it's what they can't hear because of the noise that hurts."

"Smarter than Pythagoras, he'll say," said May angrily. "And then maybe you'll fall in love with your children"

117

"May, I can't hear your birds. What I've been waiting for, hoping would happen for years, is to come home and find you singing. To come home sad 1 night, just 1 night, May, it would have fueled me for years to come home 1 night and have some rich bubbling affection for my work come out of you spontaneously, as if it would kill you if I quit physics."

"But it's your work," she said. "Not mine. How can I feel that? Does she care about your work?" She looked bitterly at Lineheardt as an enemy again.

"How do I know?" shrugged Phil.

"Are you going to be happy with her?"

"Happy?" sighed Phil derisively. "The man who burns the world with 1 giant flame?"

"So I believe in you as a person not a physicist," she said, looking guilty, as if she were letting loose an awful confession about something he had no idea was there. "But, Phil, I believed in you. I always have. I think you're wonderful. I'm sorry I hate physics, but why should I like it after what it's done to you? I'll never understand why you give so much to something which returns so little."

"I care about something too much, yes, so shoot me," he said. "What do you care about, May?"

"I care about things that can love me back," she exhaled. Her shoulders slumped suddenly in defeat.

"Did you ever wonder why I let you believe my shit statuette machine was real?" he asked.

"Come on," she said.

"In your mind, excellence in physics equals making a lot of money."

"I think you are smart enough to make a lot of money," she

118

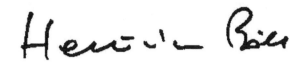

said defiantly.

"Excellence in physics does not produce money!" he shouted.

"I won't go through any more episodes of this with you," she said. "I can't."

"You should leave town."

He explained the fusion shell and Huke to her. She had no trouble believing she was in danger. She left angry, saying she would take the boys to her cousin John's in Arizona.

"Why dinnid she look at me like everyone else in this town?" he asked wryly, turning around to Lineheardt after the door slammed. "A few words to her, and she's gone."

Lineheardt laughed, delighted the confrontation was over.

"Do you know you have a speech problem?" she asked him impulsively.

"What?" he asked nervously.

"You don't pronounce your ds and ts," she said. "You say 'dinnid' instead of 'didn't.' You say 'cand' sometimes instead of 'can't.'"

"Yes," he said. "I know I have that problem."

"You try to hide it!"

"Because I cand be sure which is which," he said. "I can't remember where the ds belong or the ts."

"I knew you couldn't tell the difference between them. I knew it!"

Phil laughed. There was something pleasantly funny about her knowing it all along.

"Plus your math," she said. "That's just like Faraday. Did you know he couldn't do any math beyond simple arithmetic?"

"No!"

"Algebra stupefied him," she said.

Lineheardt was sparkling with sexuality. Phil thought about her useless girdle. The idea of it was suddenly sexy to him. The image of her bony chest beneath him when he'd screwed her came back to him with exciting intensity.

NELSON. Robt. A. 2013
STUDY FOR A RED BIRD MAN
SUMMER, LAKESIDE, OREGON

The Zemidary, **Ziraleet's** golf course, went back and forth across the western side of Trembling Peak in green ledges. The narrow plateaus looked like mountain rice paddies, except they were fairways lined with Spike's favorite devout pines. Spike went into the shop for some practice balls and took them out to warm up. The practice range was a large field of turf with limber pines behind a far away fence. He made a few easy passes with the poodle.

A tall 14 year old kid was hitting balls next to him. As Spike got up to the middle mutts, the kid turned around to watch. Spike was hitting it well. His hands felt good.

"I keep cutting across the ball," said the kid. "Watch me."

Spike watched him hit several slices with an extra long driver.

"Fuck!" the kid shouted after the 4th one and turned around to glare at Spike.

"I see," laughed Spike.

"What's so funny?" he demanded angrily.

"You. You're funny."

The kid looked at Spike with his eyes burning so bright, Spike felt like he was being speared with affection. "All I hit are these stupid fucking banana balls."

"Why do you work the big dog so hard?" asked Spike. "Why don't you try a 5."

"Big dog?" He threw down his driver and yanked the whippet out of his bag. "Golfer Jew will now try the 5," he announced, the affection gone.

He beat out several more bananas. Spike suggested turning his wide shoulders more to use his lanky golfer's build. The kid chuckled and changed nothing. Spike asked him to slow his takeaway.

"Golfer Jew thinks you might be full of shit on that one, pal."

"Let the clubhead do what it wants to," said Spike, giving it one last try. "Golf clubs are like dogs. They're bred for different work."

"What are you talking about?" asked the kid, his voice breaking in frustration.

"The 5 iron is like a whippet," explained Spike. "It's sleek and swift. It doesn't want to pull an Eskimo sled like the driver."

"Golfer Jew has had enough advice," the kid decided. "Can I hit my balls alone now?"

Spike went back to warming up. Once in awhile the kid turned around to watch, then went back to hitting his moody bananas with his 5.

Maybe it was the dry climate. Spike's hands felt so good he could do anything he wanted. He marched his shots out the range from the 150 sign to the 200, bouncing 2 or 3 balls right off the signs. By the time he got up to the driver, he was tingling all over. As good as he felt, the ball's flight still amazed him. He'd been hitting all the irons farther than normal, but he wasn't ready for this. The ball reached the top of its arc as it passed over a limber pine behind the fence. The fence had a 280 sign on it.

"I hit that 4 hundred," he whispered to himself. "I know I just hit that 4 hundred. That had to be 4 hundred. *He can really hit it, folks.*"

"What?" the kid was staring at him sullenly.

"There's something wrong with the yardage signs," said Spike. "That's it. All the signs are wrong."

"The yardage is right," sighed the kid, bored.

"Okay, watch this," said Spike.

He hit it solid again. Again the ball climbed over the top of the pine. The kid said nothing. His face was twisted with disdain.

"Well?"

"I've been watching," said the kid. "The signs are right."

"Then I hit that 400 yards," said Spike. "I hit it right over the crown like I wanted to. That ball couldn't have been more than a foot off line."

"So you're long and straight," shrugged the kid. "What am I supposed to do, blow you?"

"The signs are wrong," repeated Spike.

"Count my steps," said the kid. "I'm exactly 36" to a pace. "I'll walk it off for you."

He looked tall enough for 36 inches a pace, 6' 1" maybe, and he went right out into the practice range pacing up the line of signs, oblivious to all the other people hitting balls. Spike looked around to see if the pro was coming out to drag the crazy punk off the range. Nothing was stirring in the clubhouse. The only thing that happened was the kid turning around halfway out and glaring at someone who had hit a ball close to him. The offender quickly took a shorter club and changed direction. It took the punk 281 paces to reach the fence.

Spike realized he might shoot the best score of his life today. He felt a flash of alarm. He hadn't thought about taking that on for years. It made him sad. Who would care if he did? His father and his sister Libby? They'd probably take it as very bad news, waiting as they were for this to die. Noreen? She didn't believe in god and had ended their argument about it by telling him she was going to work. Dentists, along with banks, were open 24 hours a day, 7 days a week in Jake; and she was so mad at Spike, she was going to go to work at 3 in the morning, leaving him to return to his hotel alone. She'd walked off suggesting it was all over between them.

The kid returned to the tee. "What's your name?" asked Spike.

"Erving."

"You want to play 18 with me?" asked Spike. "I'll pay for the caddy."

"You can't get 18 in before the tournament," said the kid. "They won't let you on the course today anyway."

"There's a tournament today?" asked Spike.

"A pro-am Calcutta," said Erving.

"Oh, holy work," sighed Spike, starting back towards the clubhouse.

"Where are you going?"

"To talk to the pro," Spike called back. "I've got to get into this tournament somehow."

"I can get you in the tournament," said the kid. "My old man owns this place."

Chick

Walter Winchell & Bob Hope

125

 "I'd have to switch Bob Hope to do that," Lehman told his angry son.

"So what?" persisted Erving.

He's the funniest comedian in the country," said Lehman. "He's one of the best celebrity golfers in the world. I paid $30,000 for your team at the Calcutta dinner last night, and now you want to substitute some nobody you met on the driving range because he hit a couple of balls over the fence. Where's the per in that?"

"Bob Hope is an asshole, Pop," said Erving.

"Tony Lema doesn't think so," said Lehman. "He 's waiting to play with you and Winchell because Hope would be in the 3some. This is a celebrity tournament, bub."

"Why can't we have it my way for once?" begged Erving. "You always have something all worked out and whatever I want never fits in. Maybe I don't give a shit if we win."

"You don't want Bob Hope?" asked Lehman with a smile. "The funniest man in America."

It was obvious Lehman was pleased. His smile was spreading into a large affectionate grin.

126

"Bob Hope?" he repeated. "You don't think he's funny?"

Erving could see his father was proud as hell his son thought Bob Hope was an asshole, and the fact that it was going to cost him $30,000 seemed only to make him merrier about it.

 "Hi" said Tony Lema, gently squeezing Spike's ugly hand.

He was taller and skinnier in person than the pictures on the sports page. He liked Spike.

He acted as if he already knew Spike, but everyone in Jake acted that way towards everyone.

"We're up in ten minutes," Erving told Spike. "They've got you down as a ten handicap."

"What are you really?" Lema asked.

Spike shrugged.

"I wouldn't mind buying a bigger piece of Lehman's action," grinned Lema.

"He isn't selling any," said Erving proudly. "I got 5 per cent and that's all he's letting out."

"You did shoot that fifty something, didn't you?" Lema asked Spike.

"58." said Spike, proud that Tony Lema knew about it.

"Amazing round," Lema said.

"I'm surprised you remember," said Spike. "That was 13 years ago."

"I read that article in Life magazine 4 or 5 times," said Lema. "Not too many 13 year old kids shoot 58."

Spike looked away modestly and found Erving staring at him with new eyes. When they walked to the tee, Erving was up 1st. Hearing of Spike's 58 had changed his opinion of the value of Spike's advice on the practice tee. He tried to put everything Spike had suggested immediately to work.

"What was that?" asked Spike, astounded by the contorted twist which bore no resemblance to anything Erving's body had done earlier on the practice tee.

"Golfer Jew," said Erving, flashing a hot shamed red, "must make a few additional adjustments to his swing before attaining his staggering golfing destiny."

"That's making them dance kid," said Lema. He had a fondness for amateurs who made galleries split in terror.

For the 1st few holes Erving pestered Spike with questions about which club was what dog and why. On the 5th hole Spike hit a whippet within 2 feet of the flag for an easy bird on the hardest hole of the course.

Lema, standing right next to him, let out a happy breath. "You're the closest thing to pure talent****", but he didn't finish and began to think.

As they climbed down the wood steps from the 6th green to the 7th tee, Spike could see out around the mountain to part of Testrange 52. They walked back along the soft turf towards the far markers. More and more of the valley to the east came into view. The grey moon-like desert, which had been so dull to Spike at sundown yesterday, was glittering with millions of tiny flashes of light. The desert floor was a grey night of stars, each visible only for an instant, releasing a huge pulse of energy to send a piercing spear of blue or red light to golfers far away on Trembling Peak.

"They're the silver tailings from old mines in the mountain," Erving interrupted Spike's stare. "The wind polishes them up."

Spike felt as if all the fragments of argentite were exploding their colored light just for him. It has been a long time since golf had made him feel this way. The mountain, its beautiful golf course with the aggrieved limber pines and chrome-shiny turf, it was all magic. God, once the cruel architect, was now painting up Spike's dreams for him and even sprinkling silver stars across the canvas for decoration. To have his talent back like this, if to enjoy only for 1 glittering afternoon, it was so potent****

"He names all his clubs after dogs," Erving explained eagerly to the gallery. "Like that, the 8, It's a bulldog."

Erving, who had been hitting little spinners from 1 side of the fairway to the other for the past several holes, began to talk to the growing gallery about Spike, as if his friendship with Spike could buy relief from the embarrassment of all his little twirlers.

"See, that's a poodle," he said as Spike took a wedge out of his bag on the 9th hole. "It's a poodle because it comes in

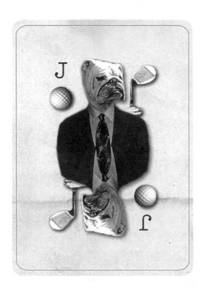

different sizes." Getting annoyed with Erving, Spike decided to hit a punch bloodhound instead of the poodle, and went back to the kennel for the nine.

"He went back to the kennel for the bloodhound," announced Erving.

There was no stopping it. The kid remembered every dog and its number. This wasn't the same thing as his secret dream about how impressive his best golf was going to be. In his fantasies Spike would beat Hogan so badly at the U.S. Open, Hogan would be reduced to chanting that Spike could really hit it, he could waffle it. No, this was not like reducing the icy Hogan to blithering adoration. This was more like playing with a urine stain around his fly.

On the last hole, Lema, who had been ignoring them in favor of Walter Winchell since the 4th hole, began to clown as if he were the radio personality, not Winchell.

"I don't think I'll hit Fido here," he said, reproducing Spike's voice efficiently. "This looks like the rhino to me."

Winchell chuckled. Lema spoke to his 4 iron as if it were a microphone.

"From anything over a mile I like to goose the charging rhino****"

He continued all the way up the fairway, Winchell and the gallery getting louder and louder with laughter.

Phil's savings didn't last long with craps. It was a stunningly fast game. He wanted to try blackjack but he needed more money. The only thing he could do was steal some. It was part of the Jake animus to steal money anyway. It was well known that half of Jake's commerce was done with money which had been stolen in 1 way or another. Jake was the hole in the bottom of the national monetary sink which all illegal money whirled down to.

Besides, it would be fun to hold someone up. **Ani-mus.** Something had changed now that he was no longer crisscrossed white with the single darting photon **TUBALLOY.** The perfectly reflecting cube of his mind was bursting with stars of piercing red crossing a night of China blue. **Animus.** It was a dizzying spiral galaxy of purple. He whispered to himself. "The animus."

He chose an out of the way spot down the mountain between 2 motels. It was called **TUCK'S WESTERN CLOTHES & CASINO**. It was a windowless plaster building stained with cheap oxblood paint. Phil circled its small block a few times before pulling into the parking

131

lot. The parking lot was full of battered pick-ups. As he got out of his car, someone with a big pot belly came out of the front door and walked towards him. He looked at Phil with hatred. **Animus.** Phil took a deep breath and walked to the front door.

There was a glaring light at the far corner of the bar but everything else was dark. 5 faces turned and looked at him with the same ugly menace the 1 in the parking lot had shown. It wasn't Phil Grethlien they hated. This was standard behavior. Their response to seeing someone they didn't know was hatred.

What was the heart and soul of this town that there were so many people in it angry to the edge of violence. How was he going to swallow such an incredible prickly **animus?**

They all watched him as he walked by towards the small casino. He had more courage now that he was inside and he met their ugly glares with some of his own fierce animosity. It seemed to calm them. 1 by 1 they turned back to the bar as he passed.

The casino was 3 blackjack tables and a row of slot machines. Beyond it was the Western Corral, a small den with a few cowboy shirts hanging from the ceiling. A pair of red leather boots stood on the floor up against the wall.

He went directly to the busiest blackjack table. There were 3 men playing. He pulled out Barbanel's gun and pointed it at the woman dealer. She was dressed to look sexy, but she was nearly 50 and had a bloated tummy sticking out against the fly of her tight cotton pants.

She registered confusion at 1st, then panic. The players turned to look at him. Phil got around to the side of the table so he could watch the bar.

"I want the box," he told the lady dealer.

"I don't have the key," she said, frightened.

"Just take it off the table," said Phil. "I'll open it later."

"That's what I mean," she whined. "I don't have the key."

"I'll get it off for you," said 1 of the players at the table.

"Are you the owner?" asked Phil.

"Hell, no," he laughed.

"Go ahead."

Phil backed up as the volunteer came around to get behind the table. The other 2 were smiling. There was something all 3 of them found enjoyable about seeing Tuck's held up. The player raised a scuffed cowboy boot and gave the box a hard kick. The table hopped and barfed a cloud of cards and chips. The wood top had split, and the black box hung by a last screw. It looked like a rotten tooth. A 2nd kick sent it skidding across the floor.

"There you go, Jack," said the player, flourishing his hand like a waiter.

The people at the bar were waking up to what was happening. The bartender was heading toward the corner where the light glared.

"Hold it!" Phil shouted, pointing the gun at him.

1 of the faces at the bar ducked, but the others just stared at him indifferently. The bartender kept on going towards the glare of the light. He was raising a shotgun straight up in the air. Phil shot in his direction. The slug went into the wallboard behind the bartender making a tremendous puff of gypsum dust. It was beautiful to watch. The pin dots of dust were shown in high relief by the glaring light. What clarity. Holy shit, he was jumping with current. He ran to the bar and shot at the bartender again. The bartender was

133

- RED

leaning over trying to get something out of a half closet. The bullet drove deep into the back of his thigh. Brilliant red, the same wet polished color as the new boots in the Western Corral, sprayed across the aluminum panel of the bar sink.

Phil looked up along the bar. The faces were angry except 1 man with a puffed big face who looked at Phil as if they knew each other. The bartender was trying to sit up. He had the 2 shotgun shells he'd been looking for. There was a lariat attached to the stock that jumped up and down like a snake as he worked to get the shotgun loaded. Suddenly he was struggling to get it up and pointed at Phil.

The bloated face shouted, "No, ROY!"

Phil shot again, this time getting him in the shoulder. Blood leaked across the bartender's dark shirt as if someone had spilled coffee on him. The nose of the shotgun dipped like an airplane in a spin and an orange tear drop of powder flame flashed out of the barrel. The shotgun roared, bucked upwards and flew completely out of his hand. The bar was silent. They all stared at the bartender. He'd shot himself so badly, his knee wasn't there any more. The bottom half of his leg lay several feet away.

"You've got to kill him now, man," said the 1 with the big face.

The bartender moaned. His head drooped on his shattered shoulder.

"Don't let him hurt like that," said the puffy fat face.

Phil took careful aim and shot the bartender in the head. He heard footsteps behind him. The 1 who had helped him get the box off the table was standing behind him to get a better look.

"Yeow."

"God damn it!" cursed Phil, going back to get the box off

the floor.

"You're some cruel bandit, aren't you?" sneered a dirty man at the bar.

"Shut up!" shouted Phil, stopping to point the gun into an eye above the sneer in a rage. "You shut up!"

Lehman was waiting with a broad grin behind the 18th green. After they putted out, someone came out of the gallery towards Spike.

"Great round, Rick," he said, clapping Spike genially on the back.

"Hi, Paul," said Spike, pleased to see a familiar face. "How did you know it was me?"

"I saw you tee off," said Paul. "How come you changed names?"

"I've got to talk to Mr. Lehman," said Spike. "Hang around."

They had reached Lehman, who was looking at Paul with interest.

"Okay, sure, Rick," said Paul. "Later."

"Why did he call you Rick?" asked Lehman.

"I knew him in Florida," said Spike.

"What does that explain?" asked Lehman.

"My cousin was in junior college there, so I went down and ****"

*Sonia out with Evy to meet Smiley and
some other jakes who seldom buy their own
drinks on 4th Street*

"Your cousin was Rick and he didn't play golf so you used his student card to get a cheap membership," interrupted Lehman.

"Thirty bucks for the whole winter," bragged Spike.

Lehman smiled, appreciating the economy. Erving looked at his father with admiration. It astonished him how quickly his father figured out all the little swindles of life.

"I spent the winter playing golf," Spike went on, seeing Lehman liked it. "I got up in the morning, read the newspaper, headed for the golf course, and then went to a fraternity house at night to drink. The next morning I'd get up and do it again. All winter."

"Let's go inside for a victory drink," said Lehman. "I've got a surprise for you and Tony."

"What about me?" complained Erving.

"You too, pal," said Lehman.

The surprises were gold Rolex watches with diamond

encrusted dials. The crowd in the bar ooed to see such expensive gifts tossed off like pens from a casino friendship kit. But their celebration was interrupted by an angry Leo Gilberg, the owner of Leo Gilberg's Hospital, who pushed his way up through the crowd, shouting over the turning heads that Spike was a pro.

"This guy is a pro!" he pointed at Spike as he reached them.

Spike felt a stab of panic. Lehman was looking at him with an intense brow.

"I'll tell you what," accused Gilberg, "you brought a pro in here and gave him a ten handicap. He shoots a 64, and you think you can get away with that in this town."

Gilberg was a chubby man in sunglasses with a dirty grey beard trimmed in Santa Claus style. He wore a brilliant diamond z in his beard.

"Who says he's a pro?" asked Lehman quietly.

"I knew there had to be a reason you scratched Hope," said Gilberg. "Harvey Penner. Harvey Penner says that this son of a bitch has been a pro for 5 years."

"I don't know Harvey Penner," Spike said lamely, as if it proved he'd never turned pro.

"Penner says that this cluck shot some incredible score when he was a kid," said Gilberg, "and he heard that he turned pro 5 years ago."

UCKER.   "Oh, he means Spike Kilmarx," said Lehman blandly. "This isn't Kilmarx. Kilmarx got sick at the last minute and couldn't play. I couldn't change Hope again so I gave Rick here, he's a friend of my boy's, a chance to play with Tony Lema. Rick, say hello to Stanford Gilberg. This is Rick****"
He stopped and waited for Spike.

"Rick Boly," said Spike, smiling ingratiatingly and holding out his hand.

139

"What?" asked Gilberg, confused.

Erving giggled and jumped up and down with delight. Gilberg against the old man. Yo ho.

"Come over here, son" said Lehman, deftly picking Paul from Florida out of the crowd.

Paul testified about how Spike was Rick Boly. He was convincing because Spike had been very scrupulous about protecting his cheap golf when he'd known Paul. Gilberg went and got Harvey Penner, but Penner had only heard of Spike. He'd never seen him.

"I'm sorry," Spike apologized to Lehman after Gilberg left. "I was a pro for all of 2 weeks. I forgot all about it. I never even played in a tournament."

"Anyone could forget that," said Lehman sympathetically. "You covered beautiful."

"Thanks, Mr. Lehman," said Spike. "And thanks for the watch."

Lehman put his arm around Erving's shoulder and took him down to the corner of the bar to explain to him how not to say anything about Spike's real identity.

Spike went over to Lema, curious about what had irritated him into mockery on the last hole. Lema wanted only to talk about the 58, confessing he'd never shot under 60. As Tony Lema listened to the story of the 58 with admiration, Spike felt his bitterness swept away. A new gleaming pride returned in its place, as if Lema's interest was like wind polishing argentite on grey alkali flats.

"Thanks for not giving me away in front of Gilberg," said Spike.

"Are you kidding?" asked Lema. "You think I'm going to get mixed up in these people's arguments?"

"I don't know. You got so mad out there." said Spike.

What the fuck is this word?

"What did I do to make you so mad."

"What are you, 28?" asked Lema.

"6."

"You can still make it," he said, getting excited. "But you've got to let golf work you without asking anything of it, without even hoping for anything, just letting it do you like you're in a daze or a spell."

"I shot 64," said Spike, hollowly. *PAY ATTENTION TO THE WAY you SPEAK; it SAYS THINGS*

"You hit so many shots pure," said Lema. "I know guys who would shoot so low hitting it the way you did to- *you never could* day****" He exhaled, as if his admiration had filled him up like a balloon. "You didn't make your right score today because you don't have all the little items that come from letting golf take you over."

"I've got arthritis." Spike lifted an ugly hand.

"Oh, okay," said Lema, twisting his mouth.

Lema walked away to interrupt Lehman and Erving. Spike watched Lehman get a tremendous pack of money out of his pocket, unsnap several large rubber bands from it, and give Tony Lema $30,000. Lema didn't even look at Spike as he walked out.

Erving came over to talk. He wanted to hear about the 58, too. He had all the questions, the same 1s Lema had asked; but the thrill of talking about it went completely dead. The new energy it had taken on with Lema hadn't been the sign of its coming back to life. It was its last brilliant flash before it died.

"Can we talk about something else, Erving," he said bitterly.

"Sure, sure," said Erving happily. "What about what Gilberg said. Did you really turn pro?"

"I guess you could call it that," said Spike. "I'd already

141

caught the arthritis and I couldn't find half the shots I hit. There was no way I was going to do anything as a pro."

"Oh, Jesus," said Erving, cursing as if it had just happened to him, and not to Spike 6 years ago. "What a fucking torture!"

"So I went to work for my father," said Spike.

"But it's not too late," said Erving eagerly. "You shot 64 today."

"My hands hurt by the 12th hole," said Spike. "I'll never be able to play 4 rounds in a row. Besides, as of today, I have an identity problem in the world of golf."

Lehman returned from a phone call. Since Spike had been around golf courses all his life, he assumed Spike had some experience with cards. He offered Spike a job in his casino.

But he didn't call him Spike. He called him Rick a few times, and then changed to Boly. When Spike accepted the job, Erving started calling him Boly, too.

Lehman was alone in the bar when Gilberg returned with new confidence. He'd had a meeting with several other hotel owners, all his cronies, and they'd voted on it. He was right and Lehman was wrong. As he explained his victory, the diamond z bobbed up and down in his dirty beard. The diamond z was a gift Ziraleet gave only to its highest rollers. Of course Gilberg would covet 1, but to wear it to a Ziraleet outing and parade it before Lehman, boasting by wearing it that he owned 1 of Lehman's prize customers; it was a difficult insult to normalize.

"You don't want to screw every powerful man on the mountain, you know" concluded Gilberg smugly.

"Really?" Lehman was suddenly alive with poisonous emotion. "Isn't that every jake's dream in this town?"

Gilberg recoiled. This was going wrong. Lehman was always expert conciliation. Lehman never got into open conflict with anyone. Lehman was subtle. Lehman gentled wolverines.

"People like you lay awake at night dreaming about how to fox this big game," continued Lehman, "and now you're mad at me because I can do what you dream about."

Gilberg took off his glasses to get a better look at the new Lehman. He revealed pale eye sockets and wide pupils.

"Go tell everyone you want to," said Lehman, waving a

hand in venomous dismissal.

Gilberg jerked back, flinching spastically before the hand as if it were a cobra.

Lehman had planned to donate the money to charity. It would have finessed everyone from getting mad about the phony handicap because charity was the 2nd largest industry behind gambling in Nevada and anything could be done in its name, including stealing the Calcutta pool.

But their sending Gilberg with the diamond z in his beard had made it too difficult to give back the money. He couldn't return even a small part of their pride to such an ambassador. The ignorant, vicious, paranoid, insulting gulls. Did they think they could turn a kid with a shotgun loose on him and suffer no reprisals to their dignity?

 After spying on Spike in the golf tournament, Noreen went home to pick out a few outfits for the rest of the weekend. She took them to Spike's room in the Dog and hung them up in his closet. She was going to marry euphoria and take it off to have with her whenever she went. She was going to pack Jake in a cold can.

But it went wrong as soon as Spike returned. He was pleased enough to see her, but he was full of purple-speak. There was no spell in it either. He showed her his new watch as if it were a bank account. He spoke of his 58 with venom. He announced he was going to work for Lehman in his casino. She was supposed to call him Rick Boly from now on. He had to go buy a tuxedo.

"All right, Rick," she said with loathing, "You go ahead and let Lehman make you rich."

Spike bought the tux, and went to his new job wearing it. The excitement of being a casino boss wore off in an hour. The way Noreen had called him Rick had sent a flash of shame through him. He stood on the casino floor dreaming. He missed his sister.

He asked Bullock (the shift boss whose dinner jacket looked like red gravel, its eye-catching ugliness a mark of high rank in the pit) could he could make a phone call? Bullock was delighted to cover for Lehman's new favorite.

His father answered the phone. Spike felt terrible. He hated the idea of ever having to go home again. Something was breaking, some something he'd always carried in the back of his mind as unbreakable.

Harry put Libby on the phone. Spike tried to explain that he might be getting married, but he was too vague so she didn't hear it breaking. But he could feel it in his stomach where it had busted. In a few weeks Harry would have her hating him for leaving.

When he went back into the casino, Noreen was sitting at 1 of the blackjack tables waiting for him. He noticed her skin wasn't pale any more. She'd turned the color of Persian melon meat from being outside. She revealed she'd been out to watch him play golf in the tournament and she tanned easily, especially this high up in the atmosphere. She looked all slick and orange. He was pleased she'd gone out to watch him play. He took her arm to touch and feel her glossy new skin.

There was a grubby looking guy playing next to her who clucked at the way Spike touched her arm. He had sloppy piles of chips arranged in a superstitious formation which he kept adjusting every time a 6 was dealt. She leaned across the table to whisper to Spike.

"You have such a splendid comfy personality," she said. She was looking at his new outfit. All the floormen at Ziraleet wore tuxedos in the casino. Her eyes said how handsome his square shoulders looked in his black dinner jacket framing a white shirt with a bulging black tie.

"It's impossible not to like you because you like everyone. Have you ever wondered about why you're so fond of dogs?"

Spike studied Noreen with newer even more potent affection. "You're sexy when you talk that way. It's so smart."

"I can see your future here," she said, enjoying his affection. "Do you wish to know your future?"

The sloppy player clucked again.

"Give me my future," consented Spike.

"The future," the sloppy player whispered to himself. Evidently, the repeated mention of the future was as terrifying as the 6 of spades because he began to realign his stonehenge of chips as if he thought the gods were coming.

"In your future Lehman will like you," Noreen said. "They will all like you. They'll give you money. It's not so much to stand around and watch people play cards for 1,000 a week, is it? Okay, but I've seen the mouths of such pals of the powerful, and their teeth are grey. They know they aren't really doing anything. They know how vulnerable they are. Your new father, Lehman, he's going to ask you a few affectionate questions once a month; and, if you ever occupy a position between him and someone else, like the gaming board or the FBI or another Lehman, he's going to use you like you're the bumper on his red Cadillac."

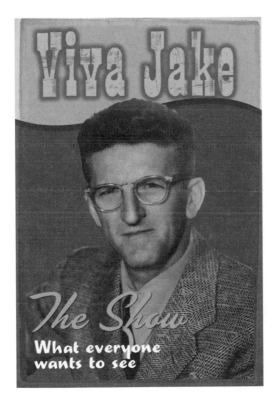

"He likes me because I won the golf tournament," said Spike.

"You think you've gotten yourself adopted?" she laced the question with astonishment. "So you'll get paid lots of money and you won't have to vomit up your guilt and eat it at dinner the way your real father made you."

"Boy, uhhh, sick," said Spike.

But he didn't really feel sick. He felt wonderful. Noreen was pouring out truth and it didn't smell like vomit at all. It was as aromatic as coffee and newsprint.

"Let's get out of here," she said. "Let's leave town the instant my divorce is final. You don't need this."

Her skin was brilliant with her sexy Persian melon glow. Last night when she'd been albino white, her breastbone had turned red while they were screwing. It had looked like neon tubing beneath her pale skin, lighting up her chest with a diffused glow. ("Oh, boy," had been her opinion during their movements then.) Now the same soft glow was all over her body, but in Persian melon orange instead of red.

"You fill my head with dirty thoughts," he said. "Why are you so smart?"

"Come on back to the Dog," she said. "I'll show you smart."

"Will you 2 make your sex deals somewhere else," said the superstitious goren next to her, putting the finishing touches on his wafer temple to the nasty gods who ordered playing cards. "Some of us are here to concentrate on our cards."

Noreen turned to look at him.

"Imagine taking a game seriously whose most difficult feature is the requirement that you be able to count to 21," Noreen gestured at the felt layout with toxic scorn. "You must be a very special person." She turned to Spike. "He possesses an intuition so powerful it can compel the hostile soldiers of Chance to abandon their weapons and line up to suck on his knee."

"I wish to speak to the manager," said the unshaven mouth. "I'll talk to the manager."

"Why don't you go get a manicure 1st." suggested Spike. "You can't shake hands with the manager using those

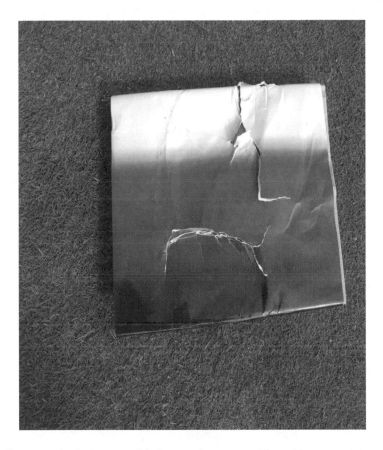

fingers. A shave would do no damage either. You want to meet the boss looking like a drunk?"

"The thought of a man and woman having sex makes this fantastic mind faint with revulsion, however," continued Noreen, her voice rising from hatred to delight. "What a filthy unsettling deed, the juicy intercourse."

The slob was waving down the pit like a Navy signalman, and suddenly Bullock had Spike by the arm.

"Hey, Rick," lectured Bullock, leading Spike away from the table, "the idea here is not to team up with your girl friend to drive people away from their play. The idea is to use your charm to welcome the customers."

"Sorry, Jack," apologized Spike. "He's got his chips all over the table in other people's way."

"Checks," corrected Bullock. "Chips are something buffalo sell to the prairie. In the pit we call them 'checks.'"

"Okay. checks," said Spike. "He's all over the table with elbows and checks"

"Huh huh?," laughed Bullock. He understood. He hated all the customers, not just 1 slob insulting a girl friend. He counseled Spike to keep his emotions under control.

"Now if he tries something neat," he concluded, "that's different. Put him on the deck and your heel on his lips. But until he does, you make him feel like this is home and you're his waiter."

When Spike returned to the blackjack table, the creep was gone. Noreen confessed she had continued discussing the juicy intercourse until he'd fled.

"Bullock says I have to be nice to assholes," he said.

"You see what you're in for?" she asked "What kind of work is this?"

"I can be nice to butt wipes," he declared. "I'll tell you what kind of work this is. It's like being a butler with the power to make credit decisions on your duke."

Noreen looked disgusted.

"Yes," he agreed with himself, pleased that he was acquiring Noreen's talent for such analysis. "A butler. That's why we wear tuxedos." He clicked his heels.

"You aren't leaving on Monday, are you?"

"Why should I?" he challenged her.

Her melon skin flushed coral with anger. This new color spread down from her neck and out across her shoulders like spilled paint.

In an instant she was gone and he felt nervous again. Now that he was divided from his family, Noreen was what was left. He ordered himself not to worry. She liked to argue and get upset, but he knew her exit was temporary. She wasn't doing anything without him. They had connected like 2 locomotives slamming into the lock position. They would chug into the future with the colored cars of their past strung out behind them in the immutable double helix of attachment known as love. She could sling her emotions into the firebox as vigorously as she pleased. The end result would be nothing more than opalescent smoke marking the twisted rails of their route to happiness.

  It was so right that there should be 40 feet of rain, Viner couldn't bring himself to stop saying it. He opened the panel's testimony with a story from a man who had survived a supernatural flood in Tennessee.

"The river was moving up my back yard like bath water creeping across your tile floor and then the dam broke," he said. "It was only 400 yards from me, the dam, and what

came down at me between the valley walls wasn't like water at all. It was a living angry thing, a black humping eel. It picked a house up here, and took it on up the street there, and put it down. It backed down the street to see if it liked it there, and she must have decided it was poor there, because she came up quick and got that house again, and took it past me another 300 yards where the house broke up because it couldn't take it any more."

The next day he saw babies floating in the dark water like dolls. It was black and tarry and it had washed around his nose and left a permanent loathsome odor there.

Viner turned to the legendary Nobel laureate Emil Lillo-Furon. Lillo spoke about the "yield of the burst."

Viner eagerly noted the recurring use of the hydro-logical word "burst" in nuclear technology.

"Phil Grethlien was brilliant in his way," said Lillo happy to be on television, the center of public interest again. "Sparks of wonderful ideas were always spinning out of him like flares off pinwheel fireworks. But sometimes his ideas were wrong."

There was silence. Lillo looked at Viner and then at the camera.

"If you think of math as a language," Lillo said, trying again, "Phil was like a child growing up in a German family, but poor Phil could only master a few phrases in German."

Silence again wafted through the studio with its unhappy smog of confusion.

"Do you believe that it is impossible for this 'implosion' to produce a flood of biblical proportions?" Viner asked.

Lillo smirked. Viner filled up with dread.

"What's funny?" asked Viner. It was a long instant waiting for what would surely be a Nobel prize winning insult.

What had made him bark the flood thing on Lillo?

"A flood," laughed Lillo. "The idea of a flood issuing from a nuclear weapon is extravagantly incompetent."

Viner began to sweat. He turned to Lanf, the public relations functionary from 52. Lanf had been angry ever since Lillo had claimed everyone in the bunker would be killed. He burst out with a passionate claim of safety and said Lillo was attempting to devalue the AWB in vengeance for his own disgrace.

"I have a notebook here I have obtained from Mrs. Grethlien," Lanf said, turning to the business of discrediting Phil with the notebook he had stolen from the empty Grethlien house.

He would demonstrate what kind of mind had given birth to the irrational vision of destruction Lillo and Viner were lieing to promote. He held up the notebook to the camera.

It was open to a drawing of a mysterious medical instrument. It looked like a soft retractor with a small engine attached. Below the strange retractor was a 2nd drawing, a rubber toy giraffe.

"Let me read to you from this notebook," said Lanf. "Remember this is the mind Dr. Lillo-Furon praises so highly."

From Lanf's reading it became clear the device was designed to process human bowel movements into animal statuettes like the toy giraffe in the drawing. Lanf went on to read from a letter Phil had written to many pharmaceutical companies.

"We shall elevate the nature of Western civilization," he quoted Phil, his voice rising and falling with incredulity. "The act of voiding, no longer disgusting because its issue can be transformed into something enchanting, need no longer be secretive. Men and women can affix this engine to the anus wherever the call comes and their intestinal production will be rendered in more agreeable public forms. Open defecation will climb the evolutionary ladder from the great apes to mankind; only now, instead of reflecting gross animality, it will exhibit the high evolution of our civilization, for what could be more civilized than making shit beautiful?"

The show just fell silent at this. Viner wasn't listening anymore so he didn't sweep in with a clean-up on the illegal word. *Lillo was sucking affection right out of him by calling him stupid so elegantly for the camera earlier. Viner often got lost in his love for brilliant minds like Lineheardt, Phil and Lillo. It was a love which he could never transfer back to himself.*

He wished God, his almighty nasty father, had given him a lesser sin to ruin his life with instead of having abandoned his country wife and their pretty daughters. A murder of a roadside pedestrian with his drunken truck, perhaps. Or sticking his letter opener in the eye of the insurance guy over the cheap repayment for a prize huge tractor melted by a lighting bolt which had split the charcoal Dakota sky with a white canal of light as wide as the federal highway. He hated himself for doing neither of these, but leaving his lovely girls instead. This hatred radiated all through him out the eyes of any young girl who trapped him in her glance.

The desert sun came in from the window behind Lehman and filled his office with white-yellow light. To Donahue, looking into the bright sun, Lehman appeared achromatic, his face silver and bronze, as if it were glazed with metal. To Lehman, Donahue was bleached colors. His powder blue sport coat was washed almost white by the sunlight, his bright hazel iris squeezed down on tiny black pearls, and his face was decorated with ultramarine veins.

Lehman's desk had a large blotter on top of its lush mahogany. Donahue could make out numbers scribbled all over it. Some were phone numbers, some were dollar amounts, and many were inscrutable. The blotter was a tear-off pad. Donahue asked how many weeks this particular sheet represented. Only 5 days, Lehman answered, noticing from Donahue's question that the sheet was full and tearing it off.

"Gilberg woke up screaming last night," Donahue said. "He dreamed he was in a car accident where he'd gone skipping across an open farm field doing 150 and hit something which pushed the engine right through his gut. He

155

was full of details describing it. Like it really happened."

Donahue was an intelligent man in his forties. Lehman respected him for his ability to catch dishonest dealers in the act of cheating. Gilberg's per at The Hospital had shot up over 30 the day Donahue had walked onto the casino floor there. Donahue had sharp eyes like Lehman himself. He didn't have to catch dishonest dealers by entrapping them with agents.

Lehman laughed to no one as he heard his thoughts referring to "dishonest" dealers. What exactly was an "honest" dealer? During his 60 years in the gambling arts, Lehman had never encountered a casino employee who hadn't stolen money on the job. That included all of his floormen, shift bosses, and casino managers. And himself.

"What does this dream have to do with me?" he asked Donahue.

"He says it's an omen," said Donahue. "That someone wants to kill him, and now that you've pulled this golf swindle, he's sure it's you."

"Your boss is a seer." Lehman's cataract glowed as he laughed. "He knows when his dreams are his future."

"I know it's bullshit and you know it's bullshit," said Donahue, "but this dream scared him stiff."

"And?"

"I found an article in Life," Donahue said. "He was only 13 but you can see it's Kilmarx."

"Really?" asked Lehman indifferently.

Donahue produced an old Life. He showed Lehman the picture of a young crew-cut Spike.

"That's him," agreed Lehman. Lehman read the article with interest. Spike had shot a 25 on the back. 8 birdies and an eagle.

"He's not any Rick somebody," said Donahue.

"Not even so much as a par on the back," said Lehman, his

head twisting with owl-like admiration. "Can you imagine going into the last 2 holes needing at least 1 birdie for a 59 and getting 2? 1 on each hole. Where were his nerves?"

"He was 13," said Donahue. "No nerves"

"Look at this," said Lehman, thumping the page with the back of his fingers. "He did have nerves. He had a headache by the 13th hole. 'I wanted to get it over with and take a couple of aspirin,' he says."

157

"A lot of people in Jake have seen this picture today," said Donahue.

"Can I keep this, John?" Lehman asked.

"It's the library's," said Donahue. "I promised I'd bring it back."

Lehman smiled patronizingly, making no move to return the magazine. "The library is not going to be there much longer."

"Sure, you take it," said Donahue quickly. "The hell with the library."

Lehman stood up, stuffed the magazine into his pocket with the rest of the day's clippings, and walked out, leaving Donahue alone in the office. Donahue went out into the living room. Lehman had disappeared.

His son was still there running engines around his toy train tracks, competing against himself. He had coaxed Donahue into a race while Donahue had been waiting for Lehman earlier. The kid had really whipped him, and then apologized for winning so big by explaining how he stayed up with his racing trains to 3 or 4 in the morning every night.

Donahue watched him making both locomotives rocket around the tracks.

Now he was making them both go much faster than Donahue had been able to do with 1. The kid knew Donahue was there, but he didn't look up from his work. Donahue let himself out and left town, deciding that if Lehman didn't like the library's chances, neither did Donahue.

 The value of having Frederic Starzinchger in residence was so high, the owner of the hotel where he'd flopped had been informed before breakfast. But Starzinchger was allowed to sleep all day in peace. Every few hours he'd wake up and call General Sensenig's driver to make a different appointment. The moment Starzinchger emerged from his room in the early evening, Gilberg was paged by his paging name so he could sneak up and intersect Starzinchger in the lobby. There a friendship was born in the early hours of the great big Jake Saturday night.

Starzinchger was fascinated with the life of the casino owner. People constantly came up to Gilberg to ask for favors ranging from simple gambling credit to finding the right doctor for a sick relative. Gilberg consistently turned to Starzinchger to consult, and inevitably the petitioner quickly divided his arguments between the 2 of them, turning the same familiarity to Starzinchger he'd been using to advance his case with Gilberg. 1 of the suitors, a young man with his foot in a cast, made several appearances but never got an audience.

When they finished the big party dinner Gilberg had instantly threw for him, Starzinchger accompanied Gilberg up and down 4th Street visiting all the other hotels. The sore foot continued to haunt their trail. He would get into position ahead of them and stare anxiously at Gilberg with his flat left eyebrow and arched right one, which made him look permanently uncertain.

Gilberg introduced Starzinchger to many important figures in the gaming industry. But these conversations were different than the 1s Starzinchger had been invited to participate in over dinner. He was not welcome in these conversations. The casino owners and Gilberg spoke openly before him, Starzinchger could hear all the words, but the sense of what they said was quite obscure. It was as if they were speaking in code.

 Lehman wasn't worried over being found out about Spike. He'd regarded that as inevitable. What worried Lehman was Donahue's saying right in the middle of the conversation, "They've found out what's going on with your dice. They all know you're dumping money to tourists."

A don't player had figured it out. Lehman laughed. He

160

could see the guy standing there betting don't, don't, don't, going hours without winning a bet. Of course. Sooner or later he'd come to the idea he was being cheated. Lehman had forgotten all about don't players. Hah. It served the son-of-a-bitch right. Why wouldn't the stupid bastard start betting with the dice and get rich like everyone else? No, not a don't player. Don't players were inflexible bilious losers. The neurotic Gilberg was a don't player.

Lehman felt uncomfortable. He had wanted to decide on when to die, but he had not picked his day yet. Now there could be no fooling around. If Gilberg knew about his unusual dice, so did Lehman's partners in **Ziraleet**. There could be no more waiting.

Sonia had taken such a big interest in the new bomb, Lehman's pockets were full of clippings about nuclear mechanics and history. She was feeding them into his reading with such insistence, he was getting fascinated too.

When he heard from his pretty lady maitre d' the Nobel winning Emil Lillo-Furon was in the crowd for Herb Shriner's early show, Lehman decided he would settle for himself the popular question of whether the bomb was going to be a dud or not. He expected he could get the answer to this mystery because mystery was another word for a secret, and Lehman had powers in matters of confidence.

He found Lillo at ringside with the pink ortolan. She was sitting in the high chair reserved for visiting celebrities. When he sat down with them, she lapped down at him from her phony throne with the usual enthusiasm entertainers have for hotel owners. This impressed Lillo and made him eager to please Lehman also. Obviously Lillo was going to ruffle the pink ortolan's feathered nether attraction. Lehman sat and talked with them through their dinner. He released significant clouds of charm across the table like a dentist discharging laughing gas into a patient.

The scientist kept looking back and forth from Lehman's eye to his hand. Finally he asked if the swollen hand had

Herb Shriner

anything to do with radiation syndrome. He mentioned a dead colleague named Barbanel, his voice textured with virulent hatred. Lehman said his hand was swollen from gout, the result of his new friendship with the chef. Lillo was pleased with this symptomatology, and Lehman found it easy to move into the line on which he intended to run the truth out from underneath the Nobel prize winner.

"I understand you are not on the best of terms with the AWB these weeks," said Lehman.

"True," laughed Lillo. "I found out only this evening they took my lecture tour as hostility against them. Thus, my hearing and my shame."

Lehman saw little shame.

Lillo stared at Lehman's startling eye. He wondered how much Lehman could see out through the cloud of glowing blue. The eye was a fascinating model of current atomic theory. Physicists had changed their notion of the atom as a solar system with the nucleus in the center and electrons revolving about it in different orbits like planets. They now envisioned the electrons as a charged almost vaporous field. Lehman's eye, a wonderful luminescent blue cloud surrounding an obscured protected black center illustrated it perfectly.

"They gave you no tickets to watch the blast then?" asked Lehman.

"Why, no" said Lillo, with surprise. The idea of attending the detonation had never crossed his mind.

"Would you like my 2 passes to the bunker?" asked Lehman.

"I beg your pardon?"

Lehman held out 2 AWB passes. Admissions to the bunker were selling in Jake at that moment $8,000 apiece. "I understand they are bringing a premium."

"That would be fun," glowed the pink ortolan. "I've never been."

Lillo looked confused. Lehman watched the famous mind whirling, asking itself questions and answering them at a speed which won Nobel prizes.

"I have someone I have to meet in San Francisco," he said after a few moments. "I'm buying a house on Baker Beach."

"Despite the doubts you showed on television," said Lehman, "You now believe that Grethlien's claims were accurate."

"No, no," said Lillo. "I believe it's going to be an unsuccessful test."

"What happens to anyone sitting in the bunker if it goes off?" asked Lehman. "Is the AWB right saying the bunker is completely safe?"

"They are quite wrong," said Lillo.

"I have become a fan of Heisenberg's Uncertainty Principle," said Lehman, recalling clippings Sonia had put in his pocket describing the findings of 1 of Germany's great atomic theorists. "I like the idea of seeing the universe in terms of probability. Einstein's assertion that god does not

play dice with the universe is offensive religious cod."

At the mention of Heisenberg, Lillo stared at Lehman with curiosity.

"Convince me in Math," said Lehman. "As a man who lives by the laws of mathematics, I'm more interested in your calculations than your assertions."

Lillo was delighted with the request. Lehman's agile mind amazed Lillo. He absorbed the inverted mechanics of matrix multiplication as if it were high school algebra.

"To recap our calculations," Lillo said, treating Lehman like a professor finding a prize new graduate student, "the fission burst ignites the fusion burst****

"And the combination of the 2 reactions is the total yield," interrupted Lehman impatiently, "6 megatons."

"Agreed," said Lillo.

They stopped to look at the white table cloth across which Lehman had scratched Lillo's wisdom like a math prodigy at a blackboard. His blue ink had wandered across open white spaces, collided with china, and branched around a giant pepper cellar out to the edge of the table and started towards the pink ortolan's fork, across and back again numerous times until the cloth displayed a cerulean army of marching alpha numerics.

The pink ortolan stared at these ant like markings as if they intended to swarm her dessert goblet and eat her blue Bavarian creme.

Lillo pulled a plastic wheel out of his pocket and worked it about. It looked very much like roulette equipment to Lehman. "The heat of thermal wave when it reaches the bunker 8 miles away is 100 calories per cubic centimeter. Which will incinerate everyone inside."

"But the heat is largely dissipated at a range of 13 miles," said Lehman, "and Jake remains unaffected?"

"Jake will suffer a few broken windows," said Lillo, then underscoring that all their calculations had been nothing more than an agreeable exercise of tutorial fantasy, *"If it works."*

"You say it won't," said Lehman, "yet you refuse my passes and a chance to sit close to your hated enemies and witness the delicious spectacle of their embarrassment."

Lillo looked at Lehman with new respect.

"I have no interest in their embarrassment," he lied.

"I think you have an idea it might work," said Lehman.

Lehman withdrew several pages from his suit coat pocket. They were from a book Sonia had been reading about World War II.

"Let me tell you a little story," said Lehman.

Lillo smiled with anticipation. He had heard Lehman was famous for telling odd little tales laced with quotations from clippings and book pages he produced from different pockets like a magician juggling bunnies.

"The great German atomic scientists, Heisenberg himself, Gerlach and others, were American prisoners when the 1st atomic bomb exploded over Hiroshima," said Lehman. "They dismissed the 1st radio announcement as a fraud. This new bomb could be nothing more than a new form of TNT, they told each other. A true atomic weapon was only very very remotely possible. The uranium problem was insoluble. It would take a lifetime of superhuman German effort to isolate enough isotope to make such an A-bomb."

Lillo laughed happily.

"You know about this," Lehman said. "You know how they felt when the details came to them on the next radio broadcast, making it clear that their lifetime of German effort had not been required."

"Yes, I do," confessed Lillo, still grinning. He loved this story.

"Their egos were crushed," said Lehman. "Even the great Heisenberg. They walked about their barracks like zombies. Their work, their pride, their grand sense of themselves was oblitcratcd."

"Yes," agreed Lillo.

"It says here they were so depressed, they stopped eating," Lehman brandished the torn book page. "Think of the poor chef. All his dishes came back to him as if the great men he was privileged to cook for thought he was salting them with rat poison."

Lillo laughed at the way chefs kept creeping into Lehman's conversation.

"You could be as wrong as Heisenberg," said Lehman.

Lillo shrugged.

"If you had to explain your conviction that Grethlien is in error," growled Lehman. "If your health were at stake. What would you say?"

Lillo jumped out of his seat with surprise at the sudden lupine threat in Lehman's tone.

"I would not say Phil was in error," he responded unwillingly, but not ready to withhold his best answer from Lehman, "I would simply say that it takes longer to produce these things than Phil has taken."

"Really?" asked Lehman cynically.

"If you look into the notebooks of Galileo and Kepler," said Lillo, feeling suddenly pensive, "you will see page after page of geometric designs. Geometry was their mode of thought because they were only beginning to explore mathematics. Phil was stuck back in geometry with them. He made forays into our world of babbling incomprehensible mathematicians like Pizarro going through Incas with a small armed party and his nerve. At Los Alamos he went deep inside us and extracted something wonderfully geometric. Implosion. Something as intellectually exquisite as Pizarro's 78 million in gold. Did you know it was 78 million? Think of it. 78 million in 1533. That would be googol billions today. He made Spain the power of the world for the subsequent 100 years."

"So will Grethlien for the U.S.," said Lehman.

"Oh, yes, we should start saying that," disapproved Lillo. "Such exaggerated praise must accrue to Phil like moons circling Jupiter. But you don't have to exaggerate like a reporter to capture him. He extracted elegant geometric solutions from a crowd of mathematical foment."

"You're not convincing me he's going to fail with such praise," argued Lehman.

"To fire it from a rail cannon?" Lillo's eyes arched. "It's all so new and we worked for 3 years, 1,000s and 1,000s of scientists****"

Lehman's relentless eyes spotted something on Lillo's corner of the table cloth. Lillo, always thinking of several things at once, had written something there while Lehman was busy scratching out equations:

(Hiroshima Complex) <=> (Gambler's implosion of self)

"What is this?" asked Lehman, indicating the mathematical symbol **<=>** between the 2 ideas.

"That is the symbol for the identity relation," Lillo explained, pleased Lehman could now share this relationship he had discovered.

"Like an equals sign?" asked Lehman.

"Yes, but stronger," explained Lillo.

"You are saying that if you have the left side of the relation then you have the right side," said Lehman.

"When I put the identity in the middle of a formula," smirked Lillo, "it's a notation that god has said it, not me, and there is nothing that can make it wrong."

Lilllo, now beyond the reach of the terrifying Hiroshima Complex, was luxuriating in being better than Heisenberg.

Lehman thought that if there were a Nobel Prize for gambling, he should like to win one.

Lehman's chauffeur

After a walk through the Chute, Starzinchger and Gilberg started back towards Gilberg's hotel. Clouds of purple carbonated light were curling down Trembling Peak. During the sunny day the peak had been an anabatic ramp which had sent passing clouds right up to 30,000 feet; but now in the cool of the night, clouds rode the katabatic vector through Jake and flowed all the way down the mountain, running a giant misty cable from 4th Street to 52.

"I'll tell you what, Fred," said Gilberg, pinching the diamond z in his beard. "Let's party all night."

Starzinchger laughed. He still hadn't gone to see Sensenig.

"Okay, I'll tell you what," repeated Gilberg, rolling the diamond in his beard between his thumb and forefinger. "We're going to party all night, but on 1 condition."

"What condition is that?" smiled Starzinchger.

"You be my expert on the bomb in the morning," said Gilberg.

"What?" snickered Starzinchger.

170

"I've got my own fallout shelter," said Gilberg. "Right up on the peak above everybody. I've got mirrors with filters and everything rigged up so you can see up out of the shelter without burning your retina. I haven't been up there for a year, but since you're here, I'm going to go tonight, and we'll take some big people, we'll call the governor and invite him, and we'll watch the bomb and you'll be the expert."

Starzinchger snickered again.

"Why not?" asked Gilberg.

"This is like having Joe Louis greet the gamblers," said Starzinchger.

"Nah, nah," said Gilberg. "We're friends. It's for fun. Joe Louis costs 1,000 dollars a night. This is a party. This isn't business."

Starzinchger was tempted. He wrestled with telling Gilberg the bomb was going to be a dud so he could get away to see Sensenig.

"All right," he shrugged, feeling a rush of greed. "We'll party all night."

"Great!" said Gilberg, throwing his arm around Starzinchger's shoulder.

"On 1 condition," said Starzinchger.

"Okay," said Gilberg.

"$500," laughed Starzinchger.

Gilberg withdrew his arm. His thumb and forefinger went to his diamond z. He looked at Starzinchger with troubled eyes.

"You want to use me as your nuclear expert," said Starzinchger, making plans for the 500 as he argued. He would try poker at the Dog. "Only you want it for free to show how sharp you are. Afterwards you're going to brag to all your cronies about how you used Frederic Starzinchger for free."

Gilberg grinned mischievously. He liked the argument. "Let's make it 1,000." He smiled happily as he took some bills out of his pocket. "You're worth as much as Joe Louis."

Gilberg soon wanted some work for his $1,000. He hailed a pair of motorcycle policemen and asked Starzinchger to explain the bomb's range to them. Evidently the police department was worried about an empty Jake vulnerable to looters, but they didn't want to be killed by the burst any more than the next guy. Starzinchger tread a careful middle ground between convincing the policemen they would be safe in Jake and not giving away to Gilberg that nothing was going to happen.

Noreen could let only 2 hours pass before she needed to see Spike again. Spike was delighted to leave the casino to take her call. She wanted him to come down to the dentist's office where she worked.

She was the only 1 there. She led him down the hall past an open office with files spread all over a table.

"Come in and sit down," she teased from inside a patient's room, nodding at the dentist's chair.

"You're kidding," he said.

She pulled him by his shirt over to the chair and sat him down. He closed his eyes and began to tremble. The dental scent in the room took on properties of burning cyanide pellets.

She put her fingers between his lips and gently touched his gums. Her clean breath relaxed him. Her fingertips walked about his gums, then disappeared. He heard a noise on the instrument tray. She showed him a metal hook, but she only tickled neatly about his gum line with it, washing him clean with little needles of air and water as she went.

When she finished, she held up a mirror for him to look, her blue eyes flashing with pride. His teeth looked like fine marble. His mouth felt clean and vibrant.

She took the mirror away and bent over to kiss him. Now that his tongue was clean, her lime flavored antiseptic mouth tasted dizzyingly powerful. Her tongue went to many of the places her fingers and tools had been. She had an inquisitive dog-like intelligence in her mouth, and she was using it to explore the new climate she'd created.

"There's a sequence everyone goes through when they come here," she said. "They get mentally drunk but its not real."

"People get mentally drunk in your dentist's chair?"

"No, stupid. Jake."

She was going to be perceptive about Jake again.

"I've just figured out why you were so good at oral sex gymnastics last night," he said. He could be perceptive too.

Casino partner

He wanted to win 1 of these match play arguments.

"Let me tell you what's going on in your mind and body" she said.

"You like to get things that give you pleasure in your mouth," he said.

"Yes, I do" she conceded the point. "And you toss and turn at night, caught in the 1st stage of sleep. You dream light boozy dreams, as if you're drunk, but you're not drunk."

"You know the menus for every dining room and coffee shop in every hotel in Jake," he countered.

"Okay, I do," she said. "When you are wide awake it is hard to call to mind the many things you wish to remember. It's hard to climb stairs. You get headaches. You were surprised to see diesel trucks parked along the side of the road when you came up the mountain into Jake."

"Oh, yeah, the trucks," he remembered.

"Those trucks had altitude sickness," she said, "and so do you. Once your body adapts and you start sleeping, you won't think Jake is so magical any more. That's why you shouldn't make any decisions on money or life changes until after your 1st magical weekend."

Spike laughed nervously. She had stuck another shot next to the flag.

"What are you laughing at, you dope," she asked playfully. "Why do you think you hit your drives so far today?"

"What?" said Spike "Oh, no! It's the thin air."

"You thought you'd discovered some new feel, some secret power, didn't you?" she asked solicitously.

"Yes." He felt very stupid. She had closed him out again.

"And the feeling of being light-headed and gay," she added.

"Shit," he said, depressed.

"You played well because you couldn't think too much," she said. "But you'll adapt in a few days. You'll be able to think again and Jake golf will be less excellent."

"It lasts only a weekend?" asked Spike morosely. "I had myself shooting 64s here for some time."

"Don't you see how depressed everyone is here?" she asked.

"No," he said. "Everyone's having a good time. Sometimes

they seem a little sad, but ****"

"A little sad?" she mocked.

"Sometimes I feel anxious and sad," he said, thinking about it.

"Krieder, my husband, was a meteorologist for the Navy in the Pacific" she said. "Sometimes he'd sail through a queer series of choppy turbulences off the Philippines. They would be out on a glass smooth sea. A strip of chop a mile wide would appear on the horizon and wash through them. It wasn't much to look at, just a strip of slightly rough water. But when they were anchored and 1 of these lines of chop came through, it would snap the anchor chains in half. Anchor chains with links a foot in diameter. He found out that the little chop on top of the water was a surface symptom of enormous underwater waves, waves over 200 feet tall which come from tides spilling over undersea cliffs in massive rips."

"How interesting. You know a lot about waves?

"Don't mock me, " said Noreen. "I'm trying to tell you that your upset is like a real storm, when the whole sea is flecked with white tops. Anyone can see it. But these guys, the Lehmans and the Jacks, they are smooth seas, and all you see on them are their little ripples, while underneath they've got 200 foot walls of emotion slamming around inside of them, breaking anchor chains right and left."

She went to the doorway and turned off the overhead light. The working light glittered down into her carefully arranged instruments.

"I said not to make any big decisions until your 1st weekend here is over," she said. "But I have to ask you to anyway because we don't have time to wait."

"What is it?"

"I want you to come away with me after we get married,"

she said. "I can't live here any more. I want to marry you, but I can't live here*****"

"I get it," he said. "Where are we going?"

"That was too quick," she said. "You have to think about it because Jake puts*****"

"Forget about Jake," he said. "I'm going with you."

She opened her mouth to talk but nothing came out. He got up and hugged her.

"We'll be happy," she swore.

He grinned at her like an idiot.

"What are you looking at?" she asked.

"You"

He blew his clean new breath at her nose.

"Let's go get drunk at Ondine," she laughed.

The casino at Ondine sang a different tune than Ziraleet. In a dull zombie chorus the player's murmur complained that somebody was cheating them out of all they cared about.

Spike and Noreen took an elevator down and walked a hall with grottoes of light illuminating weird movie scenes of fish hockey, fish chasing wild popsicles, fish carving sponge into topiary, all creations of *the Hollywood guy who had built the hotel under the impression that everyone wanted to be at the cinema all the time and that black-*

177

jack dealers didn't pass chips to agents with the approval of floormen who were getting their piece of the per.

The bar itself was crisscrossed with light from multiple projectors shining onto anything that would field light, which included Spike and Noreen, the other patrons, blank columns and walls, and large mirrors even more confused than men and women about how to handle such weird arrows of light.

It seemed impossible to decode the scene all the projectors were attempting to convey. But after a brandy, Noreen recognized on the wall a dark ocean floor which was just admitting the 1st cucumber light of dawn from above. Was this Jake after the coming of Mr. Festival's flood? The water flashed with spines of silver and then became clear with morning light. The tide was coming in. The sea was climbing the pilings of some giant dock above them. Scattered strands of sea grass swept back and forth whipping taupe-brown tendrils against the sandy ocean floor.

Suddenly Noreen was up. She swept along a long wall of sea, flipping over tables and chairs, imitating the waves turning over shells and debris in the film beyond her. Then she and the current swept back together, she mimicking a horseshoe crab which cruised along like a helmet with oars. Spike remembered her twirling her naked body above his bed like a gymnast. She was the most beautiful woman in Jake, maybe in the World. She stole melancholy from the faces of her audience at the bar, ate it, turned it into something happy and then back to melancholy, and back to pleasure, refusing to give up until she had turned it over again and again.

A new admiration for her invaded Spike and set his sense of himself back a fresh couple of clicks. She made him feel like a boy before Aphrodite. She was at this instant so potent he had no more "Holy chuck"s left to spend on her.

He was H and she was O, and the 2 between them was a steel tendon. Did that start yesterday? Or the day before? It was fresh but still felt so way long ago. The near past had expanded backwards all the way to the 1st bang, the Big 1 not theirs, and it had compressed all the old ugly things that had happened since that 1st second into a harmless film.

She fell suddenly into a chair with an exhausted laugh. The bar was a shambles, but no 1 minded, not even the busboys who had to straighten up the ruins of her performance.

"I had a physicist from 52 in my office a couple of hours ago," she wheezed, still breathing hard from her nutty dance. "They're all crazy the way they like to get close to death. They might set off a bomb that could melt Jake."

"Yeah?"

"We've got to go down there," she sat up, finally catching her breath.

"You want to go down to 52?" he asked.

"It will be fun," she said. "When we see the rail gun, we'll know if it's going to work."

"What does the rail gun have to do with the bomb?" asked Spike.

"Phil invented both of them," she claimed. "If 1 works, so will the other."

"So we see the rail gun, we decide by looking at it whether it will work or not, then we know all about the bomb," Spike thought out loud.

"Do you think that's stupid?" she asked. "The truth is always obvious, you know. If we can only see it, we'll know if its going to work."

179

"Right!" agreed Spike.

"You agree with me?" She was delighted.

"Truth is obvious," he confirmed. "It smells."

"We can rent 2 matched Appaloosas from the stables at Old Desert Top," she said. "Wait till you see them. They have huge hindquarters, just alike, both dappled with the same grey wafers, like they're twins from some Gerard Manly Hopkins poem."

"Holy work, you like horses," he said. "You really know horses. This is fantastic! Golf and horses."

"Okay, we'll play golf and go riding after we're married," she said cautiously, "but I'm not turning into any religio."

NOTHING

With the money from Tuck's, Phil went to play blackjack at Ziraleet. When he'd finally gotten the box open, he'd found $33,000 inside. Either Tuck's didn't count very often or they did a lot of business for an out of the way casino.

Walking through the lobby he saw the face of a teenager he recognized from years earlier, when he had first come to Jake.

{Erving had thoughts no one else could think so he tried them out with physicists on their way to the lounge to get drunk. One of them told him he should be a physicist. Physics was for people who could see the unseeable.

"I do that?" asked Erving.

"I just heard you doing it," Phil said. "That's why Heisenberg is wrong."

"About what?" Erving knew the name. The physicists were always quoting him.

"He said that if we can't actually measure something, it only has tendency," said Phil. "That is horseshit."

"Tendency is probability?" asked Erving. "Like dice?"

"Hmm, you're smart for 11 years old," Phil guessed his age, "but you've got to get yourself some math," he said. "Anything they want to teach you about math, you go get it. Then hang the things you see on your math."

"I'm 9." Erving corrected the stupid physicist as if he were a new private who had mistaken left for right.

"No shit? 9? You're tall."}

All the dealers at Ziraleet were old. This one's hands were cracked and raised with welts of age. He'd had his fingernails done with a clear varnish. His fingers curled up under the deck like legs on a horny toad. The horny toad was on its back, trying to struggle to its feet. It curled and jumped, curled and jumped, but all it could do was peel off layers of its geometric belly.

The hands played themselves out before him as if he were watching tv and somebody else's experience was being presented to him as a curiosity. He had been gambling and spending at Ziraleet for hours. The cocktail waitress hovered nearby, anxious to make another $50 trip to the bar. What the hell was he giving her $50 for? He hated big tips.

He lost another $500 standing on 12. What was he going to do after this money was gone? He was losing touch with his plan. He had solved the 1st part of the challenge he'd posed himself; he had sucked the homuncular of this town down into himself.

But now that he was possessed of it, he no longer gave the smallest shit about saving Jake or anything in it. His scientific energy was suffocating beneath a new tide of remorse. He'd duped himself. He had told himself he was justified in doing anything to save Jake; but, instead of irradiating the tumor of his guilt, he'd bloated it. He had less than $2,000 left. Jacks and deuces were jumping the last few fences between himself and his self-loathing like deer.

It was ten o'clock at night when Viner found him. He grabbed Phil by the arm and hustled him out to his car. Phil had just taken out a $20,000 marker on his house, and signed the note "Jake Grethlien," a piece of humor which escaped the club footed boss guy in the red gravel jacket who okayed it.

Phil admired Viner's car. Viner said everyone admired his car. It was a compulsively waxed pearl grey Nash Airflyte. The roof line was a long descending arc between modest fins. A thin string of chrome circled the rear above a rounded skirt.

"You'll never guess what's happened," he jabbered to Phil as they drove up 4th Street towards the studio.

Phil wondered if they would apply the 1,000s in chips he'd left on the table against his marker. Or would they jump into some passing pocket?

"We've touched something deep in Jake," Viner was happy. "The whole town wants to believe it's going to happen. Maybe they need to believe it's going to happen. Who knows, but we're going on camera again, and now we can really sell them on it Phil, because they want it now. Come on, we've got to hurry to make the desk."

He dragged Phil through the hallway and led him to a chair behind the news desk a few feet down from Jack Planet. They got there in time to hear Planet do a live promo about their ensuing appearance.

"This story is mine now, Phil," Viner whispered excitedly. "I started the story and no 1 can take it away from me."

They watched Jack Planet lead off with a story about the "K-war", as he called it. Koreans were dying like horse flies stuck to yellow paper. He moved the news on to a story about a cat on fire without a trace of a smile.

"Clearly, this guy," Phil whispered tolerantly at Viner, "is

183

your hero in the news business."

Phil saw Lineheardt waving happily at him from behind the cameras. Planet introduced them. The big unwieldy camera turned on them. It looked like a large video vacuum cleaner with a whorish red light glowing to signify it was busy gleaning up the specs of dirt it passed off as genuine particles of reality. Like a cat soaked with brandy and set on fire by a juvenile jake.

"Phil, we know you have a traditional scientific attitude towards this new explosion," Viner opened their segment. Oh, no, he thought inside himself as he was spoke, I'm going to blurt all my new crap about the flood now.

Phil squirmed as Viner began talking about a flood. He'd had time to think about it so he made it sound pretty good now. He was putting it all to Phil in the shape of a question.

Phil imagined all the physicists from 52 listening to Viner's sickening biblical interpretation of fusion with euphoric glee. How it must delight them to see Phil sitting at the side of an idiot as if he were a twin. Viner finally finished the question. Phil answered as if the camera were more than a video vacuum cleaner. He answered as if it were a thought tunnel to the brains of his fellow physicists.

"In the next war after Korea, we'll hate ourselves for amassing huge caches of Oriental bodies," Phil said, ignoring Viner's question. "We'll want to design weapons to reduce casualties. I don't say war will become extinct, but maybe we should take cities by firing dope pellets which send the enemy retreating in anguish from hallucinatory emotions. You know what the ultimate weapon is? It doesn't conquer a country by obliterating everything in it. It lets you march into capitols with your enemy applauding your arrival. That's how Alexander went through what he called the Orient."

Viner stared at Phil with amazement. Where the hell did

that gorgeous ungovernable idea come from? Why don't I get ideas like that? asked Viner's stunned face.

"Maybe the ultimate weapon doesn't use any kind of force," continued Phil. "Maybe it simply dissipates hostility. Maybe it's nothing more forceful than patience. Patience and the ability to communicate reality in a seduc-

tive way. Yes, warfare will become incredibly subtle. *We will invent a reality machine, sort of like something you might find in an amusement park, and then persuade our enemies to take long thrilling rides on it."*

Lineheardt couldn't stand it. He was so beautiful, so persuasive, and so sweet, she had to stop listening to him. She distracted herself by watching the hands of the signer. The station manager had bragged to her about how he always had a signer for the deaf when the public safety was at issue. Lineheardt had a deaf sister she hadn't seen for over a year. She struggled to reconstruct her ability to understand sign language.

This signer was having trouble keeping up with Phil. Phil was talking faster and faster and the hands were getting harder and harder to read, but her old facility came back in an instant when she realized the signer wasn't relaying Phil's words any more. The hands were frightened. Cross yourself, the hands said, here comes somebody with a gun; he's going to kill someone. Lineheardt, terrified, turned frantically and saw a big round man with a swollen face holding a pistol out in front of him as he hurried across the studio towards the news desk.

H

Phil recognized the over puffed face from Tuck's and saw the pistol. The pistol exploded, and he felt as if someone had taken him in a hammerlock and twisted his shoulder out of its socket. He remembered how stunned and curious the man had seemed at Tuck's, but he was trying to kill Phil now. A 2nd shot slammed into his abdomen, and he found himself jack-knifing and falling backwards at the same time. He lay on the floor out of breath. He felt painful diarrhea.

There was some noise behind him, and then Viner was cradling his head. He tried to look down at his stomach where he'd been shot.

"No, don't look," advised Viner.

"I'm going to die," said Phil, feeling stupid.

"I guess so," said Viner sadly.

"No!" argued Phil. "Am I really?"

He knew it made sense. He'd even said it 1st himself, but he couldn't get it to go down. It couldn't be true.

"You're going to die," Viner said, thinking he owed Phil the truth.

"I can't believe it," complained Phil, wanting to believe what was true. "Let me look and I'll believe it."

Viner raised Phil's head so he could see. His guts had come partially out of a hole in his back, and he could see them on the floor. There was only a thin film of blood on them. They looked grey and waxy. He could smell his own shit. The bullet had ripped his bowel open and he could smell everything that was in it.

"Oh, god," he whispered.

"Okay?" asked Viner.

"Yes."

He laid Phil's head back on a sweater Lineheardt had folded up for a pillow.

"I wonder how long it will take," Phil said up into Lineheardt's tormented face.

"I don't know," said Viner.

"Shit," said Phil.

"I'm sorry," said Viner.

"No, not about this," said Phil. "I was thinking about what
a big mistake I made. Sometimes I make mistakes and they
always seem to come back to haunt me at the worst times.
Big 1s and small 1s. They're like ghosts."

"What mistake do you mean now?" asked Viner brightly,
hoping that before he died, Phil could legitimize some
little part of the flood prediction.

"I wanted people to love my work," he said. "I wanted them
to understand it and notice some of what I put into it, just
to love it for that, but, Ow! Ow!"

"It's hurting him," complained Lineheardt.

Phil saw his end in her face. Now she was staring at him as
if he were already dead.

"There's a buzzing sound going on in my head," he said to
her. "It's painful, but it's strange because I don't feel any
more sharp pains in my gut."

"No?" she asked sympathetically, like a nurse inquiring
about his fever.

"My shoulder aches," he told her.

"I guess because it's made of bones," she suggested.
"Bones hurt."

"I'm probably going to live for a couple of more hours,"
said Phil.

"How do you know?" asked Viner.

"I don't," said Phil. "It just feels that way."

"There really is going to be something big, isn't there, Phil?" he asked. "We haven't been bullshitting them."

"We're not bullshitting," said Phil. "But don't distract yourself and them with your flood theory. It won't be that way."

"No?" asked Viner, feeling stupid and guilty.

"It's a radiant heat wave," said Phil, "followed by a shock wave, and then the noise comes last."

"I'm not going to say anything more about a flood then," vowed Viner. "I believe you."

"You believe me because I'm dying," snorted Phil derisively.

"No, no," lied Viner. He had no idea when or in what form his next flood idea was coming, but he guessed it was definitely waiting for him somewhere. "I really believe you."

"Inez, I have Barbanel's gun in my pocket," Phil said. "Would you take it away from me and hide it?"

It hurt him, but Lineheardt got it out and slipped it to Viner who hid it in his own pocket.

"Phil?"

Phil struggled to turn up to Lineheardt's face.

"Can I tell you something?" Her voice was low and full of respect, the way he'd always imagined she'd sound when she met Lillo.

"What?"

She crab-walked closer to his face.

"You know how you were always talking about how Renza or me or somebody else was going to be the next genius, the next Lillo?"

"Yes."

"It won't be Renza," she said. "It won't be me, either. It's you, Phil. It was you all along."

"Me?"

"Yes, Phil," she said, "The next genius in physics was you."

"Are you sure?" he asked.

"You've domesticated the sun."

"He's done what?" asked Viner.

"The sun is a fusion reaction," Lineheardt answered Viner while still looking into Phil's eyes. "Phil figured out how to build it here on earth."

"He did that?" asked Viner reverently. "That's what's going to happen tomorrow?"

"Inez, don't tell it that way," said Phil urgently. "I don't like the sound of that."

"But you did it," she said, baffled by his request.

"All right, I'm a genius," he said. He stopped and sighed with satisfaction. "Yes," he laughed. "There. I really am your next stupid Faraday, aren't I?"

"You are."

"Reward me for my genius then," he said. "Will you give me something to pay me off since I'm not going to live to enjoy my stupid genius?"

"What?"

"I don't want to be known as the man who invented a bomb that can blow up the whole world," he said.

"What do you mean?" asked Lineheardt, feeling a pulse of alarm.

"Don't tell it that way." he said. "Don't give me the credit."

"But all your work, Phil," she pleaded. "Your madness. So much work."

"I've had my genius for a few moments now," he said. "It's long enough. I don't want it any more. Now promise me that when Starzinchger or Huke comes to take it, you'll let him have it."

"No, I can't," she said.

"Oh, holy shit," he said. "Oh, no!"

"What's wrong" she asked, very frightened.

"I think it's happening now," said Phil. His eyes were large and filled with panic.

"Doctor!" shouted Viner, jumping to his feet. "Is he here yet!"

When he knelt back down, Phil looked dead.

"I'll do it for you, Phil," Viner shouted urgently into his face. "I can make it come out however you want it. I have the story, Phil. Whatever I say into the camera is it."

Viner punched his thigh in frustration. He was looking at Phil as if Phil were dead.

"He said he was going to last 2 hours," he complained angrily. What did it mean that Phil could be so wrong about his death? That he could be so powerless about it. Viner had recited some stuff on his show last year about an Apache medicine man who has just wiped life out of his own brain in an act of will. Viner then fell in love with exotic funeral ceremonies. Neither the kids' parents nor the station executive had noticed the festival theme morph into puppet shows of mystical death rituals.

Inside himself Phil heard Viner, heard him more directly than Viner understood. Phil watched Viner peering into him, trying to see death coming as if it were an inner tsunami that, if he just looked hard enough, he would see the wave. What a strange nice stupid man, Phil thought. He felt he should tell Viner he wasn't dying just yet, but something was taking away his interest in other people.

190

Lineheardt moved Viner aside and leaned over Phil. She
rocked back and forth between her heels and knees unable
to speak. She heard wheels creaking across linoleum behind her and turned around to see the large camera coming in to look. It approached cautiously, diffidently, like a
dog sniffing around spoiled food.

"Can you love someone who worked so hard for something he thought he'd never have," she asked the camera,
"worked so hard for it because something inside him
wouldn't let him stop; and then, when he had it, wished it
away?"

She was weeping. She wanted to say more but couldn't.
The camera backed away, confused and embarrassed by its
graceless curiosity.

Phil heard Lineheardt crying. They all seemed to think he
was already dead, but he could hear and see things around
him with astonishing clarity. Oh, yes. The clarity. He could
even hear his blood rushing through the canals of his
ears. Suddenly it was stopped. The noise of its rush disappeared.

They were still talking, and he could listen to what they
said, but the blood had stopped. This was death. There
was no uncertainty left to how long he might last now.

He no longer cared about what they were saying. He could
still hear if he wanted to try, but what he was feeling was
far more interesting. The taut fibers of his guilt were
loosening. He didn't care about killing the bartender. He
regretted it, but he didn't hurt for having done it. And
beneath that single memory, which hadn't enjoyed a long
enough life to string a web of tension through all the canals and chambers of his body, he could feel his Hiroshima
Complex, which had, suddenly slacken.

It was so obvious. It had been obvious all along. It wasn't
his fault. It had simply happened, and nobody and no

thing cared very much about why. Only himself. And he didn't care any more either now.

If he had known he wasn't going to care at this moment of dying, he would have let it go long ago. And the achievements. His genius. It was letting go, too, just like the guilt. He was surprised to realize that it was a tension also. The relief was in letting it go, not achieving it. Yes, the relief was in letting it all go. His ambition. His guilt. Even his empathy.

He saw May driving to Arizona furious with him and devastated by their brutal argument at the Dog. He was glad he was dying still married to her. He loved her again. He felt horny for her. It was her winding up the lines of his tensions he had hated, not her, and now that there was no possibility of her ever tightening his hatred of himself again, he felt a surge of affection and sexual heat for her.

All this he felt in a few instants. Lineheardt was saying something and he realized he could inspect the rhythm of his death using Lineheardt's speech as a clock. He had been hearing it all along, 1 word at a time. It was very slow. It had the rhythm of a child reading aloud before its class. She had asked Viner to call May in Arizona.

He felt an intense pain which didn't hurt. He knew it was pain, but instead of hurting him, it seemed to wash through his body in a ghostly breeze.

Suddenly he was sucked backwards through himself and things that had happened to him were lighting up, as if his experiences were a vivid Jake sign, and the hotel electrician had thrown the switch because it was getting dark. He felt his shock when his mother shrieked at him with fear and hatred for his breaking his arm; and his sorrowful weeping when he'd lied to a girl that he'd murdered her cat; Truman said, "I'll tell you when. Never."; he smelled his come when he masturbated; he recalled meeting Lillo's brother in Tennessee; he studied May's attractive brows; he puffed his only cigarette; he suffered intense embarrassment believing his dyslexia had betrayed him to a porter in a familiar train station. It was all before him. His father's short pleasant laugh when he'd asked him if he could become a farmer like Uncle Wilon; his uncontrollable anger at finding his sons violently hitting each other in their bedroom; but he was seeing only the front of things, while sensing that behind them down beautifully luminous corridors was more; there he had stored everything that had ever happened to him, and suddenly he could feel it all at once; all the images of everything came rushing up to be the same immediate thing, and it seemed much more real now than when it had originally happened, now that it was collected and all happening in the same instant, everything firing off with no proportion or order, just all together, and all very pleasurably intense.

"There can't be very much point in carting him to the hospital," Viner had just said. "Maybe you should call a funeral home if I can't reach her."

The surge of experience seemed to kill itself. His wonderful collection of himself began to blur into colors. They were all pastels. They tumbled across his persona like detergent. The darkening colors were taking his mind away.

When all that was left was a deep fluid violet, he heard some Bach. He'd been listening to Bach on the radio before he'd called Lillo, but this wasn't exactly Bach; it had some of the steam-rolling sparking qualities of Bach, but it was soothing too, in fact, it was anesthetic, and the violet was blackening, leaving only little star flares of purple behind.

In a small part of his last second, he figured out that death was not real because there was the afterlife, and every 1 had 1. His would be the way his physics would linger in the air like music after he was gone.

It was almost midnight when Starzinchger and Gilberg finally returned to Gilberg's hotel. As they walked through the lobby, Starzinchger saw Lillo with the pink ortolan. Starzinchger, who loved to play popular songs on the piano, despised this pop vocalist. In the personal mythology of his hatreds, he couldn't imagine 2 kobolds who belonged more together than this pairing.

Lillo was coming right for him, smiling as if immensely pleased to see him. Starzinchger cast an anxious glance at Gilberg and unconsciously put a hand on his thigh as if he feared that Lillo would discredit him and take Gilberg's 1,000 dollars right out of his pocket.

But Lillo was delighted to see Starzinchger and praised him to Gilberg. Starzinchger excused them and took Lillo aside where he could speak to him privately.

"How could you ridicule the Super to Truman with that crap?" he asked. He hadn't seen Lillo since their meeting with Truman many months ago. He didn't count the security hearing because he'd merely testified and had no opportunity to talk to Lillo. "You remember all that stuff with Roosevelt about how fission would have to be towed into Tokyo harbor in the hold of a ship."

"I remember," granted Lillo. The men on Roosevelt's staff who opposed the bomb had maintained it was too cumbersome to have tactical value.

"You gave Truman that same crap with your crack about building it under Moscow like a subway station," said Starzinchger bitterly.

"I used the best argument I had on hand without thought to copyrights," grinned Lillo.

"You know we can work the Super down to tactical size sooner or later," said Starzinchger. "Your argument wasn't

Paul Whiteman

fair or true."

"Of course not," conceded Lillo, "but Truman wasn't going to admit he wanted to abandon the Super because he felt guilty about Hiroshima."

"You had the hostility towards the Japanese, too," said Starzinchger, talking rapidly as he raised an issue with Lillo he'd been frightened of for 5 years. "Why do you pretend you didn't? You wanted it dropped. You wanted it to work militarily. All of us did."

"Yes," agreed Lillo blandly. "I had the momentum of 3

years work. I was, we all were, like an aircraft carrier trying to stop and turn around. There wasn't enough time."

"I don't believe that," said Starzinchger. "We wanted it."

"Less than 2 weeks passed between the test and the drop," said Lillo. " 2 weeks isn't long enough to stop 3 years and 3 billion dollars."

"You had your turn as chief, you made your gadget, and then you wanted the game to end," Starzinchger's pink face was coloring towards the red of his anger.

"Could be," said Lillo. "Yes. Probably. Yes."

"You didn't want your achievement dulled by anyone else having his turn," insisted Starzinchger.

"Yes," agreed Lillo eagerly, delighting in the fresh perspective.

"Do you know what it's like to work and work on something that nobody cares you're working on?" demanded Starzinchger, stomping his foot on the rug

Lillo's eyes dilated from interested to alert. Starzinchger stopped himself. He didn't want to talk to Lillo about this, but all the years of his dedication to the Super were festering inside him.

"I told myself I worked on fusion solely for the pleasure of finding the elegant solution," Starzinchger said. He was going to get into it with Lillo because Lillo might understand what no 1 else had. "You say, 'Well, I hope they want it,' but you try not to think about whether they want it or not because that interferes with your working on it."

"I know," said Lillo, quietly sympathetic. As the creator of fission, he'd danced the same question about with Sensenig a million times. They'd all been constantly afraid Roosevelt's hostile aides would win him back to their negative point of view that the A-Bomb would never work.

"You work and you work," Starzinchger exhaled fiercely, "and you work, and then they tell you that this thing you've poured everything into, not just your energy, but

For a good time read Charles Dickens,

everything you care about gets poured into it, your marriage, your love of music, the respect of your colleagues, your children, you take all of that and you pour it down the funnel of this thing because you feel you have to make it work, and then they tell you they don't want it. They want something else."

Starzinchger was quiet. He touched a fist to 1 of his red sideburns.

"They don't want the complete process!" his voice rose to outrage. "They want only the fuse!"

"That's finished now," said Lillo, trying to penetrate the anger gently. Starzinchger had never shown Lillo anger before, although Lillo had heard about Starzinchger's punching Sensenig. "You may work on it with all the resources you wish. You're the chief now."

"Am I?" asked Starzinchger with resignation.

"You have your program," said Lillo. "You can have your test tomorrow."

"It's not my test," said Starzinchger with disgust. "I don't have anything to do with it. It's something Huke is trying to put over behind my back."

"What?" asked Lillo, shocked.

Starzinchger laughed. "You should hear Huke talk about how this thing is going to work. Phil can't function with somebody like Huke."

"I suppose," mused Lillo.

"Phil gets ideas, but he needs people to help him," said Starzinchger. "Do you think Huke or anyone else down there can help Phil?"

Lillo smiled. "I knew it."

"They haven't even checked any of their work with Los Alamos," said Starzinchger. Starzinchger had confronted Huke again on the phone only an hour ago. "Sensenig thinks

198

that's great, claims Huke. Los Alamos needs shaking up, Sensenig says."

"How can Huke press such a young idea," asked Lillo. "Even he should know better. General Sensenig wants me to go down there tonight. Maybe I will."

"Huke has failed to grasp the nature of human intelligence," said Starzinchger, feeling suddenly merry. "Huke thinks that intelligence is like a fine silk tie 1 presents to the world with salesman-like requests for admiration. His numerous mistakes have convinced him he must be very careful not to drool soup on his fine silk tie, but what he doesn't understand is that it's actually possible to be intelligent as opposed to wearing it, and that since he isn't, he will always be spooning his physics all over himself the way a baby eats through a jar of smashed bananas."

Lillo laughed, enjoying Starzinchger's disaffection with his former minion.

"But there are many capable physicists working for Huke."

"Go talk to him. This experiment will be an exercise in shame for the AWB," said Starzinchger. "That ridiculous rail cannon won't work. They won't even get the gadget up range. They don't have a chance to detonate it."

Lillo sighed happily. "I knew it. I knew it would take longer."

"You can laugh," said Starzinchger, "I have to explain all this to Sensenig."

"I don't envy you that," said Lillo.

"How the hell did you get along with him so well?" asked Starzinchger.

Gilberg had gone into his casino and returned with some of the people they were to party with all night. They drifted over to Starzinchger and Lillo, their presence requesting an invitation to be included in the conversation of titans. Lillo and Starzinchger soon found themselves enveloped by the party which was to last all night.

Lillo took the pink ortolan's hand and excused himself. He showed more than polite affection for Starzinchger as they parted. Starzinchger wondered what had happened to the figure of ruin he'd seen at Lillo's security hearing. Lillo's eyes had been sunken, his hair white. Guilt had been radiating him with remorse. Now he ate through remorse like it was pudding. He enjoyed it. He was invulnerable to other people's unhappiness.

The sky was a muddy purple river churning with misty freight. All the lights from Jake way up the mountain shot up into the clouds in colored spears and merged there to be reflected down onto the desert of 52 in a singular lavender mist. This gaslike lavender illuminated the rail gun, a long metal needle mounted on a massive tank in the distance.

"That's it," said Spike.

The barrel was so long and slender it seemed more like a rifle than a cannon. The Appaloosas advanced across the sandy flats with nervous respect for this mystical weapon.

"My god," whispered Noreen when they were close.

Its image from afar had lied. The barrel wasn't a needle at all. It was immense. It's shell chamber door was as big as a refrigerator's. The tank was 2 stories high.

"Look, it's square," she whispered to Spike.

Their skins twitching as if trying to rid themselves of flies, the Appaloosas crept timidly around in front of the immense barrel. It was 4 feet across a mouth as square as a card table.

Lights from several jeeps appeared a few hundred yards away. Moments later they were in the grasp of military detention. Army men took the still trembling Appaloosas away and others drove Spike and Noreen to a complex of corrugated huts.

The windows looked like huge cow eyes, all glowing white with excitement. They were interrogated by Army intelligence and then led to an enormous office.

They walked past several large shuddering telephone

switchboards. A wide desk was set out before several rows of ballroom chairs. Behind a pale man at the desk were 200 women working in negligees with pencil and paper. The women looked hot, even though the cow-eyed windows were letting in cool desert night everywhere around them.

Noreen realized from descriptions of physicists she'd dated, this was Steven Huke's office. The pale man at the desk was Huke.

"*Hello!*" He came out from behind the desk and grabbed their hands with an enthusiastic left handed star handshake, the 1 Bing Crosby had made famous. "You 2 chose a novel way to get a look at my rail cannon."

Interest in the bomb was high, Huke explained. Thrill seekers had been swarming over the fences all night but only Spike and Noreen had gotten close.

"You 2 have exposed yourself to dangerous radiation riding down the range from the north," he said. "We conduct safety experiments out there, making sure bursts can't be initiated by accident. We test, but no accidents are ever going to happen. We have the odds on our side. It's like playing blackjack. Nobody will ever beat it****"

He paused and went over to look out a cow-eyed window.

"He sounds like Grethlien," whispered Noreen.

"He does not," Spike whispered back. "He doesn't give off any bit of a truth spoor."

"Grethlien did?" mocked Noreen.

"Of course he did," said Spike. "But this guy, holy chuck. Like that stuff about blackjack. I'll bet somebody figures out how to beat it someday."

"You moron," chuckled Noreen affectionately.

"Are you worried about blowing yourselves up tomorrow?" Spike called to Huke. "That would be an accident."

Huke came back to them.

"Phil," Huke said to himself. "I was watching on tv," he turned to them wistfully. "I wanted to hear what he was going to say****"

The silence was broken by the entrance of Peter Blough, whom Noreen remembered as a specialist in wave mechanics.

"Noreen!" he sprinted across the vast office. "What are you doing here tonight?"

"You know her?" asked Huke.

"She's 1 of the horseback riders?" he asked, delighted.

"So we have nothing to fear from her as a spy," Huke said.

"No, No!" protested Blough, "she's just wacky. But what mettle, for sure."

Spike laughed at Blough's talking about Noreen's mettle while staring down between her blouse buttons. Blough escorted them out to an Army car which was to return them to the Dog.

"What was he all about?" asked Spike.

"Spike, I have been charmed by other men," she said. "I think I told you that I have been charmed by other men."

"Oh, oh, okay," he said. "I forgot."

"The trouble with you is that you think men love women for sex," said Noreen. "They think they do, but it never turns out that way."

"How does it turn out?"

"They like the surrender value, not the fucking," she said, "We'll have a good time screwing for

205

awhile. We'll go through the whole thing. But the moral of it is that if something else doesn't take hold after you get bored with the surrender value, we're finished."

"How many guys does it take to learn a moral like that?" asked Spike.

"Twelve." She made up the number and tossed it out the way McCarthy enumerated Commies infesting the state department.

"All right, 12," he raised his voice. "But no more. Don't tell me later it's 13."

The Army driver was looking at them in the rear view mirror.

"Don't worry," she promised.

"Did you love any of them?" he asked.

"God," she said. "Why don't you go back to New Jersey where they grow all of this snot you're blowing on me."

"Who were all these guys?" he asked. "And stop insulting New Jersey. It's not just a turnpike, you know."

"I developed an interest in physicists," she said.

"Oh, these were science crushes," sang Spike. "You specialize in smart people. People as smart as you. I guess that's all right. It's not really love because love is when you get with someone new and different, like you and me. I'm dumb. You're smart. That's love. These science guys are more like masturbation, right?"

"A lot of them have radiation sickness, I bet," she said. "From sitting in meetings at Huke's office with the windows open. Did you see all that dust on his desk?"

"So?"

"He had several small lesions on his lips," she said. "The 1 who came into my office tonight, Jenks, he had a speckling of the same thing inside his mouth. It's little fissures, like grooves, going up and down the gums."

They had arrived at the Dog. The Army corporal held the door open for Noreen, looking at her as if he'd like to try some of this surrender value for himself.

"52 is all deluded by radiation sickness," said Noreen on the way to the room. "There isn't going to be any bomb. We've got to take a shower to get rid of any particles we've picked up."

They undressed together. Noreen stood under the water 1st. A fine mist bounced up off her shoulders into Spike's eyes.

"When Blough said you had mettle, I knew it was right," said Spike. "Even if he is a chucking scientist. He's right about you."

She laughed at the compliment.

"I thought I was in love with you because you're so smart and sexy, but that isn't even most of it," he said, admiring her wet soapy body. "It's the mettle."

Her wet blue eyes painted his face with affection and arousal. Her glossy breasts were splashing clean beneath the fine needles of the shower.

"Let's make a deal," he said. "I won't ask you any more stupid questions and you won't volunteer any more surprises."

"But I thought you wanted to know all about me so you

can love me like I grew up in your neighborhood," she said, flushing with elation. "'Giving up the truth is what fidelity is all about, Noreen,'" she quoted him.

"I don't want to know a single thing more about you." It was his turn to go to surrender and he found some relief there.

 Erving had spent the evening biting the heads off salty scallions and then eating enormous shrimp cocktails followed by chewing rare Kansas steak while watching the early and late shows in GHAZIABAD, Ziraleet's nightclub. Ed Wynn, whose jokes were not funny to Erving, rode Marilyn Maxwell around the stage on a piano built into a huge tricycle. She sang while Wynn's hands

Ed Wynn & Marilyn Maxwell

moved desperately back and forth from the piano keyboard to the grips he used to steady the wobbly contraption. Miss Maxwell's singing lacked interest but her cleavage collected his vision. She appeared at Ziraleet so often, Erving suspected she had another talent she was entertaining his father with in room 127. 127 was the room that was never rented out. Casino executives, Lehman had explained to him when he was 9, were targets for lonely women. 127 was always available for casino executives to help relieve these women of their solitude.

Erving had started evaluating 13 year old girls when he was 11 for a possible invitation to 127 to relieve him of his solitude, but he never got beyond kissing them underwater in the Ziraleet pool. He was up to 16 year-olds now with some French kissing underwater, and had recently promised himself he wouldn't be so shy when the expedition for fucking and getting penicillin shots started.

Now the tables of GHAZIABAD were deserted while the June Taylor dancers leapt through a late rehearsal on the dim stage and he ate a large branch of a chocolate tree.

"Paging Captain Chick Evans to the souvenir shop," Erving heard Margaret's voice on the public address system.

Erving ran towards the souvenir shop

"Captain Chick Evans to the souvenir shop."

He'd thought Lehman hadn't even heard the paging name request. But he had, and was having Margaret use the exact golfing name Erving had suggested. Complete with his rank from school. He thought Lehman didn't even know what his rank was.

Erving got to the souvenir shop first. The shop guy barked at Erving as he would at a stray kid who didn't know he wasn't allowed in the casino. There were thousands like him in Jake. They treated him like an asshole until they heard his name was Lehman.

"Hi, Pop," said Erving when Lehman came in.

"Howdy, Mr. Lehman," called the souvenir man obsequiously smiling back and forth between Erving and Lehman.

Fuck you, thought Erving.

"I want to talk to you," said Lehman, leading Erving out of the souvenir shop into the casino.

The casino was unusually loud. It had been that way all vacation. No wonder Lehman had asked him to listen to them yesterday. The gambler's yell Erving had known all his life was changing. It was taking on a new timbre, as if they believed they would get something for their shouting. No longer were they hollering hopeless prayers up to a patrician deity who was so entertained by gigantic catastrophes he ignored requests for boring personal service. Here at Ziraleet God was reforming his inscrutable arrogance. He had found love for the porters of his image. He was going to send them all a lot of money.

A voice boomed out "Hey, Zalman," and rushed over to talk to Lehman about something personal. Erving's father talked to him the same way he always talked to Erving. There was affection and interest in this voice. This nuncio spoke to Lehman in tones so intimate he might as well be Erving's older brother, if there was such a thing out there somewhere.

"Who was that, Pop." Was this some new bub who had wiggled close to Lehman while Erving was far away marching to and fro in dirty khakis?

"I have no idea," Lehman dismissed the entity.

Nope. It wasn't a lost brother. The whole conversation had been as reflexive as a knee jumping the foot below it because it had been hit in the patella with a hammer. Well, shit. Of course. Who the fuck called Lehman "Zalman"? No one who really knew him.

Lehman walked to BJ #12 and sat down. It was empty but a dealer appeared in seconds and Lehman laid out ten hundreds on the felt, and chips appeared in the yellow square in front of him. Lehman began playing. Erving stood silently by. He had seen this so many times, he knew 21 was as ordinary to Lehman as a giant rock was to King Sisyphus.

"You know how to drive?" Lehman raised his voice over a surge of melodic euphoria from Craps #8.

Erving sensed 1 of his father's traps. He made up his mind he wasn't going to be the fool Gilberg had been over Spike.

"I don't know anything about driving. I'm only 14." It felt good. He could feel himself projecting sincerity. His father would believe him if he were sincere enough.

"14?" asked Lehman, cocking his cataract eye while his hands continued to play blackjack on their own.

"How come you lose track of my age?"

"How come you've been cruising around the parking lot in my Cadillacs for the past year if you're only 14 and don't know how to drive?"

Erving was furious with himself for trying to fool his father. Humiliation burned through him in a powerful flame. He'd made himself as dumb as Gilberg to his father.

"How did you know that?" Erving demanded.

"Never mind, pal," said Lehman, smiling contentedly at his son's vitriolic reaction to the intelligence. "I want you to take the red car and drive East tonight. Don't tell your mother about this. She'd be against it. Here."

He handed Erving a driver's license. Erving inspected it for signs of humor. But it had the state seal. It even had a fingerprint on it, god knew whose.

"It says I'm 16," said Erving, getting excited as he realized it was real. "How did you do it? Jesus Christ, Pop, you can do anything. I don't even have to take the fucking driving test."

"You're so tall you look 16," said Lehman, as pleased with his son's elation as he'd been with his anger. "I put some money in the trunk so make sure you take the red."

His father had been promising Erving for years he was going to give him some money and a car 1 day, and Erving would go out on his own and disappear for 2 months. Erving could remember exactly when this plan was born.

{ The morning of his 10th birthday they were together in the coffee shop. His father read a clipping to him about a 13 year old African kid who had to go out and kill a lion to prove he was a man. It was like a bar mitzvah.

"When you're old enough," Lehman said, "I'm going to outfit you with a car."

His father intended to send him out across the country alone. He would screw a lot of women, get penicillin shots after every 1, and not return home for 2 months. Nothing but nothing would Lehman expect to hear from his son in these 2 months until he proved himself a man in this fashion. When Erving explained the plan for the screwing trip to cadets at school, they said that Erving had a wonderful father. Erving did not disagree. The trip became an insignia of his high rank in his father's affections. He used his fantasies of this screwing trip to sustain himself through the dull uniform winters of military school.}

But now it was upon him. Now it meant something different than what he had built up in his mind. It's prospect was frightening instead of delightful.

"I thought this wasn't supposed to happen until I was 16," he said, holding the driver's license out in front of him, afraid to put it in his wallet.

Lehman tapped the license on his new birth date.

"Yeah," agreed Erving. "I'm 16 now."

It was like being promoted to captain at school. The Commandant had the power to make cadets whatever rank he wanted them to have.

His father, far more powerful than the Commandant, could promote Erving to 16 if it pleased him, and it had, so now Erving was going out on his own to fuck women and get penicillin shots. No later than a day afterwards, condom or not. He put the driver's license in his wallet.

"Why does it say I'm from Vegas?"

"So people don't figure out who you are and take advantage of you," said Lehman. "I've got something else for you."

Lehman was carrying more clippings than usual this vacation. Erving watched patiently as his father searched his suit. The search was delayed by stops to read several of the clippings which interested him. Finally he found it.

"Take it with you," he said.

It was a picture of a teenage Spike with a crew cut. Below the picture was the story of Spike's shooting 58.

"Thanks, Pop," said Erving affectionately. They both loved sports.

"Look at this," said his father happily, showing him the red lined score card on the other side of the page. "Look what he did on the back nine."

Erving felt his father's arm on his shoulder. Lehman pointed out the birdies and eagles on the back 1 by 1. His breath was all over Erving, cigar pungent, yet sweet.

During moments like this Erving felt like a comet coming to the sun after a long orbit around deep space. Most of his life was spun out in an ellipses so long it almost merged into a straight line during its cold winter verso in military school. Now so close to Lehman, he was burned by his father's charm and powers, and he did what mammals had done with their love for their fathers since it had happened 1st in the time of squirrels or dolphins or monkeys or wherever it started. He made his father his god.

"Plant 1," Lehman said, handing the magazine to Erving and pointing to his whiskery gambling-all-night cheek as the location for a farewell kiss.

 Spike found a table in the Dog's lounge to talk so he could sell Noreen on leaving town.

"You said yourself, 'the truth is obvious,'" Spike raised his voice above Louie Prima and Keely Smith who were having their standard singing argument. "That cannon had the smell, the strange and new quality that truth has."

"Actually, truth is subtle," declared Noreen.

"You're weasling," complained Spike. "What could be stranger and newer than a square cannon on a 3 story tank?"

Noreen saw Mr. Festival, the tv personality, go up to the bar and ask Jerry the bartender a question. Jerry pointed right at her.

"Here comes Mr. Festival," she whispered to Spike. "He called us by name on television. Have you talked to him about us?"

Louie Prima and Keely Smith went on break to perform in earnest back in their dressing room what they were faking on stage.

"Who is Mr. Festival?" asked Spike.

"He looked right at me out of the television and said, 'Get out of town, Spike and Noreen,'" said Noreen, whispering. "I've never met him. Have you?"

"No."

"Hi!" said Viner, greeting them with the urgent familiarity jakes reserved for strangers. "You're Spike and Noreen?"

"You're Mr. Festival," said Noreen, her liquid blue eyes beaming out her own jake charm.

"I'm Alex Viner."

A pretty young woman with an exceptionally handsome mouth had come over behind him. Viner shook Noreen's hand and then Spike's.

"This is Inez Lineheardt," he introduced the woman. "She's a close friend of Phil Grethlien's. You 2 met him, right?"

"We met him," agreed Noreen dubiously.

"You both really impressed Phil," said Lineheardt. "He said a hundred times he'd feel a lot better if he knew he'd saved 1 couple like you 2."

"He had no confidence he was going to save the town," said Viner.

"Are you a physicist?" Noreen asked Lineheardt.

She was looking at Lineheardt's mouth with interest. Viner didn't consider such interest unusual because Lineheardt had beautiful lips with exceptionally well defined edges.

"I'm a dental hygienist," Noreen said. "Do you know there are a lot of physicists down at 52 who have radiation sickness?"

"This fusion bomb is going to be bigger than those guys down at 52 tell it," Spike interrupted Noreen.

"Because they have radiation sickness, that doesn't mean

217

the bomb is going to be bigger," Noreen argued back at him.

"Who has radiation sickness?" asked Lineheardt.

"Albert Jenks has it," said Noreen. "Do you know him? Steven Huke has it, too. I saw the lesions on their mouths. Nearly every physicist on file in our office is down for gum problems."

"I haven't been feeling very well," said Lineheardt. "I thought it was my emotions."

"Have you been bleeding when you brush?" asked Noreen. "That might be a lesion on your lip right there."

Lineheardt got out her compact quickly and looked at the spot Noreen had pointed to. It was very small but it was there.

"Phil didn't have any on his lips," she said defensively.

"The dust all over Huke's desk must be full of radioactive particles," said Noreen. "He's letting it in the windows."

"How do you know about Huke's desk?" asked Viner.

"We were down there," said Spike. "We were introduced to Huke."

"Phil wouldn't have been exposed to the dust; they barred him from the meetings in Huke's office," said Lineheardt absentmindedly. She was distracted by what she saw in her compact mirror. "It was after the last underground shot."

"The geyser of dirt," said Viner.

"What geyser of dirt?" asked Spike.

"It was a shallow burst," explained Lineheardt. "It sprayed desert everywhere."

"Radioactivity adheres to dust," said Noreen.

"Phil might have avoided exposure because he didn't go into Huke's office very often," said Lineheardt.

"That's it!" said Spike.

"How could they be so stupid?" asked Noreen. "They must have standards for their own protection."

"They do," granted Lineheardt, "but****"

"But they let Huke open windows and kill them with radioactivity," Noreen interrupted vindictively. "Then they make jokes about danger. That's what they do."

Spike and Viner looked at Noreen, surprised by her outburst. Lineheardt frowned and looked at her mouth in the compact mirror again.

"They think it's funny as hell that radiation can kill them," Noreen defended her emotion. "This 1, Barbanel, who threw himself on a whole ball of the stuff, he's a hero."

Lineheardt's eyes snapped up from her compact. "Barbanel? Phil told you about him?"

"Oh, yes," said Noreen. "He went on about him."

"I suppose he was Phil's hero," she said wistfully.

"You're all crazy," Noreen concluded quietly.

"Let me tell you what experimental physics is like," said Lineheardt.

Lineheardt's pulse was racing. She was upset by what she'd seen in her compact. She wanted to explain what it meant to spend a decade mixing a delusion with reality and attempting to extract a lucid solution. For physicists delusions were the visions the sufferer had been unable to solve and thereby raise to the status of a real problem. Intuition said you had to have a problem to figure out a solution, but it doesn't work that way. You didn't have a problem until you had a solution. What you had before you found a solution was a delusion. The horror of physics was how you could spend a whole storehouse of psychic energy and find out what you were doing was tormenting yourself with a delusion, not solving a problem.

"Once at 1 of those zeppelin ports they had back in the thirties, like Lakehurst where the Hindenburg exploded, they had a lot of them then because everyone thought zeppelins were going to be popular, a gust of wind blew a dirigible several hundred feet up in the air while 3 men were still hanging on the mooring lines."

What could this have to do with physics, asked their faces.

"1 fainted and let go while the zeppelin was still climbing. He fell a hundred feet to his death. Within 20 minutes the 2nd 1 fell. The last 1 hung on for 2 hours, 1,000s of feet up, while the wind gusted the ship back and forth snapping him around like the knot on the end of a bull whip. When I read that story it was like a silver bullet to me. 'That's what happens with experimental physics,' I said to myself. It sweeps you up. Before you know what's happening, you find out that the best you can do is hold onto that rope. Yes, you make jokes during your 2 hours. It's a way of looking down. You can't stop yourself. You have to look down. Yeah, so that's why there's all those jokes you noticed."

She looked at Noreen, hopeful, but doubting she was getting it. Only physicists and zeppelin men seemed to get it, people who'd had hold of the rope for a bit.

"Now you invite us all on the same thrilling balloon ride with this bomb," Spike said softly.

Lineheardt thought about it. The same thrilling balloon ride. Another blast of truth from an unexpected quarter. Spike was getting it.

She felt a spear of pleasure. This town was full of people wandering around boiling with fantastic visions, and on rare occasions jakes gave off reality in pungent fumes. She loved it here. She had loved it from the moment she'd arrived.

"I'm supposed to meet Lillo," Lineheardt remembered. "I have to go."

"Will you meet me back here after?" Viner asked.

"I guess so," conceded Lineheardt as she left.

Noreen watched Viner mooning over the departing Lineheardt. He looked like a teenager who had just lost the interest on a hopeless date.

"You've got to do another broadcast," Spike said to Viner. "We've got to save everyone."

"I've already tried," said Viner.

"I'm going back to the room," Noreen said to Spike. "And I'm not leaving Jake until I have my divorce."

"But somebody's got to tell them what's going on," Spike said to Viner dismally.

"What the hell do you think I've been doing?" snapped Viner. "Look, Spike, this town is different than any other place you've ever been. If you try too hard to save these people, they'll kill you."

Spike laughed.

"What's funny?" asked Viner. "You think that guy murdering Phil was funny?"

"It's not that," said Spike. "I believe they'll kill me. I just realized I don't belong here."

"You don't?" asked Viner, shocked. He and Lineheardt didn't understand how people detached from Jake. "Why not?"

221

"All along I thought I had this bad depression," grinned Spike. "I thought I was really unhappy about my life. But it's gone."

"Really?" Viner was skeptical. *"How do you get rid of that?"*

"It just went," said Spike. "I think meeting Noreen chased it, but also I think I'm not like the people who make careers out of this place. I'm just an amateur pleasure hound on holiday."

Hey !

He ran after Noreen. Again.

Lehman lay in bed with Sonia. Her lush hair flooded out across her pillow. She was still motionless, relaxing from their intercourse. Lehman's libido was inflamed. He'd had 3 different women today. In the morning he'd had a young tourist, then the actress maitre d', with the pretty face and big fat ass, whom he loved to do because she was a feverish crap player, and finally Sonia.

maitre d'

"Are you sleepy?" he asked her.

"Nrrr"

"We have to get up in a few hours," he said.

222

"Get up?"

"We're going to watch the bomb," he said. "Set the alarm for 4."

"4," she reached for the clock and fumbled with the alarm knob. "But the bomb is 5:30."

"We're going down to 52."

She was so drowsy, she wasn't paying attention. Finished with the clock she curled up against him, instantly asleep. Lehman lay awake for awhile. He took casual inventory of their bedroom. The cane for his gout stood up against the walnut dresser. Beyond it the door was open to the closet where Sonia kept his suits lined up and stuffed with clippings. He wondered if she would raise the question of the bunker being too close to the bomb when she woke in the morning.

He considered the different lies he might tell her. Entertaining beautiful lies was a favorite exercise of his, as pleasant as counting fluffy sheep jumping over a rail fence, but something else worked its way into his sleepy thoughts.

Gilberg had a grudge against Lehman. Lehman had taken Gilberg fishing on Lake Mead some months ago. On the long boat run out from the dam, Gilberg got bored. Would Lehman like to play gin, he asked. "Ok," said Lehman. He had a phrase for taking a plunger deep, and he put it to work. "Is this to waste time, or do you want to gamble?" Wasting time was 10 cents a point. Gambling was a dollar a point. After he recovered his air, Gilberg had to say a dollar. Every time Gilberg placed a card in his hand, Lehman noted its position. After a half hour of play, Lehman knew the strength of Gilberg's hand before there were 7 cards in the discard pile. This trick and 300 others he had learned over decades of playing gin removed $30,000 from the pile of assets Gilberg had brought to Jake when he retired from the business of overcharging in hospitals and came to town with his stake to prove to the wise men here how smart he is. After the gin game, Lehman had let Gilberg buy a secret 1per in Ziraleet with another $30,000. On the drive back Lehman had let him go up to a 10per for $270,000. Lehman had 7 other secret 10pers, and a German countess who had a well publicized secret 40per. All of these secret percentage owners were disappointed by the mediocre returns of their investment. "Damn it!' Lehman reproved himself in his bed. It was Gilberg who had sent the sore foot with a shotgun. How could he have missed that? The boat ride. And the partners who never made any money. Now they knew he was spraying money on tourists. Their money. So Gilberg was trying his hand at being an Italian gangster.

Hours later Lehman came up out of his deep black sleep thinking it was the alarm waking him. In an instant he remembered his plan to take Sonia to the bunker where they would be painlessly incinerated by the fusion burst and enjoy an instantaneous death, but it seemed to him that the loud noise wasn't the alarm at all. It was a supernatural engine wailing in the halls of Ziraleet, a grinding frightening sound, part of a nightmare so cogent it was waking him.

He sat up, fully awake, in time to hear the front door to his suite break open. The noise was immense. A fearsome mechanical animal was breaking its way through the living room, and suddenly 2 highway patrolmen on motorcycles were in his bedroom.

Idiotically, he looked to see what time it was. Sonia was struggling to get awake. It was 3 o'clock. He recognized 1 of them.

"What is this, Tom!" he shouted over the roar of the motorcycles. He'd gotten Tom a room for his visiting mother at Ziraleet last Christmas.

"Yes, Mr. Lehman," said Tom. "It's Tom." He had his gun out. The other 1 was already shooting. He missed Lehman with 2 shots.

Oh, no, thought Lehman with violent despair. Not this way.

"Sonia," he shouted, trying to make himself heard over the roaring motorcycles and exploding guns. "I'm sorry, Sonia! I'm sorry."

He had struggled to keep this part of his life secret from her. All the time he had been doing everything else that insulted her, fucking younger women, going off on long pleasure trips, cheating her over money, he'd always kept her unworried about criminal company, and that was more important than all the rest because respectability was a woman's 1st request. A million times he had said and done things to keep a veil over his business with criminal company and he had done it well. She believed in his non-association with criminal company more than anyone else, more even than the gambling commission itself, whose requirements on the issue were fanatical.

The bullets began to hit him. Sonia was screaming with fear and pain. The cop who had missed him had turned his gun on Sonia and was hitting her everywhere. Lehman

early Sonia

reached for her, trying to pull her under his body to shield her; but bullets kept hitting him, and the pain of their impact distracted him from his purpose. Finally he was able to roll over on top of her.

The troopers were now shooting only at Lehman. They were alarmed by all his energy despite the many times he'd been hit. They kept firing. It was comforting to feel Sonia beneath him. Protected.

"Are you afraid?" she asked up into his ear.

He realized in a flash that she had known about his dealing with criminal company all along. His proper wife had rehearsed this death in her mind. Forty years of pretending collapsed in a second.

"I'm not, I don't think," she added.

She reflected on how to explain dying to her friends, ignoring the 0 probability that she would be explaining anything to anyone ever again. Her life, she decided, was something she had wound up into a ball of pretty colored rubber bands the size of a watermelon. Death, she saw in the instant it was upon her, was the cleaving and unwinding of all her colored bands with such force that they dispersed themselves beyond the white stars of the heavens.

Lehman realized his proper wife had rehearsed this kind of death in her mind as many times as he had. She'd carried the same fears he had for decades, and she needed no explanation of what was happening. He felt a rush of pleasure and relief. The secret was out, and the release was a powerful euphoriant. His heart stopped.

They pulled him off her. He tried to speak. He wanted to talk to her about all the other things he'd done and kept secret from her. Stories of his past kept welling up into his mind, but his throat wouldn't move. Nothing in him was moving. "I guess that's it!" shouted Tom.

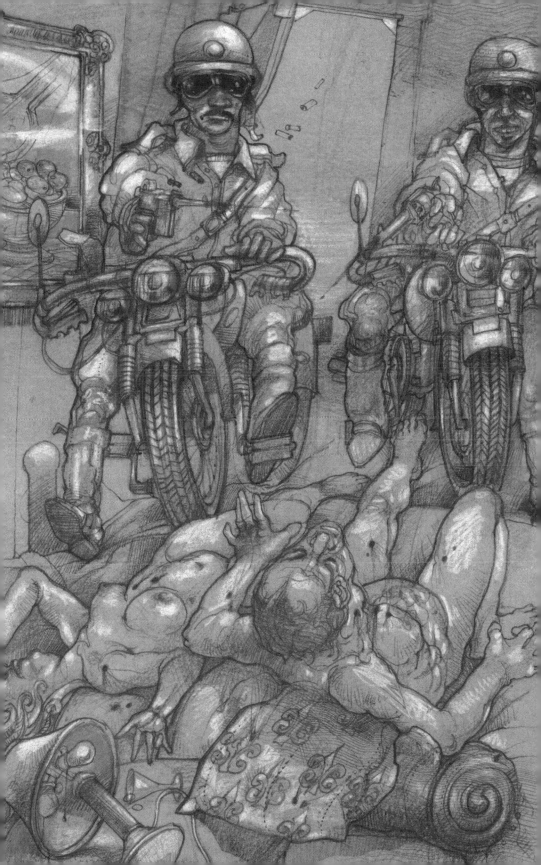

"I'd better get on the radio!" called the other 1 over the noise of the motorcycle engines.

Suddenly the motorcycles were silent. The sudden disappearance of the deafening noise purged him. Lehman felt wonderfully quiet. He saw a dream of himself. He was a quiet transparent man with clear spring water curling through his veins and cooling him with silence.

 Huke crouched down behind an aisle of files to eavesdrop on Lillo. He'd returned to his office and spotted Lynn Carol Moss Graf helping Lillo at BOIR8Min as she'd once done with Phil.

Huke had wanted to march right up to them and demand an explanation for Lillo's presence since Lillo couldn't have security clearance. But he'd heard that Lillo had met with Sensenig hours ago. It was possible that Lillo had gotten security clearance. Perhaps Sensenig had ordered the Spaniard down to 52.

There was the pretty Lineheardt, Phil's brilliant assistant, now consulting with Lillo. Her make-up was always per-

fect, and her lipstick wonderfully new. She smiled with her
pretty mouth when Lillo told her 52 would be destroyed if
the gadget wasn't moved farther up range. But Lillo insisted there was no threat to Jake. Evidently the computer
BOIR8Min had confirmed it. No threat to Jake.

But what about 52?

Huke padded quietly back out of his office. He had become
so entranced with the rail cannon, he hadn't paid enough
attention to the gadget itself. Fearing that Lillo's estimate
of the yield might be accurate, he went outside prickling
with anxiety.

The sky was a muddy purple river. He looked at the distant
rail cannon. The lights from 52 were reflected off the low
sky in a lavender glow which illuminated a long needle on
a tall pile of metal. The barrel was so long and slender it
looked like a an old black powder musket. He walked out
quickly across the flats. He loved the way its image lied
from afar. This was no needle. It was a long square throat
30 feet deep. The cannon was going to cough up a square
bomb and send it arching through the sky not at all like
a spiraling artillery shell, but tumbling erratically like a
bouncing die.

Lillo might be right. He would have to change the range.
He messed some numbers around in his mind and went
to work. He might not know the fusion gadget well, but he
had to compliment himself on his understanding of the
rail cannon.

He'd memorized every number and word Phil and his
group had put to paper, persevering through hours and
hours of drills to force his memory to retain it all. It had
been a grand intellectual effort, an effort made especially
difficult by the exquisite originality of the rail cannon. In
between long bouts of memorization, he'd worried obsessively about his vulnerability. Since the kernel of wisdom

underlying the rail gun was implosion, how could anyone claim it but Phil? But as he worked on, he reflected on the exquisite originality of the rail gun with relief. Phil was gone. There could be no dispute of ownership with no Phil. Taking pleasure in his now incontestable possession of this elegant principle, Huke happily recalled how Phil had talked of smaller rail guns.

Phil had wanted to make a rail rifle that would fire square plastic bullets through walls a foot thick. He'd wanted to build a microscope-like rail gun to fire tiny square beads down into atomic space and liberate energy from atoms.

"It would be a little different than the elegant cyclotron splitting a nucleus into neat pieces with a neutron," Phil had giggled with that strange ironic pleasure he showed when talking about his favorite ideas. *"This little rail gun would liberate energy the way dropping an anvil on a lemon liberates juice."*

Huke felt a sweet pulse of confidence as he adjusted the last capacitor with his left hand in the dark interior of the

massive tank. The cannon would fire the gadget 20 miles up range instead of 8, satisfying Lillo's objection by several miles. He could even adjust it left-handed. This proof that he had mastered the rail cannon exhilarated him. After Starzinchger appropriated the credit for the creation of fusion, Huke would stand up at the press conference and delight the nation's imagination with all the things his rail cannon could do.

 Viner had 1 manhattan after another waiting for Lineheardt to come back. The sweet corn whiskey quickly set fire to his self respect, and wild violent fantasies bothered him without respite. Maybe because he still had Barbanel's gun from Phil in his pocket.

By the time Lineheardt returned, he was certain he was right about anything and was fondling the pistol handle below the table as if he were jerking off. She sat down and began to drink like a sailor. Martinis. He tried to cheer her up by lecturing her about how great she was.

"Maybe Jake isn't in danger anyway," Lineheardt speculated, feeling suddenly euphoric. She explained what Lillo had done with the computer earlier. Halfway through she stopped. "Maybe Phil did it for nothing." The euphoric thing left, and dread took its place.

"Things could get pretty bad here even if Lillo is right," Viner responded. The suggestion that Phil had achieved nothing for Jake alarmed him.

"What do you mean?" asked Lineheardt. "If Lillo's right, there will only be a few broken windows."

"Come on outside," suggested Viner. "I want to show you something."

On the street, Viner pointed up at the rocky plug which capped Trembling Peak. Purple clouds were flowing down its face. It looked like a giant smudge pot giving off tinted party smoke.

"That's a lava dome, you know."

"Yes," said Lineheardt, brightening in the fresh mountain air. "There was an article in the Mercury which said all the underground blasts have jostled the continental plates."

"That's just it," said Viner, his head was bobbing yes up and down like a plastic fishing lure in turbulent water. He couldn't believe Lineheardt was yea-saying one of his claims.

They went down the street to Greek Hell to talk about it some more. And drink some more. Viner ordered their specialty, Greek Spit, which came in male and female colors. Lineheardt reached over to touch Viner on his left hand, which had been going back and forth from the table top to his pocket. Her thumb nestled in the crevice next to his index finger. She gently pushed down on his trembling pulpy flesh. I love you, said her thumb without her knowledge.

"Maybe a gadget this size will press so much lava up into the mountain, the top will blow off," she said.

"I'm going to get those 2 and we're all leaving," announced Viner, yanking his hand away from her and thrusting it back into his pocket. He was right, and nothing was going to stop him. He was through trying to gently persuade people. He felt as gentle as a prison guard. "They're coming with us whether they want to or not."

Lineheardt agreed to wait while he went to get Spike and Noreen. But she didn't last a minute on the street outside the Dog. She opened her compact to fix her makeup; and, when she saw the crack in her upper gum tissue, tears coasted down her cheeks to salt the corners of her wonderful lips. This was something new. It had started at the party at 52. Now she was going to weep whenever she mixed drink with fear. After a couple more vigorous rivulets of salty waste, she looked up for the great zeppelin of physics above her life and saw it shrinking. She had let go of the rope.

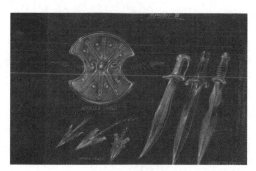

Viner opened the door to Spike's room and found them naked and having a vicious argument.

"So I want you to marry me!" Spike was shouting. "That's a little dream I've latched onto to help myself give up the idea of humiliating Hogan. You want it back? Take it."

"Screw you!" she shrieked.

A tear crested her sharp cheekbone and fell off onto her spectacular naked breast. Viner watched it leave a glittering trail as it wobbled down its stunning rounded slide.

"I tried to warn you, now I have to make you," he called to them from the open doorway. His arm was shaking. Barbanel's gun vibrated in his hand. They turned and gaped at him.

"I got the key from the desk."

He was disgusted. His hope to accomplish something noble and useful had been obliterated by the 2 lovers hurling venomous recriminations at each other like Lipan tomahawks.

"Get dressed. I don't care whether you 2 end up hating me or not. This is what Phil wanted, and I'm going to give it to his after life."

"Go away with that dumb gun," said Noreen defiantly. "I'm not getting dressed."

"Noreen," urged Spike as he pulled his pants on.

"I'm not leaving," she turned to the rapidly dressing Spike. "I'm not jeopardizing the time I've spent here on 1 of your stupid hunches."

"It's no hunch," he said. "You were the 1 who said it. Truth is obvious. It smells."

"I had to say that," she said. She spun away from Viner and Spike to confide in the wall. "So he thinks he can smell the truth the way a beagle smells a rabbit. The truth turns this way and that and Spike with his truth smeller tracks it down, blows it apart with a shotgun, and then holds up the eviscerated remains for all of us to admire."

"All right, she doesn't have to get dressed," said Viner. "We'll march her out as is."

234

"You will not," said Noreen.

"Twist her arm," Viner ordered Spike with the gun.

"He won't twist my arm," said Noreen. "He wouldn't dare hurt me. Spike! If you hurt me****"

"He's got a gun on me," said Spike.

"Give it a good yank and convince her you mean something," said Viner. "The way she talked to you, you'd be justified in tearing it off."

Spike grabbed her wrist and twisted it viciously.

"Ouch, Spike, that hurts!"

"Twist it more," Viner encouraged him. "She isn't even crying."

"She won't cry from physical pain," said Spike.

"Ow, ow. Stop it. Stop it!" shouted Noreen angrily, bending over and twisting around to relieve the pressure on her wrist.

"She was crying before," said, Viner fearfully turning away from her obscenely split rear.

"That's because she loves me," said Spike.

"Yeah, I see that," Viner indulged himself in sarcasm.

"Stop it!" Her voice had gained an angry authority.

Spike let her go. "Are you going to get dressed and come with us?"

"No."

Spike grabbed her wrist again. "I'll really hurt you this time. It's to save your life. I'll break it."

His voice was loaded with authority now. Viner watched with interest to see which 1 would win.

235

Noreen gushed with  praise for Viner's Nash Airflyte. It looked as shiny as new linoleum. He stopped to admire it himself, as if he'd just finished waxing it. The neon eye of the Dog pooled up in its polished gray and looked out at him in sad pink.

He ordered Spike behind the wheel and her up front with him. He got in the back with Barbanel's gun pointed out the window between them. He wondered if it were still loaded. He talked to himself about Lineheardt as they wound through the trembling groves of yurtville. He was upset she hadn't waited as she'd promised.

"You hurt me on purpose," Noreen whispered to Spike.

"You can't blame me," Spike whispered back. "I had to do it or he would have killed me."

"You broke my arm," she said, disgusted.

She held it up in the darkness. They were out of Jake and going straight down the mountain towards 52. A car came up behind them and she could see her arm in its lights as it whizzed past. There was a small Indian burn around her wrist, but no other sign of damage.

Spike laughed at her.

"You enjoyed twisting my arm," she said with disbelief.

"Yes, maybe I did," said Spike thoughtfully. "Yes. Good point."

"You prick."

"In fact," added Spike, "Twisting your arm was almost as much fun as the stuff we'd just finished."

"Enough of that," Viner interrupted. "I don't like dirty talk."

More cars passed them recklessly. It wasn't that Spike was going slow. They just really needed to pass him.

"They're all going to leave," predicted Noreen.

"You know why?" asked Viner. "I do."

"Because Phil was only an interesting nut to them when he was alive," Noreen answered. "Now that he's dead, they think him a prophet. A true 1."

"He was killed by Army intelligence," said Viner. "The whole thing leaked out very fast. This test is more than a bomb. The test is to see how it affects a town, how many people get killed, stuff like that."

"They wouldn't do that," scoffed Noreen.

"Oh, no," Viner agreed derisively. "They wouldn't do that."

"So people are leaving because they think the Army is going to kill them as part of a weapon experiment?" asked Spike.

"Welcome to modern warfare," said Viner, repeating the phrase a jake had thrown at him earlier. "They killed him to shut him up. So people wouldn't flee."

"And the opposite is happening," said Spike.

"How stupid are you 2?" asked Noreen. "As stupid as a man

238

with a hard-on. That's how stupid."

Viner looked down at his crotch wondering when she had seen the one that had sprung up from Lineheardt's tapping the fleshy web between his thumb and finger in the lounge.

"Before Phil was killed, he was only a physicist," Noreen went on. "When he was killed, he became a jake, and all the other jakes believed him."

"That doesn't mean the Army didn't kill him," said Viner.

"Here's a little rule for you when you think you're about to say something stupid," Noreen turned around in the seat to face Viner. "You need a little help with this because you do it so often. If what you are about to say sounds stupid, you are probably missing some information. So don't say it. Because it is going to *be* stupid."

Viner wasn't even listening because he was too busy watching Noreen's eyes to see if she had actually turned around to check his crotch for his Lineheardt hard-on.

What was his plan for himself now that he had lost Lineheardt in Jake? As she had always reminded him, he had no plan for himself. To prove her wrong, he'd planned to be Phil's Boswell. That became his plan. He'd had a plan.

It had lasted 6 hours. Then Lineheardt said she was going to write a book about Phil. So much for the Viner as Boswell plan. At least he was better than Boswell on the whore usage. Despite all the boners Lineheardt had raised in him, he had kept the "no whores" vow to himself from the instant he had made it years ago. He lacked a little of Boswell's devotion to a singular hero, so what? He forgave himself; and, remembering how eloquently Lillo had scoffed at the flood theory, he swapped Lillo in for Phil as his new Dr. Johnson.

Should I come to Jake with the girls? asked Judy inside his head for the millionth time. No, no, not, no****

The sky was a smoky blue black when the all-night party finished gambling and walked out of Leo Gilberg's Hospital. Gilberg guided the party through the empty streets towards the trail to his bomb shelter. As they walked up past the television station, they saw a figure with a heavy diving lung slung over his shoulder and flippers hanging from 1 hand.

"Hi!" he called out cheerfully to the group as they approached.

1 of the gambler's girl friends had to explain to Starzinchger what the aqua lung and flippers were for. Starzinchger couldn't grasp it, even after she'd explained it. He moved up close to Gilberg who was talking with the frogman.

"I thought I'd be the only 1 here," the frogman told Gilberg, "but I saw another diver near Horror Hall, and he said he'd seen 1 other."

"What are you doing here?" asked Starzinchger with imperious professorial authority.

The frogman looked at Gilberg as if to ask, Who's this?

"Are you from the Navy?" asked Starzinchger.

"He's a dealer," said Gilberg, having already identified the self confidence based on nothing. "Right?"

"Horror Hall," confirmed the dealer.

"Dealer. Frogman," insulted Starzinchger since he liked neither.

"I was in the Navy in Florida during the war," he said, piqued at Starzinchger. He turned back to Gilberg. "These other jerks, they've had no experience with underwater demolition. They don't have a boat standing off. They don't have anything. They think they're going to swim around in this stuff like it's the glass blue Caribbean."

He held up a long rubber light and turned it on. The dark blue sky was turning the mineral grey of false dawn. The dealer's light beamed all the way down the empty street in a luminous funnel of phosphorous light.

"They don't even have lights," he said scornfully. "They're going to swim into all the casinos, load up their underwater bags with money, and swim out. What are they going to swim to? California?"

"I'll tell you what," said Gilberg. "What are you going to do?"

"I'm going to find a place to hold on," he answered expertly. "That water is going to come in here like a high wind, with the strength of a tornado, only it's water so it will be even more destructive. They think that because it's coming from the sky, it's going to create an instant lake, like somebody's going to lower the water with a slow crane and make an aquarium they can swim around in like goldfish. They'll pop up to the surface when they're rich. No problem."

Gilberg looked to Starzinchger. Starzinchger spun his eyes.

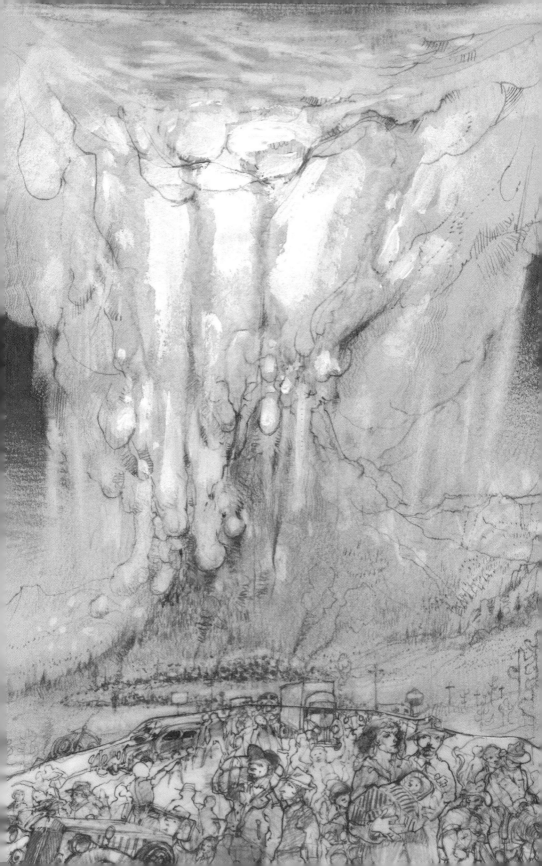

"No sir," continued the dealer, no longer caring if anyone was listening, "that water comes in here like a big wet anvil and crushes the place. Think about the turbulence. That diver standing out in the street waiting to loot Horror Hall, if he isn't flattened by the 1st crush, he's going to be tossed around like a jellyfish in the middle of a typhoon. There will be currents and whorls enough to tear his arms and legs off." He stopped and smiled to himself. "Let's see him swim to California missing an arm and a leg."

Starzinchger, at a loss to understand how the expectation of flood from a fusion burst could gain currency, went back to discuss it with the girl. She said it had happened on television. Oh, yes, he said to himself as he remembered seeing Grethlien on tv. He turned the memory on in his mind. He saw the tv host telling Phil that all the male hydrogen in the bomb was going to mate with all the female oxygen in the air and make a giant shard of hot nukewater.

The party grew nervous as it waited for Gilberg to finish with the dealer. They had all noticed the empty streets on the way up. The gambler with the nice looking girl friend mentioned the casino had been empty when they left. Somebody pointed down to the road winding through the homes and aspens. Cars were weaving and bouncing along with reckless speed. The headlights fluttered up and down like moth's wings. When the traffic reached the long straight downslope, the lights bored through the mineral grey directly at 52, as if the moths had finally locked in on a flame.

The girl said maybe they should think about going for their cars and making a run. There wasn't a soul left in town outside of them who wasn't leaving or crazy. Starzinchger looked all the way down to the bottom of the mountain where tiny white blips of light T'd off to the north and south. He started to laugh. He couldn't stop himself. He laughed so loud, even the dealer stopped talking to Gilberg and looked at him.

"Let's go!" shouted Starzinchger merrily, heading up the slope towards the shelter. "High ground is the only place to be when a flood hits."

 When Huke left his office for the bunker, he felt hot all over. He had always thought that Phil admired him. But the instant Phil had crushed his hand, a fire had started in the back of his mind. He had gotten through the night fighting it back, this fire, but in the last few hours it had begun to burn his confidence.

If Phil had hated him all these years, and with such venom, what about the rest of them? He had been fond of seeing himself as a large mass of personality which bowled through life without difficulty. But this once large boulder which had been his self, this boulder he had imagined bounding down a mountain with abandon and grace, was shrinking. It was becoming a single electron speeding through space avoiding collisions with his colleagues only by the grace of their tolerance.

He tried to tell himself that the hostile Phil was a rare nucleus which presented itself for collision only at the end of very long odds. But no matter how politely his colleagues greeted him, he suspected each was harboring his own ferocious Phil-like grudge, and he had no more power to predict when he was going to have his next trouble than an electron can predict where an overstuffed nucleus lays waiting for debate on the trajectory of its motion. This fire in his mind had burned up so much of his love for himself, Huke walked out for the burst avoiding physicists like a bum navigating teenagers with coke-bottles of gasoline and flaming zippos.

He finally reached the cool morning air and started out across the flats. The dense turbulent clouds were gone. The sky was fully extended in a deep pitchless grey. There was only a single streak of clouds above Oak Spring Butte on which the still hidden sun was projecting a hideous red.

He turned to look at Trembling Peak. It's white top was pink. He felt a new and even more powerful charge of anxiety. Lillo's prediction that the burst would destroy 52 had emptied its population. What if the technicians who were supposed to hook up the last wires had left without doing it? He was filled with hatred for Lillo. He broke into a run towards the bunker.

245

I enjoy the contrast of an inherently happy concept like love and marriage to something inherently evil & dark like atomic bombs + nuclear explosions. However, it seems that ~~it sood~~ the transition may be a bit abrupt for the reader.

You've + reader you caught it.

 Huke found Sensenig's limousine parked outside the bunker, and Sensenig inside waiting for him. There were 6 physicists in the bunker. Forty had been invited. Sensenig was in a fury about Starzinchger. Starzinchger had called him several times and set up 1 meeting after another and shown up for none of them.

As Sensenig railed on, Huke went to the control panel to inspect the detonation board. He couldn't tell by looking whether it had been wired and coded properly. He would have to input the trigger code to find out. He looked at his watch. 5:28. 32 minutes to wait. He told Sensenig to stop worrying and sit down. He'd never ordered Sensenig to do anything before. Sensenig looked at him as if he were crazy.

Sensenig wondered if he had offended Huke by maligning his hero Starzinchger. He took a seat where Huke pointed. He didn't like Huke's new self-importance. It was becoming obvious that Huke somehow hoped to supplant Starzinchger with this shot. All the signs of grand self-expectation were there, especially the imperious carriage and nervous self-importance. He remembered the same symptoms in Starzinchger immediately after the security hearings had elevated him beyond Lillo.

Suddenly it occurred to Sensenig that the only scientist he'd ever genuinely believed in was Lillo. It made him want to get to his car and get the hell away. If Lillo said this shot was going to destroy the bunker, it probably would.

He asked Huke about Lillo's prediction. Huke ridiculed the anxiety, saying he had re-programmed his new cannon to fire the shell 12 additional miles up range anyway. Sensenig lied to Huke about having to make a radio call. Huke warned him he wouldn't wait an instant past 0 to start the shot. He was so loud and wild, Sensenig took a step back, unconsciously fearing a blow to his stomach.

He went out to his car. He opened the door to get in, but hesitated. Maybe he should go back in and order Huke not to set it off. No. He was alone. His aide and driver had disappeared somewhere in Jake last night. He wasn't going to risk another confrontation with an ambitious physicist alone.

His thoughts were interrupted by the sunrise. The sun was showing a small secant of light along the butte. The mist above it was acting like a prism, stripeing the underside of a long tongue-shaped cloud with a flame-stitched watergaw.

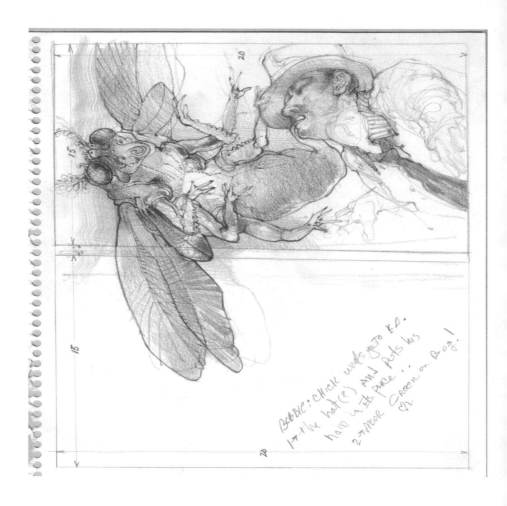

248

The wind was blowing hard as Starzinchger led the party up the mountain. Timber growth was distorted this far up. Down below, the limber pines were 80 feet tall with great arms stretching out an evangelical welcome; but here they appeared juvenile, no taller than Starzinchger, and their furry arms reached out to him only on the leeward side of their fragile trunks.

Their windward arms had been amputated by the peak's severe gales. At their knees, shrunken spruce crowded around them like dwarfs before maimed kings. These stunted and misshapen Engleman spruce, many of them over a hundred years old yet only 2 feet tall, were trying to crawl along the rocky soil beneath the ferocious winds.

They twisted along the ground in eerie shapes, their trunks contorted in agony as they looked upwards with awe at the limber pines, their inferiors 1,000 feet down the mountain, but here possessed of the courage to stand up and have half their bodies shorn off by the wind.

In the last few yards the spruce went down to tufts no taller than Starzinchger's finger. They were nothing more than a scrubby coniferous ground cover. Suddenly the tufts ended. They had reached the timberline. It was only a few hundred feet across bleached gravel to the shelter.

The peak rose up before them in a massive pink shank of rock. He turned to look down at 52. The sun wasn't up yet, but its fresh color was leaking up into the sky like red ink spilled onto a paper napkin. The nice looking girl was excited by the way the color was everywhere. She held her pocket mirror up for him to look at himself. His face was pink with reflected light.

Gilberg's shelter was sunk deep into a silver mine shaft. It had a twisting canal of mirrors which periscoped their vision up, out, and down the mountain directly at 52. Starzinchger began to ham it up about how dangerous nuclear explosions were. He dwelt on the 1st ultra-violet pulse and how it would blind them, until Gilberg interrupted him.

"The mirrors are all covered with ultra-violet screening." Gilberg said, bored with Starzinchger's useless imperious expertise.

"Marvelous!" responded Starzinchger. "We can all look without fear of injury."

Gilberg enumerated all the lavish safety precautions of the shelter, turning to Starzinchger for explanations of the dangers they were designed to counter. He had obviously paid some scientist from 52 to construct the world's greatest fallout shelter.

"In those 1st milliseconds," said Starzinchger when talk turned to the nature of the burst itself, "when the fireball is still contained by an incandescent air shell, the temperature inside is so hot, 100 million degrees, everything inside it is vapor."

"Even the stuff the bomb was in?" asked 1 of them. "The metal and steel and like that?"

"Yes," answered Starzinchger, smiling at the incredible ignorance of this group. "There is no substance in the universe which is not gas at 100 million degrees."

"What about diamonds?" asked the girl.

"If you pack bomb material with diamonds, and trigger a burst, you will turn them to gas," affirmed Starzinchger.

"Fantastic," said the girl. "Would it sparkle, diamond gas? Wouldn't it be startling to make signs out of it. Leo, they'd be much better than neon. How about rubies. Ocho Marias, tubes of sparking ruby vapor gas ****"

Starzinchger listened to some of what they were going to do with ruby vapor gas before suggesting that a nuclear reaction might be difficult to contain in glass tubes. He mentioned that if the containment of nuclear explosions were possible, space travel exceeding the speed of light might be developed using particles called tachyons whose great speed did not violate Einstein's Relativity because tachyons never traveled at a speed below the velocity of light. The theory of Relativity did not rule out such particles****

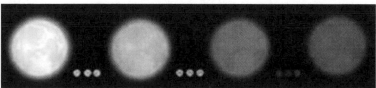

He stopped in the middle of his explanation. No 1 was listening to him. They were all talking to each other about what might be done with liquid precious gems. They had convinced themselves there was a form in between diamond gas and diamonds which could be added to cranberry juice to make glittering cocktails.

Starzinchger realized there was a whole world out there he'd been missing. He'd thought stupid people were the 1s who came to parties in New York and San Francisco to talk about physics with fan-like enthusiasms and press money into his pockets because he could calculate and learn at speeds beyond their dreams. But they weren't the stupid people of the world, after all. They were only the lowest level of intelligence in the world of physics. *There were other people out there far dumber who didn't give a tiny shit about physics, and here he was surrounded by them.*

It stunned him that people like this, who were rich, could be so stupid. He could see and accept the dumbness of plumbers and waiters because they'd had no opportunity to learn anything. But these people were wealthy. Knowledge was theirs to take whenever they wanted it. They didn't want any part of it though. Their response to his presentation of the facts of physics was to gleefully trumpet, "Aren't we stupid!" and pass their posture of deliberate ignorance off as wit. Yes, there had to be millions of people out there like these, and Gilberg was probably friends with most of them.

At the last instant, Huke faltered. Solitude hit the noise of his mind with a crushing weight. Here was a moment of loneliness so intense nothing could penetrate it. What a silence it made. Everything inside him was so quiet, it suddenly seemed seductive to not go on. But the anxiety receded just as suddenly and he felt happy instead. How many men are allowed to have the big question of their life answered? He thought of Pierre Curie alone in his lab radiating his own arm. He felt a thrill that he had at least been successful enough to bring his ambition to such wondrous focus. How could he think of stopping?

He dialed the triggering code and waited to see if the experiment had been properly wired.

In its rush to reach 20 miles up range instead of the 8 miles Phil and Lynn Carol Moss Graf had so carefully computed in order to limit the exit velocity to within the stress bounds of the new large plastic shell, the gadget came tumbling out of the rail cannon barrel and slammed up against a wall of air like a die hitting spiked foam, only harder, hard enough to go right through the end of a dice table and out the casino door, but this was air, not a single wall of sponge foam, and there was no end to it.

The gadget shell dragged 1 layer of air after another along

with it, pulling them all along in sheets, and each new
sheet of air put a bigger burden on the tumbling gadget
until it was dragging 100,000 sheets of air along at near the
speed of light, and still it kept adding sheets to its work
until it broke open like an egg and the heat which had
been created by the incredible friction of its unprecedented velocity triggered the reaction right there, 200 feet away
from the square mouth of Phil's rail cannon which Huke,
just a millisecond earlier, had watched blow apart.

Starzinchger let loose a loud
mocking "POOF!" to show them
he'd known all along it was
going to be a dud. Half of them
jumped back from the window as if
they'd been touched with cattle prods. Starzinchger chor-
tled at their reaction.

*The large pane of glass before
them turned instantly dark.*

255

The drive north had taken the beautiful Nash along a corridor of ascending mountains. As Viner, Spike and Noreen waited for the burst where they had stopped on a lesser peak, they could see how Nevada had hunched up behind them in a huge spinal column.

Far across the great lunar sea of 52, the sun was rising above a tongue of clouds when it seemed to explode.

They were wearing the special goggles which Viner, a veteran of nuclear tests, kept in his glove compartment. But despite the goggles the incredible spreading of light nearly blinded them. The sun, a small brilliant disc they had been able to stare at directly through the goggles, came rushing past Mercury and Venus, and up the horizon to Nevada, coming so fast it was as big as the sky in an instant.

Frightened, Viner turned quickly to look at Noreen. There were a hundred tiny lines on her cheeks, and between them, 1,000s of little flakes of dead skin. He could see the little skin chips with incredible clarity. He looked out the windshield of the Nash. The small scratches on the im-

257

peccably polished pearl-grey hood showed as fine white rivulets of wax.

"What is all this God-forsaken light?" Viner screamed.

For an instant the light dimmed slightly and he could see all the mountains around them. He jumped out of the Nash. The light came back up to its powerful bleaching intensity. Spike and Noreen jumped out, too.

Noreen walked stupidly towards the huge achromatic fireball, it had a shape now, it was a mammoth cloud of light climbing the sky like a balloon. It had grown so large and yet was still so near and low, it reduced the momentous humped back of Nevada to a few grey nuggets of dirt spread across a dusty desert floor.

"It's not, don't, don't" Viner heard himself jabbering. He realized he'd been shouting from the instant the sky had turned into light. "Don't, oh no, no, not this."

"The mountains look small," said Spike. He sounded far off, as if he were admiring a Hudson River landscape in a museum.

The toroid cloud of light seemed like a comet struggling to fly. The strain of lifting off was draining its energy because it lost brilliance as it labored upwards. It sparked with a luminous purple dirt. It was dragging an incredible train of smoke and ash up into the sky. A white halo formed about the sparking ball of purple and silver green. The column of dirt looked like a primitive animal brain stem shooting up into the roiling tormented cloud above it, bloating it until it began to resemble human cortex. It was a couple of miles high now and growing horizontally towards them.

"The article in Mercury was right," Viner said. He'd fallen to the ground with shock over what he was seeing and found himself now babbling from the seat of his pants. "It's a volcano. They've crushed through the earth's crust."

The bomb had ripped a hole in the earth and its guts were coming out. A minute passed. The cloud climbed until it was 6 miles high. It was growing towards them as fast as it ascended. Purple, in a rich pleasurable hue, was the color of death, and his own death was coming towards him right now in a noxious cloud of speeding gases. The sulfurous smoke the article had said would be the result of a chain of volcanic eruptions was curling over the des- ert floor like surf. It would wash a burning suffocating death over them soon.

The 3 of them looked back and forth between the cloud's terrifying advance and each other. Without speaking it, they knew they shared the same startling thought. Not only were they dying, so was the world itself. It had been punctured to its volatile core.

The instant Starzinchger saw the darkened glass, he knew an explosion of magnitude had occurred.

"We can't see!" cried the gambler's girl friend. "What happened to the glass? We wanted to see."

Everyone turned to Gilberg with their disappointment.

"I'll put the tv camera up," offered Gilberg. The shelter had a camera which went up at the push of a button like a car aerial.

"Come on!" Starzinchger was shouting frantically. "We've got to get these blocks in place right away. Overpressure goes around corners."

Beneath a study shelf under the darkened window were several stacks of cinder blocks. Starzinchger picked 1 up and slammed it into place next to the glass.

"It's going to reach down through this mine shaft and crush us if we don't put up the blocks right now!"

The panic in his voice affected them differently than his earlier histrionics. In an instant they all joined him piling up cinder blocks against the glass. A sloppy wall was up in a few seconds, and there was nothing to do but stand and stare at it and wait for a very very vigorous overpressure to punch 1 small finger of its power down through the twisted mine shaft and flick cinder blocks across the shelter like they were pebbles. Starzinchger retreated from the wall to the far end of the bunker.

"What about the tv, Leo?" asked the gambler who had brought along the pretty girl. "We missed the light. Are we going to miss the mushroom?"

"I'll put it up," said Gilberg.

"Don't put it up yet," ordered Starzinchger.

"What?" asked Gilberg, impatiently. "Why not?"

"You'll melt the camera," laughed Starzinchger across the bunker, his nervousness cracking the laugh into a cough. "The lens will turn as fast as the mirrors and the big window did. Wait until thermal radiation has passed us by completely."

"You said before that thermal radiation travels at the speed of light," countered Gilberg like an argumentative student. "It has to be gone by now."

"For the size yield that can melt glass from that many miles away," said Starzinchger, "the fireball will be dangerous ten or 15 seconds after the explosion. If you had any conception of the radiant energy required to melt glass, you'd know that this fireball is still generating 1 ardent wave after another."

Gilberg looked puzzled. He didn't know whether to believe Starzinchger or not. Gilberg hadn't helped at all in building the wall of cinder blocks because he'd heard the mocking "Poof!" and he thought he'd known what it meant.

"It's almost ten seconds now," said Gilberg, arguing with Starzinchger as if he could protect them all from danger by undermining Starzinchger's professorial authority.

"The blast wave," Starzinchger argued back, outraged he had to spend the last coins of his precious brainwork on prodigious ignorance, "that damn blast wave, the only thing from this huge burst, this is the largest burst ever exploded by man, believe me, can kill us down here, and it's going to get here very soon, so get yourself ready to ****

They were all staring at him with fear, beginning to believe they could be killed, when suddenly glass was breaking against the cinder blocks and the shelf which held their fragile wall began to tremble. A familiar breeze fanned Starzinchger's face.

"Look at your watch," Starzinchger ordered Gilberg. "Count seconds."

If they survived the shock front, he could estimate the yield by the duration of the overpressure. A thunderous noise reached down into the bunker behind the twisted finger of the shock front.

Starzinchger bounded across the bunker and seized Gilberg's watch arm. Gilberg, panicked, had stopped counting out the seconds. The bunker was trembling as if hit by a powerful earthquake. The girl was screaming and pulling at Starzinchger. The thunder was bringing home to them what the melted mirrors had failed to. The mountain's trembling grew even more pronounced. It was going to burst open like a hammered grape. 1 of the gamblers shouted that the peak was turning into a volcano. Starzinchger held onto Gilberg's arm; and, despite the girl's clawing at him, fixed all his attention on the second hand, which notched off the time segments of the blast wave like the leg of a very slow, very sick, metronomic spider.

Then the noise was gone. The shelter stopped quaking. Starzinchger felt a soaring wash of exhilaration and triumph. He looked up from the watch. Gilberg was staring at him with questioning fear.

"It's not possible," Starzinchger breathed. "I don't believe that really happened."

"What?" demanded Gilberg. "Did we make it?"

"The shock wave lasted 6 seconds," said Starzinchger. "I think it might have been 10 megatons. Or more depending how far downrange****"

"What does that mean?" asked 1 of the gamblers, the only 1 dressed in western clothes. "10 megatons. So what. What happened?"

"That would be 10,000 kilotons," said Starzinchger. "1,000 times the size of the bomb we detonated over Hiroshima."

They all, looked at him, silent with fear.

"It's far bigger than anyone thought it would be," Starzinchger said enthusiastically. "Not even Lillo thought it would be this big. Maybe Grethlien did, I guess he did. You can put that camera up now."

Gilberg fumbled with the controls while they all crowded around the television in the corner. When the picture came on, they saw Jake on fire. *The junk it was made of had offered no resistance to the extraordinary thermal radiation, and now the entire town was a single heap of ignited fuel.*

"What happened to the tires on that truck?"

There was a truck parked on the road right below them. There was nothing left of the tires. They had been incinerated; and the truck, now nothing more than a lump of swollen blistered metal, was barely recognizable as something which had once had wheels. As distorted as it was, the truck was the only thing that was recognizable. The rest of Jake was either flaming or melted. This was, unlike Hiroshima's which had taken several hours to develop, an instantaneous firestorm. The superheated fireball, which had been 4 miles in diameter and reached almost halfway to Jake, had ignited everything at once with its thermal radiation. The dry cheap materials Jake was constructed of had gone up like flash paper. Nothing which wasn't concealed in a deep buried shelter like Gilberg's would survive.

 Ten minutes after the eruption the cloud stopped growing.

It had reached a height of 90,000 feet. It was wider than it was tall, perhaps 25 miles across. They were not going to die. The only effect to reach them was a slight blowing of dust which lasted ten seconds.

The huge white cloud was to dissipating.

"I wonder what it looks like?" said Viner.

"What what looks like?" asked Spike.

"Jake," said Viner. "Maybe we should go back and see what's left. Maybe we should see if we can help anyone."

"You're not serious," said Noreen.

"I'm not sure that was a volcano," said Viner. "I wonder if it was."

"Whatever it was," said Noreen, "We should be putting more distance between it and us."

They got back in the car and Viner started east through Manhattan, Nevada. It was a small dusty town waking up to the fact that something stupendous had happened to the south. A couple in tartan pajamas were walking in their bare feet, heading up the slope to get a view of the disintegrating white cloud.

"But don't you want to see what it looks like?" pleaded Viner.

"No," said Spike, noticing that Viner's voice had a new sound in it.

"I'm really curious," said Viner in his new beautiful tone. "I lived there for ten years. Aren't you curious?"

"No thanks." Noreen agreed with Spike.

Viner guided the Nash through the people walking on the highway. They were wearing tartan pajamas, too. All of Manhattan, Nevada seemed to be taken with tartan. In his mind he suddenly saw the naked Noreen and her beautiful tits opposite Spike on their bed at the Dog.

"That's what Phil admired," he whispered to himself as he wrenched the wheel of the Nash and pulled into what looked like the only motel in Manhattan, Nevada. "I want you 2 to check in here for awhile."

"What for?" asked Noreen.

"Because it is what Phil wanted." Viner persuaded them with his rich new voice. *"May God smother Phil Grethlien in his peace. You 2 go fuck."*

Was he kidding?

"Go on." he encouraged them.

He got the gun out again.

"Okay" agreed Spike, opening the door and pulling Noreen out with him. "We're going."

They went into the empty motel office and waited inside for a moment before coming back out to watch Viner scatter the sleepy tartan population of Manhattan, Nevada as he sped back down the highway towards Jake.

 The revelers watched Jake burn and melt with a mixture of curiosity and carnival excitement. They began to talk about how lucky they were. Starzinchger could hear mania in their voices. Their delight in surviving increased their pleasure in watching the firestorm.

None of them noticed the breeze still passing through the shelter. Even if they had, they wouldn't know it was the symptom of an oxygen starved fire, a fire burning so hot and so pervasively, it was sucking all the oxygen around it into its heart, sucking it out of the shelter like a vacuum cleaner and leaving them nothing of value to breathe.

Since the oxygen supplied for the shelter was enough for only 4, Starzinchger had to wrestle with himself over whether he should explain this particular phenomena to these nitwits. Suddenly, in the back of his mind, without his even thinking about it, a solution to the moral dilemma popped free. He'd figured out what the tour of the hotels with Gilberg had been all about and why Gilberg had wanted him to convince the troopers they'd be safe from the bomb.

Gilberg's speaking in code to all the hotel owners had been like posing a problem to him, and no 1 could pose a problem to Starzinchger and expect him not to solve it reflexively any more than they could put a pond in front of a mink and expect it not to swim out and snap the necks of a few ducks. Instinctively Starzinchger had glided out into Gilberg's code and figured out Gilberg had been organizing a killing.

Not only had Gilberg been taking care of the details of the assassination, he had been lining up figures of power to support the action. If Starzinchger might have felt guilt about letting Gilberg die before the solution to the code came to him, he didn't now. He had no obligation to risk his life to save a murderer, and he thanked his wonderful intellect for relieving him of the onus.

Starzinchger quietly took 1 of the oxygen tanks off the wall. He could feel some symptoms of oxygen deficiency in himself already. He was short of breath. It was an effort to keep his mind focused. Carefully, he placed the oxygen bottle in the bathroom. He tip-toed back out into the main room, afraid 1 of them might see him. They were all too busy watching the tv. He looked about for the oxygen masks.

He was having trouble controlling his mind. His thoughts kept returning to alerting the rest of them to their danger. If he told them, and maybe he should because they're weren't all guilty of Gilberg's crime, how long would they be grateful? Especially this group. Would they allow him enough oxygen to survive? Or would it come down to a physical contest in which an alliance of the ignorant would function against the intelligent.

Of course it would, and the axis of such a treaty would put the odds of survival at 14 to 1 against him.

He found the masks in a cabinet under the 3 remaining oxygen bottles. He slipped 1 into his jacket pocket and retreated quietly towards the bathroom. Once inside he gingerly closed the door and locked it.

He slipped on the mask and breathed with deep sighs of excitement and relief. His oxygen starvation symptoms quickly abated. He felt euphoric. He began to turn Phil's work over in his mind. His own precious devotion to liquid deuterium and tritium became hateful to him. He had been more than wrong. He had held onto something crude and irreducible while Phil had developed something simple and elegant.

He worried that others would discover him missing. When their excitement with watching the firestorm stopped masking their physical discomfort, they'd notice they were all gasping for breath. In another minute or 2 they'd be turning to him for expert advice on the nature of their gasping and he wouldn't be there. He checked the strength of the door before him. It was made of heavy steel. The walls were steel also. The bathroom, he realized with a rush of pleasure, was a shelter within a shelter and impregnable to marauders who might gain access to the outer shelter. The scientist who had built this bunker had thought of everything.

He took an inventory of the items in the bathroom. He found canned foods and liquids in the cabinets. He found several issues of a new magazine whose major business was presenting veiled but visible feminine bosoms. *He studied the U shaped breasts of a woman in a sheer peignoir. He leafed through other pages. The magazine claimed that 1 30 year old woman after another was 18.*

From time to time he looked up, worried about a knock on the door. He let half an hour pass before he cracked it open.

He hoped to find them all alive. He was surprised by how powerfully this wish had affected him. Perhaps they hadn't missed him because the firestorm had moderated and all their symptoms had disappeared.

A wave of heat came in the crack as he peeked out. They were all dead. He opened the door and walked out into the heat. He felt numb with grief and guilt. They had never even figured out he'd disappeared.

Their perceptions had become so impaired from lack of oxygen, they had staggered around for awhile and then fallen over to die without even realizing what was happening. Gilberg was stretched across the sofa as if he'd lain down for a nap. His cheeks and lips were plum colored from oxygen starvation.

The television screen showed a white cloud of random light. The firestorm had melted the camera. Starzinchger moved his palm towards the wall of cinder blocks but withdrew it quickly. The blocks were radiating a ferocious heat. Sweat was already pouring off his brow into his eyes. He estimated the temperature in the shelter at 175. He looked at the blank tv screen with dismay. He had no way of telling how long the heat might last or how much hotter it might get.

A wave of dread passed over him. He was going to die, too. No matter how much oxygen he had in the tanks, the heat was going to cook him.

He felt a lessening of guilt over letting everyone else die. So what? He was going, too. But his dread quickly regenerated. He had to think of something.

The refrigerator caught his eye. Of course. How beautiful. Refrigeration. It was so elegant and pure. He thanked himself for all his dreams about refrigeration. He wondered if another physicist who had not spent the years he had scheming and working on low temperatures would have had the unconscious appetite for refrigeration solutions that had enabled him to look at this refrigerator and see in an instant it could save him from the heat.

He hurried over to it and pulled open the door. It was big enough, plenty big enough. It was a restaurant refrigerator stocked with enough meat and vegetables to last for weeks. He pulled the shelves out and hurled the food away. It had gotten so hot in the shelter, he stepped inside and was ready to close the door immediately.

"Wait a minute," he ordered himself.

He was acting too fast because he was panicked. He'd be too cold inside. He hadn't left anything inside to eat or drink. He raced about the shelter collecting the things he needed. The heat drove him like a whip. He was out of breath from his exertion. He was incredibly hot, both from his frantic work and the heat radiating from the cinder blocks, but he forced himself to take 2 sport coats off the closest bodies and put them on over his own. He was breathing still harder.

As he started to get back inside, he realized that as soon as he closed the refrigerator door, the light would go out. He wouldn't be able to see his food or anything else. He'd be waiting for who knew how long in the dark. He jumped out again. He had to find a flashlight. He fumbled desperately about different cabinets until he found 3 on 1 shelf, all in working order, and flung them into the refrigerator. The heat had climbed ten degrees in the minute it had taken him to find them. He was so short of breath, he was gasping. Suddenly he realized it wasn't his exertion which was making him gasp. He'd forgotten the oxygen.

"Good job!" he shouted.

His thinking had become impaired again. Oxygen starvation had made him as dumb as the people at his feet. He'd almost gone into the refrigerator, not only without a light, but without oxygen. Like a kid playing in some abandoned dump who gets inside an old icebox, shuts the door, and never comes out.

Blinking from the heat, he rushed to the bathroom and returned breathing from the mask as he carried the tank. He put the other 3 tanks in the refrigerator. He'd have enough to last him several days now.

The heat was so bad, he could barely force his eyes open to make himself stand and look around the shelter 1 more time. Was there anything else he'd forgotten? The dead were curled up around the room. He couldn't stand to look at them anymore. Pushing everything aside to make room for himself, he hunched inside the refrigerator and pulled the door closed.

The snap of the latch filled him with dread again. He was cold. He could feel the cold dark air on his cheeks. He shivered with anxiety.

A moment earlier, while still outside the refrigerator, it had come to him with astonishing clarity that an Army disaster team would comb every inch of the wreckage of this disaster, and they would let him out in a day or 2. But now that he was inside the refrigerator, it seemed equally cogent that nobody would even notice there was a shelter up here until they were well finished with the business of Jake itself. And they wouldn't even start there until the radiation receded. It might be weeks before someone found the shelter; and, even if it were found on the 1st day, why would any of the idiots the Army sends in to inspect such catastrophes bother to open a refrigerator door? He could see what was going to happen. A corporal would take inventory of the furniture and leave. A couple of weeks later, a squad would arrive to remove the fine restaurant refrigerator to some colonel's bungalow in Arizona.

All the stupid aspects of locking himself inside a refrigerator came to him in a flood of self hatred. Why hadn't he scratched a message on the outside of the door? Why hadn't he set the outside cold control to 50 degrees? Why hadn't he held the door open until he'd been absolutely forced to close it? He could have thought without pressure from the heat. Good job! What if the heat melted the cord and interrupted the refrigerator's power supply.

His elegant solution, which had seemed a sparkling diamond peak on the mountainous jewel-work of his physics, was an oxygen starved delusion which was going to kill him. He began to breathe oxygen through the mask in great anxious gulps, as if it could make him smart enough to go back in time and not close the refrigerator door on himself. But its profusion impaired his faculties as effectively as its scarcity. Instead of leading him to a useful perception on how to manipulate time, it made him as drunk as the bartender at the Neanderthal Bingo Station.

 Leaving Spike and Noreen in Manhattan, Nevada, Viner headed back for Jake as fast as the Nash would go. The giant cloud of after-burst was gone in an hour. He sped along the lumpy highway formulating his story for national television. A faster car bumped by him as he talked.

"Phil Grethlien, the father of the H-bomb****" he practiced various intonations of this header with a Don Pardo style and no recollection that it would break promises to both Phil and Lineheardt. He would sell this tale to whichever network had the courage to bid high enough to buy this piece. He might title it:

THE STORY OF OUR CENTURY

The road was sticking to his tires like licorice. When Trembling Peak had 1st come into view, he'd been amazed to see the mountainside glittering in silver. The bomb had collected the silver tailings from the flats, polished it, and blown it all the way back up onto the mountain. But Jake, or what was left of it, was now bubbles of glittering black and grey.

As he turned up the mountain and got beyond the severe clumps of melted asphalt, the going got easier. His ascent of the mountain was disorienting. There were no borders, no sages to mark the end of winter fat, no limber pines to take over the climb where the ponderosas faltered and shrank. The only thing to suggest there had ever been anything wood-like on this mountain were the telephone poles. Snapped off at their bases, they lay beside the road like huge consumed cigars.

The glittering aspect of the mountain, which had struck him at 1st as intensely beautiful, became suddenly frightening when he saw it consisted only of hueless shades of oxidation. There was nothing left alive on the mountain. The grey alkaline basin had risen like a lake of dust, killed everything, and then receded, leaving a residue of silver-like soap on a bathtub.

Another car passed him. Up ahead many cars were already parked where the rubble of motels made the sticky road impassable. He parked when he reached them. Fifty people or more had beat him back to Jake. A pick-up truck pulled in right beside him. Back down the mountain and out across the desert he could still see more coming. Hundreds of them were making the trek back. Above him the early arrivals were climbing the nude remains of Jake.

The pick-up driver, recognizing Viner, jumped out of his truck and started an argument. *Viner learned how he was now a giant asshole because he had been so wrong about the flood.*

He listened without argument then followed the crowd making the 2,000 foot climb to the ruins of the hotels. Even from far away he could see the Dog was the only 1 left with a wall standing. It looked like a hundred eyed monster someone had blinded by sticking brooms through its glass eyes.

When he finally reached 4th Street, he rested before the standing wall of the Dog. The concrete was laced with fissures and cracks. It looked like inexpertly worked pastry dough.

He walked down towards Horror Hall. It was gone but the light steel warehouse on the edge of its rear parking lot remained. The warehouse had been stripped of its metal shell. Its skeleton was humped and twisted like the remains of a steer that had fallen to its knees and died of thirst. A few tatters of metal sheathing clung to its bones like charred fur.

He felt incredibly dry. Jake was still glowing with heat. He was out of breath. He picked his way about, stumbling like a lost dehydrated drunk. The sun was tarnishing the silver dust. Every once in awhile he found a nugget of reality. A blistered black mailbox. A huge ganglion of metal he was able to identify as a truck because he spied a wheel rim at the bottom of it. He found a piece of a hotel sign. It was burned and melted like everything else, but there was a speck of pink in the metal. In an hour of looking, the only color he found was that little speck of pink metal.

By noon his fatigue and thirst overcame his grief and curiosity. He stumbled back down towards his car. He wondered where he should go. Going down was even more strenuous than the climb. He fell several times. He felt nauseous. Many more cars had come in and he couldn't see the Nash. Finally he found the pickup truck of the ingrate who'd pulled in after him. There was an empty space next to it. Someone had stolen his Nash.

So?

Now it was possible to go nowhere. He went back up the naked slope and wandered among the herd of social mutants stampeding around the treeless mountain. *He*

276

fell in love with every revenant jake he looked at in this busy haunting of the null volcano.

It was a little one sided, his powerful new love for jakes. The jakes were geysers of recrimination. Viner had convinced them to leave and thereby saved their lives so they hated him because he had been wrong about the flood. For the next several days, everywhere he went, they threw his discredited theory up to him with derisive triumph. He suffered in silence as they argued that he was dumb and they were smart. When they finished, he always made a quiet request for gratitude but no 1 would show him any.

1950
April 12

People continued returning to climb the hot naked mountain to the hotel wreckage. Everything was dry. The fireball had released waves of radiant heat so powerful it had evaporated every drop of moisture on the slope.

Dry or not, the Swiss, as the Army called them, found ways to lift glowing beams, scoop away the black molten goo that remained of the hotels, and search for the metal boxes which hung beneath gaming tables. Many found boxes and opened them only to discover the heat from the firestorm had rushed in through the slots in the tops of the boxes and incinerated all the money inside.

But these were only the loose boxes which had been attached to the tables in action. In hotels all up and down 4th Street, the boxes for the evening shift had been taken down and stacked in the cages when the graveyard shifts had come on at 4 in the morning. John Donahue found Leo Gilberg's Hospital's boxes stacked in a neat pyramid beneath a large mound of smoking bricks. The slots had been locked closed so the heat had been unable to enter the boxes directly. The money in the boxes on the outside of the pyramid burned anyway. But the boxes in the middle had been insulated enough to protect the money; and, since it was a Saturday night's drop, Donahue found several million dollars.

While the Swiss busied themselves looking for money, the Army put up tents and brought in trailers. Lumber arrived on flatbed trucks which struggled across the melted desert roads like oxcarts in mud. A large frame mess hall went up.

The Army tried to keep people off the mountain by blocking the road, but a lot of them had already beaten the Army back up the peak; and the rest found a way up to Jake anyway because the Swiss wanted to get back on the mountain far more than soldiers needed to stop them.

The Swiss spoke fondly of rebuilding Jake. They seemed not to notice that the glittering silver the bomb had sent up to replace the fantastic ladder of forests was already tarnished. They interpreted the return of the silver to the mountain as a sign of exceptionally potent luck, an omen that the town should be rebuilt better than ever. And since

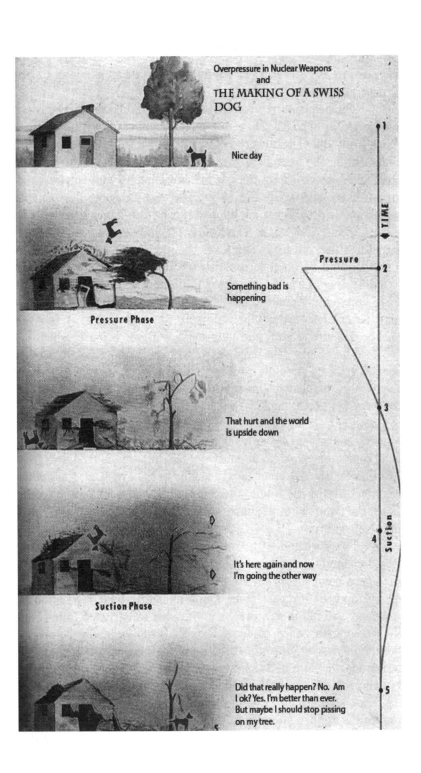

they were starting from scratch, they could at last do what they had been longing to do for decades. They could build a resort with no gambling and no whoring. This stunning beautiful mountain did not need to sell vices to attract tourists. The Swiss spoke enthusiastically of their towering lump of grey as if it were still purple and majestic and no whores and gamblers were among them.

Viner walked the grey mountain in anguish. He spent his days patrolling the ruins and peering into the talking faces of the Swiss with quiet fascination. Fortunes were being made picking through the clotted plastic remains of hotels. Donahue's millions were an inspiration to everyone. More stacked boxes were found. Underground cage vaults were exploded open by groups who formed partnerships with Army lieutenants who could have fancy explosives flown in by helicopter.

There was some awareness of a radiation hazard. Everyone knew the Army had delayed its arrival several days to avoid the radioactivity. The more cautious Army officers were walking about in special suits made of thin metal foil. The treasure hunters mocked these hot silver suits. They developed their own theory. If you didn't breathe radiation in, it couldn't hurt you. The hospital did a brisk business in surgical masks. The helicopter pilots arriving with gelignite saw the rubble of 4th Street being combed by enthusiastic ants with white fabric snouts.

The Swiss saw themselves an evolutionary advance over jakes or as God's new people in Nevada, depending on whether Darwin or God had captured their affection after the mighty event.

Many Swiss developed purple blemishes where particles of dust charged with radioactivity stuck to their skins. Viner didn't get any such patches, thereby avoiding the additional Army derogative "purple cheese," which had become the military name for Swiss with rashes. He assumed he escaped the rashes because he didn't go out stirring up dust and rubble searching for money. He hunted, instead, through the expressive Swiss faces to scavenge grief for the lost 4th Street.

1950

April 14

"It's like some union hall," a woman said to her husband as Viner sat down in the mess hall at their table. She was looking at her food and picking at it without interest.

"The trouble is, there's nothing to do," said her husband. "So everyone comes here to socialize."

Viner studied them, trying to figure out what they were talking about. It might merit a mention in his journal. It was obvious the tv networks weren't coming for

THE STORY OF OUR CENTURY.

He would have to use his notebook to write a book.

The woman said she hated it when people couldn't accept things as they were and had to negotiate for some advantage. Viner looked carefully away so they wouldn't figure out he was spying on them. His turning head brought him into the face of Lineheardt, who was sitting alone several tables away.

He rushed to greet her, his cheeks lighting up from inside as if he had just bit into a huge curl of neon. She apologized for not waiting for him the night before the burst. He could barely process her words as she explained she'd stood in the lobby of the Dog looking at her gums, then panicked and fled. She had escaped the burst by hitch-hiking out of town. She laughed at her panic over her gums, considering the beta burns she had acquired since her return.

"Did you hear about Starzinchger?" she asked.

Someone had gone up to the shelter on the peak and, seeing everything from the refrigerator thrown all over the floor, imagined that Gilberg's dying act had been to stuff all his money into the refrigerator so it wouldn't burn. Lineheardt's beautiful lip bowed up in a smile. "That guy must have been very disappointed to see Starzinchger fall out wearing 3 sport coats."

"Do you know about Sensenig," Viner tried to continue in the vein of her interest. "He was in his limousine driving away from the bunker when it went off."

"Really?" asked Lineheardt. "How do they know that?"

"He was talking to somebody at Sandia on the special radio in his car, trying to get them to stop Huke," he said. He didn't care about Sensenig. He just wanted to give her more material for her own beautiful thoughts. "I guess he was burned up inside the limousine."

"I imagine he didn't exactly burn up," said Lineheardt.

"What do you mean?"

"There's more to it than burning when you're that close," she said. "The metal of the car would explode from the ten million degree heat so the car would be no protection at all. Every kind of tissue in Sensenig's body would find its

own way to explode into flames just like the car, even his teeth, fillings and all."

"No, no, not," he lamented as if back in Manhattan, Nevada, seeing the bomb go off. Now he cared a lot about Sensenig.

"What's wrong?" she asked, curious about his upset.

"There wouldn't be any death experience?" asked Viner.

"Nothing physical."

"Everything is gone right away?"

"Yes."

"What are you doing back here?" he changed the subject.

She shrugged. "You?"

"I'm writing **THE STORY OF OUR CENTURY,**" he snickered. "How are you doing on the book of Phil? Where are you staying?"

"I'm just talking a little about him. Doing nothing on writing anything, " she complained. "I'm sleeping on the ground. That's how I got these, I guess."

She pointed at the spots on her arms. She turned around and showed him a dense concentration of pungent purple cheese on the back of her neck. She was sleeping outside because she couldn't find anyone to stay with. Whenever she tried to get a place in 1 of the tents, everyone inside wanted to negotiate some kind of group sex thing.

Viner realized the couple he'd just been spying on earlier had been talking about just that. Other conversations he'd overheard came flooding back to him. He had seen people coming and going in sexy costumes at silly hours and now he got what was going on.

"Something has happened to me," she said. "Phil was so high on that couple, Spike and Noreen, because he and I had a great screw; but now I can't stand the idea of sex. I can't even do it to survive, to keep myself off the radiation dust at night. I can't do it. The thought of it makes me sick."

"You come and stay with me," said Viner, outraged. "You don't have to sleep on the ground anymore. I have a trailer."

"A trailer!" she cried, delighted. "You know someone in the Army."

"Not exactly," he said. "When people found out I was keeping a journal for a book, I found myself in a trailer. They want me to last longer. I guess everyone, even some of the Army, want the story told."

"I'm eating a little now," she said, "I still hate sex, but I guess you can fuck me if you want to. I always liked you a lot****"

"Oh, no!" he lied, eager to assure her that they could be together with absolutely no problems. "I hate sex, too."

Lineheardt smiled distantly at his reassurance, not really hearing him. Viner's earlier question about her not leaving had stuck in her mind. Lineheardt had never even thought about leaving the fatal mountain.

She needed to talk to the Swiss and they needed to listen to her. The Swiss had a bottomless pit of ignorance about the H-Bomb, and they wanted her to throw knowledge into it. Their eyes would defocus as she explained the technical facets of the complicated reaction. They never stopped listening or started understanding. They just took it in a state of bliss. They believed that hearing the words of it from 1 of the originators blessed them. For her part Lineheardt craved an audience for the story of Phil's humiliation of the plagiarist Starzinchger, which she weaved into the physics like an apostle in love with a stammering child of god.

Cpl· Erving Lehman and Sgt· Kelly Clark demonstrate "parade rest" for Evelyn's All Girl Orchestra at Ziraleet's Ghaziabad· The Pfc sees someone in the audience so charming he doesn't hear the command·

1950

May 12

The day after Lineheardt moved in with him, Viner saw his car parked in front of the Army headquarters trailer. A corporal was sitting behind the wheel, looking at Viner, bored. Furious, Viner ran to the door, pulled it open and yanked the corporal out from behind the wheel.

"Who do you think you are?" he screamed at the corporal.

A door to the trailer opened. Someone was coming out, but nothing was going to stop Viner. He had seen so much of this scavenging, the brazen display of his stolen car had touched a fury center inside him.

"You think you can take a car because someone left his keys in it! You drive it around anywhere you like and nothing's going to happen!"

"I took your car, not him," said the man who'd come out of the trailer.

Viner turned to see a tall ugly man with red hair scattered about his head. It was Starzinchger.

Feeling stupid, Viner let the surprised corporal go. In checking Lineheardt's 3 sport coats for **THE STORY OF**

287

OUR CENTURY, Viner had heard how Starzinchger, scared to death of radiation from the burst, had run down the mountain in a blind panic, stolen the 1st car he'd come to with keys in it, and fled to LA. It now seemed somehow unreal and yet pleasing that Starzinchger had stolen his car. Starzinchger was apologizing to him, trying to explain how the blast had scrambled his powers of reasoning and morality. He ended by praising the Nash effusively.

"Why don't you keep it," Viner found himself saying. "I really don't need it anymore."

"Thanks," said Starzinchger, delighted. "That's great."

"Why was it so much bigger than everyone said," Viner demanded suddenly. "How come only Phil knew how powerful it was going to be?"

"I'm not sure yet," said Starzinchger, brusquely. "I've got to go."

Viner watched the Nash go down the naked mountain. He had hoped to be magnanimous. Exactly what was it he was reaching for with all this generosity? Such impulses had been ruling his life ever since he had met Phil. Giving the car to Starzinchger was just as rewarding as his stupid kidnapping of Spike and Noreen. And saving all the Swiss from the bomb? What had that done for him or them?

Yes, he had fallen in love with gratitude; and now that he was so infatuated with it, he was allowed to smell only the smothering dust of it. He watched his beautiful pearl-grey Nash descending the mountain like a sled sliding down fine snow. A billowing vapor trail of frosted grey blew uphill all over him. He felt a suffocating desire to have the Nash back again, even though he had no further use for it.

Inside the trailer they had asked Starzinchger several times for an explanation of the high yield. They seemed not to hear their own answers to his questions about radiation levels. The whole mountain was still a glowing heap of deadly radioactivity. The levels were so high, they didn't make any sense. The H-bomb was supposed to be a cleaner nuclear explosion than the A-bomb, but this burst had been not only the biggest thing man had ever detonated, it had also been the dirtiest. He got the hell off the mountain, determined to never come back.

It took several truckloads of exhaustively analyzed radioactive dust from 52 to figure out why the yield had been so high. In addition to what he had expected to find in the bomb residue, Starzinchger found significant amounts of Uranium 237. The uranium in the A-bomb fuse for the fusion reaction had consisted only of U235 and U238. U238, ordinary uranium, was used as a casing for the volatile U235, the fissile material of an A-bomb.

So where had the U237 come from? U237 was a very rare isotope of uranium which could be produced only in tiny amounts by bombardment of U238 with high energy neutrons. In Phil's bomb the U235 became fissile and provided

ENOUGH FUCKING PHYSICS ALREADY, ASSHOLE

the super heat necessary to trigger a fusion reaction with the tritium liberated from the lithium compounds. But these reactions would produce perhaps 3 megatons, not 10, and no U237.

When Starzinchger finally figured it out, he thought Phil must have heard the noise of the answer somewhere beneath the surface of things Phil had already known. The U237 was present because a lot of U238 had been bombarded with a lot of high energy neutrons in a way which no 1 had foreseen.

There was a 3rd step in the reaction which only Phil had sensed might be there. The unprecedented gush of neutrons created by combining an A-bomb and an H-bomb had pushed the entire U238 wrapping into its own incredibly powerful explosion. What Phil had created was a fission fusion fission reaction. The whole bomb casing had become fissile and added bonus megatons to the burst.

Starzinchger felt nervous when he went to Lillo with his solution for the presence of U237. Lillo thought Starzinchger was wrong and suggested additional examination of the lithium 7's role in the reaction. Lillo didn't mention that Phil had come to him years ago in Chicago about lithium 6 and 7, and he and Phil had nearly invented an H-Bomb then and there, but quickly dropped it because they had a hundred such ideas a day, and what good could come of that 1? They talked of Phil's genius.

"He must have known it like so many other things he'd sensed without being able to put names or formulas to them," Starzinchger said.

They both knew Starzinchger was being credited with the burst in Washington. Starzinchger waited anxiously for Lillo to ask him to give Phil some recognition. But Lillo said nothing. For years afterward Starzinchger would have rabbit ears for second hand remarks from Lillo objecting to Starzinchger's designation as the Father of the H-bomb while Phil's name disappeared, but there was never anything to hear.

Nobody in the Army or the AWB ever reproved him for destroying 52 and Jake. They were anxious not to offend him. He was asked only if he could control it better. He promised he could; but they didn't believe him, and all future fusion experiments were conducted in remote areas of the Pacific. It took him a long time to reproduce enough of Phil's work to detonate a 2nd burst and bring himself public recognition as the **Father of the H-bomb**. The burst in Nevada was destined to remain a secret from the public in order to avoid a deluge of lawsuits against the AWB.

While perfecting Phil's fusion work, our **Father of the H-bomb** woke up several times a year with startling images of vast spaces chilled to absolute 0 by tiny devices. He returned to his work on miniaturizing refrigeration. But he pursued the vision with a meandering listless mind, turning over his staff with incredible velocity, sending them on their way in wild spasms of anger. He turned away from refrigeration for good and came back to the other gem of Phil's work.

Ground Zero had been found right in the middle of 52. Not the miles and miles up the range Huke had promised everyone. Many had said that meant the rail cannon had failed. But our   suspected that the rail cannon had worked exactly like the burst. Too well. Like much of Phil's work, it had worked too well.

He spent 5 years failing to bring the rail cannon even to the same point Phil had achieved in less than a year when the 1st fusion shell had come tumbling out its muzzle with such incredible velocity Huke had been presented no chance to be surprised that he had overcooked the exit velocity. He was gratified the instant the trigger code worked, and vapor the next.

1950

June 12

Lineheardt enjoyed Viner's new fascination with uncoupling the word "delight." He had many thoughts about the badness of light.

"The subtraction of light, the de-lighting of the world, might return everything to its original state of pleasure before man was created," he offered her. "What was God's original state?"

"Darkness," she mused, thinking she wanted to fall in love with this heart-spring of exciting stupidity, but she just couldn't manage it now that the zeppelin of her physics was a dot in the sky.

"I'm worried I'm telling people the wrong things," Viner changed the subject.

Jakes had always hated tourists and their stupid state of mind. It had irritated them that visitors assumed Jake was Sodom where all the residents were engaged in perpetually thrilling vile sins. Jakes believed they lived the same tedium as those who operated auto parts stores in Chattanooga. Jakes said they went to hotels only when their relatives came to town and dragged them out. The neon which coated the skins of visitors with colored mania was only so many lights to them, as common as desert sand, they had lied. Now their grief for that missing color light tranquilized the Swiss. His favorite symptom of their loss was a new affection for Viner which had tiny particles of gratitude attached to it.

Lineheardt was laughing at him.

"No, don't, no." Her laughter scared him as much as the bomb had.

"Look, don't you know you're a different person from what you were before you met Phil?"

"I am?"

"You don't have to win arguments any more," her eyes were fondling him as if he were a pet. "You let your wild thoughts die. You'd rather listen than talk."

"No," he lied to her. "I want them to understand"

"No, you don't," she laughed again. "I'm that person."

He fussed over her for breakfast, lunch, and dinner, imitating her movements, puzzling out the intentions in her thoughts and taking them into his notebook. His Boswell instinct attached itself to her. He was a listener now. She had convinced him of it. He studied her free fall through the Swiss, conversation by conversation. She was a doctor stroking anxious limbs in a dying leper colony. There was no hope for a cure. There was only her care in caressing the deformed bones of the victims.

After she died, Viner put his notebook aside. It was valueless, a patchwork of praise for Phil, Lillo, Jake in its death spiral, and finally Lineheardt who had become his greatest living hero, chaste in manner and gorgeous in deed. He'd been wrong to promise her he hated sex. He had wanted her the 1st night they'd been together, and every night afterwards. A good-bye kiss from her wonderful mouth was all he'd had of her. He hated himself for not asking for what she said she would give to him while denying all others.

He introduced himself to a woman with beta burns in the dining hall and took her back to the trailer. He touched her on 1 of her purple burns, feeling it like a puzzle he could solve if he stroked it long enough. When she left, he was visited by Lineheardt's ghost talking to him about Einstein. Her ghost was everywhere the rest of the day, mixing in with the memory of the woman he'd made love to. By night they were the same, and it was as if he'd made love with Lineheardt.

Curious about what was happening in his distended gut, Viner went to the hospital library to read how the doctors said he was supposed to die. Lineheardt had told him of Queequeg from Rokovoko, probably a Maori prince, who had mistaken the moments of his imminent death so that God could provide a coffin for his best friend Ismael to use as a float against drowning. Was there somewhere in this report a coffin he could use to float past these death officers who called themselves doctors?

Because everyone thought of him as the reporter who was going to tell Jake's story, he had no trouble persuading the WAC nurse to give him access to the medical files.

He was distracted by his boredom with the medical terminology and a fear of the stench which was everywhere in the hospital, an unmistakable smell which seemed to bother the nurse not at all.

He found 1 long report, dog-eared from repeated handling. It was entitled Acute Radiation Syndrome. It was several hundred pages long. The symptoms and deaths of several victims of accidental acute whole-body irradiation were described in medical language. The cases were dated and the patients were referred to as Case #1, Case #2 ****

Halfway through Case #3, he sat up alert and sweating with excitement. It had to be Phil's friend. He was reading about Barbanel. Case #3, 1945, had thrown himself on 2 small lumps of fissile bomb metal and tried to pull them apart. He had used his body to protect the other physicists in the room. It was definitely Barbanel. There was a picture of him from the neck down. He was sitting in his bed with elephantine hands displayed in his lap.

They'd packed Barbanel's hands in ice to control the swelling. Cyanosis resulted. Cyanosis, the nurse responded to his question, was a blue jaundice. The report compared Barbanel's radiation burns to flames. The difference seemed to be that with radiation the flesh was slow to recognize the burn. The blistering and swelling might take days to develop.

Barbanel had a punishing ileus. He was monstrously distended from gas. Ileus, the nurse said, impatient with his persistent medical ignorance, was a blocked intestine. They put gastric suction down his nose and sucked out a green fluid with a fecal odor.

"It smelled like shit," Viner whispered to himself in horror as he read the report. "He just lay there and they vacuumed shit up out of his guts through his nose."

The suction relieved Barbanel's pain. The report was surprised by the large amount of fluid coming up. The 1st night they took 2 quarts of it out of him. They kept taking it out until he died because it was his only relief from the pain. They had tried morphine at 1st, but his pain was much stronger than the largest dose of morphine they could prescribe without killing him.

The patient complained of pain along his tongue. 1 of the gold inlays in his teeth was alive with radiation. It was frying his gums and his tongue. They capped it with foil. Viner saw Lineheardt's ghost showing him her neck sprinkled with hot silver tailings.

Barbanel complained also of a sharp pain in his testes.

"This was the original atomic hero," Viner said out loud. He looked up, anxious not to attract more attention from the irritable nurse.

He read on, admiring Barbanel as if he were a favorite ancestor. Barbanel had given Phil something which, through Lineheardt, had passed on to him. It was the stupid love of gratitude which shrank the survival instinct to something puny and disgusting.

On the 8th day the patient's lips turned cyanotic. Viner arrived at something in the report called the Gross Protocol. The Gross Protocol described the patient's build and nutrition. Barbanel's nutrition was good. The Gross Protocol went on to say the patient's flesh was still warm except for the hands which were cold from treatment with ice. He realized he was reading now in a time past Barbanel's death. This was an autopsy.

The Gross Protocol said rigor mortis had set in so strongly the jaw could not be pried open. It also said that the patient had liver mortis on his buttock, his back, his neck, and even his right ear. It occurred in irregular mottled spreads of bluish purple. Except his ear, which was solid purple. There were fissures in his gums. The Gross Protocol went on about Barbanel's skin, about hair loss, and other details.

Viner began to see the pathologist at work, as if it were an event taking place in the present, right before him. He watched surgical gloves peeling back dead eyelids.

The pathologist bends over and looks in. He announces the eyes are sunken and hemorrhaged. He pulls back the lips so that Barbanel looks like a frightened ape. He notices the vertical fissures in the gums. He struggles to pry open the jaw but can't. He feels about the abdomen. It is swollen and purple. He slices it open. Immediately the small intestines protrude, distended with gas. There is a sour odor. All of Barbanel's abdominal organs are bathing in the fecal liquid they'd been vacuuming up his nose. Even his lungs are full of it. The pathologist makes a slight incision in the protruding intestine. It shoots fluid up in his face.

"Ugh!" he says dodging quickly aside.

He stands at a distance cleaning himself and watching it spray like a slit garden hose.

"That poor son of a bitch must have hurt."

1950

June 14

Viner walked through what was left of Jake, a few trailers and a hospital, taking the pleasure of the afternoon spring air. For the last month people had approached him with mementos they wanted him to have. No one was still pretending that the world would ever give a shit about the story of the century. Just now someone had given him a key chain from the Dog, and clasped his hand around it with gratitude and no mention of Viner's duties as their journalist.

All he had left of Lineheardt was her good bye kiss when he'd visited her in the hospital against her wishes. Like he was going to respect that request? It was in the same class as "Shall I come to Jake with the girls?"

The night before she committed her body to the doctors they both hated, she had told him to stop worrying about Queequeg's failure to die on his own schedule.

"You will granulate your kind spirit into dense particles and cast them to the other side. The same way distant novas send us spider lattices of gravity filaments."

Lineheardt held his hand across the wobbly table in the Airstream. They were drinking Jack Daniels he had mixed with ink to make resemble the color of their favorite Greek Spit. She still liked holding his hand when they were getting drunk. She went on talking about the death of his own volition, using the same affectionate tones she wasted on her worship of Phil.

"Who is so wrong now?" Viner mumbled. "She is barking shit physics here."

He wanted to see into her eyes to check for lieing, but she was wearing the busted pair of sunglasses she had rigged up with the spandex from a white watch band. He had to settle for watching her mouth. He was helpless before it. He believed everything which exited this pretty opening. He went back to swilling his toxic ink with his head down.}

Her endorsement of his death plan made it possible. She was as smart as any of them.

He no longer felt like talking about the things he had done so wrong. He reviewed a few of the things he might never talk about again. Like trying to make Phil look stupid so everyone would believe it was a flood. He went into his trailer and put the Dog key chain in his red metal box. He thought about not screwing Lineheardt. He came back out.

What about his foolish love of gratitude, like saving Spike and Noreen? That was a kidnapping risking a lifetime in jail for a matched pair of bimbos. Giving the car to Starzinchger, worse than stupid. Coming back to be with his people, fatally stupid. No, no, not. Stop it. He must not indulge this recreation of judging himself. He could ease himself away giving up such fun.

This beautiful afternoon the remaining Swiss smiled at him as if he were a minister. The hours passed with quiet pointless talking to the few left in Jake.

Viner had thought that after he had divided the sex professionals from his life, the remainder which kept him in Jake was the glorious squirming color everywhere - the neon, the cars, the clothes, the slot machines**** But now he knew it wasn't that. Now, looking at this grey sex-dead ash mountain where the last few dying lavished their affection on him, the final mystery of his life bloomed open for understanding.

He had been unable to sever himself from Jake because jakes delighted in him. They loved his wrong-minded shit even while they hated him for being wrong. After radiating death had scorched everything out of Jake anybody could advertise as pretty, there was still this 1 thing left over for Viner which made Jake wonderful and bound him to it. His desperate unsuccessful efforts to save all the jakes had made him the Swiss hero; and they all, brilliant and dumb, forgave his histrionic errors and loved him for starring in the blindstorm they were lost in.

He stopped near what had been the timberline of Trembling Peak, and thought back to Lineheardt's face smiling at him when he brought her into the Airstream. He felt himself turn grateful he had never troubled their friendship with sex. And coming back to die with the Swiss as their pastor without portfolio, what was so bad about that? Suddenly, he didn't even regret giving his beautiful car to that asshole Starzinchger anymore.

Many of the wonderful things he had said on his tv show fell through his mind like snow falling on a hot volcano. These exquisite perceptions had been so beautiful, each in its own instant, but now there was no way to ever see or care about them again. They were melting on the ghostly heat from the columns of lava he had promised Lineheardt would be blowing up Trembling Peak through the 100 years of tunnels the miners had built.

He sat down on a flat rock. He studied the clouding sky.

Wads of grey cloud cotton lolled across the twilight. A mood started deep in his limbic system, rising lazily to creep across his brain. This frontier of calm blotted his apprehension 1 dot at a time, as if crossing in time with the cotton clouds, until his ears were red and a smile leaked up his cheeks. Tens of minutes passed as the grey cotton moved. The sky became a dome of it, and then it was night. Black and peaceful. Moonless. A world without thoughts of light or unhappiness.

1950

Sept 1

Late that summer Spike and Noreen went back to Jake. They caught sight of the grey peak early in the afternoon. At 1st they thought all the grey meant the mountain was covered with hardened lava. They saw clusters of glinting hives where Jake had been. When they got close enough they saw that the silver hives were Airstream trailers. They drove up the mountain and found the Army busy bulldozing what was left of Jake into a smooth bed of rubble. The Airstream trailers were being hooked up to jeeps and pulled away.

They went into a large frame building filled with picnic tables. A lieutenant told them the Army was winding things up. He seemed to think they were relatives of somebody from Jake. Relatives of the Swiss tended to pass themselves off as residents, he said. Noreen insisted she was a Jake resident. The lieutenant smiled. He said the Army would soon extend the perimeter of Testrange 52 and close the gates to all civilians, whether they were Swiss or not.

"What does he mean, 'Swiss'?" asked Spike as they walked along the ruined 4th Street.

Noreen shrugged.

They wandered into a pole building which looked like a hospital. A single guard pointed like an automaton towards a room down the hall.

Inside they met a talkative clerk who went on about how the Swiss had turned from going through the hotel rubble to picking through homes. This searching mechanism was different than the treasure hunting. As the clerk talked, Spike realized that the rows of bins behind the clerk contained all the things the Swiss had left behind for whomever cared enough to make a claim for the best of the items their lives had left behind.

"That guy Viner, he was some kind of a moron, he told me to start this department," the clerk said "It got me out of the wards. Everyone pretended to have a nose full of Novocaine, but it was so bad**** That's the way cholera smelled. Did you ever know that cholera, the great disease of the West, is a disease where people pour diarrhea out their asses faster than they can drink water? That's the disease of the West. Pouring liquid out your bottom until****"

Noreen looked at him with hatred so he became quiet with embarrassment.

"Do you have anything back there from that guy Viner himself?" asked Spike. "The moron."

"Yeah," apologized the clerk . "It was weird how he went. He just laid down on a rock and died. He just turned off the switch, like 1 of those Apache Zen guys who can turn off their hearts. Did you know him?"

"We had the honor," said Spike fiercely.

"Sorry," said the clerk. "I never knew that."

There was a letter from Lineheardt to Viner between the pages of Viner's notebook, which, according to an un-

signed note beneath it, had been written with her favorite colored ink from the bottles supplied to Viner by the

Army for THE STORY OF THE CENTURY.

Found on table unfinished. A.V.

Dear Lex,

Don't visit me.... I knocked my head on the
door trying to go outside. It made me so dizzy
I had to sit down and then I threw up in my lap.
Something I never told you. It was cold sleeping
outside before you took me in; I've never
known anything so cold. Phil used to talk
about standing at the point of their woods in
Wisconsin in February waiting for the bunny
to come out when he was a kid, how cold it
was,
well, that's what it was like at night here lying on the
dust. So Thanks.

About physicists combing up greatness for
themselves. They say that if you shear off a
mountain at sea level, a new one the same size will
work its way up in the same place in a few thousand
years. Think of the vast spread of pressure in physics
which lifted Einstein and Hilb so high. We may
look at the white gleaming spike Relativity and
admire it as a glittering snow peak atop a
volcanic foment of science, but it is not, as the
newspapers would have it, the whole amazing
mountain. The Einsteins, like generals, let other
people fight anomalously while they award
themselves medals.

Don't visit me

"Is it true about mountains?" asked Spike.

"I don't know," said Noreen.

304

She flipped through Viner's notes, trying to find clues of what else had happened to him. Lineheardt died in the hospital and was cremated. Limbs swell up, Viner's handwriting said with Fs which looked like Ts. Eyes too, until they're twice their normal size. It is a problem for people who want sex. People try to hide their deformities when they make matches, and arguments break out when swelling or burns are revealed at the disrobing. People are anxious to avoid the syndrome where a couple turns out to be too sick to make love or vomit blood because the excitement is too much. But usually no matter what horrible sight comes out during the disrobing, they go ahead anyway.

Noreen looked up for Spike who had wandered away to look out the window. The window's yellow screen of light made his face gold on 1 side and grey on the other.

"Did you see this?" she called to him.

"What?" he asked, coming back.

"The spots on women's skin have a piercing emotional appeal," she read in a whisper so the clerk couldn't hear. "Most of them are all dappled with purple now."

To
One of my favo
bosses —
With sincere
admiration
Dottie

Dorothy Lamour

They found more artifacts of Swiss life in Viner's red metal box. A key chain from the Dog, which Spike sneaked into his pocket. A toy roulette wheel from Horror Hall. A scorched family bible. People had given them to Viner to save when they were ready to die. Noreen slid Viner's notebook up her back under her lavishly cabled purple sweater. The clerk watched her hide it. He didn't say a thing. He didn't care. She could have walked out waving it like a ball park hotdog.

They left Jake soon after, driving down the mountain in a trance, not talking for hours. Evening showed them a giant roof of chrome with a single pearl stud, Venus. When they reached Arizona, Spike opened up like a beer can dropped from the 20th floor. What a pair Phil and Viner were. It was a lot of gibber to Noreen, sprinkled with far too many "holy chuck"s. It seemed like there was a race in Spike's mind for who was better, Phil or Viner. And after an hour of blather, Viner won.

"Did you ever notice that Viner said some pretty dumb things along the way?" Noreen had always found Viner decently stupid.

"Sometimes us stupid people get it right," Spike puffed his own stunted mental powers. "All the brain power in the world won't make your emotions smart. To get it right, to be right, you have to solve the emotions and that is not a brainy deal; it's a different system of stuff."

"Oh, ok," said Noreen. "I turn off my brain and I'm an emotional genius."

"All the brainy stuff you wizards have, that's just shine you buff on what you do after you do it," he said petting her arm on the seat. "If your emotions stink, so do you, no matter how smartly you lay it on."

"So I stink because I'm right most of the time?" she laughed. "Holy chuck."

"No," laughed Spike. "1 day, you'll get it because you love me."

"Get what?"

"How Viner got so good after he was so wrong."

"I can't wait," snorted Noreen.

"That guy was a saint, stupid."

Erving won the Mid-Amateur at Saucon Valley which resulted in the amazing sight of Doctor Professor Golfer Jew wandering down fairways in the Masters at Augusta National

1950

Nov 1

Erving came out to the street with his eyes blinking to recover from the darkness of watching **ROCKY MOUNTAIN**. He walked along the long line attracted to its next screening. He was nowhere near the primary mandate of his manhood trip. He was returning to **ROCKY MOUNTAIN** day after day because many teen lookers were going to this movie to admire the sincerity of Patrice Wymore. But none of them would talk to him very long. He wasn't spellbinding them in supermarkets and department stores either. Connecticut girls were unlike the Eastern girls who appeared at the Ziraleet pool.

Of course not, he lectured himself. He was acting as wild as a physicist with expensive machines and no theory. Girls were excited, isolated and fearful in Jake, just like new cadets at **E.N.M.S**. But here in Connecticut, they were as comfortable as a 2nd lieutenant. He knew how to make 7th graders drill like they were at West Point, but he needed something for the female who would never be going to military school. It had nothing to do with leadership. In this war, the girls were Tallyrands, vulnerable only to ambassadors from rich foreign nations.

Walking past them on the sidewalk, he was taunted again by their indifferent presence. Was their only role in his life to soak up his admiration as if he were as distant and mute as a cold star?

No! Something new and wonderful came into his knowing pool. When he reached the end of the line, he got in it again, now with no intention of seeing the next show. He had hit upon an experiment in pretty girl physics which had something smart to it. They won't be able to move away, he thought, as he planned his new tactic. Plus, he would have something they wanted.

{Pollyte's father taught Greek and Latin at a Connecticut's best Quaker prep school. She had always loved her father's Greek books, playing with them as a toddler.

He responded by reading them to her. They could play together in this manner for hours. At 3 she was a favorite at the golf club pool for babbling to herself in Greek. By the time she was 7, she was seeking out diner owners in their kitchens to chat with them in a mixture of ancient and modern Greek about her lunch.

Out of her admiration for her father and her love of Greece, her high school junior year project was "The Young Quaker's Journey to Ilium," a story about a teenage girl who translated passages from THE ILIAD in the darkness of movie theatres. This girl, who looked like a priestess with gorgeous hands, furnished Ingres-like images of Trojan war events along with citations of how shamelessly Hollywood copied Homer's story devices.}

Today was All Saints Day which was a no school day on her unofficial calendar so she was waiting in line for a matinée, smoking L&M's with her pretty friend Rhonnie. As a 2some, they often locked up the vision field of passing custodians of the male hormone. She noticed a tall young-ish guy walk up to the line about halfway to the ticket box. He had a nice tie tucked between the buttons of a French blue dress shirt like he was in the Army. Was he wearing cuff links?

She watched him talk for a while and then come down the line to stop and talk again. He was wearing perfectly tai-lored grey pants. No loose fabric around the hips and lower thighs. He was stopping to talk to girls. There was a 3some about his age, 15 she guessed, but they just giggled at him so he moved on down the line. He stopped for a presenta-tion to a woman in her twenties. They exchanged hostili-ties and he moved on.

"What's he doing?" Rhonnie asked.

"He will talk to us," guessed Pollyte, blowing smoke rings which suggested this was not her 1st cigarette. "He's a little young."

He did have cuff links, each a brilliant silver star like she might see on a military uniform.

"Look, he wants to be a general," Rhonnie had noticed the cuff links, too. "I want him. You have your Yalie boyfriend."

"He's not my boyfriend."

"He was Tuesday when you had your hand in his pants."

"He thinks I should squeeze his sex aneurysm because he dresses well," Pollyte laughed at the boyfriend who was losing more status the closer Erving got. "Why is Jeff so proud of his clothes? His pants are too baggy, and he stuffs so much stuff into his pockets."

Rhonnie whinnied.

"Now look at this 1," Pollyte compared Erving to Jeff. "Those slacks are snug."

The well tailored athletic warrior stopped for a girl who ignored him. He was standing so martially straight, he looked like Achilles telling Brises to kill Agamemnon.

"He's kind of young," repeated Pollyte as he approached her and Rhonnie.

"Are you tired of waiting in this line?" Erving asked Pollyte, his eyes lit with hostile charm.

"What about me?" demanded Rhonnie turning her bosom a little. "What if I'm tired?"

"I have tickets for both of you," he said. "Let's go in."

"Do you play basketball?" asked Rhonnie, blowing out starlet smoke.

"Yes," conceded Erving.

"I have a friend who knows Ed Leede on the Boston Celtics," bragged Rhonnie.

"I'm from Las Vegas," said Erving, getting out his phony driver's license to prove it. "How are you're going to do in a name dropping contest with someone who lives at the Last Frontier hotel in Las Vegas?"

Pollyte smiled and her eyes brightened with aquamarine neon.

Rhonnie grabbed the license.

"I mostly play golf," added Erving while they inspected his driver's license with the same doubt Erving had shown his father 3000 miles earlier.

Pollyte

"You live at the Last Frontier Hotel?" asked Rhonnie, looking at him as the physicists had at the ski lodge years ago. "What kind of person grows up in a hotel in Las Vegas?"

"Nobody grows up in Las Vegas," shared Erving. "You have to leave first."

"This is a fake." Pollyte said, handing back the drivers license. Her smile and tone said she liked the deception.

"Who do you know then?" asked Rhonnie.

"Jeff Chandler, for one" said Erving, pointing at the nearby poster for 'Broken Arrow with Jeff

Jeff Chandler

Chandler as Cochise !!!!!' ."

"You know Jeff Chandler," squealed Rhonnie. "I love his big lips"

"Herb Shriner, Marlyn Maxwell, Howard Hughes, Tony Lema, the golfer." Erving was smiling now, looking at Pollyte even though he was talking to Rhonnie. "Johnny Van Neuman, Xavier Cugat, Tony Martin and Cyd Charise, Hildegarde, and Ralph Leach."

"Who is Ralph Leach?" Rhonnie asked. (Did that mean she recognized all the other names?)

"Vice Chairman of the Morgan Guaranty Trust Company," bragged Erving. Did no one understand that even huge figures in the world of finance could stop by Ziraleet independently of but on the same day as the President and First Lady of Turkey?

"She plays golf," Rhonnie informed him, assuming the role of Pollyte's wing honey. "And she speaks Greek."

Rhonnie had bigger breasts and was graded prettier than Pollyte in everyone's slam book, but there was something in Pollyte which both sexes of all ages craved. Maybe the effortless friendliness. The exquisite fingers. Or the luminous skin? Uh, huh, but there was more. She always had some magical pearl she would whip out from a secret pocket and hold forward in her palm to say "look at this" and anyone would be mesmerized.

"You speak Greek?" asked Erving, getting excited. "What do you know about Santorini?"

"Η Σαντορίνη ήταν δεδομένη από Triton στη Λιβύη για την Ελληνική Αργοναυτική Εκστρατεία Euphemus, γιος του Ποσειδώνα, με τη μορφή ενός Ψλοδ ανδ στιψκινγ βρωμιάς," said Pollyte. "Euphemus ονειρευτεί ο ίδιος τις ακαθαρσίες με γάλα από το στήθος, και ότι οι ακαθαρσίες μετατράπηκε σε μια όμορφη γυναίκα με τους οποίους είχε φύλο." Η ομοιότητες εδώ με την καταστροφή της Τροίας είναι λογοκλοπής. Ι επιστροφή της έντασης χωρίς να τελειώνει. Ο οποίος, από το δρόμο, βρίσκεται ο Βιργίλιος."

"What the hell is that?" Erving howled.

There was the pearl. Different for every person but easy to tell it had come out by looking at whom she was showing it to. Erving sounded like a Siberian Husky meeting the moon.

"Greek." said Rhonnie "That is Greek."

"What did you say?" he demanded of Pollyte.

"Santorini was given by Triton in Libya to the Greek Argonaut Euphemus, son of Poseidon, in the form of a clod of dirt," she translated the Greek mythology. "Euphemus dreamed that he nursed the dirt with milk from his breast, and that the dirt turned into a beautiful woman with whom he made love."

Erving laughed so loudly he sounded like Santorini, the volcano itself, blowing up with a huge laugh that could carry across continents and darken the world with merriment. But today it only darkened the face of the 20 whatever beauty Erving had challenged earlier. Pollyte watched Erving field her scowl and instantly return hatred, again like Achilles, but this time more like Achilles staring at Hector for killing his best friend. His volcanic glare mixed in with the stentorian laughter as neatly as cream in coffee.

"How many tickets do you have in your pocket?" asked Rhonnie.

"Ten."

"Ten?" disapproved Pollyte, initiating the cross-fertilization of their positions on money. "Why would you think you had to spend so much?"

"Might have seen a girl I liked out with her volleyball team," Erving answered in a flash, "You want to go inside instead of waiting another half hour out here?"

"Is the offer good if I'm going steady?" asked Pollyte.

"Duh," mocked Erving. "I never thought of that"

"I'm not."

"Does that equal yes."

"Yes."

"Do you say yes to lots of stuff," asked Erving.

"Yes," argued Pollyte.

Erving was a tiny tachyon approaching an object of immense gravity faster than the speed of light. She wasn't what Lehman had sent him to find. Lehman didn't even know such females existed.

"Do you say yes to everything?"

"Try me," she smiled, taking his hand and leading him out of the line towards the movie with Rhonnie tagging along behind, flushed with devotion to her best friend.

"When she was 9," Rhonnie told Erving as they sat down inside, "she was the New Haven junior junior champion in golf."

Erving was bored by the movie since he had seen it 6 times already. He whispered the story of a massive Russian caldera called Kurile Lake until Pollyte quieted him by shoving her tongue into his mouth.

To her delight, he was staying with friends of her parents who had found him playing golf alone. This happy accident gave him a high social ranking despite the Las Vegas origin. She took him to parties and taught him the Twist. In less than a week she got him drunk, deflowered, and hooked on L&Ms.

"I'm not going to be a physicist," Erving answered Jim Roman with disgust.

{ Lehman took Erving to the ski lodge to meet physicists because Lehman thought Erving was interested in physics.

All the physicists came kissing up to Lehman, and 1 after another they were astounded that Lehman, the pleasure obsessed degenerate, could muster enough domestic interest to have a son. They looked upon Erving as a biological oddity. Like he was a 3 armed dwarf. Even when Erving talked their physics, they didn't listen, but looked back and forth between him and Lehman.

Erving liked physics because it had been around him for as

317

long as he could remember. Even before he had been sent away to military school, he had enjoyed watching the physicists who came to Ziraleet to gamble. He liked that they were so Eastern. He eavesdropped on them in the lounge. They were non-stop weird when they were drunk and trying to impress B girls with bomb lore. Well after the ski lodge injury, he still liked to listen to them even if they were all assholes. He explained to Sonia it was possible to like physics without being an asshole yourself.}

"Except for you, physicists are assholes" Erving confided in Jim, considering it something of a favor he was doing for Jim not to paint him with their dirty brush.

"How can you say that with such conviction?" asked Jim. "Physics is always coming out in your thinking."

Erving stared at Jim's black and grey hair, his thin pointed nose and slender neck. The tight mouth, through which he hissed when he was upset, was relaxed. Jim looked over and caught Erving staring at him with affection. His own deep set eyes fired for an instant, but he quickly turned to look out the windshield again.

"I'm a vulcanologist," Erving mocked.

Jim laughed happily.

"All the girls I meet here, and everyone else, they're all full of questions about Las Vegas," said Erving. "What's it like to grow up in such a sinful town, and all that shit. They believe everything I say, but you never ask any of that."

"No," said Jim, getting out of Erving's Cadillac.

Erving got out too and they started inside.

"Except 1," added Erving. "She doesn't believe anything I say."

"That would be Pollyte?" asked Jim.

318

"What about her?"

"She's the 1 who doesn't believe you."

The mashed potato clouds were starting to leak. The wind whipped cold darts of rain into their faces. They hurried across the lumpy stone patio and in through the kitchen door.

"What were you 2 talking about out there?" asked Janet.

"He was giving me some advice," said Erving. "He thinks I should be a physicist."

"He brings out the worst in people when he gives advice," said Janet.

"And I'm pretty sure he likes Pollyte," added Erving.

"I'm going to start a fire," said Jim, stepping quickly into the keeping room.

"I thought you made a rule you were never going to give advice to anyone ever again," Janet called after him.

Erving went to help Jim roll newspapers for the firebox.

"You don't know very much about me," said Erving. "But you're adopting me. That's what you've done, you know. You've adopted me."

"We like to think it was the other way around," said Jim.

"You don't even know me," said Erving. "You don't know the 1st thing about me."

"We know a lot about you," said Jim, laying twigs on top of the rolled newspapers.

"Sure," said Erving. "You don't even know if I'm really from Las Vegas. You looked at my watch like it was from Mars."

The day they'd met on the golf course, Erving had caught Jim staring at the diamond scabbed Rolex as if it were a huge boil. He'd vowed that thing was never getting on his

RUFF Nº 2

wrist again. "Maybe I'm from Brooklyn. Maybe I walked into Yeshiva Used Cars and held them up for their star car, the week's receipts, and the owner's watch."

"I don't have to ask questions about your past to know who you are," said Jim, putting the last of 3 large birch logs on the twigs. "Everything that's important is perfectly visible in you now."

"Oh, come on," said Erving. "You don't know me."

"I know you have grown up with distant parents," said Jim. "You've always had a lot of time on your hands. I know that you don't trust anyone and hate money. I know you fear nothing, even though you should."

Jim looked about for the box of fire matches. Erving found them on the candlestand.

"I know that you have fantasies about a thug coming to hurt Janet so you can throw yourself at him like a wolverine," said Jim, opening the tall polka dot box of matches. "Most of your attractive character was visible the 1st afternoon we met on the golf course. The 3 of us enjoy each other's company, don't we? Why should I threaten that by probing a past which obviously makes you uncomfortable?"

Jim struck the long match and touched it to the corners of the rolled newspapers.

"You think your father is the smartest person who ever lived, but I imagine he's no smarter than you, if he's even your equal."

Jim gave Erving a smug look which suggested that as a Yale physics professor he'd had some chances to see what smart was.

"But what about the money?" asked Erving. There was a sharp pain in his temples. "Don't you wonder about all the money, about where I got it?"

"Hrnssngrsss!" hissed Jim, his calm suddenly tainted with anger. "I know where you got it."

"Where?" demanded Erving, angry back.

"Your parents gave it to you."

The birch bark began to snap like tiny firecrackers.

1950

Nov 2

That night Erving dreamed he was living alone in Hawaii in a seedy apartment building exactly like the Vogue in Jake where he had lived for awhile with Lehman and Sonia when he was a sergeant, and the family was so busted from too much gambling they owned no hotels. There was nobody he knew in this dream of Hawaii. He was walking down a street pitted with bottomless shadows, so fucking lonely, there was nobody to know and nobody to talk to. He went into his building and up to his apartment.

There were a lot of people in his apartment, and they were all getting ready to have a party but he knew none of them. They all seemed to know him. They greeted him like friends. There was a girl who knew he was faking his age. She thought it was funny that he was only 14. She pointed out the window with beautiful fingers.

He'd been doing a lot of reading about volcanoes with Jim's Yale library card so when he looked out the window, he recognized the cloud right away. It was a nuée ardente blooming through all the colors of the prism and then settling on purple. Its dirty stem was lined with crimson-lake

Master Erving Lehman home from Elsinore Naval & Military School where he has reached the rank of sergeant

lavender while a darker mineral violet mixed around inside its head like purple clothes in a murky washing machine. He was in Hawaii so a volcano was blowing up into the sky. This 1 looked bigger than Tambor. It roiled upwards as if someone had gutted the earth to its magma and all the ugly shit inside the globe was squirting out.

He shouted to his guests that the volcano had exploded. They'd better hit the floor and hope the poisonous gases don't kill them.

At 1st they didn't believe him. They discussed it among themselves, all with puzzled and anxious looks in his direction like he might be crazy. They looked out the window and back at Erving on the floor several times before they scrambled to get flat on the floor themselves. He had 1 last second to look up out the window. Shit. He felt awful. He was going to die and this fucking volcano was going to make it like he'd never been there, and there would be nothing left of the Hawaii everyone was so used to. He felt a deep penetrating sadness, as deep and black as the terrifying pits of shadows he's passed by on the sidewalk. Oh shit****

He sat up in the cold Connecticut night. The wind was still blowing hard and the old house had hundreds of little wind canals. Janet had left the window cracked. He wanted to get up and close the window, but he couldn't face walking naked into the big razor of cold air knifing in through the cracked window.

He lay in bed shivering. He was rattled by the dream. He felt the panic and sadness of it again, and saw the ghost of the Hawaiian volcano. He couldn't shake the emotions and memory of the dream. It was too vivid. Even though he hadn't really known any of his party guests in Hawaii, he felt a fierce sadness, as if he'd really known them all well, and he was going to have to learn to live without them. It would be like when he'd landed in military school for the first time. His dreams were sending him back.

He was in a purple mood at breakfast.

"If a girl comes to you and talks to you in your dreams," Erving asked Janet, referencing a tamer part of the dream before it had lashed him with a panic so powerful it was still scaring the shit out of him. "I mean it's like she's right there and she's talking to you like she can see through you all the way to Hawaii, does that mean I'm in love with her?"

Janet smiled at him with delight.

"She touches me a lot," he said. "Like on the back of my neck or my forearm."

Janet obviously knew which girl he was talking about. She kept smiling. Nothing to say. Just a smile the size of Tennessee.

Jim and Janet worked on cheering him up, but the fear was

so strong it was making holes in his lungs. Oh, shit, something was going to amputate his past again. He couldn't breathe. He couldn't stay at the breakfast table. He had to get up and go stand by Jim's morning fire gasping with fear. Everything he knew was going to be severed from him and there was nothing he could do to stop it.

He turned on the tv. Jim came out into the keeping room. It was unusual for him not to go directly to his office with his coffee to review the day's lecture. His look of patrician understanding was missing. His coffee was a trembling storm of creamy tan. The fucking tv had a program on about Trembling Peak.

"My favorite volcano," Erving said to Jim bitterly.

Up to now he'd avoided the smallest reference to the volcano with them. He always turned aside any chance of conversation about it by brusquely asserting he'd never been to Jake. He had been letting a fine talent go without development because he was getting to be a wonderful liar. The narrator on tv was quoting the Mercury. He described how an unheralded vulcanologist had saved the people of Jake by studying continental plates and seismic graphs.

"The mountain blew off and kept blowing off," said an eyewitness.

"Listen to this asshole," said Erving.

"You're from Jake, aren't you?" asked Jim. "Not Las Vegas."

"It must have been half a minute before it quit," went on the face in its hillbilly accent. "There was light everywhere from it, like the mountain was a sparkler, but a million times brighter than the brightest sparkler you've ever seen, because everywhere I looked I'd see things I couldn't see before."

"Half a minute?" objected Erving.

"It was so clear, so clear and such clean silver light****"

continued the hillbilly.

"Who is he?" asked Jim.

"I don't know him personally," said Erving. "I saw him on tv with Lex Viner."

"In Jake?"

"Yeah," admitted Erving. "This guy went along with Viner's nutty theory about a flood because he'd been in 1 some place. I was on Viner's kiddie show once when I was 10."

"The top of the mountain blew off into the sky," the hillbilly voice continued behind film of a volcano. "It was so fast, it all happened at the same time almost. The fire came out and you could hardly believe that much mountain was going up into the sky. What a miracle gusher of dirt it was, and it was blowing up hot."

The narrator came back on and said the Trembling Peak fireball came from a Pelean explosion. A Pelean eruption lets loose a cloud of brilliantly colored incandescent gases called a nuée ardente which lifts into the air at scorching hypersonic velocity.

Pelean volcanoes are the most violent form of volcanic eruption possible. In 1816 Tambor, a Pelean volcano in Sumatra, created tidal waves 300 feet high. Tambor poured so much ash into the atmosphere no 1 along the equator saw the sun for a year. The dense cloud of ash lowered temperatures all over the world. New England had summer snow storms. Half the world starved because growing seasons were catastrophically eliminated. So said the mouth in the tv.

It annoyed Erving that the narrator hadn't mentioned Santorini. His readings at Yale library had shown that Tambor was big, but Santorini was his favorite.

"Trembling Peak is quiet now," said the narrator. "But

when will it raise its radiant trunk again? And what if there are no westerlies to carry the debris out to sea when it does?"

"I'll tell you what will happen if there are no westerlies," Erving said to Jim. "Santorini dumped ash 7 feet deep for hundreds of miles all around it."

Jim was staring at him.

"It was a miracle this volcano erupted on a remote atomic testing range and no human lives were lost," said the narrator.

"What about Jake?" sneered Erving. "I guess there were no human lives lost because it's still up there spinning in the sky waiting to come down like boulders that fall on fucking gas stations."

"You're not going to work?" Janet had come in and was amazed to find Jim drinking his coffee and watching tv. Jim never touched his coffee until he was inside his office.

"What the stupid hillbilly said isn't right," said Erving. "Half a fucking minute. No sir."

Jim looked at Janet nervously. As a prominent member of the physics community, he knew the volcano story about Jake was a fabrication. It was rumored that young Phil Grethlien had figured out how to fire a fusion burst.

"Where are you going?" Jim asked the rising Erving.

"For a ride."

"Wait a minute," said Jim. "Listen to Truman."

A special news conference had suddenly come on. The president was announcing that the Russians had exploded their own A-bomb as if it had just happened yesterday instead of last year.

"I told you," Jim said to Janet with vindication.

"You knew about it last December!" said Janet, outraged.

327

"He's lying."

The United States was no longer the sole nuclear power on the globe, the president was saying, but our nuclear physicists, led by Fred Starzinchger, were nearing perfection of a bigger bomb called the Hydrogen bomb. It was a new super bomb****

"I've got to go out for a ride," said Erving, going abruptly out the door.

He always checked his money before he went anywhere. It was a habit, like some people press their pocket to make sure their wallet is there. He opened the trunk. The lockbox was right there, like it always was. He flipped up its metal tongue. Maybe he'd go into New Haven and buy a blue blazer to impress the Quaker girl-friend who had visited him in his dream. Jim was at his shoulder.

"There's something about Jake I should tell you," said Jim. "I've been waiting because****"

Erving picked up a handful of hundreds to put them in his pocket. He'd never let Jim see this before. He felt embarrassed.

"Look at that!" shouted Jim.

"It's money," said Erving angrily. "It's money, that's all."

"This is unbelievable," said Jim.

Erving looked back down into the lockbox wondering what was so astonishing about hundred dollar bills and saw something different. He looked at the bills in his hand. Half of them were 1,000s. He looked back at the pile he'd taken them from. The Rolex was lying on the pile next to it, its now useless band splayed open. He would never wear that fucking thing again. The pile of bills he'd fetched the handful from was the lowest, about a 3rd of the way down. He could see now that all the rest of the bills in the stack were 1,000s. He realized in a flash all the other stacks were the same. The hundreds were only topping. A beard for the 1,000s.

"What were they like?" asked Jim, his voice calming with wonder.

Erving stepped back from the trunk. His hands came up to his face. He could feel his fingers trembling against his cheeks. He wanted to throw up. He ran inside to the bathroom. He leaned over the bowl shivering. He wanted something to come out, but he couldn't throw up.

He got up and looked at himself in the mirror. His face was a contaminated grey. 1,000s were not what Lehman should have given him for his sex expedition. 1,000s were what his father collected with a passion. Beneath the disguise of hundreds was probably every 1,000 his father had, all of them representing many many stories to Erving about how Lehman had come by them. A packet from a banker who plays roulette. 1 from an old lady in a knit dress. 5 in a game of panguingue. Someday, his father said at the end of every such 1,000 story, Erving would have them all.

"He knew it was going off," Erving said to his own strangely colored face in the mirror.

Evelyn and Phil Spitalny

Men had had something to do with this volcano, and where it came to secrets about what men were going to do, Lehman had powers. He had known the bomb was going to destroy Jake.

Jim was talking to him as he got ready to leave but he didn't process a word of it. He'd remember rips and snatches of it later. There was a loud noise filling up his head now, so loud it saved him the trouble of having to think. Janet kissed him good bye as if he'd been drafted for service in Korea and would soon be going up Pork Chop Hill without ammo in his piece.

He got out the book about atomic weapons that Ralph Carlisle Smith from Los Alamos had autographed for Lehman. Lehman had carefully placed it on the front seat of the Cadillac the night Erving had left Jake. Erving had stuffed it in the glove compartment and left it there undisturbed. Now he stared at it decoding a thank you for dice shooting lessons. What was all this supposed to mean?

He started West at a speed certain to insult the police. If they stopped him, he would throw some of the fucking 1,000's into their lifestyle.

"Jesus, Pop!" He rolled down the window.

"Thanks a lot for the book. It just explains everything beautiful," he shouted out the red car across the universe to his far away father.

The Effects of Atomic Weapons

PREPARED FOR AND IN COOPERATION WITH THE U. S. DEPARTMENT OF
DEFENSE AND THE U. S. ATOMIC ENERGY COMMISSION

Under the direction of the

LOS ALAMOS SCIENTIFIC LABORATORY

Los Alamos, New Mexico

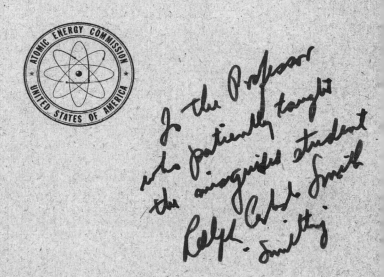

To the Professor who patiently taught the unorganized student.

Ralph Carlisle Smith — Smitty

BOARD OF EDITORS

J. O. Hirschfelder, *Chairman*   David B. Parker

Arnold Kramish   Ralph Carlisle Smith

Samuel Glasstone, *Executive Editor*

For sale by the Superintendent of Documents, U. S. Government Printing Office
Washington 25, D. C. - Price $1.25 (paper bound)

1950

Nov 4

He stopped only for gas. He didn't get out of the car much until he reached the new gate for 52 far south of the old 1. There was a new fence and a larger gate on the other side blocking the road up to Jake. The guard said the Army had expanded Testrange 52 to include the dangerous volcano and a large buffer zone. How could he find the people who had lived in Jake, he asked. Everyone survived, the guard chanted. The records of new addresses were in Carson City.

"Fuck you, Carson City, you lying son of a bitch!" screamed Erving. "I'm not going to any fucking Carson City"

"So don't go to Carson City," said the guard, looking at him with mild surprise. "Fuck you, kid."

"Yeah, fuck me, bud," Erving shouted to himself as he drove to Carson City, where he set about getting the stuff he'd need to get across the desert to the peak. "Fuck me."

He drove the Rover he'd traded the Cadillac for across desert pathways to reach the northern edge of 52. The only things he'd taken out of the Cadillac were the lockbox and the stupid fucking book Lehman had left him, which he had flung into the glove box of the Rover like it was garbage he had to keep despite its putrid spell. He entered through a barbed wire fence and headed south for Jake.

It was windy, and wind in Nevada meant the weather moved across the sky fast. It was different from the Connecticut wind he'd left behind, where the clouds moved so subtly he'd had to study them to make sure they were moving. These clouds humped across the sky like giant caterpillars, each taking no more than 20 minutes to make the whole sky and disappear beyond the Cactus Range.

He wasn't going to make it in 1 day. He'd hoped to get far enough south to catch at least a glimpse of the sun setting behind Trembling Peak.

It was always such a big thrill to catch that 1st sight of the banded mountain standing above the grey desert like a barber's pole of purples, maroons, and greens.

{ He was 7 the first time he returned from **E.N.M.S.** The top of the mountain was hidden in a banner cloud.

A banner cloud is caused by moist air climbing the windward side of a high mountain and condensing near the top. The winds blow the condensation out and over the leeward slope in a pennant stream of white which reaches out a mile or more before it tatters and disappears in the rising warm dry air of the desert.

This 1 hooded 4th Street in white. It was as if the stripes of cactus and forest were reaching up to nothing. It scared the shit out of him. The security deputy driving him home explained that the top of the mountain had not been amputated. It was a banner cloud. Everything was still there inside it. Not that he didn't believe the deputy, but it was very sweet to drive up into that banner cloud and find luminous color saturating the mist as if it were being sprayed about by huge pulsating paint guns.}

Marilyn Maxwell

He'd seen the mountain coming home a hundred different ways since then; the sun setting on its tip sparkling with argentine streamers, at mid morning when the slope's huge striations were as brilliant and distinct as the sergeant's stripes on his sleeve, in the rain which turned it into dull checker-work, and his favorite, the early twilight when the neon peak was laid out against a backless lavender sky.

But he wasn't going to make it in 1 day. The sun was all gone before he could see past Thirsty Canyon. He kept going, deep into the canyon. Finally he stopped. He got out and lit a L&M. In the late desert twilight, the Cactus Range was a majestic comb of mineral grey. The sky turned dark blue. The atmosphere was giving the moon an unusual ring, hundreds of miles in diameter. The moon was an ashen fruit in the center of this giant navy colored pie. A jet from Nellis had scrambled to get close to it and flew straight up like a knife cutting through the pie and leaving a vapor trail like whipped filling behind it.

When he woke up, he could see the peak. He bumped across the desert at reckless speed. Jake was miles away and the fucking desert stretched out in front of him like an endless grey sieve. Suddenly something new mixed in with the grey. It was solidified droplets of rusty iron. The rusty pellets got thicker and thicker, then disappeared where the grey sand became freckled with green. He stopped and jumped out of the Rover.

He picked up a handful of sand and let it run through his fingers. It looked like smashed Ziraleet ashtrays. As he drove on, more and more green mixed in with the grey, and traction became difficult even for the Rover. He was sinking down in grey green sand.

He looked up to the mountain. There was no sign of Jake. He scanned this new kind of grey green desert. Where the hell was he? He should at least be able to see the buildings

335

of 52. Where were the huge refrigeration plants and the spaghetti complex of corrugated tunnels? He opened the Rover door and looked down. The sand was all the way up to the top nut of the front wheel. He stepped down. The grey green powder came right up to his knee, his foot going through it as if it were a cloud.

What in the world was this powder? He'd been to 52 20 times and never seen this. He tore open the glove compartment and ripped out the Carlisle Smith book on atomic weapons he hated so much. He flipped through it until he found what nuclear weapons could do to sand. Fucking A, this new dust was a product of the first awesome blow from reconfiguring a few hydrogen atoms. It was the desert itself, renovated a little by Phil Grethlien's idea to turn a lithium bug loose in an equation.

He was driving right at the heart of the burst crater. He was still in the outer collar of the ejecta. If he continued driving another quarter mile, he would reach the edge of the crater itself and plunge down its slope to disappear beneath 400 feet of pulverized sand and suffocate. The iron pellets he'd seen earlier were what was left of 52's labs and offices. After the burst the sky had rained everything that had been metal in 52 in hot liquid drops.

Now he knew enough to turn away from the deep sand. Had Lehman seen this? Seen his son crossing the desert to find home and worried about his plunging down a hole of dust? That would explain his planting the book in the car.

"Okay, Pop, I got it. How you knew I'd get it, I'll never figure out. Man, your fucking powers**** Oh, sure, I'm smarter than you. You ****" he continued in spurts for an hour.

He went around the crater, a detour of 2 1/2 miles since this lake of nuclear dust was 5 miles in circumference. Finally he was heading up the mountain for Jake.

There was no color, no fucking color at all. He felt dizzy

driving up the slope. The mountain's nakedness magnified its height.

He couldn't stop looking back over his shoulder. It felt like there was nothing to hold him on the slope. The higher he got the more fearsome the long grey incline appeared.

Where was the botanical ladder? He stopped when he reached the turn-around. This was where he always got the 1st smell of 4th Street, which was the reeking heat of cars and diesel trucks who'd worked their engines red climbing the last 3,000 feet. He remembered vividly that sour odor of a cooked diesel now that it had been erased by the smell of fresh ice in the air.

Though he could see that it was gone, Erving couldn't make it pass through his mind. Jake wasn't there. He could say that to himself easily enough, and he did several times, but he couldn't put it in his brain to stay. It wouldn't go in to be in the same place with what was real. He stared at the bed of rubble below the sunrise face of the rocky peak. He felt like he was staring at cold peas in the mess hall of **E.N.M.S.** He knew he had to eat them before they'd let him leave the table, but he couldn't bear to put them in his mouth. He sat and stared while the peas grew colder and more nauseating.

Finally he got out of the Rover and walked the rubble. He looked off at the familiar mountains, Black Mountain and Shoshone Peak, like a sailor trying to figure out his location from the stars, but it didn't work. He couldn't fix where things had been. A few fragments jumped up in front of him when he got himself positioned just right on the distant landmarks, but it was only jagged scraps of what had been, like photographs torn into pieces which he couldn't keep in his mind long enough to put together.

He sat down on a pile of debris he guessed was **Ziraleet**. He could see proof now that man had something to do with

337

staging this volcano. A wall of the Dog was still standing. Whoever had bulldozed everything else couldn't bear knocking over this 1 last wall.

Where was everyone he knew? Jack, the floor boss who let him shill 21 when Lehman was out of town, Margaret Moore, Lehman's school marm secretary who always called him Master Lehman****, they weren't on the list in Carson City. There wasn't one name on the list he could recognize. And of course, no Lehman or Sonia. No way was his father going to tell some stupid Carson City clerk what he would be up to next.

Erving understood that his father often lied to people to get them to do what he wanted them to. Afterwards they weren't mad because it was always obvious the lie had been for their own good.

The whole time he'd been in Connecticut, Erving hadn't been mad at all that Lehman hadn't tried to find him after the volcano, how fucking hard could it be for Zalman Lehman to find a kid in a red Cadillac who'd blazed a trail across the country throwing hundred dollar bills at people with a diamond encrusted Rolex on his wrist, yes, he'd seen that the lie had been for his own good and he'd decided he wasn't going to see through that particular benevolent fucking lie until he'd wanted to, but since that damn tv had come on with all that bullshit about a volcano, he'd been forced to look through this lie whether he wanted to or not, and god, what did it mean? He had all the money and there was no clue where Lehman and Sonia were.

He went back to the Rover. The whine inside his head which made it impossible to think began again. He convinced himself he felt nothing. It was a peculiar kind of nothing which buzzed up his arms and arc'd across his back in prickly heat. When he got back to the Rover and headed down the mountain, this arc of nothing climbed back and forth across his shoulders and then ascended his neck with a paralyzing white voltage.

Pollyte was charmed by the mystery of where Erving actually came from. Before he disappeared on his run West, he hadn't told her anything. Then he came back and told her everything in amazing bursts. From the ruin and the grandeur, she built him into the son of a Nevada Ozymandias. She couldn't get enough of his talking about the burnt Jake. The unusual Western words and phrases about his other-worldly home were cool, and the sound of his voice grew more and more pleasing as she formed his exotic civilization into something she could recognize.

At parties her friends found him impossible to follow, as if he were Homer with all those lost modifiers. She decoded him effortlessly, but it continued to surprise her how sweet his anger was to her. Bad ideas social innocents worshiped, Erving tore into like a lion ripping the head off a zebra. She fell deeper in love every time he lit up on a deficient commandment and destroyed its tiny value with smoking wit.

During Erving's years in prep school and college, Jake became a myth. A popular song unified its diverse stories into a tale about a tame volcano that poured lava down its slope in a spreading orange delta which the Swiss sailed across on special sail craft with heat-resistant metal skis while wearing brilliant silver asbestos suits. The song said that these heroes, who stayed to ski the lava slopes of

Trembling Peak until the last orange coal had blackened, were 1 with nature in a way no other race of men could be because they took thrilling slides across the hot oozing neurojuices of the Earth.

1 best seller, edited and adjusted by historians and geologists, gave the full story from a lost manuscript which the Swiss called **THE STORY OF OUR CENTURY.** ■ Additional history was constructed from the memories of people who had talked to Swiss on radio long distance.

Reading it, Erving was confronted with the ghost of Viner. He felt transported back 15 years, when as a 10 year old, he had sat in a peanut gallery to listen to a man in a silly costume rave at a tv camera about how to die while he danced like a spastic Geronimo. This central character wasn't even identified as Viner. He was represented by "▲ • ⌐□ □ ⫽• ⌐ ⌐□ ⫽⌐¬□ ∨ ⌣⌐." some Mr. Festival thing Viner had jotted in a notebook.

The book said the jakes were all going to go off and die in secret from their own purple agony anyway. Who is born, grows up and old in a gambling town I'd like to know? asked ▲ • ⌐□ ⫽• ⌐ ⌐□ ⫽⌐¬□ ∨ ⌣⌐. This isn't a real human place, preached the nacreous Virgil. This is God's nasty stadium for a mood you're in. It can last for days or 20 years, but it's still only a mood. You come and try to lift your party up to Jake's, and you leave when you're willing wake up and get out of your rented bed.

So said ▲ • ⌐□ ⫽• ⌐ ⌐□ ⫽⌐¬□ ∨ ⌣⌐. Viner had been elected a gambling-life epic tenor with a purple halo by an ever growing number of experts on the opera up the magic mountain.

341

After calling Lillo to invite himself to visit, Erving asked Jim for his cash back. He still didn't know how much it was. Back from his 1st return to the West eleven years ago, he'd given the whole box to Jim to take care of until he could attain a majority of 25. Jim had used it to pay for Erving's education and support. Jim was penurious, and required explaining to extract things like an extra hundred dollars to send a limousine to bring Pollyte to Princeton for a party weekend.

Now 25, Erving braced for Jim refusing to give him all his money back, but there was no objection. They fetched the empty lockbox down from the attic, went to Jim's safety deposit box, and loaded the bills back in the same way Lehman himself must have done it. 2 feet deep in 1,000s with the remaining hundreds on top.

"Did you ever count it?" asked Jim

"No."

"You never knew how much it was?" he asked. He was disappointed.

"Who cares," Erving dismissed the idea.

"The original amount you left with me was just over 6 million dollars," reported Jim with obvious disappointment in Erving's trust. He wanted Erving to know that none had been personalized by Jim. He wanted his honesty proven out with a count. He didn't understand that Erving was giving his honesty Jake's highest compliment by declining one.

Erving bought a new red car, drove to Vegas in 40 hours, and checked into the Flamingo under a paging name. He had considered going to the Golden Nugget where Lehman had started in the gambling business long ago, but decided he couldn't spend enough money at a Fremont Street sawdust joint. He needed the Strip for more grandiose akraisia in the service of his vengeance. He had the lockbox brought in from the trunk. He was invited into the cage to watch the money counted. This count he observed like Bullock watching a crap shooter with too many rings.

It came out to $5,900,000 plus some cigars. All his education, clothes and rides for Pollyte had cost $100,000. He hadn't made much of a dent in the Lehman wad so far.

He checked their faces as they counted. The head cashier looked familiar. All casino employees looked familiar to him. He never saw games or tourists when he was in a casino. He saw only the people who worked there.

He had signed in with the paging name he had spent most of the nicotine drive inventing, Hogan Chuck Montmorency. They quickly figured out there was no such thing as a Hogan Chuck Montmorency.

But they accepted the need for the paging name. Gambling towns were the drain in the monetary sink which all illegal fortunes whirled down to. When men in cash business stole their own cash, such cash came to gambling towns. When men who didn't own any part of cash businesses stole cash from those who did, that cash also came to gambling towns. So did proceeds men derived from selling dope, swindling widows, and kidnapping for ransom. Mr. H. Chuck Montmorency's money was as welcome as any from other adventure executives; and a similar story about his wealth soon conceived itself purely out of the casino officers' need to have an inside explanation for everything.

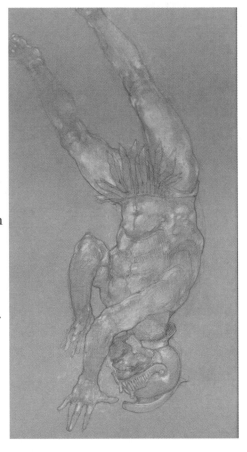

H. Chuck, pit bosses repeated all over the Strip, had robbed 41 banks in Mississippi, Rhode Island, and Idaho. Only the Flamingo's head cashier knew who was dating whores without touching them, going to every show in town, and gambling away hundreds of 1,000s of dollars by the hour.

Erving developed a laugh as he went through his Vegas experiences. Being in gamblingville brought it back from somewhere. It was more a question than a laugh. He couldn't figure out where it came from, but he knew he liked it. "Huh huh?" he laughed to himself, trying it out again and again. He especially liked it in casinos. He knew what the crap officers were doing when they complimented him on his play. They said he was a savvy player. They'd never seen anyone run a hot hand like him. He laughed, "Huh huh?", as if their praise and friendship were genuine.

He had a strategy for craps, but it wasn't for the game itself. He was playing his own game beneath the craps. He measured his success on any given night by how upset he got the men in the pit. He didn't care about losing so long as he could get 1 streak going and make his chip racks look like swollen dark leeches. The casino officers would stare at him then, some morose, some hostile, but all distant. None wanted to come up and chuckle ingratiating phrases about his manliness and skill then. The best nights were when they had to summon the hotel owner himself to help watch H. Chuck scare the piss out of everyone in the casino. It was only after he'd 7ed most of it away that they came over to grin and say what a savvy player he was and make him laugh his new stupid laugh.

An investigative reporter had recently found Viner's actual notebook of his days in Jake after the bombvolcanofloodwhateveritwas, and published it with beautiful graphics. It was for sale everywhere in Vegas. He studied the pictures and read it obsessively at night, after he got rid of the evening's date. In a few days he knew it all by heart.

"To the Swiss this dead heap of black lava," Erving recited to his date 1 night on their way out to party with Wilbur and Toni Clark, "is not unlike a purple tower of Joshua trees, conifers, and lights. The beauty was always inaccessible to them****"

The date got all excited. She recognized ▲ • ⌈☐ ☐ ⫽• ⌈ ⌈☐ ⫽—|☐ ✔ ⌣⌈. Viner quotes were repeated so often in Vegas everyone recognized his style right away. Her favorite person in the story was the virgin Lineheardt. The date had no idea who Viner actually was, but she said she knew someone at the Frontier who'd been there, who'd survived the volcano. She described someone he thought he knew.

"You've balled Starzinchger," laughed Erving. It was well known in physics circles that Starzinchger was a compulsive gambler who made frequent trips to Vegas and Reno. "But he can't be at the Frontier now. He died recently."

"Who?"

"A tall guy with a long thin face," said Erving. "Fred Starzinchger. He has a prominent chin; it makes his face looked scooped out. He's like a shovel standing on its handle with red fuzz on top of the spade. Or he was."

"Oh, yeah, I know Starzinchger," she said. "Nasty date."

"Huh huh?," snorted Erving. "Does anyone ever notice how much Starzinchger loved himself for spewing all that money at cold tech for fusion, like making a huge incredibly expensive error was endearing."

"But this guy is not Starzinchger", she objected. "This guy is a dealer at the Frontier. He worked at Horror Hall in Jake before the volcano, but he didn't go Swiss."

"He's not a physicist?" asked Erving, puzzled.

"Well, he was a deep sea diver," said the date, hoping diving had something to do with physics.

Erving caught the diver on his break and took him to the Canary Room for a cup of coffee. A student of hotel decor, Erving was taken with the Canary Room's thick yellow linen. This was his first visit to the address on the old driver's license he got from Lehman. He played with a heavy silver fork. He checked to see if it was real silver. A flash of Ziraleet went through him. 1 of the favorite stories of Jake mythology was the night they gave away silver chalices at Ziraleet. He liked that 1 because he had been there to see Lehman doing it and had wondered what the fuck his old man was up to.

The diver said he'd met Starzinchger climbing the peak with Gilberg.

"Where were you when it went off?" asked Erving, brushing the mention of Gilberg quickly aside.

"You mean when the volcano exploded."

Erving laughed.

"I was in the basement of the Dog holding onto a pipe," he said. "The next thing I knew there was light everywhere, the hotel collapsed, and the basement started filling up with water. I could tell it wasn't the flood because it didn't come in with any turbulence. It was just a broken water main dumping water into the basement. It filled up the basement, which was a good thing because the hotel was on fire above me."

He had stayed underwater with his diving lung. He'd had only 3 hours of air so he swam up after a half hour to see what was going on and found the fire burning hotter. The top of the water was almost boiling. The fire was heating the water as if the basement were a big kettle and he was its lobster.

He dove the 10 feet back down to the bottom. He crawled about and tried to occupy his mind by playing with his underwater flashlight. He was convinced he was going to die. When he ran out of air, he burst to the surface. The fire had moved on. The water was cooler. He hurried outside and found Jake gone.

He hated himself for surviving. He wanted to go into anything that was left and save somebody, he wanted it very badly, but there wasn't anything he could do. He scrambled down through the dying fires and found several people standing at the bottom of town watching.

They were all from Jake, and most of them would die from the radiation flakes which were swirling around in the air

like charcoal snow. He survived because he still had his wet suit on and because he got out of there. He had heard that the Swiss had survived the 1st days drinking the water he'd hid in. Every other drop of water on the mountain had been evaporated by the fires and the volcano.

"You really think it was a volcano?" asked Erving. The diver seemed not to understand the question. Erving had thought the guy was joking before.

"What kind of volcano kills people with radiation?" persisted Erving, now deeply frustrated with minds which ate in everything offered without checking for poison. "Why the hell weren't you blown 20 miles high along with the rest of the peak if there was a volcano?"

"I don't know," answered the diver. "A slow volcano? The radiation came out with the fumes and gases, yes?"

Shit, next he was going to start singing verses of "God Only Knows," the song about the stunning virgin with band-aid sunglasses on the album JakeTown.

"Do you know me?" Erving asked him, wondering if there was anyone left in the world who could recognize the son of the great Lehman.

"What do you mean? No. I didn't hear your name too well when you said it."

"Chuck Montmorency," snickered Erving, remembering he was talking to a dealer. "H. Chuck Montmorency."

"Oh, hell yes, you're the scary crap shooter staying at the Flamingo," said the diver. "Sure, I've heard of you. You almost closed the El Rancho Tuesday. Red Caddy convertible, yes?"

Erving gave him the same look he'd given the souvenir shop guy at **Ziraleet** ten years ago. He wanted to say "Yes? Yes what, you fucking moron," but he had attained his majority now so he was trying to leave his talents for profanity and taunting idiots behind him.

He went back to the Flamingo to lie down. He dropped off. The inevitable virulent dream came on swiftly, and he tore up his bed when he saw himself going into military school for the 1st time. The guard from **Ziraleet** led him into the Navy dorm. He stared at a gigantic Micky Mouse painted on the wall. The paint was chipping. The huge mouse face was spackled with a plaster rash. The mouth was opened in a cruel diseased smile. Everyone in the Navy dorm was making their beds. They all knew how to make their beds, but he didn't so they all looked at him with hatred. His pulse was pounding and he couldn't breathe. He fell down on the Navy dorm floor. The room spun and he started to see vivid colors.

"He's dead," said a bald adult in sharply pressed khaki slacks and military shirt.

He woke up trying to scream but emitting only "Uhhn, uhnnn, uhnnn." His room was throbbing with pink light from the Flamingo's neon tower of champagne. His pillow looked like he had attacked it with a mace and left it for dead.

"McCafferty," he said to himself, identifying the gruff authority who had pronounced him dead in the dream.

He got up and lit a cigarette. He had started smoking again driving through Kansas. It was something to do while piloting the fun new Cadillac. He had stopped smoking so long ago, a fresh cigarette could still make him dizzy and euphoric. He had enjoyed speeding through New Mexico with the top down, high on nicotine from L&M's.

McCafferty was the former Marine drill instructor in charge of the Junior School at **E.N.M.S.** 1 day, after Erving had put in 5 long years getting McCafferty to like him, McCafferty had disappeared. Nobody had a word to say over what or where to. McCafferty was just gone, and Erving never saw him again. Maybe they fired him when they found out about his lining the cadets up and examining all their dicks and balls twice a year because a jap had shot off one of his nuts at Iwo Jima.

His cigarette finished, Erving reflected on his ability to survive while figures as powerful as McCafferty and Lehman dropped away. It suggested there was something awesome and indestructible about himself.

Sleep rushed through him. The nicotine from the cigarette sparked a series of new euphoric dreams in which, instead of suffocating beneath the gases of fearsome authorities like McCafferty, he paraded through the territories of his past like Alexander the Great touring the Orient. His blood vessels coursed with a magical luminous liquid so potent it beamed a supernatural pink aura out his skin.

NELSON, RObt. A.

\NDER THE GREAT ABOUT TO START UP HIS EGYPTIAN MADE DOUBLE HORSE ROMAN RIDER
SUMMER - LAKESIDE - OREGON 2009

2 days later he went to the Flamingo cage and found his
lockbox empty, even though he had left it still holding a
couple of million the night before, when he had reloaded
for a volley of purple chips through the Nugget.

Tonight the play at rou-
lette was monopolized by
a large group of men, all wearing
the same red blazer with identical corpo-
rate emblems on the breast pocket. They
made the roulette pit look like it had the
measles.

They played roulette as a team sport. They
elbowed back and forth from table to table
between the other gamblers, calling aloud to
each other on their progress, cheering wildly
when someone hit a number on the nose, as if they'd all
jumped over Clyde Lovellette for a slam dunk.

Donahue knew the sense of each game backwards and for-
wards. Each 1 had it's language of numbers, and he could
hear its results in chunks. Their meaning vaulted into
his head without any effort of interpretation on his part.
In blackjack 4,6,8,2 meant 20. 9,5,2,4 was its synonym. He
knew how to fracture and reconstruct 3:2,6:5,2:1 in multi-
ples of 2, 5 and 10 so he was fluent in craps. For roulette he
carried the dictionary of multiplication for 35,17,11,8,6,5
times any common bet. All the permutations of a game's
numbers were the vocabulary of its language, and he knew

353

how to say them the way a chef can cast cuisine names in French.

But ever since Jake had gone up in gas and smoke, he could detect nothing odd in any game. He could walk back to the monitoring room where all the spy cameras reported and scan the screens for signs of a bad move; but, even if he focused on 1 table which informants had turned in for dirty, he saw nothing.

Desperate during 1 graveyard shift months ago, he had climbed the catwalk through the lattice work of the Flamingo's ceiling dome and peeked down into the casino below. The tables looked like green amoeba with disembodied protoplasmic hands floating around their rims. The roulette tables were a school of geometric squid, each with a giant whirling tartan eye. He got dizzy from their motion so he turned to spy down on the blackjack formation. 2 great arcs of felt kidneys. More hands. The hands were like filaments in a primitive digestive system. They were whipping the chips and cards into a uniform, digestible but undecipherable mush.

He understood the language of dice, cards, and chips all right; but the slang of motion which cheating dealers cheated with had become babel. He climbed carefully down from the dome and asked to be assigned to the cage.

Which assignment had proved to be no fix at all. Now he dreaded the count because each box looked like a land mine to him. When the box was opened, he would have some relief if the bills came flying out like leaflets from a bomber. But when a box was thumped on the bottom like a ketchup bottle and nothing came winging out but 5s and a few payout slips, he felt like his nails were being pulled off with pliers.

His grief for his loss of expertise exploded into fear when he saw Lehman's son, now 25 years old, come striding into

354

his cage with an old Ziraleet lockbox full of money. Donahue recognized the style of play that followed immediately.
H. Chuck Montmorency might have thought he was doing
something new, but it was obvious to Donahue, obvious
even to Cafiero and the others. Anyone in casino manage-
ment knew this pattern. H. Chuck was playing like a casino
owner.

The game was to torment a rival. To make it look like he
was going to put them out of business with a gigantic win.
This kid was damn good at it. Too good. Donahue wasn't
going to say anything, but then they wanted to drill the
kid's box, as if the kid weren't losing it fast enough. They
didn't like the punishment. They hated the anxiety he
made.

"He plays all up and down the Strip," rationalized Cafiero.
"We pay for his entertainment, and then he takes money
out of here to other joints."

"We ought to do a little more work on finding out who this
is," Donahue hinted gently.

They paid no attention to that weak suggestion. They
drilled the box without finding out H. Chuck was Zalman
Lehman's son who could call on vengeful friends all across
the gambling industry using his murdered father's name.

Seeing Erving had also brought back pleasant memories
of Donahue's meeting with the potent Lehman. He remembered thinking that he'd better get right out of Jake
because Lehman had indicated it was going down to ashes.
He had come directly to North Vegas and a hardware store
for equipment to plunder the ruins. After which he had
taken a long ride up on Gilberg's money. Followed by the
other thing.

He had played some pretty nice hands on his way back
down. His favorite was a straight flush wheel in high-low
near the end of his money. Now he was back to work. Rich-

er only in experience, he watched others make his mistakes hours on end, and then after work, he went out and made a few more of his own.

Since he was the cashier, Donahue had to lead the kid to the empty box. Cafiero's idiots had replaced the old drilled drawer with a completely new 1. Donahue had to say, "See, it's empty," and show him a drawer of slick virgin metal. The old 1 had been tarnished and full of nicks.

The kid just looked in it and snorted his huh huh laugh. Then he flung the drawer across the vault room. It clanged off the steel door and lay on the carpet like a dead cat.

"I'm sorry," said Donahue.

The kid started out, but Donahue stopped him. "You can bluff them into giving it all back," he said, suddenly deciding this was more important than his job, "They'll be scared to death if you tell them who you are."

"Who am I?" sneered the kid.

"We played racing trains ten years ago."

The kid looked at him, then got embarrassed, as if Donahue were looking right through the Loro Piana suit and seeing him in the nude.

"Oh, yeah." Erving's chin went up as he looked at him intently. "Donahue."

"They don't know what happened to your old man for sure," said Donahue. "You tell Cafiero your old man is hiding out somewhere."

"My old man is dead," he snickered. "He was killed by a new kind of volcano which features no lava, no crater, no nothing but radiating silver dust."

Donahue laughed, and suddenly the kid knew Donahue had been there afterwards and was full of questions about his father. He asked if his parents had died on the mountain from the bomb.

"Who knows?" Donahue knew Gilberg had 7ed them out in bed, but he couldn't tell the kid that. "It doesn't matter anyway. All you have to do is say 2 words, and all that money grows back in your box. 'Zalman Lehman.' That's all you need."

"Huh huh."

"What's so funny?" asked Donahue.

There's 2 things I never want to do," said Erving.

"Okay?"

"Fuck a whore, and ask a mob asshole for a favor."

"Yeah." It was Donahue's turn to laugh, "Got a few of both on my calendar."

"Huh, huh?" Erving repeated his favorite new laugh.

"Yeah," confirmed Donahue, throwing in a little respect. "But why did you pick up that dumb Jack Bullock laugh?" he asked jealously. "He wasn't the sweetest guy in the world."

"He was to me," recalled Erving, instantly remembering the laugh of his casino mentor now.

Looking at this young ghost of Lehman, Donahue thought back to the last words of his conversation with that mysterious figure.

"You are risking your hotel. And yourself." Donahue had said to the great gambler. "Why are you giving away money?"

"To make god's head hurt so much, I'll hear the son of a bitch moaning."

Donahue had believed Ben Goffstein was the fastest pony in gambling until Lehman's down curling smile showed he was fooling with the mysterious Asshole who jobbed the spots on dice while they were still rolling, not blindly like most jakes, but for the pleasure of taunting Him back.

Erving went back to his suite and packed. He didn't bother to check out. He didn't even tip the bell captain who came for his bag personally.

He just got in the red car and started driving again.

Lehman and Sonia had grown up back East. They had considered themselves visitors to the West on a business mission. They had told him bluntly he was supposed to think he was from the East, too. And sometimes not so bluntly.

{ When he was nine, coming home on vacation from **E.N.M.S.** after his promotion to 1st Sergeant, he opened the door to his room to find a woman standing by his bed dressed for a nap and a man in the bathroom wearing an undershirt.

He ran to the drawers and opened them, looking for his stuff. The man shouted at him. The woman looked puzzled. He felt a wave of panic. Had the deputy brought him back to Ziraleet like part of a machine that keeps on running even after it had been turned off? Maybe he'd been brought back to Ziraleet even though it had been sold, and Lehman and Sonia were somewhere in Reno running a new hotel.

His stuff was still in the drawers. He looked up again at the woman. She was wearing a nearly invisible sheer thing over her purple underwear. He flashed back to conversations he had heard last vacation between waitresses about Esterlene who had been promoted out of the coffee shop uniform into the purple underwear in which she could make a lot more money. The Ziraleet erotic workers wore purple underwear. Was this 1 Esterlene? he wondered as he yanked out the upper drawer

and threw it across the room at the woman. It moved in slow motion towards the shrieking whore. Did she like her purple get-up more than the waitress ruffled yellow bib? He took an instant to think on how angry he was that she was in his room, and then he was sprinting into his parent's empty suite next door in search of Sonia and whatever wild lie she would have ready to explain this latest insult to his comfort.

When he finally found Sonia in the beauty parlor getting her hair carbonated, she explained he was supposed to stay in a different room for just that night because 111 was taken. Didn't he know 111 was often rented while he was away at school? He didn't expect them to keep a room empty for no reason? She said the deputy was supposed to tell him to wait for them in their suite. The deputy had failed to explain it to him.}

So did Sonia's explanation fail as he analyzed it with a couple of extra decades of experience. His stuff had still been in the drawers. Why? Because that couple weren't really staying in the room. They were using it for an afternoon transaction, unaware, until his drawer had hit the wall, they were getting lascivious in a 9 year old's bedroom.

Even now, Erving still thought of 111 and Jake as home. He couldn't help himself. Home was where you wanted to be when you were somewhere you didn't want to be. Jake had been all he thought about at **E.N.M.S.** Now he thought about it all the time no matter where he was. He was the person ▲ • ⌐□ ⁄⁄ • ⌐ ⌐□ ⁄⁄⌐ ✔ ⊃⌐ had said there were none of.

He was the poor motherfucker who'd been born in Jake and grown up with it as his home, and finally it was coming to him that this place, his home, Jake, was now nowhere at all. There wasn't even any record of it, unless you counted all the Viner elaborations, which he didn't since Viner's observations and the expert critical derivatives on them diverged a few million parsecs from his own experience. He wished Jake had been preserved in a magazine like Spike's 58 with the exact numbers.

Erving treasured the Life magazine as his last real keepsake from Lehman. The lockbox full of money had failed to qualify for emotional attachment. Jim had erroneously thought Erving was going to spend them 1 at a time for the rest of his life, so he had refused to invest the 1,000 dollar bills in impersonal securities where they would lose their paternal value. The Ralph Carlisle Smith book on atomic weapons Lehman had put in the Cadillac to say "watch for the giant hole in the desert and this is good bye" was still around somewhere, but it froze his fingers as if it were liquid tritium whenever he opened it.

Now there wasn't enough of the real Jake in any of the books or the songs to recognize as part of his life there. Jake was gone and what was left was a mythology so wild the real place was non-existent. Fuck. Non-existent except for the Gordian imagination of a minatory Golfer Jew driving out of a different stupid gambling town inside another wild red car.

"What's so funny?" his voice mocked back towards Donahue a few times at the top of his lungs as he sped away from Vegas on 95 towards Lillo in San Francisco.

Billy Daniels

It hadn't occurred to him he would be driving right past the old Testrange 52 until he saw a chained gate with a worn sign forbidding entry. His neck jerked to the other side of the road. Another chained gate and a ruined highway. Up there was the high pile of waste that remained of Jake. Up there maybe the ashes of his mother had been wandering around lieing to the wind for a decade because Lehman had left his wife out of his new life as well as his son?

There are a few milliseconds when the initial energy of a nuclear burst is emitted as very high frequency X-rays. So high is their frequency and therefore their energy, they travel only a few feet at the speed of light before they are absorbed by the startled atmosphere and re-emitted as

the ultra-violet light which gives the fireball its 1st purple.
Erving felt the treasured segments of Jake he had captured
from his capricious memory run away across the gorgeous
Nevada sky above him. He fell into a waking dream and
saw a ghost of the finishing H-Bomb which had destroyed
his home now moving backwards. It was retreating from
its full extension out to Viner, Spike and Noreen, moving
across the vast Nevada sky, and shrinking into its brain
cloud all the treasured memories of his life in Jake. A massive turbulent column reformed below it and imploded the
hottest spike men had ever made down to a few very radiating inches inside Erving where it came to lodge next to
the same organs Barbanel had used to cradle his mistake.

"What's so fucking funny? Bullock wasn't funny? Come on. Didn't you like the way he walked like a sore pony. That was funny****" his shriek reached back at Donahue again and again, until he was bored with sharing his newly fissile hatred with the fresh but still unfeeling red car.

1961

Aug 26

Erving climbed the stairs of the cliff rapidly. The choppy Pacific unfolded a blue and white check beyond Baker Beach, spreading to the horizon like a peaked cotton table cloth. He entered Lillo's walled courtyard. He looked aimlessly about as he waited for an answer at the door. He saw the Pacific again through a crack in the wall, a streak of checkered blue lightning shooting down the stark white wall.

He wanted to rush back out beyond the high white walls and see the whole vast table of blue and white ocean again, alive and distant, before it was taken away from him forever. Oh, shit, he couldn't stand any more of these surges.

"It's hypnotic, that spike of ocean in the wall," said Lillo behind him. Erving hadn't heard him open the door. "It's more exciting than the panorama."

They went inside. Lillo padded across the terra cotta floors in cashmere stockings. Erving followed him, pleased with Lillo's warm feelings for him. From the time he'd called,

364

RUFF 2

Lillo had been very pleasant. He had even offered to pay Erving's plane fare to California, saying he knew how it was between money and young physicists. Erving replied that Lillo didn't know everything about the relationship between money and this young physicist.

Master Erving Lehman invites other cadets from Elsinore Naval & Military School to holiday dinner at Ziraleet·

Lunch was served by Lillo's new Croatian wife. She was eager for Erving's praise. He could tell she and Lillo had been fighting. She seemed determined to make something up to Lillo by being nice to his guest.

She served scallops on a bed of jasmine rice. Erving praised its keen sulfur yellow sauce.

"Your father was a brilliant man," said Lillo.

"You think so?" argued Erving.

"He understood modern physics with very little explication," said Lillo.

"You think so?" he returned again.

"I was astonished that he could grasp Heisenberg's Un-

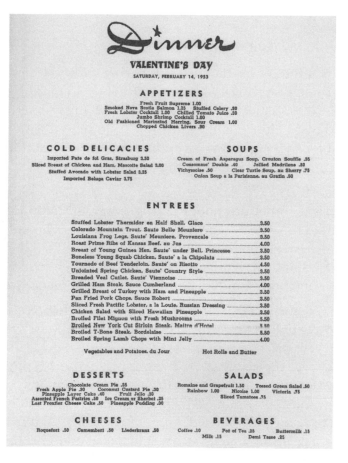

Dinner

VALENTINE'S DAY
SATURDAY, FEBRUARY 14, 1953

APPETIZERS

Fresh Fruit Supreme 1.00
Smoked Nova Scotia Salmon 1.25 Stuffed Celery .50
Fresh Lobster Cocktail 1.00 Chilled Tomato Juice .30
Jumbo Shrimp Cocktail 1.00
Old Fashioned Marinated Herring, Sour Cream 1.00
Chopped Chicken Livers .50

COLD DELICACIES

Imported Pate de fol Gras, Strasburg 3.50
Sliced Breast of Chicken and Ham, Mascotte Salad 3.00
Stuffed Avocado with Lobster Salad 3.25
Imported Beluga Caviar 3.75

SOUPS

Cream of Fresh Asparagus Soup, Crouton Souffle .35
Consomme' Double .40 Jellied Madrilene .50
Vichyssoise .50 Clear Turtle Soup, au Sherry .75
Onion Soup a la Parisienne, au Gratin .50

ENTREES

Stuffed Lobster Thermidor en Half Shell, Glace	3.50
Colorado Mountain Trout, Saute Belle Meuniere	3.50
Louisiana Frog Legs, Saute' Meuniere, Provencale	3.50
Roast Prime Ribs of Kansas Beef, au Jus	4.00
Breast of Young Guinea Hen, Saute' under Bell, Princesse	3.50
Boneless Young Squab Chicken, Saute' a la Chipolata	3.50
Tournedo of Beef Tenderloin, Saute' on Risotto	4.50
Unjointed Spring Chicken, Saute' Country Style	3.50
Breaded Veal Cutlet, Saute' Viennoise	3.50
Grilled Ham Steak, Sauce Cumberland	4.00
Grilled Breast of Turkey with Ham and Pineapple	3.50
Pan Fried Pork Chops, Sauce Robert	3.50
Sliced Fresh Pacific Lobster, a la Louie, Russian Dressing	3.50
Chicken Salad with Sliced Hawaiian Pineapple	3.50
Broiled Filet Mignon with Fresh Mushrooms	5.50
Broiled New York Cut Sirloin Steak, Maitre d'Hotel	5.50
Broiled T-Bone Steak, Bordelaise	5.50
Broiled Spring Lamb Chops with Mint Jelly	4.00

Vegetables and Potatoes, du Jour   Hot Rolls and Butter

DESSERTS

Chocolate Cream Pie .35
Fresh Apple Pie .30 Cocoanut Custard Pie .30
Pineapple Layer Cake .40 Fruit Jello .50
Assorted French Pastries .50 Ice Cream or Sherbet .25
Last Frontier Cheese Cake .50 Pineapple Pudding .30

SALADS

Romaine and Grapefruit 1.50 Tossed Green Salad .50
Rainbow 1.00 Nicoise 1.00 Victoria .75
Sliced Tomatoes .75

CHEESES

Roquefort .50 Camembert .50 Liederkranz .50

BEVERAGES

Coffee .10 Pot of Tea .25 Buttermilk .15
Milk .15 Demi Tasse .25

certainty," Lillo insisted. "Einstein never accepted it."

"My father understood probability and dice, not physics."

"We had a long conversation," persisted Lillo. "When we finished, he had a grasp of atomic mechanics."

"My father had a wonderful talent," said Erving, "but it didn't give him the ability to understand your version of the atom. It gave him the ability to convince anyone and everyone that he understood exactly what they were talking about, though in fact he cared very little about what you were saying."

"Such shallow magic would show through quickly to an

expert in the field," said Lillo.

Lillo could see a spurt of pride in Erving for his father. Lillo thought Erving was happy to accept the compliment on his father's grasp of the atomic. But Erving was actually proud that Lehman had gathered in Lillo so well with his talent for sucking in images and ideas like cards, shuffling them around, and then dealing them back out as if he'd just invented blackjack.

There was something about Erving powerfully familiar, Lillo told himself. Maybe it was the signals of Lehman, like the fine Henry Poole suit; but he found himself talking to Erving in a way he would not have talked to Lehman at all. It was somebody familiar, but not Lehman, somebody else.

Lillo had inspected Erving's prominent new theoretical work long before he'd called. Erving's work supposed there were discrete containers of gravitational fields which spilled over their walls at high levels of agitation. It might take years of intense work for Erving to prove enough to change the course of physics; but Lillo imagined that once this crude idea was turned out in handsome glen plaid, a whole new fashion of physics would be cut and sewn by sweatshops full of Renzas.

Lillo had also inspected Erving's private life through his vast network of friends in physics. Erving was well remembered at Princeton as the brilliant student who antagonized Einstein and wore a vicuña coat to football games. Lillo was thrilled to discover that Erving's wife was a Greek scholar, and began immediate preparations for Erving's visit by hiring someone named Burt from Harvard to fly out twice a week for Greek lessons. By the time Erving arrived, Lillo could sight translate any part of THE ILIAD and had some theories about Erving he had derived from scholarly articles Pollyte had published on Homer.

Erving asked Lillo what it was like to work for the govern-

Burt from Harvard

ment. Lillo thought he knew what this question meant. Erving had to make a living and he was worried about the consequences.

"It's not the technology of weaponry that matters," Lillo told him. "The technology of destruction is as inevitable as human ambition. What matters is the technology of human behavior. In the end, the mood is the only thing that's controllable. Weapons are scapegoats we talk about a lot because we fear containing the wild purple moods inside ourselves."

Erving saw himself splitting the nuclei of his own life without respite in order to make his way towards a whirling confusing fantasy as secret and ungovernable as the infantile narcissistic wish of the 1st atomic scientists on the Hill who wanted to obliterate their country's enemies.

This flash of his future began to mix with the moment he had 1st landed in military school and seen the diseased mouth of Mickey Mouse on the wall. Instantly the past, the future, and the present were so mixed up they became the same thing.

It had happened to him like this 1,000 times, and it always made him feel like he was breaking. He stood mortified in the Navy dorm. He was as famous as Bohr, but a hostile adult sergeant, McCafferty, approached, ordering him into a squat, and he would have to squat until his legs caught fire, or McCafferty, delighted to have an insubordination to make an example of, would slap him around the dorm. Erving couldn't move. Would this be the big blow, the 1 he knew McCafferty packed for some worst offense, like hitting out at McCafferty himself?

Yeah, hitting McCafferty! The blow coming for that would not only amputate his past, that 1 would sever his future, too. There would be no hell to wander around in trying to get promoted to major after he drove his fist into McCafferty. That 1 would bring an end older than mythology. That I would bring the last second of personal time up for private review.

"Einstein saw himself riding up an arc of light when he was 7," said Lillo, oblivious to Erving's spell and Einstein's lie.

Erving had to struggle to make himself breathe. He tried to focus on what Lillo was saying in order to escape the terrifying dissociation. Lillo was leading him into the living room. Erving walked behind him like a dog.

"Dick Renza was visiting me the same day you called," said Lillo, "He's nothing more than a brilliant mechanic. Like Starzinchgcr and that poor monkey Huke. They don't understand the true nature of experimental physics."

"No."

"You know what physics experiments are like?"

"What are they like?"

"Physics experiments are like making tv series," said Lillo brightly. "You work and work and work to get 1 isolated natural process set up so you can repeat it again and again. So what have you proved, when you've done it? You have proved that you can make 1 experiment repeat itself, that's all."

Erving began to grin. The vision of McCafferty receded.

"What that has to do with reality may be very little," continued Lillo, grinning too. Now they were both delighted with his leitmotif. "Rather like Zorro on tv, don't you think, where the director lines up the events of interest to produce the desired ending with the same single-minded purpose as an experimental physicist."

Erving boomed out the stentorian Santorini laugh which so impressed Pollyte every time it came.

"You're going to be a fine physicist," Lillo approved.

"I'm glad it's so obvious," smirked Erving, clearly not believing Lillo.

"You have the genes of great intellectual ability."

"You think?" The glow of pride in Lehman Erving had felt earlier now turned to resentment.

"Jake was our Troy, do you see?" he asked Erving. Had Erving's wife never told him this directly? wondered Lillo. "The H-Bomb was a Trojan horse we led into your town."

"Troy?" asked Erving. "Where do you get that?"

"Some day you'll need to unsay this wrath," Lillo referenced Achilles telling the Myrmidons why he was giving up his hatred of Agamemnon, which Lillo had just studied with the Burt from Harvard. Translating THE ILIAD was supposed to be difficult, but Lillo found the intellectual requirements quite familiar. Elegant poetry was the beautiful sister of a handsome math proof. "You may wish to emulate the forgiving of Agamemnon by Achilles."

"Have you been talking to my wife?"

"I read her papers," confessed Lillo. He decided he would surprise Erving with how much he could understand with very little to go on. "Why do you need to be so angry with your father?"

"Because he gave me all his money and sent me away for good," said Erving, triumphantly bitter. Here was Lillo working his father's trick, as if just mentioning it to him gave him mastery of it. "And it was no fucking accident."

"You'd rather have died with him?" asked Lillo.

Erving's hand leapt to his mouth as if to cap the grief that wanted out. To die with the magical Lehman, oh Jesus, where do such gods go when they die?

"You're damn right, I would have died with him." shouted Erving. "What's so hot about this ugly parade of accidents? You know what life is?"

Since Lillo loved pretty leitmotifs as much as Lehman had loved clippings, Erving was ready to give him a new 1, 1 of the many which came to him when lying in bed pretending to Pollyte he was asleep.

"God takes a huge B-24 with a rubber band under it and

Lisa Kirk

winds it up until it is twisted and knotted enough to fly, then puts you inside and turns it loose," Erving lectured in tones raised a few grades beyond professorial. "This bomber squirts viciously upward. We try to make a course. We get violent responses. The bomber veers with incredible sharpness to the slightest pressure on the rudder, but then refuses to correct at all to the wildest wrenchings of the stick. We look out our cockpit with horror and panic. We turn to our copilot, that long suffering inner being of ourselves that has to listen to every stupid fucking thing we say, and we remark, 'Handles rather well, doesn't she?'"

"Your career." Lillo agreed eagerly.

After Lillo said good bye to Erving at the door, he returned to his office and made a note to leave Erving some millions of dollars. Lillo hated foundations and the way they worked so he wasn't about to create 1 with his enormous monies. He made notes and left different sums and percentages to people he liked. It was far better to be randomly whimsical and possibly quite wrong with his gifts than to generate a building-full of bureaucratic groznicas who would only disperse his astonishing fortune to other twits like themselves.

Twits. He'd let that 1 in from somewhere. It was a nice word. It buzzed around his head like an insect looking for food. **Twit**. It sounded so cool. **Twit**. The little word began gobbling up the thoughts from the back of his head.

Erving stopped in the courtyard to stare again at the ocean through the hypnotic crack in the wall. He felt a spear of sadness for Lehman. The jagged elongated z of distant water reminded him of his father. Lehman had been a zoetrope. It was effective, oh, yes, how it worked, but what an effort to keep his walls up so high and show only opaline flares of charm for an instant. Shit. Who had Lehman spent most of his time on? The same people Viner and

374

Phil had been sucking up to. Tourists.

Erving envied Macbeth. Macbeth didn't go to sleep so he didn't have dreams. Erving didn't have to sleep to have dreams. They came flying into him in daytime halfway through a sentence. So he might as well sleep and dream.

So he did that night and saw something newly frightening and ridiculous as he slept in the plane on the way home to Pollyte. Phil was pulling a huge sled of physicists who were jumping up and down and howling for faster more exciting turns around a track he recognized as a full scale version of the racing trains rig he'd used to make a fool of Donahue years before. Racing against him was Viner pulling a grandstand full of kids who weren't kids. They were the

Master Erving Lehman, a First Sergeant at **ENMS***, with the sons of other prominent Jake hotel owners· This group contains a graduate of Harvard· He's the one out front·*

Swiss.

Fuck this, he decided in his sleep. He wasn't going to pull 1 of those sleds. When fame called him on the phone, he was going to head out and hit golf balls until fame stopped ringing. People like Phil and Viner could buy the world its free drinks; and Lehman, who had charmed legions of stupid tourists while hiding beneath a paging name, could give them every fucking thing he had.

He arrived home with only the cash from selling the car, which he handed to a puzzled Pollyte as if it were radioactive.

"Lilllo has been reading your papers," Erving told her. "He tracked you down because you're married to me. He loves THE ILIAD now. He says, Jake was our Troy and I am the Achilles of the West. You're going to get a letter from him. Tell him I am no fucking Greek jock with a big knife."

Pollyte saw a lot but heard nothing after Erving said Jake was Troy.

Looking at Erving's eyes on fire, shining with rage like the Achilles he claimed he wasn't, Pollyte fell into a beautiful idea which was to last her the rest of the decade as a formula for the fallen city of Jake. The picture of Troy exploding in a nuclear fire rocketed up her cortex, crashed into the top of her skull plate and exploded against it like frozen colored perfume. Slowly, deliciously, a liquid of exquisite odor melted through the canals of her thoughts until its chill made her shudder with pleasure.

As for Erving, the vision of the H-Bomb cloud which he had sucked out of the Nevada sky into himself would burn like a fusion cell, driving his intense pursuit of golf and physics not unlike the divine power which drove St. Soandso The Ascetic to spend 20 years of the 3rd century standing on his left foot in a dark hole while loving Christians chucked food down from the noisy world above.

2 people with unquenchable ambition found paths for it which allowed them plenty of time to wrap a blanket around a sweet natured baby with globular brown eyes.

Pollyte fell towards THE ILIAD like a goose with folded

wings returning to its home pond.

Erving acted out his hatred of other people's naked ambition by not going to meetings, symposiums, academic conventions and department parties. He worked only with graduate students who never missed appointments and he always left early for the golf range to hit practice balls followed by evenings with Pollyte and Kacy.

Whenever something went bad, he would sink into his work like Dr. Manet trying to reroute the French revolution by cobbling shoes. In one of his long periods similar to the whacking of slender nails into leather with a tiny hammer, he constructed a linear accelerator which, instead of whistling mesons through space on the crests of radio waves at 99.999% of the speed of light, accelerated space itself.

Erving became a youngish full professor at Yale. He liked teaching Physics101.

"Science books love to talk about Relativity," Erving blistered 70 freshmen, "with Einstein's picture of a man on train a speeding towards someone on a the platform. Their vision of the same thing is not identical because one is moving and one isn't and this makes their observations Relative. It makes a cute picture. But beware of cute pictures. They are only tacked on at the end of a long discovery process. What happens first is the physicist finds something new no one has ever measured before. Then he falls into mathematics and tries to invent a manipulation which allows him to predict the measurement before it is made. Only then do the wits among us come up with pictures and images. They are not science. They are blather. The science is measuring the process and predicting its result. When you can accurately predict outcomes in this manner, you can build rocket ships, bombs, and cars; and some physicists can make a living with bullshit."

"Professor Lehman," asked a raised hand. "Are you refer-

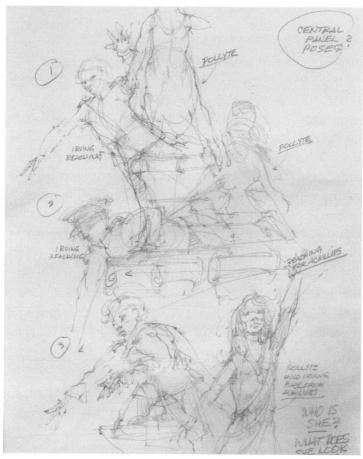

ring to thought experiments when you say 'bullshit.'"

"My peccadilloes precede me," granted Erving. "A thought experiment is a non-experiment. It is something somebody thought up for the newspapers. It can't be tested because it is only a thought, which is a distant ancestor of something which has come out the proven side of an experiment. If a thought experiment proves anything, it is that everyone involved in it is an asshole."

"Does that include Einstein and Bohr, Professor?"

"You can stop calling me 'Professor,' " Erving's hatred of rank exploded. "And, yes, Einstein is an asshole. Haven't you studied the work of The Virgin Lineheardt?"

Erving won the Mid-Amateur at Saucon Valley which resulted in the amazing sight of Doctor Professor Golfer Jew wandering down fairways in the Masters at Augusta National.

"It should be said," a paper by 1 of Erving's admirers read, "that Dr. Lehman's reality can become as widely dispersed as milk from a glass thrown against a laboratory wall because a sophomore skipped an appointment he'd begged for, to name one of the young professor's more legible comments on over-confident Yale students." Spilling milk with horizontal velocity was Erving's revenge for all the Sundays he had spent in parade formation knowing Lehman would break his promise to come to **E.N.M.S** on visiting day and take him out to buy jam.

After Erving's influence ran its course, and mentioning his name became as embarrassing as wearing a wide tie, a new physicist named Aiz Rugad found that Reality had crystalline events as dense as neutron stars. Rugad acknowledged a great debt to Erving when claiming there was no such thing as time and never had been. Time is a spurious device for impeding Reality.

"While the minds of men are eager to stuff nature into such artificial vessels, Reality itself does not suffer it," Rugad writes. "These fluctuations, I hasten to warn science fiction magazines, are nanonic and in no way support trips back through Reality as if it is a zoo where you may divert yourself feeding a brontosaurus waffles. The chance of man manipulating these spontaneous natural fluctuations are equivalent to 0. "

It's feasibility is comparable to the chances that anyone will figure out a way to beat roulette**** Blackjack is no longer the example of choice as idiots all over the nation are beating blackjack as flat as chefs hammering veal for eager diners who believe it tastes better than pork which costs 1/4 of a young calf and doesn't look as cute.

1967

Feb 27

After Erving's return from Las Vegas, Pollyte was interested in Viner and the new book created from his notebook. She seized Erving's marked up copy and asked him many many questions about Viner. She was fascinated with how the book came to be.

1 morning Kacy invited Erving onto the floor with her elegant fingers. He pushed her yellow truck into her belly a dozen times while she repeated the same squeal. Pollyte came in and announced she had bought an airplane ticket to Greece and disappeared for a week, leaving Kacy to him.

They were both impressed with the results. Erving mothered Kacy like a terrier with a puppy while Pollyte was gone. She came back with an arcane Greek manuscript 800 years old. She was so pleased with his maternal instinct, and he with her adventure, she took many more trips to Europe.

In the next 5 years she created an illuminated translation of THE ILIAD in her own hand. Erving declared her flying purple and red W the most exquisite letter in the history of fancy manuscripts.

A day after Lillo died, Erving was watching Kacy talk to the family in her doll house when a lawyer called to tell him Lillo had bequeathed him 7 million dollars in honor of his father Zalman Lehman.

"Jesus Christ, Twist, here it comes back again," Erving hung up and marveled to Pollyte. "My father can cross bor-ders no 1 else can. I throw his money away, and it comes right back to me. Shit, you have to be a hero in a religious story to keep coming back across the River of the Dead the way he does."

He called her "Twist" from their first week together because her dancing style would go briskly wild when Chubby Checker or Joey Dee and the Starliters were singing. Erving had spent a few of his early years studying the movements of the June Taylor chorus girls on the stage of Ziraleet, but he had never seen any of them dance like a rearing race horse on mystically lithe female legs.

"What are we going to do with this installment?" asked Pollyte. "Put it through the shredder, and use it for packing?"

"Oh, yeah, Quaker princess, fuck you with that Yankee tightwad shit."

"Me?" returned Pollyte. "What about the asshole who thinks money is flash paper for emotional bonfires?"

The President and First Lady of Turkey

"You give me Greek Hell for shooting all that money up into the air in Vegas," Erving shouted "and you spend 5 years and your inheritance from your grandmother's paintings into a book only 6 people have read? And 33% of your fan club is Lillo and some Burt asshole who flies out from Harvard on Lillo's personal jet twice a week to explain it to him. It shouldn't be too hard for you to find a way to understand that Vegas trip someday."

"When will that some day be?" shouted Pollyte back. "The day after you understand it."

"It wasn't his money!" Erving exploded like the sun erupting a giant flare of starry night from its core. "He lifted it from the walking dead." Then quietly. "So I threw it back at him and his fucking kind."

"I heard he gave a lot of it back at Ziraleet before you learned how to do it," she challenged him again.

"Well I gave the rest." his voice faded and his anger fell.

"So your father gave you another gift," Pollyte lowered her emotion to catch his quiet despair. Listening to him talk about his father like this was like watching oil from a gutted tanker bloom across coral. "But since he didn't even know he was giving you this 1, let's give it a chance to stick. If he didn't know he gave it to you, we can keep it. Double maybe we shouldn't even have to make any such rule. Whatever he gave to you, take it because there was no 1 he wanted to give to as much as he wanted to give to you."

Erving knew that Pollyte used "double maybe" to introduce the self evident. It was like a double negative to her

which made the possible indisputable. Emerging from the fog of his anger, he concluded mathematically that his wife wanted him to save this money which his father had wired to him through Lillo from the afterlife.

"Your father didn't really care about the idiot who bumped into you with the silver cup from his trophy room, did he?"

She was pressing the "double maybe" further towards the realm of immutably correct, but the pressure imploded his disappointment back into fury.

"How the fuck do I know what he cared about?"

"Make up what he cared about then," gleamed Pollyte. "And let it be you."

She was always her finding a contradiction in his emotional structure which destroyed the whole fucking thing from axioms to polynomials.

"What about the truth?" he countered. "We are supposed to love the truth. You and me, Twist. How about it?"

"The truth?" mocked Pollyte, as she found his idiotic contradiction instantly. "Fuck you, Golfer Jew, with that 'truth' song. I've read your papers. You are the guy who re-wrote Reality for all your physics friends. You make up the 'truth' all day long."

"Ouch."

"We should keep this shipment from the dead gambler," she concluded. "Maybe Kacy can use some of it."

The mention of his wonderful daughter, whom everyone loved without reservation, who was growing up sheltered by Pollyte's shadow from the neon halo of his rage, imitating only his caring and affection to a large tribe of adoring friends, destroyed his plan to set his father's indelible ghost on fire with torches made of money.

"Ok." he surrendered to her, suddenly seeing in full the

naked stupidity of Lehman's hatred for his own money. "She can have it. You, too."

"Me, too? I'm not in it for the money, dimwit," she smiled her mischievous erotic smile at him. "It's more about the beautiful tailoring."

Erving giggled. He hadn't been called a dimwit since **E.N.M.S.** When would she learn he was almost as smart as Darwin?

"What were they?" she asked. It was for his own good. They both knew he would be so much better off giving up their spell. "Sonia and Lehman. The people you've introduced me to who knew them, they all say Zalman and Sonia were wonderful."

He wanted to stop blotting out their memory with anger. He wanted to unsay his wrath. He wanted to be like Achilles and make up with the bad king.

"They were**** Pop didn't **** " He broke at the start of his unsayings. He was no fucking Achilles, and he was never going to unsay his wrath because Lehman was no Agamemnon. Lehman was 1 of the gods not some dirty gambling warlord. "What were they thinking when they sent me away?"

He was shouting at her again, blowing out hot sulfur nuggets like the volcanoes he had been so fond of studying when she had 1st met him. He was so attractive then, the boy man full of exotic eruption names like Changbaishan, Kikai, and Aniakchak, a tall noisy punk showing off a phony driver's license with angry pride.

Her seduction of him with her willowy hot twist, hard drinking, and sexual aggression had extinguished Erving's interest in finding #2 on his teenage fucking trip, and now in his thirties, he still hadn't incremented his total of sex partners. The flood of amazing Greek which she had showered on him in the line to the movies had so permanently

Sophie Tucker

startled him, he never pursued romantic interest in any other female.

She was just as dazzled by the sparking other-worldly personality which alternated between furious recriminations and beautiful understanding. That this alternating current of compassion and rage could surge on for decades beneath constant thunderbolts of affection mesmerized and confused her.

Erving and a superior officer after a ride in a Cadillac from Beverly Hills

1968

Oct 19

Pollyte asked him to come with her to the local Friend's Meeting. They had left Kacy behind with Pollyte's parents for a vacation drive through Pennsylvania, and Sunday called her to her Quaker god. He didn't mind. He liked Meeting.

In the parking lot Erving saw a young cadet with twin silver bars on the grey shoulders of his school's military uniform. Erving jumped out the car and went over to him.

"Good morning, Captain," he said with the military voice from his 7 years at **E.N.M.S.**

"Sir," replied the cadet, recognizing the sound of an officer.

"Are you the ranking officer at your school?"

"No, sir. I'm in charge of K Company."

"How many men in your command?"

"32."

"Two platoons, squads of 8?" asked Erving.

"Yes, sir."

His mother appeared from behind Erving. She wore a Channel suit in powder blue. It was appropriate for a Quaker Meeting if her son's uniform was.

"You come to Meeting with your son in uniform?" Erving put on his best charming Jake smile as if this were a curiosity to him.

"His father left us," she recited, bored. She had heard the question before. She thought she knew every line on both sides of this discussion. "He needs male values. He likes it in military school."

The point of evil in her life was her husband's departure and she was harvesting revenge for the misdeed in many ways, including the destruction of her son's youth. An imperial narcissist, she had her story about her choices, and it was a recreant cow pie.

"He hates it there," said Erving.

The cadet captain's face looked like Erving had taken the pins out of several hand grenades and dropped them on the ground to practice soccer.

"He doesn't tell you because cadets who tell their parents they want to come home never get higher than sergeant," Erving kicked one of the grenades of puerile military confinement at the smug-blue Xanthippe.

"You always said you liked it," the mother accused her son of lying.

"We had to write a letter each week, peppered with happiness," Erving shared from his years as a cadet. "My mother collected them as if they were post cards from Vachel Lindsay."

"I thought he liked it," the woman said again, now reporting directly to Erving.

"He liked it as much as the great Victorian physicist Charles Dickens liked being sold into a shoe blacking factory."

The woman grabbed and pulled her twelve year old away by the gold braid on his sleeve. Erving watched them approach the old door to Meeting as if he were seeing himself leaving Jake for **E.N.M.S.**, the event of evil in his own life. Everyone marks such a point in their life to excuse all the shit they spill around. Her hurt point was the exit of her husband. His was his arrival at **E.N.M.S.** She dragged the captain all the way inside the stone Meeting house. If that woman's excuse for being an asshole was bullshit to him, his was the same thing to everyone else.

"In Dickens' London there was a woman who slept on the sidewalk and made a living wrapping dog turds up in old rags and selling it to factories who used it for fuel." Erving turned to Pollyte. "When social workers came to rescue her from her squalor, she wouldn't leave. She loved her life, she said. That woman living on the proceeds of selling dog shit, and me at **E.N.M.S.**, and this kid," he indicated the straight backed kid now inside, "we have all committed the same sin against ourselves."

"Sin?"

"We accepted a heinous thing because we didn't have the vision to change it."

"How could you know to change that?"

"We made ourselves swallow something hideous, so now when we try to explain how horrible it was, we sound like idiots because, if it was so bad, why didn't we destroy ourselves trying to get away."

Pollyte touched Erving's cheek as a cat would pat a human face with the soft part of its paw.

"But we did destroy ourselves," he said. "By destroying each other. The major activity of that life was inflicting pain."

"You could never see that from inside of it," insisted Pollyte. "That's what the story about that London woman and her innocence means. Not that you were a monster. This is why you can't go to department meetings. Because you fear the sin of not being able to see back to yourself from the future. You work alone. No group will ever make you peddle those dog logs wrapped in rags. You're never going to get trapped in a shared illusion like **E.N.M.S.** again."

"Shared illusion," wondered Erving. "Would that be like a Nevada resort? Voices crying in the desert?"

Inside at Meeting, the Quakers were bored. Many eyes were shut, supposedly rolled up backwards to check their inner light, but more likely halfway into an inner nap.

Erving looked through a window, cut out of the Meeting house in 1742, to a huge oak tree, probably planted a week after the window was framed. He studied its giant structure to keep from falling asleep. The leaves were a deep green contrast to all the fall colored maples and walnuts beyond it. This giant senator gave fall no quarter. It was large and vital enough to treat with later more imposing wintry temperatures.

He dozed off looking at the tree, and the oak changed into a black walnut in his sleeping head, turned its leaves yellow, and shed them in a mental wind like a dog shaking water. The yellow chips cascaded off the tree in torrents until the woman in crystal-blue began to speak about the progress of her 20 years' commitment to the quiet faith.

The aggressive details of her devotion included committees she had chaired and the quality of her service. She
was talking directly at Erving, her voice firing bullets at
him like a Browning automatic rifle. Her son in uniform
was gone, and Erving asked the god who lived in Pollyte's
Meeting houses to cut the child officer loose from his toxic
military service.

"If there were an exam to become a Quaker," Erving whispered, "she'd flunk it."

Pollyte touched the back of his forearm to ask for a more
Quakerly silence from him, but her touch lingered with
affection because she was more in love with his long
standing loathing of self-admiration than with Friendly
decorum.

A soft invitation to enjoy Quaker restraint was soon offered
by a man embarrassed by the Chanel conceit. The concise
Quaker then sat down with his hand over his face, and kept
it there, as if embarrassed to have spoken out, not sure if
the Quaker god wasn't as shamed by him as by the blue
Chanel officer of committees. Erving wanted to go over to
him and pat the tidy shoulder of his modest sport jacket.

When Erving looked back to the blue Mom to see what
she made of this Friendly invitation to notice her ego, he
saw instead, a row behind her, a 9 year old face of exquisite
beauty and stinging familiarity. It took several seconds to
process her image into Spike Kilmarx, but that was who
she looked like, an angelic young female Spike. She was
sitting next to an equally gorgeous platinum head of hair
who had to be her mother since they were leaning playfully up against each other. And next to them was the father.
And he was Spike Kilmarx. 17 years older than the day of
the golf tournament.

Erving jumped out of his seat, and stepped quietly about
the Meeting house floor.

"Spike?" he asked him. It was bad form, but he couldn't wait until after Meeting.

Spike smiled, recognizing the fulminating teenager he had never stopped thinking about in the 17 years which separated them.

Erving dragged Spike outside.

"My wife is going to kill me for this," said Erving.

"Mine is going to kill you too," said Spike. "We're trying to get Clare into their Friend's School."

"Why aren't you wearing the Rolex?" mocked Erving. "It would make quite a flash at Meeting."

"Sold it for a house full of furniture," laughed Spike. "Where's yours?"

Erving shrugged. It was at the bank where Pollyte kept it. He would give it to Kacy when she turned 21 so she would have something of her mysterious grandfather.

"How is your golf?" Erving inquired.

"I can hit it," Spike taunted himself with a grin. "I can really lash it."

"What happened to you?" asked Erving. "I thought you were dead."

"I thought *you* were dead," agreed Spike. "Until I saw your name in the paper for the Mid-Am."

"My old man sent me away so I wouldn't get killed," said Erving.

"Wow!" said Spike. "How did he know it was going off?"

Erving laughed. "He had a way with secrets. How did you get out?"

"That guy, Lex Viner, the Voice of Jake from all the books, he came after us with a gun and drove us 200 miles out of town."

They exchanged their histories. Erving claimed he wasn't quite the Golfer Jew he used to be. 4 years at a Connecticut prep school and 4 more at Princeton, all in the company of charismatic wasp teachers had extinguished his inner menorah.

"Are you still in love?" asked Erving, wondering how a marriage made in Jake would survive beyond it. "The devotion thing. How is it?"

"If I make her cry," said Spike, "which you'd guess would be impossible, but no, not even hard because she's just a beautiful teary pie face, when it happens, I beg God to let me go back 5 minutes so I don't feel like opening the front door, putting my left arm in the door jam and slamming it shut with the right."

"Does that work for you?" grinned Erving.

"How's your wedlock?" asked Spike. "The perfect temper control. How does anyone marry that?"

"You're just an emotional genius," said Erving. "Aren't you?"

"Next to you, I am."

"She gets pretty upset when I lose my spin," conceded Erving, now calculating that his rage might be a transformed negative of Noreen's beautiful tears. "I give her lots of opportunities for that. But when it's over, she pats me on the neck and touches down my arms."

They were interrupted by how-do-you-dos because Meeting was over and wives wanted to know more about the husband's friend. But soon their talk went back to Jake, reeling off stories until Noreen insisted everyone come back to their house.

Erving was pleased to see how much beautiful furniture the Rolex had bought.

Spike and Noreen understood why Erving had gone back to

Jake, and they grieved together over the inanimate dust left below the arching trajectory of so many wild lives****.

Spike told Erving about the artifacts Viner had treasured. He still had some of them. Noreen had lent Viner's notebook to a reporter years ago and never got it back. After the 1st book about it, someone had paid $34,000 for it and donated it to the New York folk art museum.

All 4 of them had loved reading the volumes which followed that 1st collection of Viner's scrivenings for **THE STORY OF OUR CENTURY**. The more pop scholars studied him, the gentler he got. Then anyone could write anything about Jake, get it published, praised and believed. Many of these books made no mention of Lehman who had always hated the press and refused to talk to them.

Spike liked that the fiercer aspects of Viner, like the kidnapping, were cooked out of his life by the students of his life. Even the abandonment of his family had been forgiven.

But not by Erving who found himself spouting all nuée ardente over how stupid it was to glamorize someone who had left two daughters in favor of a gambling town. Spike replied with respect for Viner's dodging modern medicine by lying down on a rock and sending what was left of his life up to the sky like an Apache holy man.

Then Spike began to speak of Phil with awe because of what he'd invented and because he'd saved their lives****

"You stop fucking lionizing him," Erving interrupted in a fury. "He was just another gambler who exhausted his life making love to a fucking monster."

"He put Jake's life on like a shirt," Noreen agreed, referring to a decision point of Phil's decline. "Trying on high risk gambling as if it were a physics experiment."

"Oh. shit, that's wrong," Erving emitted more hatred. "He already knew everything there was to know about big risk gambling. He wasn't trying on anything. He had been in there screaming at dice for years. He shot a plastic bullet at the moon. Do you think that was a rational fucking physics experiment? What about the H-Bomb itself? That might have been a gamble, turning that little baby loose, huh, huh? He rolled that one out hoping it wouldn't hurt humanity too much? Then he thought he could rescue it all by acting out his fucking fantasy to be a super Jake. Jesus, he was supposed to be smart, but what he did was immensely stupid. Do we let all that pass because he had a sweet personality? Fuck that."

His rage, as usual, silenced the room. Clare looked with respect at her father's friend who was allowed to shout dirty words at the top of his lungs. He was looking at her mother like he wanted to fight, and she was glaring back like she was going to rip away his bedtime book, and turn off his light.

"Easy, Erving," Spike moderated. The 14 year old punk he had met on the golf range still inhabited Erving's mature physiology. "This isn't a golf lesson."

"Yeah, this is nothing like a golf lesson," Erving sneered. "This is a gratifuckation lesson. That whole town was built out of erectile tissue. The hotels, the gas stations, the houses, everything! And everybody in it was walking around with an intellectual, physical, and emotional hard-on, hell bent on gratifuckation"

Clare wasn't sure what this new word "gratifuckation" meant, but she knew Erving had just added

something new to the already impressive ledger of his profanities.

"And the Swiss." said Noreen. In the years which had followed her exit from Jake, the Swiss had been her favorite animal of Jake's social evolution. Because she and Spike had turned out to be a surviving sub-species of Swiss, she never tired of analyzing them. "They were sorting through lethal radioactive nuggets in search of thrills."

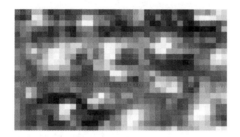

"Yeah, in Vegas you can see revenant Swiss now." Erving agreed, recognizing her as a colleague in Jake science. "If I hear 1 more jake from Vegas say he doesn't like to go to the Strip, I'm going to set his fucking moustache on fire."

Clare giggled. She had reached the mirth point of Erving's continuing devotion to explosions, fire, and curses. Was he permitted this flame-throwing dirty diction because his wife stared at him with the same face of worship her mother turned on her father?

"You know, I'm Swiss." Erving suggested to Noreen, smiling at Clare with affection now that he could detect her finding him funny. "I just didn't get back to Jake in time to be killed. I had to go to Vegas to eat my radioactive biscuits."

"Okay," sighed Spike. "But what about the generosity. Your

dad was so generous. What was that all about, if he was selfish?"

"Generosity?" Erving hissed like his hero Jim Roman. "Nobody in Jake ever gave me anything without a sneaky self-serving reason." But Jim Roman had given Erving so much for mystifying non-aggrandizing reasons, Erving had applied most of Jim's mannerisms to his own person, especially the hiss of disgust.

"So they have to have a right reason to be generous?" asked Spike. "Wrong reason, not generous?"

"Erving's right," Noreen came out for Erving. "Hitler gave Eva Braun lots of stuff. Does that make him generous?"

"Hitler?" asked Spike.

"It's just an analogy," instructed Noreen.

"You can take that analogy and shove it," smiled Spike playfully. "And all the other analogies you are so fond of. She thinks analogies are some kind of holy wisdom water. She sprays them about like John the Baptist so everyone who gets wet from her analogies will be a lot smarter."

"I'm sorry," blushed Noreen. Color washed across her pale cheeks like a Nevada sunset. "I shouldn't do that. You're right."

"He's right?" demanded Erving, incredulous. "He's not right. You're right. That was a cool analogy. Much better than his about holy water. All your analogies are no good because he's too dopey to understand yours?"

"Yes," laughed Noreen, smiling and blushing as if Erving had just now overheard Spike's 3rd marriage proposal as Phil Grethlien had years ago on Trembling Peak.

"What kind of shit is this?" Erving demanded. "No matter how right you are and how wrong he is, you take it his way?"

Noreen continued smiling and blushing as if Erving's seeing into this secret gave her a guilty embarrassing pleasure. Clare came over to help her mother stand up to the funny interloper.

"He's swimming in self gratifuckation, he's so right," sang Erving. "And what the hell are you getting out of it?"

"I don't know," shrugged Noreen. Clare took Noreen's hand and interlaced their fingers.

"The hell you don't know," shrieked Erving. "You big liar. You know exactly what you're getting."

"Yeah?" asked Spike, "What does the big liar think she's getting?"

"You." smirked Erving.

"She's got me, all right," conceded Spike.

"But he's not swimming in your gratifuckation," Pollyte volunteered. She was going to put another page in her long history of incisive dismemberment of Erving's treasured perceptions.

"Okay," sighed Erving, the air going out of his anger. "What is he swimming in?"

"The same thing you are," beamed Pollyte. "The admiration of his wife."

Clare smiled to see them all laughing.

"Phil was like his own favorite creation," Spike posted on the silence which followed the solution of their keen emotions. "What was his favorite invention? If you've read the words of The Virgin Lineheardt, you know what it was."

At the same time Noreen said "The rail cannon," Erving said "Rail particle collider."

"Rail everything" completed Pollyte.

"That's it," Spike turned to her. "He was like his rail things because he blew himself up firing a shell at something that couldn't be hit."

Phil's path across Jake suddenly sounded to Erving a lot like his own trajectory through Las Vegas ruining his father's money. Had he driven himself into the same pit of nuclear powder which had trapped Viner and his father?

"Is that something you need to hate?" Spike asked Erving.

 { **E**rving followed the boy in front of him who was following boys beyond them down a dark stair towards a single brilliant light bulb hanging from a ceiling 50 cadets ahead.

He reached out to touch the rough plaster wall to steady himself. On his opposite shoulder a fist darted against the junction between his shoulder and biceps, expertly directed at the vulnerable bone there.

He turned toward the older boy who had hit him, shouting with pain.

"Shut up. Hands at your sides," ordered the 8 year old corporal.

He had learned the previous afternoon, his 1st at **E.N.M.S.**, there was no chance of changing this much larger cadet's hatred of him. He had learned in 1 afternoon that any effort in that direction made more pain for himself. In all his 6 years he had never encountered anyone who had the right to hit him, let alone a host of them, who would all do it again and again because they enjoyed it. Each and every insult was backed up by a huge bald man named McCafferty, whose eyes glowed with hatred when he saw tears.

At 5:45 this morning he had woken up in the same hell. Jake and his royal experience there was a continent far away from this Amazon.

He closed off the pathway to his self pity and looked back at the corporal with hatred of his own.

He continued down the stair toward the blistering white hot bulb. He felt it bleaching his past out of him.

He took the anger which was boiling through his body into his head and spread it across his thoughts like Achilles putting on a gleaming helmet to avenge the killing of his best friend. Except for Erving, the friend he set out to avenge was himself, the lost son of the great Lehman.

He passed under the exploding white light towards the mess hall for the 1st of 1,000's of times on a journey through his own cruelty in the name of leadership to the ultimate security **E.N.M.S.** had to offer. By his 11th birthday, he would be the Commanding Officer of the Junior School. Decorated with officer insignia, 6 rainbow colored ribbons, and 5 brilliant yellow hash marks, he had acquired the fear and respect of every cadet who might wish to hurt him.}

It was near midnight when Erving and Pollyte walked towards their country inn.

"Isn't Clare a beautiful young girl," admired Pollyte.

"Yes," agreed Erving. "I miss Kacy."

"You've been away from her for all of 30 hours."

"Going to military school from Jake was like crossing the river Styx to be with the dead in Hades." said Erving, thinking about Clare and his absent daughter and still under the spell of THE ILIAD, which Pollyte and Lillo had cast into him.

He stopped and looked up into a night cloud shedding a fine mist across a solitary moon.

"I was a boy Achilles in hell with an arrow in his foot."

"I think I was wrong about that," She had been thinking on this for a while, but now was her instant of change. "You were not Achilles. You are not Achilles."

"I'm not?"

"DESCENUS AVERNI FACILIS, JANUA ATRI DITIS PATET NOCTES ATQUE DIES; SED REVOCARE GRADUM, QUE EVADERE AD SUPERAS AURAS, HOC OPUS, HIC EST LA-BOR."

Again Pollyte threw the beautiful fabric of enigma over him in an ancient language.

"Jesus, I love you, Twist," he howled up to the enveloping sky. "But what the fuck did you just say?"

"Going down to hell is easy," she translated the challenge of the Sibyl to Aeneas. "The gate to Pluto's dead world is open all day and all night; but getting back up to living air, such ambition, this will be your struggle."

Pollyte had left Achilles' shade behind in Greek Hell and fallen in love with Aeneas fighting up from the Roman Underworld with a golden branch in his fist. A stunning illustrated Virgil, dedicated to Emil Lillo-Furon and costing many 1,000s of dollars to produce a solitary copy, was spraying another perfumed storm across her brain. Now working in Latin, she would outfit him with the finest cloth of love and affection to protect him from the storms of his blind self loathing.

Erving could see the huge change in Pollyte as her eyes studied him. In the quiet of this new night, his mind strayed far from his physics. A lot of his progress in physics had been made by his imagining things no 1 else could see. Now, guided by Pollyte's unveiling of her admiration, he brought that gift of indirect seeing to himself. He slipped into Pollyte and then his young daughter's eyes and looked back out at himself.

He saw Kacy's father, so different from what lived in the mirror. And he saw his wife's idol instead of Dickens lecturing himself to Death. Globs of hot confusion melted down his face as if he were Lineheardt or Noreen.

"That trip to Las Vegas and what you did there, and what you saw there," said Pollyte slowly to the weeping man who was still half boy, "That was another crossing."

He stared at her like a child lost in a train station.

"Your father gave you the gift of learning how to leave behind dark worlds where they sell dog logs wrapped in gauze. Something he and a few other people in your story couldn't do. **E.N.M.S** was awful but stop falling on it's sword. Who do you think you are, Viner? Phil? ****"

"All of them. I'm all of them."

"You're not. Listen to me, I know heroes, and you conquered strange and savage children at **E.N.M.S.** From then on you knew you could make anything work. That's how you face hostile incomprehensibility with your beautiful smirk. So now accept the hero in yourself as your father's gift and fight your way out of the dark world of hating him as your newest and greatest deed."

Jesus, she could sing like Homer. Thoughts about the ugly blue divorcée had been pinging him ever since they had left Meeting. Whenever that bitch saw something she really wanted, she had a lever in her head she could pull to get it. Her lever was this "my husband left me" thing. Her son was an inconvenience at home, so she pulled her lever and won the right to park her son in military lockup while she collected cherries for her bowl. She wasn't the only one who had this lever thing. Everyone had one and they were all pulling on it now and then. Erving looked back along lives from his past and saw many who had pulled this lever at the wrong moment. Phil Grethlien. Steven Huke, Shit, every fucking big asshole in Nevada.

Lehman, too, he had one. No one knew what it was because he gave nothing away about himself, but you only had to watch him 20 minutes to know he had pulled the lever on an h-bomb of "i am a god." You could see it in how parasites sucked up to worship him. That's what he was pulling his lever under the table for. Erving had one, also. It was the other side of the puff-blue lady's coin, but it was the same thing. Whenever he had to have something, he pulled the "they sent me away to military school" lever; and he took whatever it was he wanted just like the poison-blue bitch did. Thus, mathematically, the personal slot machine mounted inside his head was the same self indulgent bullshit as hers, Lehman's, and the physicists at 52.

"And now you talk about Jake and what you hated there to Spike," Pollyte whispered in the low call she used for talking lullabies to Kacy, "Your parents were already the wrong way across the Styx. In Hell. Right there in Jake. They were thinking they were sending you back the other way. That money you got for that stupid sex trip. Nobody gives their son 6 million dollars to go lose his virginity. He knew all along he was going to be sending you away. The sex trip story was a cover he built up through the years knowing what he was going to do. That money was for your education. And for getting you admitted to a different life. To lift you out of the living hell he'd wandered into."

Erving stared up, letting fine dots of moisture dilute his salty cheeks.

How like Lehman to know and do like a god.

"You're not Achilles," Pollyte repeated, singing now like Virgil. "Achilles was so Swiss, all in love with his own death. You got away from the dying city."

Thus Pollyte showered him with hot specs of affection. Too bad St. Viner couldn't see this volcano light up because he would have loved seeing it the melt the snow this native jake had watched fall across his life. What Pollyte loved in him, which she had taken into herself behind his awareness, was gathering for the gentle blazon of a new Aeneid with sparking orange and gray dropped caps.

All the bad things which had wound up inside him for decades began their unwind. This relaxation was more leisurely than the light speed implosion of pain from the Nevada sky 10 years ago. He began with an examination of his father as a displaced warlord like the Queequeg in Viner's notes. Had Lehman salted coffins across the future to save his son? There might be puzzling items in his father's behavior coming back to be solved in Lehman's favor through new decades. He could inspect them beneath the same fusion lamp which had illuminated the Ralph Carlysle Smith book at the exact moment he needed it to save him from driving into a deep suffocating pit of nuclear pica.

He could take his rage and partition it into his past where it belonged. He could stop acting like a released prisoner who smuggled the corruption of prison out into society

and loosed it there. He had been a convict knifing unsus-
pecting citizens over offenses fatal behind bars but barely
offensive in civilization.

"Look at the sky, Twist."

The mist was acting like an atomized water lens across the
black well of night so the moon was refracted into several
terms of a brilliant proof. Each argent wafer was brighter
and cleaner than the 1 before it, the series finally solving
into the great white disc itself.

The End

Kacy   Pollyte

Inkpies, Inc.

Works by Chick: Paranoid Blue, Street Life, "The Year of Hitting Golf Balls", Ondine, and other crap.

ISBN 978-0-9819314-3-2 (paperback)
Printed in the U.S.A.   LCCN 2015955097

Answers:

The physics are a metaphor. Skip them wherever they get in your way.

The modernity of ›H comes from my cultural advancement at Faber College where I learned lots of wonderful new shit while lacing scholarly inquiry with profanity and lust.

Writing something like ›H is not about starting with a full bottle of ink and dipping into it to scratch out pages until the ink is gone. It is more like looking at what you have just written, scanning for a pretty spot of ink which is still wet and scraping it back up with your pen and nocking that tiny dot of moisture into a jar. It takes a long time to fill that jar halfway. You go through hundreds of ink bottles. When a dot of ink added makes the jar overflow, you have the book. It's in this jar of gorgeous ink, not all that black spit they sell in bottles.

The best things about this book are the things not there. It avoids the banal as if it were vomit. It despises the explicitness of tv. It's agita goes into your reading lung like colored smoke from an exotic cigarette.

The trunk of the story curls down a tree among leaves of graphic art, photos, and graffiti.

▯ ╱╱ ⼚,▯▯◣ ╱╱ ╱╱ �つ▯∨ Ⲥ Ⲥ▯◣ • ∨ ◣▯▼ ■ Ⲥ⡄? • • ◣◺ ╱╱▼▯ ╱╱▼ Ⲥ Ⲥ⌈_⫽ ╱╱●▯▼?▯∨ ●_⫽つ∨_⌉⌈▯
● ◣▯∨⌈∨▼◣ • ⌉▼ Ⲥ▯A● _⫽◺ ╱╱▼▯◣ ╱╱ ╱╱.

FROM THE IMBONGIS:

"To be a good writer I think you have to be a good talker and the very best talker to me is someone I call Chick. I know not which is more remarkable; the insane lucidity of his conclusions, the humorous eloquence of his language, or his power of method. He transmigrates into the views of others, turns questions inside out and flings them empty at you on the ground."

"You are a very skilled writer, in fact the literary prowess you bring to bear on it is staggering. The story is necessarily multi-faceted and its artistic-viability seems almost predicated on your ability to color outside the lines"

"A. M. gave me your manuscript and I read it with great interest. Wow! You have a strong voice. Sexy. Irreverent. Fascinating. It was fun for me to read a well crafted and beautifully written novel that has such a definitive style. Thanks for sending it to me. (By the way, when I was a little girl, I used to visit Las Vegas when it was a small town with one or two streets of casinos and joints and an acre of land sold for $1.00)"

"I am reading this fucking book, man, or maybe I have already read it. It is definitely a very enlightened book, man, because most of the time I get so lost in the word pictures that I forget what is happening, so I have to go back, and then I find more word pictures, until I am in a fucking maze, man -- YES! I am a-mazed, man, but I know somehow the Great Magnet will finally lead me to the cheese. There is a lot going on in this book, man, and if you are not very fucking careful, it can get you so zapped that you forget to refresh your internal supply of essential alkaloids, which leaves you shaking so much that the *print begins to jump up and down, man, or maybe it is the book that does that· In my condition, man, it can sometimes be hard to tell·"*

*"****unlike the cookie cutter novels out there you cannot guess what the characters will do as shown by one of my favorite parts where the character's greatest desire is to prove something impossible thus becoming the person that all other future failures and impossibilities will be measured against·"*

"a parable about life in the modern era that follows in a great tradition of folk tales in its apparent hyperbole, with the exception that everything that happens in the story is either based on details culled from true events, or is well within the realm of plausibility· It is historic fiction that takes the most outrageous elements of the history of the atomic age and blends them together into something of Paul Bunyan proportions without inventing any giants·"

FROM THE DEAD :

"Chick may fool you with the way he chunks down long sentences with periods, but you can still see that the structure of thought is stolen from me." Jack Kerouac

"The transfer of meaning up from the page to the aha region of a reader's brain is eased when the writer invests the voice rising from the print with an operatic authority. Chick hides from his public to let such an aura infest his sentences. As opposed to letting the reader see what an asshole he is." Anthony Burgess

"Some sentences in >H aren't straightforward. But neither is anything new. Cliches are straightforward." Dylan Thomas

"You have to be a like a silver miner when you read >H. You need to sink some tunnels down the core of a mountain to get the money." Thomas Berger

"I got so carried away with character I missed things I should have done with the story. In <u>Bleak</u> <u>House</u> I let the law writer and the daughter he had never known occupy the same building without passing each other. And worse, I let the law writer die of opium without a clear tipping event. The event was right in front of me and I missed it. They needed to face each other on the stairs. The daughter sees a ruined man she will never recognize. The father sees his daughter and recognizes two things in the same instant. The face of himself and the most stunning beauty in London all contained in one visage. And his helplessness to speak then or ever to this amazing creature. I never did say why he smoked himself to death that night because I didn't know why when I wrote that episode out. Now I know why. And so would the reader had I not missed when it should have happened." Charles Dickens

"Yes, it's good about the inside of casinos and all the people in or about casinos, but that's not what makes it ring. The little stuff happening in the lines, that's what pings you over and over again. Like the bell on an old Smith Corona chopper, it rings again and again." James M. Cain

55 ◯

11,500 - a few scrubby Sort Tala

TIMBERLINE - 11,000 ———— LIMBER PINE
· Engleman Spruce

HOTELS + EVERYTHING SCRUBBY.

10 M

·18°

BUSINESS DIST — TALL LIMBER PINES

A FEW PONPEROASA.

·67°   8.

LARGE SPEC. BELT OF   7500 Engle
TREMBLING ASPENS - TIGHT GROVES   Spru
RES. AREA.

6 M.

3°   PON DEROSA
                                    lack of undergro

PINYON   MOTELS. DOWTOWN JOINTS

4 M
S.A. Sagebrush,
also greencurro
                                    Winter fa
3 M
DESERT
creasote
CACTUS.

2000   HIGWAY

Robert A. Nelson

from Louise Nelson:

OK! Yes, the black board is already up on 2 Easles & has been for longer than it should have! Bobs show sort of threw him off track & then life &... well you know! Stuff! I think the black board will be a wonderful contrast to all Of the others. The serfice is really excellent, but since it's really good paper one needs to try and avoid erasing to often! It takes colored pencil quite splendidly & I suspect Bobbie will get moor of it in smaller sizes to work on in the future. We usto use a good black heavy paper for printing & drawing, a "rives b. F k. Black, but over the years we have noticed it simply falls apart. It gets brittle, so unless it's under glass, I would expect most of that older work, on it, is not in good shape. I don't think you have any big black paper drawings, but if you do & you see a water mark with a "bfk" or arches, it should be backed and permanetly attached to a quality acid free board! Bob has salvaged some of the works in peaces but others we just tossed! Loads of people used that paper & I would guess it's a universal problem. I have done some short term color fade test on it & so far in the last year of sun hitting it almost every day, it's excellent. We don't take the best care of our older work & that's a project iam going to work on over the winter! We have lots of big file drawers we don't even know what's in them! Time to bring them into the house & rescue what we can! I do have one portfolio containing my personal collection of r. A. Nelson's, I keep under the bed! Any how this wonderful sheet of black board will be the perfect serfice & we thank you for going through all the problems of Ordering it for bob. Some days I wonder how we made it this far.. 2 totaly financial retarded adults...... Luck or the will of the gods, who ever they may be or not! Enjoy your Holliday with family!

Love you guys & give Cheryl a big hug for us! L.